Valley Melodies

BONNIE LEON

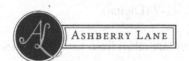

This is a work of fiction. All characters and events portrayed in this novel are either fictitious or used fictitiously.

VALLEY MELODIES

Ashberry Lane, a division of WhiteFire Publishing
13607 Bedford Rd NE
Cumberland, MD 21592

ISBNs: 978-1-941720-40-0 (Print)
       978-1-941720-41-7 (Digital)

All Scripture quotations are taken from the King James Version.

DEDICATED
to
The brave men and women
who dared to leave what they knew
and travel west where their faith would be tested
in the Oregon Territory.
It is because of your resolve and courage
that my Oregon life is possible.

Chapter One

Oregon Territory
April 1856

The sun slid behind the mountains, and evening bird song quieted as Emmalin and Jacob approached Deer Creek, the town she had grown to love and thought she'd never see again. Henry barked at something in the brush and darted off the trail.

Trepidation nibbled at her joy as Emmalin grasped Smoke's coarse mane more tightly as if the dappled gray could provide the steadiness she needed.

Earlier today she'd been in a wagon set on returning to Philadelphia and the life of ease she'd had there. The idea made her stomach ache. Then Jacob caught up with her, convincing her to go with him to his burned-out place on the river—leaving Mr. Henderson to continue to Oregon City without her.

As she and Jacob stood where the blackened forest ended and the heavy greenery of woodlands closed around them, he had asked her to be his wife, to rebuild the cabin destroyed by fire, and to start a life together. It had been a beautiful moment, a dream, but now reality drew near. Did she have the strength required to be a pioneer wife?

"Almost there," Jacob whispered as they moved past the grist mill. The paddles slapped the water, the wheel groaning as if in tune to Emmalin's emotional disquiet.

A cat, perched on the top step of the schoolhouse, stood, stretched out its lean golden body, and yawned. It eyed them as they rode toward her father's mercantile. *Her father.* Heaviness seized her as she replayed the last months. Her mother had died of fever, and Emmalin set off with her uncle to Oregon Territory in search of a father she didn't know existed until her mother's death. Emmalin had only been in Oregon City one day when her uncle was killed in a freak accident. With the help of Jacob, a mountain man, she traveled to Deer Creek and found her father.

Anger simmered inside her as she thought about Collier breaking off their engagement only to follow her to Deer Creek when he discovered she was now a wealthy woman.

Emmalin took a deep, steadying breath. While her life had been riddled with suffering, good things had also come about. Good things like discovering she was an heiress to her uncle's fortune. And good things like Jacob Landon.

The mercantile was dark, but lights glowed from within Margaret's café. Jacob maneuvered Smoke to a stop in front of the café, dismounted, and tied the horse to a hitching post. Henry padded up to the door and waited.

"I'll bet Margaret's got something good to eat," Jacob said as he reached up to help Emmalin down.

"I hope so. I'm starved." She swung her right leg over the horse's back and dropped to the ground, standing in Jacob's arms for a brief moment, wishing she could remain there feeling the safety of his strength.

His lips had settled into a soft smile as he gazed down at her. Though drawn in by his love, she stepped away. A public demonstration of affection would be improper. Her mother would have been shocked by such a display.

"Are you ready?" Emmalin took his hand.

Jacob gave it a squeeze. "I am if you are." He grinned. "Have to admit, I'm a little nervous to face Samuel. I might work for him and have known him a while, but I didn't tell him about my feelings."

"He'll be happy for us. He thinks very highly of you."

"That's good to know."

Emmalin pressed a hand to her stomach, trying to quiet the sudden flurry of butterflies. How *would* her father accept the news? The last he knew, Emmalin was headed north to Oregon City to join the wagon train going east.

And what of Mr. Henderson? What would he think when she didn't arrive at the campsite? When Jacob had come for her, she'd been so surprised and had behaved recklessly, taking off on a whim with a mountain man the way she did. Mr. Henderson must think her mad.

Jacob held the door of the café open, and Emmalin moved inside, the aroma of roasting meat and vegetables greeting her. Her father sat at the table nearest the kitchen with their good friend, Margaret. They looked up, surprise on their faces.

Samuel stood, looking taller than his six-two height. Her father's blue eyes were dark with interest. "Emmalin? Jacob?"

Margaret bounced to her feet. "I can hardly believe what I'm seeing." She tucked chestnut brown hair off her face. "I thought you'd be miles from here by now."

"I was." Emmalin glanced at Jacob. "But Jacob caught up to Mr. Henderson and me. And, well, he took me to his place on the river."

"What about Philadelphia?" Samuel asked. "I thought you were set on returning to your fancy life?"

Emmalin felt the jab and accepted it, remembering how that life had betrayed him many years before. "Jacob convinced me I was making a mistake." Emmalin tossed a quick smile at Jacob before turning back to her father.

Jacob stepped forward. "I meant to ask you properly, but all of a sudden, I knew what I needed to do and there was no time." He removed his hat. "I'd like to ask you for Emmalin's hand in marriage, sir."

The question hung in the air.

Samuel furrowed his eyebrows, then finally broke the silence. "Marriage? What in tarnation?"

"I know it's sudden, and I do apologize. I should have come to you before asking her, but I was up at my place when I realized what a fool I'd been. I had let her go without telling her how I felt, so I went after her."

Jacob stepped closer to Emmalin. "Samuel, I love your daughter and I want to marry her. I'll do my best to make her happy."

Samuel looked from Jacob to Emmalin, then to Margaret, who stood with her hands pressed together, an expectant expression on her face. He finally settled his gaze on Emmalin. "This is what you want?"

"With all my heart."

"All right, then." Samuel reached for Jacob's hand. "You have my bless-ing." The two men shook, and Samuel let out a laugh. "I was beginning to think you'd never come to your senses." He slapped Jacob on the back in a friendly way, then moved to Emmalin. "And I'm sure glad you'll be sticking around."

"This is where I belong." She looked at Jacob. "When he came for me, I knew."

Jacob took Emmalin's hand and gave it a squeeze. "I'm already working on our home."

"Oh," Margaret said in a gush. "Thank the Lord! I was thinking you two had missed out on the beautiful gift God had given you—each other." She pulled Emmalin into her arms. "I'm so happy for you. And thank-ful you'll be living here. I couldn't imagine how I was going to manage without you." She held Emmalin away from her, the fine lines in her face deepening with her tender smile. "Deer Creek is better with you in it."

Emmalin's heart swelled. "Thank you. It feels like home." Her eyes sud-denly filled with tears as she realized what had almost happened. "I nearly made the biggest mistake of my life."

Margaret gave Emmalin's cheek a pat, then moved toward the kitchen. "You must be hungry. I made chicken and vegetable pie. There's plenty."

"Sounds good." Jacob draped his coat on a hook on the wall, then placed his hat over it. "I'm starved."

"Chicken pie sounds perfect," Emmalin said as she removed her cloak and handed it to Jacob who hung it next to his.

"Have a seat, you two, and I'll get you some."

Emmalin and Jacob took their places at the table while Margaret spooned dinner onto dishes, setting the steaming plates in front of them. "There's chocolate cake when you're done. I was feeling low, so I did some extra baking. Now it feels like a celebration."

Joy bubbled up inside of Emmalin and she sent a "thank you" heav-enward.

"Coffee?" Margaret asked.

"Yes. Please." Emmalin took a bite of chicken.

"Sure." Jacob scooped up a forkful of the vegetable pie.

Margaret filled their cups, then refilled hers and Samuel's. She set the coffeepot back on the stove. "Oh, Mr. Henderson. What became of him and your luggage?"

"He's on the road north. I figure I'll ride up in the morning and let him know what's happened," Jacob said.

"But what about your things, Emmalin? How will you manage?"

"I'll be fine, Margaret. I didn't pack all my clothes and necessities. After all, so much of what I wear here wouldn't be acceptable in Philadelphia."

A look of surprise touched Margaret's face.

"So many of the people there don't know a thing about being practical," Emmalin said in a hurry, hoping not to offend her dear friend. "And whatever I need I can purchase from the mercantile. Expense is no concern."

"Oh, of course," Margaret said.

Jacob shifted in his chair.

Why did he look so uncomfortable?

Samuel rested his elbows on the table. "So, when do you two plan to have this wedding?"

"I figured around the end of summer." Jacob glanced at Emmalin. "If that's all right with you?"

"Of course."

"I have the cabin to build. It's a big job."

Emmalin held back her disappointment. September seemed so far away.

"You can get it done sooner with some help. I know several men who'd be more than happy to give you a hand," Samuel added.

Jacob's mouth became set. "I guess we'll see."

"At least we have plenty of time to plan the wedding and make your dress." Margaret reached across the table and patted Emmalin's arm.

Emmalin pressed a hand to her chest. It all seemed so real now. She was actually going to become Jacob's wife. Here in the wilderness of Oregon. Feeling disquieted, she glanced toward the windows, dark now that the sun had set. How was she going to manage? She'd been here less than a year. Could she truly step into the shoes of a pioneer woman?

"I'll get busy downing more trees and building us a good sturdy house." Jacob leaned back in his chair and circled his arms behind his neck.

"Can we have chickens and a garden? And perhaps some roses too?"

"We can have anything you want. It's going to be your home."

"This is going to be a glorious summer." Margaret clapped her hands together. "I have so much to teach you, Emmalin."

Emmalin caught a glimmer of what it could be. It seemed almost perfect. She couldn't imagine a better beginning. Margaret would continue to teach her all she needed to know about keeping a house, and her father would steady her and help her with things like farming. And Jacob...well, Jacob would love and watch over her. With him at her side, she could do anything.

As long as they stepped into their future together, they would have the strength they needed. She reached for Jacob's hand and grasped it. He smiled at her and dropped a kiss to the back of her fingers.

Yes. All would be well. This was right.

Chapter Two

Emmalin stirred, caught in those moments between sleep and wakefulness. She reached her arms over her head and released a slow breath. A sense of well-being settled in her. She rolled onto her side and snuggled beneath her quilt. Just a little more sleep.

All of a sudden, she was wide awake, her thoughts tumbling backward to a restless night. Her mind had spent the hours jumping from plans, then dreams and the what-ifs of her future. There'd been little time for sleep.

And then she remembered Jacob and hugged her pillow. They were getting married!

Emmalin pressed a hand against her tumbling stomach as it all came back in a rush. Their ride across the meadows and into the hills east of Deer Creek where Jacob had told her he loved her. She never thought she'd hear those words from him. And their first kiss…it had been so tender, as if out of a dream.

She sat on the edge of the bed and dropped her feet to the floor. The wood was hard and unforgiving. Cold. The air was chill. What had happened to the previous day's warmth? She stood and moved to the window and lifted the floral cotton drapery.

Emmalin studied dark heavy clouds. The smell of rain was in the air. Had she yielded too quickly? She had been completely deceived by Collier…and others. Her mother and father had lied to her. All her life she'd believed her father had died. Her grandfather and her uncle had known the truth and they hadn't told her.

Her mind edged toward a question she didn't want to ask. Could she trust Jacob?

She pushed her feet into silk slippers, padded to the armoire, and lifted out her dressing gown. She threw it on, then tied the gown in front only now aware of a throbbing headache. She massaged her temples as she headed for the door.

The aroma of coffee and warmth from the woodstove was a comfort. Her father had kindly thought of her before heading into town. She opened the firebox on the stove and added wood, then poured a cup of coffee and stirred in milk and sugar. It was just what she needed. She sipped the coffee as she moved to the rocker near the open hearth and settled into the chair. Resting her head against the wooden back, Emmalin closed her eyes, breathed deeply, and attempted to quiet the uneasiness humming through her. Why the anxiety? Of course she could trust Jacob. He had no reason to deceive her. She should feel nothing but bliss.

Perhaps the unease was simply because the realizations and proclamations of love had happened so suddenly and unexpectedly. Jacob had literally swept her off her feet. It had been so romantic, like a love story. But real life held no promise of a happily-ever-after ending. Rather, it was full of obstacles and privations.

Of course Jacob loved her, but had she made the right decision? She'd not taken adequate time to give thought to what she was agreeing to. Life as a pioneer wife sounded romantic, but it was more about hard work, taking risks, and facing dangers with determination and grit.

There was no need for her to rush into marriage. She was financially capable of caring for herself. With her inheritance, she was now a wealthy woman. A life of luxury could easily be had. She rested a hand at the hollow of her throat where she felt the rapid pattering of her heart.

Jacob's handsome face, his hazel eyes that made her catch her breath, and his charming smile swirled through her mind. He was the finest man she'd ever known. Of course, she should marry him.

Comfort and wealth meant nothing without him. But choosing him meant living in the Oregon wilderness, far from creature comforts. Even

Deer Creek was a fair distance from Jacob's place, taking more than an hour on horseback, and there were no neighbors to call upon in time of need. Was she truly prepared for such an existence? There would be no turning back.

When Jacob asked her to share his life, she'd been swept up in the magic of it all. It had seemed like a grand adventure. But in the light of day, she couldn't ignore its harsh realities. There would certainly be hardships and danger aplenty. Plus, there would be things to fear. Emmalin knew that all too well.

She opened her eyes and took another sip of coffee. Oh, how she loved Jacob. Was love enough to overcome all they would face?

"Howdy, neighbor," came a call from outside.

Emmalin startled, nearly spilling her coffee. She'd been so wrapped up in her thoughts she hadn't heard anyone approach. She pushed out of her chair and walked to the door. When she opened it, her friend Charity bounded up the steps. "Charity. What a lovely surprise."

"After hearing the wonderful news, I had to come." Wearing a bright smile, Charity gave Emmalin a massive hug. "I'm so happy for you." She stepped back. "I had no idea. I mean I wanted you and Jacob to fall in love, but you didn't say a word."

"When I set off from town yesterday, I had every intention of traveling to Oregon City and signing on to a wagon train. Though I must admit my heart was heavy at the thought of leaving. And then Jacob came along and, well, I couldn't resist his charm." She laughed.

Charity clapped her hands. "I want to hear all about it."

"I was just about to make some breakfast. Would you like to join me?"

"I've already had breakfast, but I'll take a cup of coffee."

Emmalin stepped inside and held the door for her friend. "Do you take cream and sugar?"

"Just black." Charity dropped onto one of the hardbacked chairs.

Emmalin filled a cup with coffee and set it on the table. It was nearly nine thirty, too late for a real breakfast. A slice of apple strudel would do well. She cut a piece, placed it on a plate, and sat across from her friend.

Charity studied her with wide blue eyes. "Are you all right? I don't mean to be rude, but it's late and you're still in your nightdress."

"I'm fine. I just didn't sleep well, with all the excitement."

Charity brushed a strand of blonde hair off her face. "I wouldn't have slept a wink. I'd be over the moon." She smiled. "Have you set a date?"

"Sometime in the late summer. There's a lot to be done."

"Of course." Charity glanced around as if looking for someone. "I'm surprised Jacob's not here this morning."

"He's hunting down Mr. Henderson who has all my luggage and has no idea what became of me yesterday after I rode off with Jacob. It seems inappropriate to just let him keep wondering."

"Oh yes. I heard about how Jacob chased after you." Charity leaned forward. "How romantic. And he asked you to marry him there at his place on the North Umpqua?"

"He did." Emmalin couldn't help but smile at the memory. "He took me quite by surprise. In recent weeks we've both known that we love each other but refused to admit it to ourselves. It all just seemed so complicated. And I truly couldn't entertain such an idea without Jacob announcing his feelings to me first."

"Thank goodness you did the right thing. I'm so happy for you. The two of you belong together."

"Yes, we do. Tomorrow we are going out to his place and finalize plans for our home. He's building it himself." A swirl of excitement felt as if it might lift her off the chair. Their home. It didn't seem possible.

"It's all so perfect. Jacob is a good man and so handsome." Charity brightened with a delighted smile.

"That he is." Emmalin set her fork on her plate. "It's just all quite unexpected."

"Everything will work out. And the surprise of it all only makes it more romantic." Charity sighed. "I wish I had a suitor."

"I thought you and Pastor Miller were courting."

Charity frowned. "I don't know how he feels about me, or if he feels anything at all. We've shared a few picnics and he once took me to dinner at Margaret's café. But he's still not made his intentions known. I'll likely stay an old maid forever."

"You'll find someone who is perfect for you. And perhaps it is Pastor Miller. He's rather reserved and doesn't seem the type to blurt out his feelings in a rush. He just needs a bit of time." Emmalin eyed Charity's trousers. "Of course, it might help if you dressed a bit more modest." She smiled sweetly to lighten the criticism.

"I know you're right, but I'm not about to be someone I'm not. I wear what's appropriate to the task. And this morning I had work needing done in the barn. A dress would have been completely ridiculous."

Emmalin pressed her lips together, holding back a response. How she loved Charity, but her choices might be the end of her. "I hope he comes around. You are a perfectly lovely woman and would make a fine wife."

"I do hope he can love me, just as I am. Otherwise, I'll never have a home of my own or children. I've always wanted children, lots of them." Her tone had turned wistful.

Children. Emmalin's mouth went dry. She hadn't thought about that part of marriage. Of course, Jacob wanted children. But she didn't know how to be a mother.

"You and Jacob will have beautiful babies."

And then what would she do? All of her life, she'd known that when the time came for her to be a mother, she would have a proper nanny to help her. She'd never imagined a wilderness life where mothering would be something she did on her own.

"Emmalin. Are you all right? You're white as a ghost."

"I'm fine." She took a drink of coffee. It went down in a large, hot gulp. What if she and Jacob did have a lot of children? She couldn't possibly manage. Two or three little ones would be adequate.

"Are you certain you're not ill? You look awfully pale."

Emmalin cast what she hoped was a convincing smile at Charity. "I've never been better."

⁕—⁕—⁕—⁕—⁕—⁕

Smoke splashed through the shallows of the Umpqua River and lunged up a trail leading to the roadway. Jacob pulled back on the reins when they reached the top of the bank. Smoke stopped, and he stroked the horse's neck. "You're in high spirits today." He sat back in the saddle. "Likely feeling my happiness."

Jacob didn't feel completely happy. He'd rather be spending the day with Emmalin instead of tracking down Mr. Henderson. If he kept up a brisk pace, he might have time to ride out to Samuel's when he got back to town. Emmalin would be looking for him.

His gaze swept across the rolling countryside. Deep green grasses danced in the breeze as shadows of sun and clouds drifted across the meadows. He was reminded of a lush green carpet he'd once seen in a fancy hotel in Oregon City.

What was the name of that hotel? Maybe Emmalin would like to visit there one day after they were married. He was sure it wasn't as fancy as the hotels in Philadelphia, but it would likely please her. They could dress up, eat at a fancy restaurant, spend an evening at the theater, and then retire in luxury. Maybe he could arrange something like that for their honeymoon. It could be a surprise.

His mind returned to the previous day. When he'd gone after Emmalin, he didn't know what to expect from her. She was wealthy with no need of financial support from him. A life of plenty awaited her in Philadelphia. Even with doubts taunting him, he couldn't let her leave the Umpqua Valley without telling her how he felt. If he let her go, he would likely never see her again. He had to take the risk.

Thank the Lord he'd found the courage. Still, worry niggled at him. Emmalin loved him now, but how would she feel when she was actually living in a rustic wilderness cabin instead of a Philadelphia mansion?

His mother had managed to find contentment in a small cabin alongside the river. She hadn't been an heiress, but she had lived a congenial life in Canton, Ohio before setting out for the Oregon Territory to be a missionary with his father.

Jacob smiled, imagining how pleased she would be to know he'd found someone to love and who wanted to spend her life with him. Even in the midst of life's practicalities, his mother had always been a bit of a romantic. She was the one who introduced him to poetry and the pleasure of getting lost in a novel. His father was a good judge of character and would be well pleased with Emmalin.

Jacob set his eyes on the gray sky. His parents knew of his good fortune. He was certain of it. But what of his native family? Those who took him in after his parents died. Would they ever know? Heaviness wrapped itself around his heart. They were likely imprisoned at the fort in Grand Ronde. On his search after the fire, he didn't find them, but did discover that most of the local natives had been detained at Grand Ronde. At least it was in Oregon Territory, close enough to travel to. But that was for another day, today was a time for jubilation.

Jacob turned Smoke back onto the road, tapped him in the sides, and settled into a relaxed gallop. The horse skillfully maneuvered the rutted lane. Furrows had been cut into the soil by the many wagons that had traveled through.

Black, white-face cattle grazed on a hillside, likely part of the Anderson family's herd. They had a sprawling ranch that took most of their time to maintain. They were rarely seen in town. In years past, he'd helped them run cattle south. The journey to the California stocks was arduous and slow. Though the money was good, he probably wouldn't make the trip again, now that he was getting married.

Married. The word sizzled in his mind. It was almost too wonderful to believe that Emmalin was going to be his wife. He wasn't sure what a woman expected of a husband. He mostly knew the native way, which might not set well with Emmalin. He'd be needing God's guidance on how to be a respectable husband.

He spotted a wagon ahead. It must be Mr. Henderson. Jacob tapped Smoke lightly with his heels, and the horse picked up his pace. "Hello there. Mr. Henderson?" The wagon kept moving. "Mr. Henderson," Jacob hollered more loudly.

The driver looked over his shoulder, then pulled back on the reins as Jacob rode up alongside the wagon. The aged man smiled at him. "Hi there. I been wondering what happened to you and Emmalin."

Smoke danced and Jacob pulled up on the reins. "We're getting married." He smiled broadly.

"Hah! Can't say I'm surprised, the way you two looked at each other yesterday."

"It took us a while to get our feelings worked out, but we finally found our way." Jacob thumbed his hat up a notch. "I was wondering if you'd mind keeping Emmalin's trunks with you until you get back to Deer Creek."

Mr. Henderson glanced at the back of the wagon. "Sure. I've got room for them plus the load I'm picking up in Oregon City."

"I'm obliged. Thank you."

"Anything I can do for a young couple in love. It's been a long while since my wife and I were starting out, but I haven't forgotten what it's like." His blue eyes twinkled with mischief.

"When you get back to Deer Creek just leave the trunks at the store. I'll take care of them."

"Sure thing. When you two planning on getting hitched?"

"After I get our house built."

Mr. Henderson nodded. "Let me know if there is anything me and the missus can do to help out. Probably won't be all that long before you have a family to look out for."

"Sure hope so." Jacob grinned. "As we grow, I'll have to add on to the cabin."

"Me and Mrs. Henderson had a whole passel of kids. They all have families of their own now. They been a real blessing to us. I hope you two can find as much joy."

"I'm counting on it. And I know Emmalin will make a fine mother."

Chapter Three

Emmalin dipped an earthenware bowl into rinse water, then wiped it dry and set it on a shelf. She rather liked the simplicity of her father's dishes, but when she managed her own home, she hoped to purchase quality glassware for special occasions. She didn't intend to leave all of her Philadelphia ways behind. Perhaps she ought to order a table set with a tureen, platters, and serving bowls. It could well take months to arrive, and it would be splendid to have them in her new home right off.

She glanced out the window, trembling with anticipation. Jacob would arrive soon. This love for him was powerful, reaching deep within her soul. Her mind seemed always to be full of him.

Today they would ride to his property and lay out the design for their future home. She closed her eyes and envisioned them together in that forested place along the river. The home would be a bit rustic of course, but she would bring refinement to it in her own way. The location was delicious, sitting along the river. The one drawback—it was far from town and friends.

Her father stepped out of his room. Settling a hat on his head, he moved toward the front door. "I'll take care of the milking and get Sassy ready for you."

"Thank you. I'd rather not meet Jacob in a disheveled state." She lifted her mouth in a teasing smile. "He should be here soon."

Samuel grasped her shoulders in his strong hands and looked straight at her. "It's a big day for you. I wish I could go along, but this is something a couple should do on their own."

"You'd simply be bored with all of our planning anyway. However, once we are living there you will always be welcome to visit." She gave him a quick hug.

"I'm counting on it." Samuel took a deep breath and slowly let it out. "Don't rush through this part of your life. These are consequential days that you can never get back. When a young couple discovers how they feel about each other and begin planning their future they tend to feel they have to hurry to begin. Don't. Before you know it, this time will be a distant memory." His brow furrowed. "I remember such days."

"I know you do. And I'm so sorry you and Mother lost each other." An ache settled at the base of her throat. How wonderful it would have been if her parents had found a way to share their lives. Instead, her father ended up in Oregon Territory alone—her mother would not make the trek to join him—divorced, and with no knowledge that he had a daughter. They'd lost so much and so had she. "I wish Mother were still alive. She would be delighted with how everything has turned out."

Past sorrow touched her father's eyes. "I shouldn't have given up on us so easily." He disappeared within himself for a moment, then tenderness replaced the sadness in his expression. "It does no good to dwell on the past. Best to celebrate the present. And there is much to commend. These are good days. I'm happy for you and Jacob. Let me know if there is anything I can do to be of help."

Emmalin gave him another hug. "I will. I'm sure we'll need assistance. Even Jacob doesn't know everything. And what I understand about wilderness living and being a wife would barely fill a thimble."

"I don't know anything about being a wife, but Margaret sure does, and she will be happy to come alongside to help you." Samuel moved to the door. "I better tend to that horse of yours." He stepped onto the porch and pulled the door closed.

Emmalin finished up the morning dishes, tidied the house, then packed a lunch to take along for the day's adventure. She glanced out the window. Still no sign of Jacob. She hadn't seen him since they'd ridden down from the hills and into town to share their news. Now the minutes they spent apart passed agonizingly slow. What if he had simply been caught up in the moment and no longer felt the same? Her heart squeezed in anguish.

Emmalin's mind recaptured the moment he told her he loved her. Had it been only two days since? She closed her eyes, reliving the feel of the strength in his arms, the surprising softness of his lips, and how she had responded to his kiss, pressing close to him as she answered his longing with her own. Heat flushed her cheeks. She'd never been kissed that way, not even from her ex-fiancé Collier. His love had been a sham—how could she have felt the same?

The sound of footfalls on the steps swept her back to the present. Jacob?

She hurried to the door and swung it open.

Jacob stood with one booted foot on the top step, hands tucked into his pockets. A smile lit the gold flecks in his eyes.

Happiness welled up within Emmalin. How could she have had any doubts? He was the one for her.

He set a small satchel on the porch, took the final step, and, in one lithe move, pulled Emmalin into his arms. "I've been thinking about this moment ever since I left town yesterday." He brushed a strand of hair off her face, then kissed her soundly.

Emmalin's heart battered inside her chest. She felt faint. Their lips parted and she looked into Jacob's ardent gaze. "I'm so glad you're here." She hugged him hard around the neck.

"I missed you." Jacob squeezed her tightly. "I want to do this for the rest of my life." He half chuckled.

Remembering her father was still about, Emmalin stepped back just enough to allow space between them. Wearing a coy smile she said, "I hope you do." She looked beyond him to the barn. "My father is still home."

Jacob glanced over his shoulder. "I don't see him."

"Well, he's here." Emmalin rested a hand on Jacob's arm. "Did you find Mr. Henderson?"

"I did. And he was glad to keep your trunks. He won't be back for about six weeks. I hope that will be all right."

"I can wait."

"You ready to head out?"

Emmalin stepped inside. "Absolutely. I just finished making our lunch and my father is saddling Sassy for me."

Jacob followed her into the kitchen and leaned on the counter, regarding her tenderly. "This is going to be a fine day."

Emmalin returned to his arms. "It's going to be fun." She pressed a light kiss to his lips. It felt strange to show such affection, though she did like it.

"Hey there, you two," Samuel said as he walked into the house.

Emmalin lurched away from Jacob. She felt heat in her face. "We're nearly ready to leave. Just need the lunch sack."

"You're blushing." Her father chuckled. "Love's not easy to restrain. I remember." He turned to Jacob. "Glad to see you made it back all right."

"Got in last night, sir."

"No need for the sir." He looked at Emmalin. "Sassy is saddled and ready to go."

"Thank you." She took her coat down from a hook on the wall.

"Coat's a good idea. Spring weather is nothing if not unpredictable." Jacob helped Emmalin with the wrap. She pushed her arms into the sleeves, then looped the top button.

"We'll be gone most of the day," Jacob told her father. "We've got good weather so it's a fine day for a ride."

Emmalin picked up the bag that held their lunch and a flask with water and stepped through the doorway.

Samuel stood there as they moved off the porch. "Don't worry about dinner. I'll probably eat in town at the café."

"I'm sure Margaret won't mind." Emmalin cast him a playful smile, thinking it would be nice if they were to get more serious about each other.

"I hope not. I kind of fancy that woman."

"I'm sure the feeling is mutual." Emmalin's step was light as she moved to her horse. Sassy nickered. "Good morning, girl." Emmalin stroked her neck, then took the reins in her hand, and with ease pushed up into the saddle. What a difference from the attempts she'd made when she first learned to ride astride. She arranged her skirt so it modestly covered her legs.

With one swift move, Jacob threw himself onto Smoke's back and settled into the saddle. "Now, where did Henry get off to?" He glanced about the property, then put two fingers to his lips and whistled. Henry appeared from behind the barn and trotted toward his best friend. "There you are. Don't need you getting into trouble." Jacob looked at Samuel. "I'll make sure to get Emmalin back before dark."

"Appreciate that." Samuel stood on the porch and watched as the two headed toward the road.

Feeling carefree, Emmalin turned and waved. Her father lifted a hand in response. He looked relaxed, which gave her confidence. She trusted his judgment. If he was satisfied with Jacob, there was no reason to question the match.

It didn't take long for heat and moisture to build up under Emmalin's collar. "Just a moment." She pulled Sassy to a stop, unbuttoned the coat, slipped it off, and draped it over the front of her saddle. "The sun is warmer than I anticipated."

Jacob glanced at the clear sky. "Warming up, all right. This time of year, the weather's changeable, never know what it might do."

"Remember the terrible storm we had on our first fishing trip?"

"Yep. That was a bad one." A look of mischief touched Jacob's face. "But I didn't mind spending the night at the cabin."

"Oh, you rascal." Emmalin laughed. She rode up to Jacob and grasped his hand. She liked the feel of it—strong and callused. "I can barely believe I'm here and we're planning our future. We're actually riding out to *our* place." A flutter of excitement mingled with a dash of trepidation caught flight within Emmalin.

Jacob kissed the back of her hand. "I nearly lost you—fool pride of mine."

"I was just as prideful, and afraid to tell you how I felt."

A soft smile settled on Jacob's lips. "Well, at least God got ahold of me before I made the biggest mistake of my life. Though sad to say, He pretty much had to grab me by the scruff of the neck." He squeezed her hand before releasing it. "We better get a move on."

They followed the road for a while, then turned off onto a trail that meandered across an open meadow. Wildflowers of every hue swayed among tall grasses. Emmalin breathed deeply, savoring the mingled aroma of sweet grass and fragrant flowers. She reached down and plucked a tall black-eyed Susan. "I think these are my favorites. They look so happy. I can imagine them singing praises to God." She twirled it between her fingers, then broke off the long stem and tucked the flower into her hair.

Gazing across the sweeping meadow, Emmalin listened to the melody of the birds who sang as if they were as happy with life as she was.

"I don't think I've ever known a lovelier place than this. If only my mother could have seen it." Familiar sorrow pierced her heart. "She missed so much of life. Everything would have been much different if she had joined my father all those years ago. I think she would have been happy here." She turned her eyes to the hillsides. "This would have been my home." Her throat tightened with emotion. It would have been marvelous.

Jacob shifted the reins in his hands. "Samuel would have had a richer life, with a wife and child. But what would you have been like if you'd grown up here?"

Emmalin shrugged. "Certainly, I would be more suited to frontier life." She sat straighter in the saddle.

"True. But I love you just as you are." A crooked smile appeared. "Your upbringing had a lot to do with the woman I love. You're accustomed to more than just this." He swept his arm out as if presenting the scenery to her.

Since arriving in Oregon, Emmalin hadn't considered her privileged upbringing to be a positive influence. Most of her life she'd taken easy living for granted, but the months on the trail as she traveled across the country had opened her eyes to how sheltered she had been. Soon after arriving in Deer Creek, it became an embarrassment. It hindered her. Her years spent as a socialite became something to overcome.

"You should be grateful for it all—your past and your present."

Her eyes stung. Jacob accepted her just as she was, even though she was ill-equipped for life in the wilderness and still struggled with the effects of her upbringing. She blinked away the tears. "Since arriving here I have endeavored to conquer my overindulged youth, never considering it an asset."

"You have a gentle heart. Part of that comes from your years spent at your uncle's house. And it's one of the things I love about you. Here in this place, women become hardy souls early in life. Sometimes it seems too much of the genteel part of a woman drops away, stolen by the ruthlessness of the world. I'm thankful you still possess those gentler qualities. You'll get tough soon enough."

Emmalin felt as if she'd been immersed in mercy. "Thank you, Jacob."

He reined in his horse, stopped alongside Emmalin, and closed the gap between the horses, then he grabbed hold of her saddle horn and leaned close. "I love you, even the part that is spoiled and willful." He grinned.

Emmalin laughed. "I doubt you'll remain grateful of such traits. They can be trying even for me."

Jacob and Emmalin remained there for a few minutes while the horses grazed on spring vegetation. Henry plopped down in the deep grass and rolled onto his back. A breeze rustled through the swards, accompanying the sound of bird song echoing across the meadow.

The warm hum of spring caressed Emmalin's soul. "Nature has its own song, don't you think?"

"What do you mean?"

"There are the obvious songs, like the trill of birds, though they aren't always the same. And the morning bird calls are quite different than their evening choruses."

"That's true."

"And there's the gentle whisper of grasses in the wind, the buzz of insects, and the sound of the tree boughs dancing. Even the rain sometimes reminds me of a melody." She closed her eyes and listened. "When I lived in the city, nature's songs were muted, drowned out by the noise of people, barking dogs, and traffic on the streets. I rarely heard the lovely melodies of the countryside."

"I never gave it much thought until now. We have all our lives to listen to the valley's melodies." Jacob looked at her with adoration. "Together."

Emmalin giggled. "You try to conceal it, but you are truly a romantic."

His smile slid into a sideways grin. "Wouldn't want the secret to get out." He nudged Smoke forward and Emmalin rode alongside him.

As they moved into the trees and followed the trail into the hills, clouds blocked the sun, and the forest turned dark. All of a sudden Emmalin felt isolated. They were far from town. She took a deep breath. It would take a bit of getting used to, living so far from people. A shiver of apprehension moved through her. How would she manage?

Chapter Four

Jacob and Emmalin both turned quiet as they approached the burned-out cabin and barn. The fire had been cruel, taking everything in its path. A swath of forest had been left blackened. Emmalin stared at the gnarled, dying trees and could very nearly hear the torturous screams that were emitted as they were overcome by flames.

Several logs lay stacked, ready for building. There would be a new beginning.

Jacob pulled to a stop and studied the burned remains. "I'll tear down what's left of the house and barn after I get our new place built."

He dismounted and hurried around to Emmalin to help her dismount. Henry ran ahead. "I think he's ready for a dip in the river."

"I might be too. I'm a bit overheated."

He lifted a brow. "Really? You know how to swim?"

"No, but I might be convinced to wade."

"When I was a boy—before the fever took my family—my brother and I swam nearly every day during the summer." Jacob led Smoke past the burned-out cabin and a small canvas tent and moved into the clearing where the new house would be built. "The new place will be closer to the river than my parents' cabin. It'll be easier to haul water."

"Perhaps we can have plumbing put in. That way we will be able to pump right into the kitchen."

"Sure. I can do that. Just never seemed necessary."

"We have plenty of money."

"You have plenty of money. It's not mine."

"But after we're married—"

"No. I will work for our money."

Emmalin was shocked by the harshness of his tone. Did he see her inheritance as a threat?

Jacob eyed the clearing. "Plenty of good timber here for a sturdy cabin."

Maybe she was imagining things. No need to discuss it now.

Emmalin looked up into the branches of cedar and fir. "The trees are so large. How do you cut them down and get them ready for building?"

"It's a lot of work." Jacob patted the reddish-brown bark of a cedar tree.

"Isn't it dangerous?"

"Can be. But I know how to fall a tree so it goes down where I want it. It's all about the angles of the axe cuts."

"I've never understood any of that," Emmalin said, fear prickling over the surface of her arms.

"When I get back to it, I'll show you."

"I'd like that." Even though Emmalin said the words, she dreaded the idea. Falling one of these huge trees was rather terrifying. "Perhaps I can be of help."

"I'm not sure what you can do about bringing down a tree."

"There must be something."

"We'll see. You might do some limbing."

Emmalin studied the heavy limbs of a huge fir, and a shudder shook her insides. Even the best logger could make a mistake. "Perhaps we should consider using planed lumber. We could order it and have it hauled in by wagon."

"No reason for that. And it would cost a pretty penny."

"I'm sure it would be easy enough to get a shipment from Oregon City." Emmalin knew not to speak about costs, but she quieted her voice anyway and added, "I do have more than enough money."

Jacob compressed his lips and closed his eyes in a long blink. "No need for anything other than what God's provided. And logs help keep the cold of winter out."

"But wouldn't it be easier? And safer?" Emmalin took a breath and waded into what she knew could be trouble. "I've seen my inheritance as God's provision…" She let the sentence drop off, fearing Jacob's reply.

Turning away from her, Jacob acted like he was studying the layout of the house. Emmalin's stomach clenched. She'd upset him.

Jacob stepped into the center of the clearing. "So, do you still think this is the best spot for the cabin?"

"Yes. I think it's perfect."

"We'll have plenty of room for a barn over there." He nodded toward the north end of the clearing. "And I'll put up a new outhouse at the edge of the trees."

Emmalin didn't want to upset Jacob further, but the idea of traipsing all the way to the forest edge to use the outhouse made no sense to her. "Could we have the necessary built nearer to the house? That way we don't have to walk so far, especially if we get up in the middle of the night." She hated using outdoor facilities. If only they could have indoor plumbing.

"We could do that, but I'd rather walk a little farther and not have to smell it."

"Oh. Yes. Of course." Emmalin studied the distance between the house and trees and spoke, even though she knew it would be wise to remain silent. "An indoor necessary would be so nice, much easier."

Jacob looked at her with a furrowed brow, then picked up a couple pieces of wood and walked several steps and stopped. "This should be plenty long." He set a chunk of wood on the spot, made a turn, and walked several more steps where he set another piece of wood. "I'll hammer in stakes next trip up here and set out some lines to mark the rooms." He nudged his hat off his forehead. "This place will be bigger than the one my father built." He studied the space and moved along an invisible wall. "I've been thinking more about the layout since we were up here a few days ago. What about the kitchen here?"

Emmalin's mind was still on the necessary and Jacob's somewhat reckless response to her suggestion. He seemed so set. "I suppose so." She moved away from him. "But I prefer to have the kitchen here. I thought we had decided. There's a lovely view, and it would be so pleasant to look out the window while I'm cooking or washing dishes."

Jacob joined her. "Sure. We can do that."

Hoping to drive away the iciness between them, Emmalin said kindly, "Thank you."

He circled an arm around her waist. "I can already see you in the kitchen making some of my favorite blueberry pancakes."

Emmalin chuckled. "Don't expect too much, at least not at first. I have a lot to learn about cooking."

"You'll do just fine."

"I need more lessons from Margaret."

He pulled her closer. "I'll make sure you have a fine woodstove for cooking."

"A white enamel stove would be nice and could be placed right here." She held out her hands to indicate the setting.

"White?" Jacob screwed up his face. "I don't know about that. We're going to need something that can hold a lot of wood, and I figure you'd like four cook tops."

"Of course, but can't we get that in a newer style of stove? They are so much prettier. And they have a warming oven too. We can order one from Oregon City."

"Don't see that something fancy will be necessary all the way out here."

"Perhaps not." Emmalin didn't want to argue. "But it would be nice. And it would brighten up the cabin."

Jacob didn't respond for a moment, then said, "If that's what you want." He took strides toward the river. "I'll put in a hearth and fireplace here." With a smile he added, "And I'll make sure you have a rocker so you can sit here and do your sewing."

"I do love embroidering. And reading," Emmalin added. "What about you? Won't you have a rocker too?"

"Never enough time in a day for me to sit and rock."

"Not even when the sun's gone down and the day is done? I thought you enjoyed reading."

"I do, but I like to do my sitting on the porch. And by the end of the day, I'm worn out. If I get my nose in a book, I'll likely fall asleep, and then I'll be snoring."

"Snoring? I don't recall you snoring when we were traveling from Oregon City."

He shrugged. "I've been told I do. Guess it depends on how tuckered I am. And after I hang up my socks by the fire neither one of us will want to sit near them." He lifted an eyebrow, looking slightly embarrassed.

Emmalin wrinkled her nose. "There won't be any smelly socks in my front room. I'll see that they are laundered every day. And you'll have a clean pair each morning."

Jacob chuckled. "That'll be something new." He moved toward the front of the cabin space. "We'll need more than a couple of bedrooms. Maybe one here. And another one over here." He stepped toward what would be the front door. "And we can put our room on the opposite end of the cabin. That way we won't be sleeping next to the children."

Emmalin wasn't sure she wanted to talk about children just yet. But now that he'd brought it up there was no avoiding the subject. "I'd rather be near the little ones. What if they need me in the night?"

"Of course. I can see that. I just thought it might be nice to have some peace and quiet."

Emmalin balled her hands into fists. This wasn't what she had imagined. In her mind this time of planning out their home would be romantic, and she'd been confident they would agree on most everything. It had seemed that way when they were first making plans for the house. "In truth, Jacob, I've never taken care of children. I don't have the first idea what to do."

"Isn't it something that comes natural to a woman?"

"I suppose. Do you want a lot of children?"

"Sure. I'm hoping we can have a whole litter of them." He grinned.

Emmalin's stomach tightened. A litter? She wasn't some kind of farm animal.

"Emmalin? You all right? You look pale."

"I'm fine. Just tired." She turned her gaze to the slowly moving river.

"I have no doubt you'll be a good mother. And I can teach our boys to hunt and fish. This is a good spot for fishing." As if sensing her uneasiness, he moved to her side. "We'll have a good life here on the North Umpqua."

Emmalin didn't want to talk about the house or family anymore. She stepped out of the imaginary cabin and away from Jacob. "What about a garden? Where should we put it?"

"I think the best place is there to the north. The ground is good. My mother had a garden there." He took Emmalin's hand and led her into the garden area. "How about an orchard? Right over there." He nodded to the east of the garden.

"I'd like that—fresh fruit whenever we want." Emmalin's excitement revived slightly. "We can have plums and apples, maybe even a cherry tree or two."

"And how about pears?"

Jacob circled his arm around Emmalin, but the trepidation that had crept in didn't quiet. There was so much to think about and plan. And to overcome? She and Jacob had such different ideas about how things should be done. Living all the way out here, she wouldn't have the support of Margaret or Charity. They'd be so far away. There would be no surprise visits for tea and a chat. A breeze rustled through the trees, raising goose-flesh on her arms.

"We'll be happy here." Jacob gave her a squeeze.

"Yes. We will," Emmalin said, but she felt unprepared and vulnerable. She leaned against Jacob. She needed to feel his strength. Being a pioneer wife wasn't going to be easy.

Chapter Five

Glad to have the dishes done, Emmalin lifted off her apron and hung it up. The smell of overcooked pork hung in the air. It hadn't been her best dinner effort, but her father had eaten it with gratitude anyway. He was a good man, a good father. Thankfulness washed through her. She'd nearly missed ever knowing him.

He sat at the table, bent over a set of traps. Each must be cleaned and repaired before being put away for the season. He glanced at her. "All done?"

"Yes. Thank goodness." She moved toward the cabin door. "It's nearly dusk and I haven't collected the eggs yet. The day got away from me."

Samuel put the trap he'd been working on in a box. "Margaret said she'll take any extras we have."

Emmalin picked up a basket from a shelf near the door. "I'll be taking some into town tomorrow. I'm counting on Margaret having time for a chat over coffee and pastries." She lifted her eyebrows in good humor, then stepped outside.

The day had been warm but was rapidly turning cool. Long shadows reached across the yard and trees stirred in the breeze. Frogs croaked a loud chorus from a nearby pond and within deep grasses.

Stopping at the bottom of the steps, Emmalin searched the early evening sky for stars. Here in the Oregon wilderness, when the world prepared to sleep, it was an especially lovely interlude. She closed her eyes and breathed in the fragrance of spring—damp soil, sprouting grasses, cedar and pine, and a hint of sweet wildflowers.

Emmalin meandered across the yard, swinging the empty egg basket. What might the morrow bring? Perhaps Jacob would visit. Remembering the thrill of his lips on hers, she felt the warmth of a blush. Though she still felt shy about sharing things like kisses, she looked forward to experiencing more of Jacob's affection.

Emmalin wrenched her mind back to the present. She enjoyed gathering eggs. In Philadelphia it had been a chore done by servants. She'd never known the satisfaction of searching them out, sometimes reaching beneath a friendly hen and gently grasping her day's offering in her hand. Counting the number of eggs collected was peculiarly satisfying.

She hadn't known how friendly the fat, plucky fowl could be. In her father's flock there was only one sassy pullet. She was black and white, easily stirred up and quick to let Emmalin know she didn't appreciate anyone stealing her eggs. Only when in the biggest hurry did Emmalin risk snatching one out from beneath her because the attempt almost always resulted in a sharp peck from the hen.

Pulling open the door that led into an outer portion of the chicken house, Emmalin grabbed a handful of cracked corn from a barrel, before entering the nesting area. She was met by the pungent odor of birds, hay, and ripe manure. She wrinkled her nose. Though sharp, the smell no longer repulsed her.

"Hello, ladies. Did you have a nice day? Were there a lot of bugs and grain to be had on your outdoor foray?" Her father teased her about how she chatted with the birds, but she rather liked it and ignored his joshing.

The hens greeted her with clucking and deep burring sounds. They knew she'd likely brought something good to eat. Emmalin liked to imagine they enjoyed her company, although common sense told her what they really cared about was the grain in her hand. She tossed out the ground corn.

"There you go."

The rooster jumped into the middle of the brood but didn't partake. Rather, he watched over his ladies while they ate up the evening treat. "Ah, you're a fine bird, always protecting the flock." As if he understood the compliment, he ruffled his feathers and targeted Emmalin with a sharp gaze.

Emmalin moved to the nest boxes. The hens each had a favorite nest. Emmalin couldn't imagine how they decided which was best. They were identical in size, and each held fresh grass to cushion the hens and their eggs.

She collected a total of eleven eggs. The last box held a golden-brown hen who burred at Emmalin and refused to move. "Oh my! Are you broody?" Emmalin smiled. That meant they would soon have new chicks.

She checked to make certain the water container had an adequate supply, then she slid the hen's gate closed and stepped to the door with her clutch of eggs held closely. "Good night, ladies. Sleep well." She met the rooster's gaze. "And you too, sir." She stepped out and pulled the door closed, then glanced at the basket of eggs. When added to what they already had, there would be more than enough to share with Margaret.

Emmalin had made it halfway across the yard when, out of the corner of her eye, she saw something move. She stopped. There was a shadow along the edge of the chicken house. The hair on her arms prickled. Surely it was nothing, a rat or the farm cat. She stared into the darkening gloom, willing her eyes to see. And then she did see. A cat moving toward her? No. Not a cat—a cougar!

She couldn't breathe. What should she do? She had no weapon.

Her mind whirled with instructions she'd been given if she were ever to come face-to-face with a predator. Don't run. She wanted to run. But no. That would only encourage the big cat to chase. And it would easily overtake her. She knew not to scream for fear of sounding like prey. If only she had a gun. Why didn't she have one on her? Standing straight and tall, she stared at the huge cat.

With a glance at the house, she calculated how many steps it would take to reach the porch. It was at least twenty yards. She'd never make it before the animal would be upon her.

Emmalin remained still, taking shallow quaking breaths. The cougar didn't move, except for the twitching of its tail. Emmalin was reminded of the farm cat facing down a trapped mouse. The mouse rarely survived the standoff. Would that be her outcome? She tried to swallow, but her mouth was dry.

Keeping her eyes on the animal, Emmalin took a step in the direction of the house. The cat perked up and leaned toward her ever so slightly but did not attack. All right. Maybe she could make it. *Move slowly. Face the creature. Never take your eyes off it. Do not run.*

She took another step. The cat also took one but did not close the distance. Emmalin chanced another. The animal watched her, its golden eyes glinting in the fading light. Emmalin took a step forward. The cat came closer. Emmalin's breath caught in her throat. She felt as if she were being smothered by fear. Her body buzzed with terror. She hugged the basket of eggs. Could she offer them up? Surely, he wasn't interested in eggs.

Maybe she could call for help? No. Her father would never hear. The windows and the door were closed. And her cry might goad the cougar into an attack.

Trying not to show fear, yet certain the animal could smell it, Emmalin maintained her stance and edged toward the house. Crouched low to the ground, the cat followed while maintaining its distance. Emmalin was nearly to the porch. Just a couple more steps.

So close now. She almost shouted her relief when her foot touched the bottom step. Still clutching the basket, she moved her free arm very slowly and grabbed hold of the railing. The cat stayed put, watching, not retreating. If she tried to hurry onto the porch, would it leap on her? Emmalin could feel the power of the animal and imagined the piercing of its claws and teeth. It could be on her in a moment. One more step, then another. The cat glared at her, its tail twitching.

She was nearly at the door. Taking a deep breath and trying not to quake, she readied herself. In one swift motion she leaped to the door, opened it, and threw herself inside, slamming it closed behind her. Holding the basket of eggs against her abdomen, she leaned against the solid wood of the door and gulped in oxygen.

Her father propelled himself out of the chair. "What is it? What's wrong?"

Emmalin pressed a hand to her chest. "A cougar! It stalked me! It's in the yard!"

In two strides her father crossed the room and seized a rifle from its rack on the wall, grabbed a handful of shells from a box on the hearth, and slammed one into the chamber, then another, and cocked the gun. Pushing the remaining shells into his pocket, he hurried to the door. "Stay put."

He disappeared into the near darkness. Ignoring her father's command, Emmalin followed onto the porch where she stared into the deepening nightfall. Her father ran to the edge of the yard, then stopped, raised the rifle, and fired. He gazed into the gathering darkness, then cautiously walked into the field. Emmalin held her breath. Finally, he stopped and yelled, "I got him." He prodded the animal with the gun barrel, then knelt beside it.

Emmalin quaked. Her legs felt as if they were about to go out from beneath her. She set the basket of eggs on a step, marveling that she hadn't broken them. Gripping the railing, she whispered, "Thank you, Lord."

Her father returned to the yard, dragging the big cat behind him. He hauled it into the barn, then reappeared a few moments later. "I'll skin it out tonight."

"I-I thought he was going to kill me."

Her father draped an arm over her shoulders. "It likely wouldn't have."

"The way it looked at me. And it followed me to the house." Emmalin's tension was suddenly released in uncontrollable sobs.

Her father pulled her close. "He can't hurt anyone now." He gave her a gentle squeeze. "Was he at the barn?"

"No. After I collected the eggs and stepped into the yard, that's when I saw him. He was standing next to the chicken house, in the shadows. I thought cougars stayed away from people."

"They usually do. But this one's young and too lean. Likely hungry and decided chicken would be an easy target. You just came along and got in the way."

"Will it happen again?"

"I can't promise it won't, but it would be a rare thing if it did." He smoothed her hair. "No need to be afraid."

Emmalin stepped away. "I should keep a gun on me when I'm out. Could you help me with some shooting practice?"

"Sure. But I thought you were able to handle a weapon. I mean, you killed an Indian when you and Jacob were attacked last summer."

"I did, but I need more practice. I think that was a lucky shot."

"All right then. I'll get you a pistol to carry if that will make you feel safer."

"Thank you. It's a good thing I didn't need it tonight."

"You used your wits and you ended up fine." Her father grinned. "I have to say you looked like you'd seen the devil himself when you came through that door." He chuckled.

Emmalin smiled, but she wasn't up to laughing about it just yet. "I felt like I had. And I won't feel safe until I have my own pistol and rifle, and know I can trust my ability to use them efficiently if needed."

"A lot of folks around here are armed most of the time. Don't see why you shouldn't be too. You just need to be careful that you know what you're aiming at before you take a shot."

"I'll use the utmost caution, I assure you." Emmalin let out a slow breath and closed her eyes. Terror stayed with her. She would never forget what it felt like to be prey.

Her mind went to Jacob's home. It was likely more dangerous there than here. But she would be ready the next time something like this happened. She shuddered and burrowed her face against her father's cotton shirt. When she straightened, her gaze went to the trees and the deep shadows that lay beneath the boughs. Was there an animal there? Waiting?

Chapter Six

Emmalin poured herself a cup of coffee. "Would you like more?" Her father held up his cup.

After filling it with the dark draught, Emmalin set the pot back on the stove top, then sat at the table. She dipped a teaspoon of sugar from a delicately painted porcelain bowl that had been one of her mother's pieces Emmalin had brought across the Oregon Trail. It seemed out of place in this rustic cabin. Her mother would have never imagined her glassware or her daughter ever living in such a place. And soon Emmalin would move to an even more remote house. The now familiar sense of insecurity draped itself over her. Was moving so far from town the right thing to do? She hadn't been raised for such a life, and after the cougar encounter the night before the idea was terrifying.

Emmalin added milk and stirred it in, while trying to quiet the trembling in her hand. She didn't want her father to know how frightened she was.

"Will you be going into town?" Her father slurped his drink.

"I need to get a few items from the store, and I wanted to get some eggs to Margaret."

He took another swig of coffee. "I'll hitch up the team for you."

"I'll need to learn to do that for myself." She set the spoon on the table.

"When we get some time, I'll teach you."

Emmalin sipped her coffee, her thoughts, once more, returning to the previous night. She hadn't been able to get the encounter out of her mind.

"You look tired. You all right?"

"I'm fine. Perfectly fine. But I didn't sleep well. I couldn't stop thinking about what happened. I kept imagining what might have been."

Her father reached across the table and patted her hand. "That's to be expected. It was scary. But you'll have to let it go."

"I'm not sure how to do that. It was so distressing. I barely made it back into the house. And even though you believe all would have been well, we can't know that for certain." She placed her cup on the table in front of her. "What if it happens again?"

"I've been living here more than half my life and that's the first time I've ever seen a cougar come that close to the house."

Emmalin blew out a controlled breath. "Of course, you're right. I'm being silly." She took two more sips of coffee, then pushed away from the table. "I best get ready." She took her cup with her, had a final sip at the sink, then set the cup in a porcelain washing bowl.

Samuel sopped up the last of his gravy with a biscuit and pushed it into his mouth. "I'll get the wagon ready," he said around the mouthful of food. He swilled down the remainder of his coffee and set his plate and flatware in the sink. "I'll wash these later."

"Thank you." Emmalin hurried to her room. She stood in front of the bureau mirror and splashed her face with cool water from the basin, then using toothpowder, she cleaned her teeth. She detested the flavor but wasn't about to end up like so many others who lost their teeth to decay. The front door closed with a thud. She'd hoped her father would be going into town, thus alleviating the need for her to go in. The idea of it made her heart skitter.

Emmalin brushed her hair, gently tugging out small tangles. Her cheeks had more color than usual. Likely from lingering stress. It was a good thing she needed to make the trip into town. Margaret was always level-headed. She'd calm Emmalin's nerves.

Emmalin tied her hair back with a ribbon and let it fall past her shoulders in soft waves. A chignon would be more acceptable, but she didn't want to take the time and her hands were still trembling. She pulled on a dark blue knitted shawl and pinned on a matching hat. If she were in Philadelphia, gloves would be an expected part of her attire, but here they only served to set her apart.

Finally ready, but still apprehensive, she talked to her image in the mirror. "You have nothing to worry about. The horses are sensible and strong."

Once in town she would have a marvelous chat with Margaret and feel much better. Emmalin walked purposely to the front door. From the porch, her eyes returned to the place where she'd first seen the cougar, half expecting to see it crouching and gazing at her. Of course, there was nothing to see. She looked about the yard. Nothing frightening, only a handful of robins hopping about in search of worms in the damp grass.

She took the steps casually to the barn, barely managing not to do a continuous surveillance of the property just in case of predators. The wagon was ready to go.

Her father checked the lines, making sure they ran freely over the backs of the bay geldings. He turned to Emmalin and handed the reins to her. "All set."

Grasping them firmly, she climbed into the wagon and settled on the wooden seat. "Thank you, but after this if I'm going to become a more independent woman, I must learn to harness the horses myself."

"You already told me that once this morning."

"Yes, I know, but it's important so needs to be repeated."

Her father offered a kind smile. "We'll do it soon. It's a little complicated, but once you get the hang of it you won't have any trouble."

"All right." Emmalin straightened her spine. "I should be back by late morning or early afternoon."

"If you get home early enough, we can have lunch together."

"If I have any appetite remaining after coffee and pastries." She turned the horses toward the drive and whipped the reins lightly. "Come on, now." The horses stepped into a trot, and the farm fell away behind Emmalin.

The farther she traveled from home, the more anxiety she felt. She quieted her breathing and tried to focus on the beauty of the open fields and distant green hills adorned with oak and fir. It was pleasing to the eye and to the spirit. God had created it and watched over it all. And He would watch over her as well.

Emmalin's thoughts returned to the day her father taught her to drive the wagon. She'd been afraid then too, thinking the team would run away with her. But they hadn't. She'd quickly learned to handle the horses, and the confidence gained had bolstered her sense of independence.

Was she ready to tackle the life of a pioneer wife? After what had happened, well, the cougar had stolen what confidence she possessed. Now she felt nothing but vulnerable and unprepared.

She turned her gaze to a sky with white clouds sweeping across its blue canopy and the shadows beneath them that swept over the meadows. The Lord was here. She breathed deeply, her apprehension ebbing. This was indeed a splendid day. Even the horses seemed happy, tossing their heads, and stepping lightly.

Though more at ease, Emmalin still kept watch of the open fields and dark tree line, just in case a predator waited there. She'd known the dangers were real, in fact she'd faced many already, but the cougar came at her in a place she felt safe. Her father's cabin was relatively close to town. Jacob's, on the other hand, was far from anything civilized. She wouldn't be afraid when Jacob was with her, but what would she do when he was gone and she was there alone?

She spotted the Olson place at the edge of town. The small one-story house wasn't much to look at, but it was sturdy and it had been built with planed lumber. Sophia Olson was sweeping the porch and offered up a small wave. She was a tiny thing and quiet. Emmalin had never gotten to know her. "Good morning," she called, thinking she should make a greater effort to meet the woman. One of her little ones peeked out from behind her mother's skirts, then ran inside the house.

Emmalin turned her attention back to the horses and the road in front of her. She'd made it without incident, just as she had many times before.

The town blacksmith stepped out of the livery. "Morning."

Emmalin pulled back on the reins. "Good morning, Mr. Fulsom."

He took a glance at the blue sky. "It's a fine day."

"Yes, it is. How are you?"

"Good. Just taking a breather. Say hello to your father for me."

"I certainly will. Have a good day." Emmalin lifted the reins and the horses immediately moved forward. They knew exactly where to go and plodded along, stopping directly in front of the mercantile. She'd been silly to worry.

Emmalin climbed down from the seat and tied the team to a hitching post. Making sure to carry herself with confidence, she retrieved the basket of eggs from the back of the wagon. First, she'd get needed supplies and then drop in at Margaret's café. She turned toward the store, but the café door opened and the aroma of freshly baked pastries wafted out. Emmalin changed course. She could get supplies later.

The mingled smell of coffee and sweet scent of baked goods warmed Emmalin's insides. It was past time for breakfast and the café had only two customers, men who looked like miners, likely from down south. Emmalin couldn't imagine how they tolerated endless hours of panning along the riverbanks. Some used shakers to separate gold from the rocks and mud, but it was still backbreaking work.

The two men sat near the back wall, hunched over plates of eggs and pancakes. Without speaking, they shoveled in their meals.

Emmalin moved toward the kitchen. "Margaret?"

Her friend opened the oven door, then straightened and flashed a smile at Emmalin. "Good morning. What a pleasant surprise."

"I've been thinking about your delicious pastries, and I'm in need of your company. Do you have time for a guest?"

Margaret glanced at the nearly empty café. "The morning crowd is gone. It's the perfect time. Just let me pop a couple of pies in the oven first." She picked up two pies from the kitchen counter and, holding one in each hand, stepped to the stove where she slid them into the hot oven and closed the door. "I'll be glad for fresh fruit. I'm nearly out of apples."

"Won't the cherries be coming on soon?"

"Not soon enough for me." Margaret wiped her hands on her apron. "I'm ready for another cup of coffee. How about you?"

"Yes. Thank you."

Using an oven mitt, Margaret lifted the coffeepot off the stove, grabbed two mugs and walked to a table at the front of the café, near a window. "And how about one of my fresh cinnamon rolls?"

"Sounds wonderful." Emmalin set the basket on the counter. "I brought you some eggs."

"Oh. Thank you. I can always use more." She filled the cups with coffee, then returned the pot to the stove. "I have two cinnamon rolls left, one for each of us." She transferred the rolls to two plates along with a fork for each and carried them to the table. "I'll have to keep a close eye on the clock. I'd hate to overbake those pies."

Emmalin grabbed the sugar bowl and creamer and headed to the table. "Oh, I've been needing this." She sat and added sugar and milk to her coffee.

"Any special reason for your visit?" Margaret sat across from Emmalin.

"I always enjoy your company, of course, but I do have something I want to talk with you about." Emmalin took a sip of coffee. "Mm. I don't know what it is about your coffee, but it tastes better than anyone else's."

"It's just plain old coffee. Maybe it's my company." Margaret laughed.

"That's it, I'm certain."

Margaret cut into her roll and took a bite. She closed her eyes as she chewed. "You'd think I'd get tired of these, but I never do. If I'm not careful I'll get fat."

"You? Never. You work too hard for that."

Margaret set down her fork. "So how are things with you? And Jacob of course."

"Jacob is fine, at least I think he is. He's at his place working on our cabin."

"I expect he's anxious to get that done so you two can get married."

Emmalin felt a flush touch her cheeks. "We both are." She rested her arms on the table. "A few days ago, we made a trip out there and put together some plans for the house."

"That must have been fun."

"Yes." Emmalin couldn't conceal the disappointment in her voice. "However, we don't exactly see eye to eye on everything. But I think we came to a somewhat agreeable compromise."

"No couple agrees on everything."

"Of course, but he insists on using logs taken from the property. And I truly worry about him falling trees up there by himself."

"He knows what he's doing. And he's been on his own for a good long time."

"That was obvious when we tried to find commonality about our house."

Margaret smiled, cheeriness in her eyes. "I expect with your different backgrounds that your visions for a home will differ."

"Certainly. I do understand that." Emmalin hated the shrill tone in her voice.

Margaret reached for her hand. "Whatever you end up with it will be the place where you begin your lives together. As you go you will find your way. Surprisingly, as the years pass you will think more and more alike." She gave Emmalin's hand a squeeze. "Jacob said late summer, but have you set a date?"

"No. Jacob insists the house must be complete before we can be married."

"I think he's right about that. You two will need a house after the wedding, your forever home."

Forever? The muscles in Emmalin's abdomen tightened. Did she want to live so far from town forever? "I will just have to be patient I suppose."

"You'll manage." Margaret cut off another bite of roll. "How is that father of yours?"

"Good. He's working on our place today. I think he wants to make sure the chicken house is secure."

"Oh?"

"That's what I needed to talk with you about." A rush of adrenaline pumped through Emmalin at the thought of last night's encounter. She pressed a hand against her chest, in hopes of quieting her rising heart rate. "Last night, just before dark, I went out to collect eggs." The scene washed over her, the fear and panic fresh. "After I'd gotten all the eggs, I stepped out of the chicken house and saw a shadow alongside the building. At first, I thought it was a feral cat I've seen about our place, and then it came out of the shadows." Emmalin's voice was hushed as if she were now facing down the animal. "It was a cougar!"

"Oh my!" Margaret abruptly put down her cup. "So close to the house? Was something wrong with it?"

"My father said he was rather skinny and young. He was probably going after the chickens. But he came after me."

"He attacked you?"

"Not exactly. I backed up toward the house and he followed me, matching my steps. He never took his eyes off of me. He kept pace until I reached the front steps of the house. I was so frightened I could barely breathe."

Margaret leaned on the table. "Something like that would scare any person. What happened?"

"After what seemed like an eternity, I made it onto the porch and into the house. I could barely stand I was shaking so hard. My father shot him."

"Thank the Lord! In all the years that I've been here I've never had to face down a cougar, especially not by my house. A skunk and a possum, and one night I watched as shadows of a wolf pack paced around my place, but never an aggressive cougar. You poor thing."

"I'm all right. But I must admit at being a bit shaken up. And now," she lowered her voice, "the thought of moving all the way out to Jacob's place has me feeling a bit frazzled. It's even wilder out there. And I'll be on my own a lot of the time. My father, you, and Charity will be so far away."

"It is isolated, but you'll get used to it. And we're not all that far away. Not much more than an hour's ride." Margaret leaned back in her chair. "Any animal you'll encounter up there you can see here close to town too. It's not that different."

Emmalin nodded and let out a breath. "Do you think Jacob might possibly consider moving closer to town?"

Margaret cradled her cup in her hands. "I doubt it. He has deep roots there. His family is buried on that place."

Margaret was right. She couldn't ask such a thing of Jacob.

"Maybe you'd feel better if you were more equipped to face the dangers."

"How do you mean?"

"I know you can use a rifle, but are you a good shot? Do you feel comfortable using it?"

"I'm just barely adequate."

"Well, that's it then. You need to get yourself a firearm of your own and do a lot of practicing. After my Edgar died, I didn't have anyone to rely on but myself. In those early days, I felt small and weak out at my place all alone, but I didn't want to leave. It was our place, the home we shared. So, I did what I had to. I got stronger, better. I learned what I needed to know about running a ranch. And I practiced my shooting. I'm a good aim now and any animal that comes on my place better not mess with me." She laughed. "You can do it too. I know you can."

Emmalin felt a surge of confidence. "Of course I can. And my father said he would give me instruction." She grabbed Margaret's hand. "I'll do it."

Chapter Seven

Jacob sat easy in the saddle as Smoke moved along the trail. It was a good day to be out. As he passed through the forest and meadowlands, a profusion of birds serenaded him. A coyote was so intently focused on prey it didn't notice Jacob's approach. Jacob tugged on the reins and stopped to watch. Henry stared, quivering with interest. "Stay put," Jacob told him in a hushed voice.

The coyote's tail twitched in anticipation of a meal. All of a sudden it leaped upon an unsuspecting squirrel. With the meal clasped in its mouth, the coyote glanced about, spotted Jacob, and sprinted into dense underbrush.

Henry stepped forward as if ready to give chase. "Henry. No. No time for that today." The dog looked up at Jacob and remained in place. Jacob grinned. "Looks like he's got himself some breakfast." Henry whined. "You already had yours."

Jacob studied the sky. The sun had burned through the morning haze and the air already felt warm. He swept off his hat, used his forearm to wipe sweat from his brow, then replaced the hat. Tall grasses swayed and whispered a soft melody as they bent in the breeze. The air was heavy with their sweet fragrance.

He'd always valued life in the Oregon Territory, but with Emmalin at his side it was better than he'd believed it could be. She helped him see through new eyes—her eyes, which were the same deep blue of an afternoon sky. The shimmer of her hair reminded him of the ginger-colored flowers that grew in the upper meadows.

A passionate ache swelled in his chest. He'd been resigned to living out his life as a bachelor, just him and Henry. He'd been content, but now he knew life would be incomplete without Emmalin to share it.

The power and beauty of God's blessing swept over Jacob in a great wave. They would have a future together. He envisioned her helping him in the garden and tending to their children while she worked in the kitchen. Their wedding day seemed far away. If only he could build the house faster. If one of the young men in town could work with him to fall the trees it would be a big help. Growing season was a bad time to try and find help. Emmalin's suggestion of planed wood nudged him. If he didn't have to cut the timber and prepare it for building he'd save time. But purchasing wood meant he'd be trading a strong sturdy house for a few months of waiting. That would be foolish. Also, he didn't have the money to buy the wood. Using Emmalin's new inheritance didn't seem right. He understood that after they were married, they would share everything, but they weren't married yet. And relying on Emmalin for financial assistance didn't set right.

He tapped Smoke with the heel of his boot and the horse moved along as Jacob's mind wandered to his parents. What would they think of all that had happened?

The sorrow and loneliness of the small boy who had lost his family pressed down on him. He'd been only ten when his parents and younger brother died. The memories were still vivid, close. Life had been rich, filled with all sorts of adventure and loving relationships. His mother had seen to that. And then all of a sudden, they were gone, and he was alone. He couldn't imagine what would have happened to him if the local Umpqua tribe hadn't made him a part of their family. He'd lived with them until his eighteenth birthday when he'd returned to the cabin in the woods that his father had built.

Considered an oddity, it had been a struggle to re-engage with the Deer Creek community, but he'd managed. And now, unbelievably, he'd captured the heart of an amazing woman. His mother would have been taken with Emmalin.

Blossom, his native mother, would disapprove. She'd wanted him to marry Wild Dove, his childhood friend. Wild Dove had grown into a beautiful woman, skilled in the ways of the Umpqua and she had a good heart, but she wasn't the one for him.

The memory of her disappearance and the rest of the tribe cast a shadow over him. If they had been captured and were living on the Grand Ronde Reservation, they were living a life of sorrows.

Was there any way out for them? Unlikely.

A bark from Henry cut into Jacob's thoughts. His friend trotted ahead. They were nearly there. "I'm coming." Jacob leaned forward in the saddle and allowed Smoke to break into an easy lope.

When Samuel's cabin came into view, Jacob's anticipation intensified. Emmalin. She stepped onto the porch. Was she as eager to see him as he was to see her?

She hurried down the steps. "Jacob. I was beginning to worry."

He stopped and dismounted. "No need." He pulled her into his arms and held her for a long moment, then gave her a respectful kiss, aware that Samuel was probably about.

"The hours since seeing you feel like eons." She looked up at him, her eyes alight. "Today will be fun. We haven't gone fishing in ever so long."

"I have a new fishing hole to show you. It's not far from here."

"Wonderful! I'll get my wrap and our lunch." She disappeared indoors.

Samuel emerged from the barn, leading Emmalin's horse. "Good morning." As he walked around Smoke, he patted the horse's hind end. "How you getting along?"

"Good. Just doing some fishing today, me and Emmalin." Jacob hesitated, wondering if he should invite Samuel.

"She told me. Sounds like fun. Wish I could join you, but I've got a delivery to make." He tipped his mouth up on one side. "And I doubt you two want my company anyway."

Jacob grinned. "You're always welcome to join us."

Samuel tied Sassy to the porch railing. "I'm going to need your help. Planning on putting in a prune orchard."

Jacob arched a brow.

"Supposed to be a good crop for this part of the country. With any luck a man can make a tidy profit. But I'll need to get beehives. Course they won't make a difference this year, but it's not every day a local has hives. I came across a fella up in Oakland who said he'd be willing to sell me some. I'm loaded up with deliveries elsewhere and was wondering if you'd mind picking them up for me sometime this week."

Emmalin appeared, carrying a saddlebag. "Get what?"

"Bees. I bought four hives."

"Aren't they dangerous to have around?"

"Not really. And they're good for pollinating. I'll need them for the prune orchard."

"Oh. Of course."

"I can go to Oakland and get them for you," Jacob said. "You've been kind of easy on me lately. Been a while since I made a haul for you. I ought to be able to get there and back in a couple days—fifteen miles isn't that far north, just a little slow in a wagon on those rutted roads."

Hefting the saddlebag onto her horse, Emmalin asked, "Would you mind my going along? I've never been to Oakland."

Jacob loved the idea of spending more time with Emmalin, but while transporting bees? "Might be dangerous."

"But Father, didn't you just say bees are not dangerous?"

"Yeah, but I wasn't talking about when they're being jostled around in the back of a wagon." He lifted his hat and scratched his head. "There are methods to keep the bees trapped inside the hives. And if you get a real early start back in the morning it shouldn't be too risky."

"I'm sure it can't be that bad. Jacob's a good driver."

"I'd be glad for your company." Jacob glanced from Emmalin to Samuel.

Emmalin settled a beseeching look on her father.

"I suppose. But you'll probably have to leave before daybreak."

"It should be fun."

"All right, then." Jacob gave a nod.

Securing the saddlebag, Emmalin gave her horse a light pat. "This is today's lunch."

"With any luck we'll be eating fresh roasted salmon today." Jacob quickly added, "I'm sure your lunch is delicious, but I was—"

Emmalin broke into laughter. "Fresh salmon will be delicious."

"I better get a move on," Samuel said. "I'll be back late, so don't hold dinner for me."

"Where are you going?"

"I've got a delivery to make to the Sanderson farm."

Emmalin dropped a kiss on her father's cheek. "You be careful."

He gave her a quick hug. "You too."

With a little hop, she hauled herself onto Sassy's back. Taking the reins, she cast a playful smile at Jacob. "What are you waiting for?"

Jacob had been so busy admiring her that he was still standing alongside Smoke. "Oh. Nothing." He pushed up into the saddle, tipped his hat to Samuel, then turned his horse toward the road and set off at a canter.

Emmalin was quick to overtake him. "Catch me if you can." She laughed, the wind tossing her hair and her skirts into a frolic.

Jacob chuckled as he leaned over Smoke's neck and urged him forward, chasing Emmalin down and surpassing her. "I'll see you at the river," he called over his shoulder.

"Oh, you're wicked."

After a good sprint, Jacob slowed Smoke to a walk and Emmalin sidled up alongside him. Jacob sized her up. "You've definitely mastered riding astride, like a real Oregon woman."

"I thought I was until I met up with a cougar a couple of nights ago."

"What?" Jacob leaned forward in his saddle, alarm firing off.

Emmalin told him the story of what had happened, the fear in her voice rising as the tale unfolded.

"I'm glad your father was there."

"Me too."

"I hate the idea of you being in that situation without me to watch over you."

Was Emmalin miffed? Her expression seemed annoyed, and she didn't answer right away.

Sassy chewed at her bit and tossed her head. Emmalin held the reins tight. "How far to the fishing hole?"

"Not very."

Riding side-by-side they ambled along a trail leading away from town.

Happiness spread through Jacob. He hadn't known this was what had been missing in his life, someone to love and to share this place, this life.

Henry padded along between the two of them, his tongue lolling. "I think Henry's had about enough." Jacob pulled to a stop.

Almost immediately the big white dog dropped into lush grasses and lay panting.

"You need a drink, boy?"

"Poor fellow." Emmalin frowned.

Jacob dismounted, grabbed his flask, and knelt beside the dog as he poured water out for him. Henry stood and lapped up the water as it spilled out. "Sorry, old boy. I forgot about you."

Jacob recapped the canteen, looped it over the saddle horn, and remounted. "We're nearly to the cut off."

The trees closed in around them, leaves rustling in the breeze. A covey of quail scattered in front of them and disappeared into the brush.

"I adore quail. They are the most darling birds," Emmalin said.

"Tasty too, but not worth shooting. There's barely more than a mouthful."

"I suppose we can be thankful for that."

The air was cooler in the shade of the trees. Jacob leaned back in the saddle and looked up into the branches. "Hot for this time of year. Maybe we can take a swim."

"That would be refreshing, but what shall we wear?"

Jacob hadn't given that much thought. He'd always skimmed down to his underclothing with no thought of the opposite sex. His face heated from embarrassment. "Maybe some other time…after we're married."

Emmalin blushed. "You haven't taught me to swim yet."

"I will. I promise."

"It would be a good idea, especially since we'll be living at the river. And if I'm going to be independent it's one more thing I'll need to know."

"You don't need to know everything. I'll see that you're safe."

"Of course you'll do your best, but I can't depend on you to always be close by to help. Especially after what happened a few nights ago, I need to be self-reliant." Emmalin tipped her chin up a notch. "I'm not about to be one of those weak-kneed females who can't do for herself."

Jacob decided the best course was to be quiet. There would be opportunities to talk more about this. Taking care of Emmalin was an honor. He looked forward to the day when she relied only on him.

They continued on, without speaking. The trail narrowed and cut deeper into the forest and down a bank. Jacob pulled Smoke to a stop. "From here we walk." He dismounted, but before he could reach Emmalin to assist her, she was already on the ground. Why did she have to be in such a hurry? "Follow me. It's a little steep so watch your step. If you want, you can tie Sassy here and I'll come back to get her."

"That won't be necessary. I'm capable of getting her down the trail."

"Suit yourself." Jacob felt a flush of irritation. Why, he wasn't sure. He should be glad Emmalin wanted to be independent. Boldness was a good trait here in this wild place. But the more liberated Emmalin became the less she would need him.

He moved along the trail, setting his feet with care so not to fall. He soon heard the sound of the river tumbling toward the ocean. The trail grew steeper, the grass more damp. He glanced behind to check on Emmalin. "Almost there."

"I can hear the river." Her voice resonated with delight, but the next sound out of Emmalin wasn't gleeful. "Oh!" she squealed.

Jacob reeled around just in time to see her tumble backward, falling hard against the grassy bank. "Emmalin!" He left Smoke and ran to her. "Are you all right?" He kneeled beside her.

"Oh dear." She pressed a hand to her chest and sucked in a sharp breath. "I'm fine. Just startled. And I got the wind knocked out of me."

He helped her sit up. "You scared me." He glanced at Sassy who seemed just fine.

Emmalin held up the reins. "I might be clumsy, but I did manage to hang on to my horse." She pushed to her feet and brushed dirt and debris from her skirt.

"You sure you're all right?"

"Yes. Just embarrassed. I should have been more cautious."

Jacob smothered a laugh. "You were quite a sight, with your feet flying out from underneath you the way they did."

Emmalin gaped at him. "It was *not* funny."

He gasped, working to shut down his laughter.

"Well, I guess it was a little funny." She grinned. "I don't suppose native women ever had any such difficulty."

"They did some of the time." Their present plight returned to haunt him. "Right now, I'm pretty sure they're struggling and wish they were on a jaunt to go fishing."

"Oh, Jacob, I'm sorry. I didn't mean—"

"Don't apologize. Just something I have to work out. Sometimes I worry about them."

"I do too. I can't imagine what their life is like now."

Jacob took in a deep breath and gave her a half-smile. "We're almost there. You going to be all right?"

"I'm fine." She planted her hands on her hips. "But, Jacob, don't baby me. If I'm going to be your wife, I won't be whining over a small slip."

"I'll try, but this new role will take some getting used to." He returned to his horse and continued on, only more slowly than before. He was glad when they finally made it out of the forest cover and onto a rocky beach along the river.

"My goodness. The water's high." Emmalin stepped onto the rocks.

"Spring runoff. Normal this time of year."

Henry found his way to the river's edge, got a good drink, then set off in search of adventure. After giving the horses a drink, Jacob and Emmalin tied them to tree branches, then Jacob got out the poles and bait. "I figure we'll start with salmon eggs. I remember how you disliked crawdads last time."

"They were dreadful, but they seemed to work well."

"I have some." He opened a rusted metal canister that held crustaceans.

She glanced at them and wrinkled her nose. "I think I'd rather use eggs. And I'm sure I can set up my own pole and bait the hook. I remember how."

Jacob handed her a pole and tackle, then went to work on his own set up. By the time Emmalin had finished with hers, he already had his line in the water. She made her way gingerly over the rocks to the river. Jacob kept an eye on her, while trying to mask his attentiveness.

"There's a nice pool right out there, just below the rapids." Jacob pointed toward it.

He fought the compulsion to offer Emmalin help. After a couple of failed attempts, she managed to cast out the line. He was proud of her efforts but hoped she wouldn't become too independent. He liked watching out for her.

It didn't take long before they'd each caught a salmon. Jacob built a fire and roasted one of the fish for their lunch.

"It smells delicious." Emmalin retrieved fresh baked bread and tea cakes.

Oil dripped from the fish, sizzling in the flames. Jacob checked the meat, careful not to overcook the meal. "It's just about right."

The two settled down on the bank to enjoy the small feast. Jacob was so comfortable with Emmalin even though there was little conversation while they ate. There was little conversation while they ate. He appreciated that Emmalin didn't feel the need to talk all the time. Women who prattled got on his nerves.

"I've been thinking about sharpening my skills as a marksman." Emmalin wiped her hands on a towel. "My father is going to teach me. Would you mind giving me a few lessons too?"

Jacob lifted the last chunk of meat from a bone. "As I recall, you're a pretty good shot already."

"Adequate. I want to be excellent. I need to know I will be able to hit what I'm aiming at, especially in an emergency. I don't want to find myself in a predicament like I was with that cougar."

"I'll be glad to teach you."

"Wonderful." Emmalin pushed to her feet. "Can we begin now?"

"Sure, but I don't see the hurry. I'm always going to be here to protect you. You don't have to be afraid."

Emmalin furrowed her brows. "Jacob, I appreciate that you care and want to keep me safe, but I need to take care of myself."

"Using a weapon to kill isn't something you should be spending a lot of time thinking about."

"Have you forgotten that it was my shot that saved your life when we were attacked by Indians last August? I didn't want to kill that man, but I had no choice. And I did it." She planted her hands on her hips and drilled him with a hard stare. "And I would rather you not decide whether it's appropriate for me to fire a weapon or not."

Jacob felt as if she had slapped him. "I didn't mean to speak for you."

She softened her stance and smiled.

"And I remember that day. That's when I first realized how strong you are. You can do anything you put your mind to." He gathered his thoughts. He needed her to understand how he felt. "As your husband, I should be the one to defend you and watch over you."

Emmalin crossed her arms over her chest. "I'm not a withering flower. I love that you want to protect me, but I also need you to understand that taking care of myself is important to me. I never want to come face-to-face with any kind of predator and not be able to do that. I don't want to live in fear."

"I don't want that either, but if you're never afraid then you're not likely living in reality."

"Of course." Emmalin pursed her lips, then continued. "If I can take care of myself, it will help."

"All right." Jacob fought the need to pull her protectively into his arms. He knew that a woman alone in this territory needed to be afraid some of the time, and she needed a man to look out for her. But today wasn't the day to convince Emmalin of that.

Chapter Eight

Emmalin folded a powder blue cotton fabric and set it out for display. It was lovely, splashed with a delicate floral pattern. She ran a hand across the material. It was good to be back in her father's store. When she'd left town heading for Philadelphia, she thought she'd never see this place again. It felt like home.

She held up the fabric. It would make a fetching blouse. If only she knew how to sew. She could barely imagine accomplishing such a task. Perhaps Margaret or Charity would teach her?

In the months ahead, she and Jacob would both be in need of clothing. In Philadelphia she'd had a seamstress who created stunning gowns and accessories. Only on rare occasions had she purchased readymade. Here in Deer Creek, there were few readymade dresses and no seamstress. Women made their own clothing. She would simply have to learn.

Her father looked up from a ledger he'd been working on. "That looks nice. You're good with the displays."

"I don't know what you did without me." She tossed him a teasing smile.

"You're good with the customers too. They tell me you're much prettier than me." He grinned. "And I'm often told what a beautiful smile you have."

"I'm flattered."

"I agree with them."

"Thank you." Emmalin looked at her father. "You do know that you have an extremely friendly face, don't you? It's the first thing I noticed about you."

He raised a brow but did not reply.

Emmalin propped her hands on her hips and studied her work. "Once upon a time, I had a lot of experience with shopping. Philadelphia has some of the finest shops in the country. I suppose I gained a sense of what caught a customer's eye." She glanced around the store as an idea flitted through her mind. "You know, it might be a good idea to make some improvements here, possibly even expand. I'd be more than happy to pay for any changes."

"Oh, I don't know." Her father frowned. "The store has been just fine, and this is a very small town. We don't need a lot."

"I suppose, but it is going to grow, all of the Oregon Territory is."

"Well, we'll just have to wait and see."

Emmalin flounced inwardly. She wanted to help others and now she could, if only they would let her.

"Once you get married, I don't know what I'll do."

"When I come into town, I'll be happy to share my ideas. And you can always ask Margaret." She stepped away from the display. "Do you need me to do anything else?"

He glanced around the store. "I think that's it for the day."

No longer distracted by work, Emmalin was suddenly aware of the hollow feeling in her stomach. "I think I'll stop in at the café." She crossed to the door. "Can I get you anything?"

"No thanks. But I'll be hungry by dinner." His blue eyes glimmered with a challenge.

"How about chicken and dumplings?"

"Sounds good."

"I have a recipe I want to try. It's Margaret's of course."

"Can't wait." He returned to his work.

The talk of food had intensified Emmalin's hunger. She'd been so busy she'd missed lunch. As usual, when she opened the café door, scrumptious smells greeted her.

"Hello, dear." Margaret dried her hands with a towel. "So nice to see you."

"And you." Emmalin smiled. "I smell something yummy."

"I just took some cookies out of the oven."

Emmalin closed her eyes and breathed in the fragrance. "Applesauce spice?"

"That's right. Have a seat. I'll get us some tea to go with our cookies." She disappeared into the kitchen while Emmalin sat at a table near the front of the café. She liked this spot because it offered a view of the town. Mr. Powell, a farmer who lived north of town, rode up on a black, heavy-bodied horse and stopped in front of the post office. He slung himself down, tied off the horse, and walked inside.

Emmalin rarely had reason to use the post office. When she left Philadelphia, she'd discovered she didn't have any true friends, except for Tara Richardson. As it turned out, even Tara hadn't reached out to her, never answering a single letter.

Margaret reappeared carrying a tray laden with light brown lumpy cookies and a small pot of tea. "I was looking for an excuse to enjoy some of these." She placed the tray on the table and set out teacups. "I already had tea steeping in hopes you'd stop by." She filled both cups.

Emmalin spooned out sugar and stirred it in. Taking a sip, she closed her eyes in appreciation. "I've been waiting for this. I'm starving. And I have so many things to talk to you about."

"I imagine so." Margaret's eyes danced with humor as she took a sip of tea.

Emmalin served herself a cookie just as the café door opened in a rush.

A man strode in. He looked frantic. "Margaret! Thank the Lord you're here!"

"Mr. Sullivan. Are you all right?"

"It's Alice. She's having the baby, but something's wrong. Can you come?"

Margaret was on her feet immediately. "Of course. I'll get my bag and be right there. Tell Alice I'm on my way."

"Thank you." With a slight nod toward Emmalin, Mr. Sullivan hurried back out the door.

Margaret bustled into the kitchen. "I'm so sorry to have to put off our visit." She searched through a cabinet in the back.

"I just hope Mrs. Sullivan is all right."

Gripping a carpet bag, Margaret hurried toward the door. She was just about to step out when she stopped and looked at Emmalin. "Would you like to come with me? Have you ever attended a birth?"

Emmalin didn't answer right away. She would rather not be part of it, but if she were going to be a pioneer wife, it was something she would need to know. "I've never been at a birthing. But I'd like to come. Will it be all right with Mrs. Sullivan?"

"I'm sure she won't mind. Another woman at a birthing bed is usually welcome. Make sure to get a wrap. It may be late by the time we return. And tell your father where we've gone."

Before Emmalin knew what had happened, she was riding out of town alongside Margaret. She had to remind herself to relax. After all, having a child was a perfectly normal occurrence. It would be valuable to better understand the process.

Several women on the wagon train came to their time while on the trail. Emmalin was not closely involved in any of the births, but she couldn't escape the sounds coming from women who labored. She also observed the worry and stress of family and friends. The emotion was always intense, like static in the air. Finally, a tiny cry would pierce the hearts of those waiting and cheers of relief and congratulations went up all around the camp. Sadly, not all labors resolved in exultation, some ended with tiny coffins being placed in the earth and others included a husband kneeling alongside the grave of his wife.

Emmalin's stomach ached. May the Lord have mercy on Mrs. Sullivan.

The cabin wasn't far from town. When it came into view, it looked cozy huddled in the midst of an oak grove. Like most homes in the valley, it was small.

Margaret pulled back on the reins as they approached the house, then stopped in front of a hitching post. She quickly dismounted, secured her horse, unlashed her traveling bag, and hurried up the porch steps.

Emmalin rushed to catch up. She grabbed Margaret's arm. "Have you done a lot of these?"

"A fair number, yes." Margaret's lips lifted in a knowing smile. "I know what I'm doing. But I also understand that the outcome doesn't always go the way we hope."

"Do all the women in the county rely on you to help them birth their babies?"

"No. Some have family or friends attend them. Still, I can't count how many of the children in this community were born with me at their mother's side." Her eyes were lit with a special delight. "I'm privileged to be a part of it." She patted Emmalin's arm. "Try not to worry. Nature seems to know how this is done. And our heavenly Father is always here to help."

She took the final step and knocked on the cabin door.

It creaked open and a tow-headed little girl with large, frightened eyes peered out. "Miss Margaret. Thank goodness you're here." She swung open the door. "Mama's in the back bedroom. She's needing you."

"All right then, Rachel." Margaret briefly rested a hand on the little girl's head. "Your mama's going to be just fine." Margaret strode across the cabin and rapped on the bedroom door before opening it.

With a smile for Rachel, Emmalin followed Margaret and quietly slipped into a small bed chamber. It was dark, with the shades drawn. A lantern sitting on a bureau offered the only light other than what leaked in around the edge of the draperies. Emmalin stood against the wall and stood quietly, trembling inside and hoping her apprehension didn't show on her face.

Sweat beaded Alice Sullivan's face. Her eyes looked like hollowed spaces above sharp cheekbones, and her hair which would normally have been pinned up nicely, had been woven into a thick braid that hung over her left shoulder. She'd always had the look of someone who was overworked, but she was now clearly in a state of utter exhaustion. She lay back against a hill of pillows, eyes half closed.

Sympathy sank into Emmalin. Birthing a baby was arduous, painful work, but clearly Mrs. Sullivan had gone beyond what should be asked of any woman. What could be wrong?

Alice reached for Margaret's hand. "Praise be. I was beginning to give up hope."

Continuing to grasp the woman's hand, Margaret sat on the edge of the bed. "I'm glad to be here. Now, what seems to be the trouble?"

"This time isn't anything like my first two." Alice blew out a breath. "The girls' labors were short. They were born with no problems."

Mr. Sullivan cut in. "She's been laboring since last night."

Alice managed a wan smile for her husband. "It feels like something's wrong. This child just doesn't want to be born." All of a sudden, her jaw tightened and she rolled forward. Clutching Margaret's hand, Alice let out a guttural groan.

Margaret rested her free hand on Alice's abdomen and circled her other arm around the woman's shoulders. "Take a slow, deep breath, dear. Try to relax your body."

Alice blew out a breath followed by a slow inhalation.

"Good. That's better."

When the contraction ended, Alice lay back, eyes filled with worry. "Something's wrong. I know it."

"We don't know that. Every birth is different. I'm sure everything is going to be just fine." Margaret glanced at Mr. Sullivan and the older daughter, Elizabeth, who stood beside him, clinging to his arm. "May we have a few moments of privacy?"

"Oh." John Sullivan cleared his throat. "Yeah." He placed a hand on his daughter's back and guided her out of the room.

Emmalin started to follow.

"Not you, dear. I'll need you."

"Oh yes. Of course." Emmalin's stomach rolled. What could she possibly do? She edged closer to the bed.

"Let's see how you're progressing. I'll have to take a look."

Biting her upper lip, Alice nodded. "Another pain is coming," she managed to whisper. She tightened her grip on Margaret's hand and squeezed her eyes closed. "I feel like I have to push."

"You just go on ahead. We'll get through this contraction and then I'll have a look see." Margaret returned her free hand to Alice's abdomen. "Keep breathing, dear."

Alice groaned as she bore down. The groan became a low growl as the pain intensified. Emmalin pressed her back against the wall. Why was she here?

Gradually Alice relaxed and her breathing became slower, shallower.

Margaret checked her progress. "This child wants to come out backward." She looked up at Alice. "That's the hold up."

"Backward?"

"Feet first. It's called a breech birth. Sometimes it takes a little one longer to make their grand entrance, but all should be fine. It's almost here. I can see the feet." She glanced at Emmalin. "If Alice doesn't mind, I think you should see this."

Alice pushed her head back into the pillows and looked at Emmalin. "It's all right by me."

"Through the years I've only attended a handful of women with breech births," Margaret explained.

Emmalin edged forward, her hands clasped tightly in front of her. She couldn't deny that she was curious but terrified at the same time. She dared look. "Oh! Dear!" The words popped out before she could stop them. She pressed a hand to her mouth, embarrassed at her outburst. But she'd never seen anything quite like this.

"Another pain!" Alice gasped.

"Go ahead and push. Your baby's coming. Keep pushing—gentle and steady." Margaret grasped the baby around the torso as it descended. She glanced at Emmalin. "Can you get me that towel on the nightstand?"

Emmalin handed it to Margaret.

"Please dear, can you help her sit up? Get behind her and support her back."

Emmalin scooted onto the bed and moved in behind Alice, helping her to sit up. "Is this all right?"

Alice nodded. "Ah. Another one."

Margaret held the infant gently and maneuvered the arms free of the birth canal. "The shoulders are coming now."

Alice let out a screaming type of growl and pushed. "Get him out! Get him out!"

"Almost there. Keep pushing." Margaret took a firm hold of the baby just above the shoulders and turned it slightly. "Push! Now! Push hard!"

Alice bore down, grabbed hold of Emmalin's hand and squeezed until Emmalin wondered if she might break it.

Emmalin pushed her into a more upright position. "Is that better?" Her voice quaked.

"Your baby is almost here, Alice. Just one more big push."

Alice let out a heavy groan and then leaned back against Emmalin, clearly spent. At first Emmalin was frightened. What had happened? Why had she given up?

And then Margaret held up the child, turned it onto its stomach and gently slapped its bottom. A tiny quaking cry emanated through the room. Margaret wore a big smile. "It's a boy! You have a son!"

Alice laughed as tears coursed down her cheeks. "A boy. We have a boy!"

The fear and anxiety Emmalin had felt only moments before was swept away in a tide of joy. The baby was here! It was a miracle.

Margaret cut the cord that attached the child to its mother and then she wrapped the towel around him and handed the infant to Alice. "He's a big boy."

Tears spilled onto Emmalin's cheeks. She hadn't expected to feel such deep emotion.

Alice held the child against her. "John. Where's John?"

"I'll get him." Emmalin gently moved out from behind Alice and hurried to the door. As she opened it, she called, "Mr. Sullivan, you can come in now."

He hurried into the room, followed by his two girls. "Alice, are you all right?"

"I'm just fine. Margaret knew what to do."

"He was breech, feet first, which is a little trickier than usual, but Alice did just what she needed to." Margaret planted her hands on her hips and smiled at the exhausted mother. "She's a strong woman."

John moved to his wife's side. "She is that, all right."

Alice smiled up at her husband. "John, we have a son."

"A boy? We have a boy?" He leaned over his wife, smoothed back damp hair, and kissed her brow.

All of a sudden, Emmalin felt out of place. This was a private moment, just for family. She silently stepped away and left the room, making her way to the front porch. She leaned on the railing and, gazing at the lush green fields, took a deep cleansing breath. The air was sweet and pure. What she had seen was brutal, but it was also beautiful. One day it would be her agony and her joy to bring a child into the world. The idea thrilled and terrified her.

Chapter Nine

Emmalin's stomach knotted at the sight of the North Umpqua. The river was swift and deep. She'd never liked river crossings.

Jacob held the reins taut to slow the team as the wagon rolled downhill toward the Winchester ferry. "Water's running high."

"I don't recall ever seeing it this wild." A huge log rolled to one side as it floated in the muddy surge.

"Spring runoff. Temperature warms up and melts the mountain snow. More water, more powerful." He looked at Emmalin with soft eyes. "We'll be fine. The fella who runs the ferry knows what he's doing."

Releasing a breath, Emmalin nodded. She could trust him.

The team remained sure-footed as it moved toward the riverbank and the waiting ferry. Henry put his front feet on the edge of the wagon and whined. Was he also frightened?

A tall, skinny man with a scraggly beard stepped up to meet them.

"Hi there, Jedediah."

He smiled up at Jacob. With a touch to the brim of his hat, he gave Emmalin a nod. "Good day to ya."

"Good day," Emmalin said, thinking that if he'd trim his beard, he might be attractive, but who could actually know with so much hair hiding his face. He had friendly eyes.

"How've you been?" Jacob leaned forward and rested his arms on his thighs.

"Can't complain." Jedediah glanced at the rushing waters. "Course the river's high this time of year so the work is harder."

"Any reason we shouldn't cross?"

"Nah. I'll see you get a gentle ride." He sized up the team and the wagon. "But I'll have to charge you twenty-five cents."

"That's reasonable." Jacob took coins from his pocket, counted out the required number, and dropped them into Jedediah's outstretched hand.

Emmalin prayed Jedediah was as good a ferryman as his confidence projected.

"Where you heading?" Jedediah put the payment in a small leather pouch hooked to his belt.

"Oakland. Picking up some beehives for Samuel."

Jedediah cocked an eyebrow. "Glad it's you and not me. Got no need for bees."

"We'll be fine. Just need to respect them and take it slow."

Jedediah moved to the flat-bottom scow and motioned Jacob forward. The horses were used to the transfer and stepped onto the ramp, loading without incident. Jedediah closed the gate behind them while Jacob climbed down from the wagon. "Need some help?" He joined him on the rope. "With this current, figured it couldn't hurt."

"I'm obliged to you."

The two men set to work pulling the cables that ferried the barge across the river.

Emmalin gripped the edge of the seat. Though she hated river crossings, she was grateful for the ferry. Still, her heart pounded hard beneath her ribs. On the trail across the country, she'd seen more than one wagon get swept away by turbulent rivers.

Henry's cold nose snuffled her cheek, then her neck. She turned and smoothed the top of his broad head. "Ah. Hello there." She scratched the scruff of his neck, and feeling slightly better, she turned to face the river.

Thankfully it wasn't an extremely wide river at this location, and Emmalin breathed out her relief when they reached the north side. Jedediah let down the ramp while Jacob climbed up beside Emmalin. She tucked her arm into his and leaned against him, feeling instant comfort.

Jacob took the reins in hand. "Thanks, Jedediah. I'll see you tomorrow."

"I'll be here."

"Thank you, Jedediah," Emmalin said, truly grateful for his skill.

The horses plodded forward. Jacob slapped the reins and they moved faster.

Recent rains had been light so the road was not mired with mud, though the ruts gave them a good jolt from time to time. Emmalin kept a hand on the edge of her seat to brace herself.

As they headed north the road narrowed into little more than a trail, which cut its way through broad grasslands. Emmalin especially enjoyed the spacious meadows with their rich, sweet fragrance. Oak trees stood like giant green umbrellas sheltering cattle from sun and rain. Cedar and fir crowded together in groves on rolling hills.

"I remember being so frightened when I first arrived in Oregon Territory." She felt quiet settle inside her. "Now it looks and feels peaceful and hospitable."

"I remember when you first got to Oregon City. I was intrigued by the young woman who came from Philadelphia." Jacob grinned. "I thought you were foolish, but I also knew you had to be brave to continue your journey to Deer Creek on your own."

"I was severely frightened. My dear uncle…well, what was I to do?" She blinked back tears. "I miss him. He was such a kind man." She stopped to give herself a moment to ease her emotions. "I'm glad I came. If I hadn't, I wouldn't have met you."

Jacob gave her a side hug. "I guess we were meant to be."

"We certainly were. But I do worry about my uncle's estate. I won't be there to oversee it."

"Can you contact the attorney representing your uncle's holdings?"

"I did that almost immediately when I learned of my good fortune."

They moved along in companionable silence. Emmalin's mind returned to the many adventures she'd experienced since leaving Philadelphia, remembering the day she first saw this expansive countryside. She'd left her home seven months prior and was doubting her decision to have come at all. With no idea what lay before her, she'd been afraid and couldn't imagine what her new life would be like in Deer Creek. There had been many surprises. Her mind snapped back to her most recent experience.

"Oh. I forgot to tell you."

Jacob looked at her, a question on his face. "Sounds important."

"Well, yes. And no." She shook her head. "It's just that I helped Margaret deliver a baby. Mrs. Sullivan had a little boy."

"You were there?"

"I was." Emmalin pressed her palms together between the folds of her dress. "It was amazing. And terrifying. When I saw Mrs. Sullivan holding her brand new infant, I realized that one day it would be me and you." She let out a slow breath. "I don't know if I'm brave enough or good enough to do what she did."

"You're one of the bravest women I know. And strong. And determined. I'm pretty sure you can do anything you set your mind to."

Emmalin let out a little laugh. "More likely you are suffering from blindness." He narrowed his eyes in a question. "You know, love can be blind."

Jacob chuckled. "Well, I do love you. But I have good reason to believe in you."

Emmalin's heart swelled with delight. How wondrous it was to be loved by such a man. She cuddled against him. "You make me better."

Wearing a look of contentment, Jacob kept his arm around Emmalin while skillfully handling the reins with one hand.

Even though the wooden seat was hard, and the wagon bounced repeatedly as they rolled along the rough terrain, Emmalin was content to ride beside Jacob all day. She was almost disappointed when they reached the small hamlet of Oakland.

Jacob pulled up in front of a roadhouse.

"I had no idea there was such a convenience here. Why didn't we stop when we were traveling south last summer?"

"We were close to Deer Creek. So no need. And it would have meant traveling out of our way." He jumped down and Henry leaped out of the back. Tail wagging, he rubbed against Jacob's legs. "Good boy." He patted the dog, then came around and gave Emmalin a hand down. "I could use a cool drink." He glanced at the glaring sun.

"Lemonade would be splendid."

"With any luck they'll have some." Jacob allowed Henry and the team to drink from a watering trough. When the horses had slurped up a sufficient amount of water, Jacob secured them to a hitching post, then taking Emmalin's arm, he stepped up to the door, pulling it open for her.

It was dark inside after the brightness of the afternoon sun, and Emmalin thought she caught the scent of a cigar.

A short, round woman appeared from a side door. "Good afternoon. Are you looking for a place to stay?"

Jacob removed his hat. "We are. But I've got a big thirst. Do you by chance have something cool to drink?"

"I absolutely do." She stepped through a door and reappeared a few minutes later with a glass pitcher. "Lemonade. Made it just this morning."

"It sounds wonderful." Emmalin set her bonnet on a small wooden table and sat down.

"I'm Martha Walker," the woman said with a kindly smile.

"I'm Emmalin Hammond. And this is Jacob Landon."

"Oh. I thought you two were a couple. You look like you belong together."

Jacob flushed. "We are a couple, just not married yet."

"It's so nice to meet you." Martha grabbed two glasses out of a cupboard and filled them with the pale lemonade. She set the glasses on the table. "What brings you this way?"

"I have business with a local farmer, a Mr. Hasper."

"Oh, sure. He has a place just east of here. Big ranch."

"Is it far?"

"Not at all."

"I'd be obliged to you for directions." Jacob took a big swallow of lemonade.

Emmalin sipped hers, fighting the desire to gulp down the whole glass. "This is delicious."

"Just water, lemons, and a little sugar." Martha propped her hands on her hips. "Will you be needing supper tonight?"

Jacob looked at Emmalin as if for affirmation. "We'll likely be hungry come dinnertime."

"Good. I have a big ol' chicken roasting in the oven. There should be plenty for everyone. I'll make sure to keep some for you two if you're not back before we serve."

Emmalin's gaze roamed over the room. It was plain with little ornamentation, except for a rather ornate upright piano standing against the front wall. "You have a lovely piano."

"That was left here by a family traveling south. They needed to stock up on supplies more than they needed music. We made a trade. Sadly, I don't play."

Emmalin pushed to her feet and crossed the room to the piano. She rested a hand on the rich dark wood. "It's a handsome piece." She longed to sit and stroke the keys. "Would you mind if I played something?"

"No. Not at all. No one plays around here."

Emmalin pulled the bench away from the piano, its wooden legs rasping against the oak floor. She sat on the hard seat, lifted the fallboard, and rested her hand on yellowing keys. She hadn't played since before leaving Philadelphia, yet her hands felt at ease on the ivories. She played the scales up and down, satisfied to hear that the piano was very nearly in tune. Her mind wandered through an array of songs that had languished in her since before her mother's death.

Without deciding on any particular piece, her hands moved spontaneously over the keys, and the haunting melody of "Moonlight Sonata" came to life beneath her fingers. Caught up in the power and beauty of the song, her location and circumstances faded. She closed her eyes and played through the piece to the ending crescendo.

With the last note, the room fell silent, then Martha broke out in applause. "That was amazing! I've never heard such a beautiful song before."

Suddenly embarrassed, Emmalin turned to look at her audience of two. While she played, she'd been unaware of them.

"Emmalin." Jacob said her name as if in reverence. "I had no idea."

She glanced from him to Martha. "Forgive me. I forgot myself."

"Don't apologize. Such a gift. Do you have a piano?"

"No. Actually, I haven't played since leaving my home a year and a half ago."

"You must miss it terribly."

Emmalin hadn't realized how much. She stood and stepped away from the piano. "Perhaps one day I will have one of my own again."

"I didn't realize you wanted one," Jacob said, almost sounding apologetic.

"Neither did I." She shrugged. "I'd forgotten how much I love to play."

Jacob frowned.

Was he feeling badly because he didn't have the funds to purchase a piano? Emmalin hurried to end the discussion, grabbing her bonnet from the table again. "It's of no concern. Shouldn't we be going? If we're to speak with Mr. Hasper while there's still daylight."

"Right. We better get a move on."

"I'll have your rooms ready for you by the time you return," Martha said.

"Thank you. Sure appreciate that." Jacob moved to the door, opened it, and guided Emmalin to the wagon. He gave her a hand up, then climbed onto the seat beside her. He lifted the reins. "Come on, Henry." The dog leaped into the back, his tail flagging his enthusiasm over another leg to the day's journey.

Martha stood in the doorway. "All you need to do is stay on this road, heading east, then take the first turn south. You can see Mr. Hasper's place from the road. It's the only one down that way, about a mile after the turn."

"We should be back before dark." Jacob slapped the reins, and the wagon rolled down the dirt road.

Martha's directions were simple and clear. It didn't take long before Mr. Hasper's ranch came into sight. The place was nothing special, just a small log cabin with a couple of outbuildings. To the west, cattle grazed behind fenced acreage dotted with oak trees. To the east, a burgeoning orchard proclaimed its presence, trees heavy with vibrant white blossoms.

A bald man with a round face stepped out of the cabin. He lifted suspenders up over his shoulders as he strode toward the wagon.

Jacob pulled the horses to a stop. "Mr. Hasper?"

"That's me. You can call me Tom."

"I'm Jacob Landon. I'm here to pick up some beehives for Samuel Morgan."

"Sure. But he didn't pay for them yet." He spat a stream of tobacco juice.

"I've got that for you."

"All right. Let's have a look and you can tell me if you still want them."

Jacob helped Emmalin from the wagon. "My fiancée, Emmalin Hammond."

"Good to meet you." Hasper barely glanced at her as he strode toward the orchard.

Jacob and Emmalin fell into step beside the rather rotund farmer. "Is it far?" Jacob asked.

"Nope. I put the bees just beyond the house in this orchard. They been busy with all the trees blooming out."

Emmalin had to watch her step as they made their way over the damp, uneven ground. Thankfully it was little more than a five-minute walk. Emmalin had never seen anything like it. In a meadow, alongside the orchard, there were at least a dozen hives. They looked like miniature multiple story homes. Mr. Hasper had been honest when he said the bees were busy. Their hum filled the air as they flew among the blossoms and buzzed in and out of their wooden houses. The sweet fragrance of flowers was heavy, making the air feel thick.

"Samuel said he wants four hives." Mr. Hasper tucked his thumbs into his suspenders. "He told me he knows how to take care of them."

"He's all set up." Jacob folded his arms over his chest and studied the bee activity. "So, what keeps them from stinging me when I move them?"

"You have to wait till nightfall. After dark they settle down inside the hives. And when I'm collecting honey, I use a contraption called a smoker. Smoke keeps the bees calm. I've got one I can throw in on the deal. Samuel's gonna need it."

Jacob rubbed his day-old whiskered chin. "I was thinking I could leave real early in the morning before the sun comes up."

"I'd advise against it."

"So, I have to drive these bees to Deer Creek during the night?"

"That's how I'd do it. Bees are a lot quieter at night. You're less likely to get stung."

Jacob turned to Emmalin. "Guess we'll head back tomorrow night. Are you all right with that?"

"Certainly." She smiled, but inside felt uneasy. So much could go wrong, traveling at night with bees. If only she hadn't induced Jacob into bringing her along, although she imagined he would be bolstered by her company.

"I'd sure rather not drive the road between here and Deer Creek in the dark." Jacob compressed his lips.

"It's up to you, but that's what I'd do."

"I guess there's no way around it." Jacob rubbed the back of his neck. "I'll be back before nightfall tomorrow."

Hasper gave him a nod. "All right. See you then."

Jacob and Emmalin returned to the wagon and headed toward the roadhouse. Jacob, unusually quiet, was clenching his jaw.

"Is it safe to travel after dark?" Emmalin asked.

"Just have to take it slow. We'll be fine."

Emmalin was unconvinced. Jacob hadn't even looked at her.

The tantalizing aroma of roasted chicken greeted them when they arrived at the roadhouse. Martha hustled between the kitchen and the dining room, serving their meal of chicken, along with creamed baby potatoes and peas. After they'd finished eating, Martha cleared the table while everyone retired to the living quarters.

"I'll wash up the dishes later." Martha sat in a plush chair. She was silent for a few minutes, then said, "I've been thinking about that piano. There's no reason to keep it here. No one plays it. I was wondering if you might be interested in buying it, Miss Hammond?"

"Oh." A thrill shot through Emmalin. "Really? You'd sell it to me?"

"Absolutely. I'd like to see it go to someone who would actually use it."

Emmalin turned to Jacob. "Would it be all right to take it with us?"

Jacob didn't answer right away, then he said, "It's big and heavy, plus we've got the beehives." He scrubbed his chin. "I guess we could do it. But I'll need a couple of men to help load it."

Emmalin turned back to Martha. "I would love to purchase it. How much are you asking for it?"

"I don't really know. What do you think it's worth?"

"I have no idea. I'm ashamed to say I never had to consider such things while growing up."

Martha studied the piano. "Would fifty dollars be too much?"

"No. Not at all. But I'll need to have a bank note drawn up. Will that be all right with you?"

"Of course." Martha smiled broadly. "Oh, I feel so much better about that."

Jacob leaned forward on his thighs and pressed his palms together. "Well, I guess we'll be taking a piano back with us tomorrow, along with the bees. Could be an interesting trip."

Jacob grinned, but Emmalin thought she saw concern in his eyes. What did he mean by *interesting*?

Chapter Ten

With the sun low in the western sky, Jacob secured the piano inside the wagon bed. He ran his hand along the dark mahogany top. "It's a nice piece." He removed his hat and wiped his forehead with his shirt sleeve. "Time to get the hives and head for home."

Martha hustled out of the roadhouse door, a woven basket in hand. "It's going to be a long trip back so I made you something."

"How kind," Emmalin said as she took the basket. "Thank you."

A soft smile settled on her lips. "My pleasure."

Jacob shifted his hat on his head. "Thank you, Martha."

"Anything I can do for friends." Her smile brightened. "I hope to see you from time to time."

"I do hope so," Emmalin said. "And thank you so for releasing your piano. It will provide me with many pleasant hours."

"Perhaps the next time I'm in Deer Creek, you'll entertain me with a few songs."

"It will be my pleasure."

Martha took a step back. "You two be careful, now. I don't want to hear that you've had an unfortunate accident along the way."

"We'll be fine. I have absolute faith in Jacob."

Emmalin cast Jacob a loving smile, and he felt a worrisome pang in his chest. Taking care of her was the most important thing in his life.

Trying to ignore the tension in his body, he gave Emmalin a hand up into the wagon. The hours ahead would be challenging, and the responsibility of getting Samuel's bees and his daughter home safely weighed heavily on him. Traveling country roads at night was no easy task. If he'd known the trip back meant making the journey after dark, he would never have allowed Emmalin to join him.

He climbed into the wagon and took his place on the stiff wooden seat beside Emmalin. "Get on up here, Henry." The dog leaped into the back, and Jacob lifted the reins. They should make it to Mr. Hasper's place before dark. He slapped the reins. "Get up."

<hr />

When they approached Tom Hasper's cabin, the stout farmer emerged from the barn and gave them a wave. "Just in time. Last I checked, the bees were settling down for the night. Just drive the wagon on over and we'll load up the boxes." He tramped toward the orchard.

Jacob drove the wagon along behind him. Several yards from the hives, he pulled up the team and leaped down. "Henry, stay put. I don't need you nosing around."

"Just need to take a few minutes to make sure they're inside." His arms folded over his chest, Tom watched as the last stragglers buzzed around their homes. "I'm guessing all but a few have gone to bed. I cut some grass to pack the entrances so they won't escape." He grabbed handfuls of grass and went to work wedging it into the hives.

Jacob joined in and worked his way around another hive.

"Once they're set up at Samuel's place leave the grass as is for a day, then start removing it a little at a time. That way enough bees will stay inside to support the hive while they get acquainted with their new surroundings."

Jacob could hear the hum of bees inside. "I'll do my best." He chuckled. "Don't want them finding their way out too soon."

With one man on either side of a hive, they carefully moved it to the wagon and slid it into the bed. Jacob swiped at a lone bee buzzing about his head.

"Looks like you've already got a load." Tom pushed the hive farther into the wagon. "Might be tight."

He glanced at Emmalin. "We'll manage. The piano is important." Emmalin's happiness was worth any extra effort.

They managed to load all four hives without difficulty. After they were strapped in, Jacob stepped back and studied the load. "That ought to do it. Just enough room left for you, Henry." He gave the dog a pat.

"With the sun down, you won't have to worry about them getting overheated," Tom said. "Just make sure to get them to Samuel's place before the heat of the day tomorrow."

Jacob walked around the wagon and double-checked the ropes that secured the load. They were snug.

"I wish you luck. It's a bit of an undertaking to make the trip back in the dark."

"Yep. Long night ahead." Jacob glanced at the sky. The light was rapidly fading. He took a bank note out of his jacket pocket and handed it to Mr. Hasper.

Tom glanced at it, then folded it in half. "Tell Samuel I'll be happy to do business with him any time."

"I'll do that." Jacob climbed into the wagon. He looked at Emmalin. "You ready?"

"I am." She tied her bonnet more snugly, then sat with her spine rigid and straight and her hands pressed against the seat at her side.

Was she scared? He hated the thought, but there was nothing that could be done about it.

Jacob slapped the reins and the team moved forward. No need for the lanterns yet. "With any luck we'll get back to Oakland before we have to light the lanterns." Jacob glanced at the partly cloudy sky. "Hope the clouds don't pile up. Moonlight will make the trip easier."

"Have you ever done anything like this before?" Emmalin's voice wavered.

Jacob considered lying. He didn't want to frighten her, but he settled on the truth. "I've never hauled bees before, but I've driven a wagon at night, plenty of times. It's always easier during the day, but we'll be safely back in Deer Creek by morning." He tightened his grip on the reins. The morning light would be welcomed.

Gradually darkness draped itself over the earth. By the time Jacob and

Emmalin reached the edge of town, only a shimmer of daylight remained above the hillsides. "Do you think you can drive the wagon while I lead the way using a lantern?" Jacob asked Emmalin.

"I can manage a team quite well, but I've never driven at night." She gazed down the road. "It's really getting dark, but I can do it."

"All right, then." Jacob handed her the reins, pressed a kiss to her cheek, then climbed down. Reaching into the back he took out two lanterns and lit them both. He hung one from a hook at the front of the wagon and kept the other with him, holding it aloft as he walked ahead of the team. "I'll take it slow and stick to the best part of the trail."

Emmalin gripped the reins tightly and let out a shuddering breath, wishing her stomach would stop tumbling. The stretch of road just outside of Oakland was in fair condition, but the farther they traveled south the worse it got. Each time a wheel dropped into a hole or hung up in a rut, Emmalin stiffened as the buzz of the bees behind her grew more intense. What if they escaped? Would they attack her? She tried to stay focused on Jacob. He moved from one side of the road to the other, holding the lantern high and calling instructions, pointing out upcoming rough patches.

Emmalin's hands ached from holding the reins too tightly. She rolled back stiff shoulders, but it did nothing to release her tension.

Jacob stopped. "You doing all right?" He studied her from behind the lantern light.

"Yes. Fine." She made an effort to keep her voice light. Nothing good would come of worrying him further.

"If you need to stop let me know."

"I will."

He turned and moved on. When the front right wheel fell into a hole and the wagon momentarily tipped at a precarious angle, Emmalin gasped. There were cliff sides along the way, but she wasn't certain if they'd reached that part of the trip yet.

"Stay right behind me. I won't let you drive off the road."

"I'll do my best." Emmalin's voice wavered with dread and fatigue.

The night deepened, but finally moon glow reached into the sky, washing Emmalin with relief. It cast light over the hillsides and across the roadway. Thankfully there were no cliff sides, at least not yet.

Emmalin's respite was short lived. They soon crested a hill where tree branches arched over the road, allowing only patches of moonlight to shine through.

Jacob stopped and walked to the wagon. "There's a long steep grade coming up so I figure it's a good time to take a break. And I'm hungry."

Emmalin was suddenly aware of how empty her stomach felt. "I am too. I've been concentrating so hard I didn't realize."

Jacob gave Emmalin a hand down, then tied off the horses to a tree branch. Henry leaped out of the back and set off to investigate the forest. After checking to see that the bees were secure, Jacob and Emmalin sat side-by-side on a log.

Emmalin opened the basket of food Martha had given them. "Are the bees safe?"

"Yeah. Stirred up a little. But they haven't escaped."

"And I hope they shan't." Emmalin took out a sandwich, made with freshly baked bread and chicken left from the night before. She handed it to Jacob, then took one for herself. "It smells delicious. Reminds me of Martha's warm cozy kitchen." Emmalin's mind trailed back to the roadhouse. If only she were there now instead of parked alongside a rutted trail surrounded by the dark of night.

Jacob bit into his sandwich and chewed. "Mmm, good."

Henry returned, sniffed the air, then sat in front of Emmalin and stared at her.

Jacob laughed. "He knows which of us has the kinder heart."

Emmalin broke off a piece of her sandwich and gave it to the dog. "There you go." She glanced at Jacob. "I don't mind sharing."

Henry gulped down the mouthful and returned to begging.

"That's enough," Jacob warned sternly. The dog moved to Jacob and lay at his feet.

Emmalin took a bite of her sandwich and gazed down the road where it disappeared into the dark. "How much farther is it to the river?"

"We're about halfway."

She wanted to get the crossing over with. "Will Jedediah be there?"

"Probably not."

"I didn't think so. But I was hoping."

Jacob reached out and grasped her hand. "We'll be fine."

She nodded. "It seems like we've come farther than halfway." Emmalin tried to keep her voice uplifted. Then as much to encourage herself as Jacob, she added, "Well, we can be thankful to have half the trip behind us. We've done perfectly well so far."

"We have." Jacob turned quiet.

"What are you thinking about?"

"Being out here on the trail at night just reminded me of a time when my native brother, Songa, and I were hunting. It was a good trip." He let out a long breath. "I wonder how he's doing and my mother, Blossom, and the rest. I need to make a trip up to Grand Ronde to see if that's where they are and if they're all right." He took another bite of his sandwich.

"Will you go soon?"

He spoke around his food. "I want to get further along on the house and have a better idea how long it's going to take to finish, and then I'll go."

"I hope they're doing well."

"Me too." The worry in Jacob's eyes revealed his doubts about their well-being.

Throughout the evening, Emmalin's mind had dragged her to the river crossing. And now she dreaded it more, knowing Jedediah wouldn't be waiting for them. If only they could have traveled during the day.

After finishing their sandwiches, Emmalin retrieved oatmeal cookies from the basket and handed one to Jacob. She also gave one to Henry and kept another for herself. It was soft and sweet.

A breeze blew through the trees. Emmalin shivered. "I'll be glad to get into town and someplace warm."

"No need to be cold." Jacob walked to the wagon and grabbed a quilt out of the back. Taking long strides, he returned to Emmalin and draped it around her shoulders. "This should help."

"Thank you." She pulled it closed. "I didn't really notice the chill air while I was driving the team."

"Hard work keeps a person warm."

"That's true." Emmalin glanced at the wagon. "This will all be worth it when the bees are settled and the orchard comes into bloom next spring." She closed the quilt around her neck. "And I can't tell you how thrilled I am to have the piano. In Philadelphia I used to play nearly every day."

"I figure the good Lord knew how much you needed it."

"He knew even when I didn't." Emmalin smiled at the thought of her Lord watching out for her and caring enough to provide a perfect gift.

Jacob stood. "Need to move along."

He took hold of Emmalin's hand and pulled her to her feet. He gazed at her. "You look extra beautiful in the moonlight. You sure don't look like a pioneer woman."

"What do you mean by that?" Emmalin feigned irritation. "Pioneer women aren't pretty?"

"No. Of course they are, but they seem a little more frayed, maybe from all the hard work. And you're just unusually pretty."

She felt a warm flush touch her cheeks. "Oh. You. I was just about to get cross, wondering if you were disparaging the local women or that you didn't think me capable of becoming a real pioneer woman."

Jacob pulled her into his arms. "You're a fine woman, pioneer and otherwise." He held her for a long moment before releasing her and then lifting her into the wagon.

The springs of the seat creaked as Emmalin settled on the wooden bench and picked up the reins. She'd much rather have remained in Jacob's arms. His strength made her feel safe.

"It's going to get steep." Jacob checked the harnesses. "Don't let the horses move too fast. You don't want them to get away from you."

"I won't." Emmalin tried to sound confident, but she was more frightened than she could even admit to herself and especially Jacob. She didn't want to disappoint him.

Every step down into the valley was taken with trepidation. Emmalin's nerves prickled. Part of the time, Jacob kept a hand on the horses' head-halters to steady them. Occasionally he'd stop and walk out in front, checking the road, then move back to the team. Henry stayed beside him.

The moon gradually slid toward the edge of sky and what bit of light it offered was often hidden behind clouds and trees. Darkness closed in with only the limited light of stars to show them the way.

"Jacob, how far now?" Emmalin was nearly spent.

He pulled up on the horses, then moved to the wagon. "Do you need to rest?"

"No. I can keep going."

He grasped her hand. "We're almost to the ferry."

"Thank the Lord." Emmalin was conflicted about reaching the river. It meant they were nearly home, but the idea of crossing without help, and in the dark, set off sparks of fear inside of her.

As they approached the landing, the clouds parted. "Take it easy along here," Jacob called over his shoulder.

The road steepened dramatically. Emmalin tugged back on the reins. "Are you sure I can do this?"

"I have no doubt."

Emmalin wished she were as confident as he sounded. She could see the river in the muted light. It was moving fast and was higher than when they'd crossed before. The wagon bounced over a ridge in the road, and she glanced back at the wagon bed. A furious buzzing emanated from the hives. If only they would stay secured.

She kept the reins taut as they descended to the river. When they reached the ferry, Emmalin exhaled slowly, only then realizing she'd been holding her breath much of the time. They were nearly home. The worst of the trip would soon be behind them.

"I'm going to need your help getting the ferry across from the other side."

"Of course." Emmalin put on the brake, tied off the reins, and climbed down.

Jacob got ahold of the pulley. "Can you grab the line behind me?"

Emmalin joined him on the rope, pulling hand over hand as they dragged the heavy barge toward them.

When the ferry bumped against the bank, Jacob jumped aboard and let down the ramp. "We did it." He held out the lantern. "This is a little tricky. Can you hold the lantern so I can see clearly while I drive the wagon on board?"

"Yes." Emmalin pressed a hand to her chest. "Thank goodness. I was afraid you'd make me do it."

Jacob chuckled. "You've done well, but you're going to need a little more practice before you do that." He climbed onto the seat. "Hold the lantern up high."

Emmalin straightened her arm above her head, the lantern swaying. "Is that all right?"

"Perfect."

The horses snorted and stomped their feet.

Jacob lifted the reins and clicked his tongue. They trod forward. "Good boys."

Their steps sounded hollow on the wooden decking. They didn't hold back as Jacob guided them aboard. When the wagon cleared the ramp, he drew back on the reins and stopped, then leaped down and pulled the ramp closed. He grabbed hold of the pulley.

Emmalin was immediately beside him. Together, they hauled the ferry across the rushing waters. Emmalin was concentrating so hard on the task she nearly forgot to be afraid.

"Glad it's not raining," Jacob quipped.

"That would be dreadful."

When the ferry reached the opposite side of the river, Jacob let down the forward ramp. "You go ahead with the lantern. I'll drive the team."

Emmalin did as asked. Careful to follow the smoothest section of road, she walked up the bank, holding the lantern high. "Can you see well enough?"

"Yep."

"It's quite muddy. Stay to the right."

He slapped the reins and the horses stepped across the ramp and onto the mucky bank. It was steep and rutted. The horses stopped hauling and tossed their heads. "Hah! Get up!" Jacob whipped the reins. The team danced before finally starting forward. Rocks gave way beneath their hooves. The gelding on the right lost its footing and nearly fell. Terrified it reared in the harness.

"Whoa! Whoa!" Jacob sawed at the reins. The horse came down and the wagon rolled backward toward the river.

"No! Jacob!" Emmalin screamed.

The bank cut away, and, with a hard thump, the wagon dropped into the wash. With the splintering crack of wood, the piano broke loose of its ties and slammed against the hives, clanging notes filling the night air.

"Jacob!" Emmalin ran toward the horses. She needed to get ahold of them. Two hives and the piano slid off into the water with a splash.

Emmalin reached the team and grabbed ahold of one halter, then the other. Using the most commanding voice she could muster, she cried, "Forward! Move! Get up!"

Jacob stood and steered the team onward. "Hah! Hah!"

Emmalin dug in her heels and hauled on the harness, wrestling the animals forward. They finally found their footing and moved up the bank, dragging the back of the wagon out of the river.

When they reached level ground, Jacob pulled back on the reins and set the brake, then jumped free of the wagon. "Emmalin! Are you all right?"

"I'm fine." She tried to catch her breath.

The two of them hurried back to the river. The piano was half in and half out of the water and the hives were being carried away in the current. Silhouetted in the misty light, they bounced in the wash.

Sickened by the sight, Emmalin grabbed hold of Jacob's hand. The piano was ruined, and two hives were lost. "Oh, Jacob."

"It's all right. The team is safe and so are you. That's all that matters." He pulled her close. "I'm so sorry about your piano."

"It's not your fault." She leaned against him and circled her arms around his waist. "I was so afraid."

He smoothed her hair and held her close. "We're safe and the team is safe. We can be grateful for that."

Emmalin gazed at the ruined piano. She was grateful that she and Jacob weren't hurt but couldn't help but feel disheartened about how difficult life was. The battles never seemed to end. What would she face next?

Chapter Eleven

Late spring sunshine warmed the world and added to Emmalin's anticipation of another good day. She leaned forward on the wagon seat.

Margaret slapped the reins across the team's hind quarters. "I was so sorry to hear about what happened to your piano."

"It was disappointing, but I suppose it wasn't meant to be."

"At least neither you nor Jacob were injured."

"I was so frightened. But Jacob kept his head and we made it back safely. I'll find another piano one day. Poor Jacob blames himself. There was nothing he could do to avoid what happened.

"My father said that, for now, two beehives will be adequate. And I can promise you, if I can avoid it, I'll never travel at night again."

Margaret nodded. "I agree with you on that. I've never liked it."

Emmalin scanned the blue sky. "It's such a lovely day for berry picking. I've never actually picked strawberries before."

Margaret flashed an inquisitive look at Emmalin. "Never?"

"We always had servants for that sort of thing. And last year the season for strawberries was long past by the time I arrived."

"Did you grow your own berries at your home in Philadelphia?"

"No. We got them from a farmer who lived outside of the city. It was not considered ladylike to spend time doing such things. And I dared not expose myself to the sun in such a way as to get a tan. Even a bonnet couldn't offer enough protection." She feigned outrage.

"My goodness. Now I'm doubly glad I grew up in the country. I was always a bit brown. My mother didn't approve of me climbing trees and such, but I did, every chance I got." She laughed. "I was a handful."

"I'm not surprised. You have a strong spirit. And though that might have made for a turbulent childhood, it's all part of who you are now." Emmalin draped her arm around Margaret's shoulders and gave her a squeeze. "I love you just as you are. And I am blessed to have your friendship." She settled her hands in her lap and lifted her face to the sun. "I like having color in my cheeks."

"You're a beautiful woman, Emmalin."

"Thank you." She gazed out over the fields. "I know it's silly, but I'm excited. I'll get to spend time with Charity, but I'm also going to do something new, and it will be one more thing I can do for myself." A smile touched her lips. "When Jacob and I get settled in our own place, I plan to grow oodles of strawberries."

"You have good ground up there with space for a big garden." Margaret turned the wagon onto the lane that led to the Sutton farm. "Since moving here, I never took the time for my own berry patch. No need, not with Charity's family farm. They have the best berries in the valley."

With a wave, Charity stepped onto the drive, woven mats draped over her arm. She walked toward the wagon. "Good morning. How good to see you both." A gust of wind threatened to sweep away her bonnet, so she captured it beneath her hand. "This is such a treat."

"For us, too," Emmalin said, eyeing Charity's cotton summer frock. "No trousers today?"

"They're not necessary for berry picking." Charity smiled, the blue in her eyes looking like a reflection of the sky. "But I'll be mucking out stalls tomorrow. Would you like to join me? You can bring your own trousers."

Emmalin wrinkled her nose. "I think I'm going to be busy."

The three women laughed, and Margaret said, "I doubt you'll ever get Emmalin into a pair of trousers."

Charity chuckled. "You're probably right."

Margaret pulled the brake. "It's a good thing we got an early start. It feels like it's going to be warm this afternoon."

"Yes, but hot weather is good for the berries. Makes them sweeter. And the plants are loaded this year. The weather has been perfect for them. May is very early for strawberries to be ready."

"I'm glad they are. They sound marvelous." Emmalin stepped down from the wagon.

Charity caught her in a one-armed hug. "I can't imagine how you can even think about something as mundane as berry picking with your wedding coming up."

"If only it were sooner, but building a house takes a dreadfully long time." Anxiety flashed through Emmalin. She wanted to get married but the idea of living so far from town was still rather terrifying. Pushing aside the thought, she took one of the baskets out of the back of the wagon. "And what about you and Pastor Miller?"

Charity blew out an exasperated breath. "I'm not sure there even is a Pastor Miller in my future. I declare, that man hasn't a romantic bone in his body. I'm beginning to wonder if he's confused me with his sister."

Margaret laughed. "Oh, I'm certain that's not the case. Give him time. I've seen how his eyes light up when he looks at you."

"Do you think so?" She smiled. "I hope you're right. He is such a fine man. And I truly care for him."

Margaret rested a hand on Charity's back. "He'll come around." She turned to look at the sprawling berry field. "We have a lot of work to do. I'm so glad to have your company. It will make the labor easier."

Charity handed Margaret and Emmalin each a mat. "These will help keep you out of the dirt." She took two baskets out of the wagon and the women walked to the berry field. "Have you any word about the natives? Sometimes I still worry about the possibility of skirmishes." She turned to Emmalin. "I thought Jacob might know something."

"He doesn't talk about it much, but I know it's on his mind." Emmalin's heart ached at the idea of Jacob's native family being locked up.

"Most have moved off to other territories," Margaret said. "Or are housed on reservations."

"Jacob said some have moved into the mountains and will hide as long as they must. I can't imagine how difficult it is to not know what's become of one's family."

"I feel awful about what happened," Charity said. "But I must admit that I sleep better at night, knowing we don't have to worry about an attack."

"I think it is just plain sad. The local natives never caused any trouble. What happened to them is an injustice." Margaret tucked ginger-colored hair into her bun. "I haven't given up hope. God knows what is happening to those poor people. I just pray Jacob will find his family one day. Do you think he will go up to the reservation?"

"He hopes to." Emmalin felt the twist of a knife in her heart. Why had it been allowed? The local natives were decent people, with lives that mattered. Were those in authority without feelings?

When they reached the berry patch, Margaret walked toward the first row. "Is it all right to begin here?"

"Yes. The first several rows haven't been picked in a couple of days."

Emmalin moved to the next row and Charity the one after that. Kneeling on the mats, the three friends worked while chatting. Early morning dew glistened on the leaves of lush green plants, and the sweet fragrance of berries hung in the air. Plump red fruit rested among the leaves.

Birds sat on a hedgerow watching and warbling, likely hoping to snatch a delectable fruit at the first opportunity. Emmalin smiled as she recalled Beethoven's *Symphony No. 6*. She hummed the lively melody and popped an especially perfect berry into her mouth. Sweetness splashed her tongue as she chewed. "These are delicious. I don't think I've ever tasted any so sweet."

Charity sat back on her heels. "We pride ourselves on having the best berries in the county."

"Possibly in the country." Emmalin ate another, closing her eyes as she relished the luscious flavor. "If I'm not careful, I'll never fill my basket." She returned to work.

The morning passed pleasantly with Beethoven's 6th meandering through Emmalin's mind and heart. By midday, she and Margaret had filled four large baskets. "This is all I can manage today," Margaret said. "If I want to get any of these preserved, I need to get home." She pushed to her feet, dusted the dirt from her hands and skirt, then loosened the flask tied to her belt. She opened it and took a drink. "Are you ready, Emmalin?"

Emmalin stood and pressed her hands against the small of her back, rubbing out the ache burrowed there. "Yes, I'm ready, but I've so enjoyed myself. Thank you, Charity, for allowing us to pick."

"Come back any time. We have more than we can possibly use."

Emmalin looked at Margaret. "Do you think we can?"

"Of course. How 'bout the end of the week?"

"I'll be here," Charity said. "But I do have a picnic scheduled with Arthur on Wednesday." She held her arms out from her side.

"Does Pastor like strawberry pie?" Margaret asked with a mischievous smile.

"He does. I plan to bake one for him."

Emmalin asked Margaret, "Will we have time to bake pies this afternoon?"

"Absolutely. I planned on it." Margaret ambled toward the wagon. She gave Emmalin a bright smile. "I'm pretty sure your father will enjoy some strawberry pie. What do you think?"

"I think he will be eating pie tonight." Emmalin laughed. She set her baskets brimming with fruit in the back of the wagon and climbed up onto the seat.

Removing her straw bonnet, Charity waved it as they drove off. "I'll see you on Sunday."

"Sunday," Emmalin called.

◆◆◆◆◆◆◆◆◆◆◆◆

Margaret pulled the wagon to a stop in front of her house where she and Emmalin unloaded the baskets of berries and set them on the porch. "I left cookie sheets and cheese cloth on the kitchen table. Can you get them while I put the horses away?"

"Of course. Where would you like me to put them?"

Margaret scanned the yard. "How about there on the wash table." She drove off toward the barn.

Emmalin hurried to the house. This should be fun. Mother and Uncle Jonathon would be astounded at how much she'd learned. She smiled at the idea. If only she could share this new life with them. If only. She was tempted to embrace the pain of their absence, but instead she swept it away and went inside where she quickly found the needed items and carried them to the wash table.

With the horses in the paddock, Margaret strode back to the house. "We'll need a couple of knives."

"I'll get them." Emmalin returned to the kitchen and retrieved two paring knives from a drawer, then stepped onto the porch where she joined Margaret. "I've never done this before."

"It's easy, but time consuming." Margaret picked up one of the baskets. "I'll set these aside for jam and pies. Oh, we'll need bowls." She moved past Emmalin and into the house, then hurried back with an assortment of bowls. She handed one to Emmalin and set two on the porch, and with a bowl in her lap, she sat in one of the wooden rockers. "First we need to slice them."

Emmalin sat in the other chair.

"So, all we do now is cut off the green tops and slice the berries into quarters. You can toss the tops on the porch, and I'll sweep them up when we're done."

Emmalin watched as Margaret topped a berry and then sliced it into four pieces, then she did the same. It only took a handful of berries before her hands were stained with red juice. Some of the berries had dried mud on them. "What should I do about the dirt?"

"Just set those aside in this bowl." She placed one on the porch between them. "We'll wash them later. Maybe use them for fresh eating."

"When I was young, I used to do this with my mother and two sisters," Margaret said. "I've such fond memories of our working together and chatting all the while." She closed her eyes as if capturing the images from days past. "Then just as now—perfect weather and the sweet smell of berries." She opened her eyes and picked a plump berry out of a basket. After slicing it, she dropped it into her bowl.

"This will become a precious memory for me," Emmalin said, choosing a strawberry.

Time passed quickly as the two friends settled into talk of the weather, recipe sharing, and ideas about the upcoming wedding. Emmalin imagined what her wedding day would be like, and her excitement built. If only the cabin could be built more quickly. "I can hardly wait to be Jacob's wife." She felt an unexpected shiver of apprehension. "I hope I'm not a disappointment to him."

"You? Of course you won't be." Margaret smiled softly. "But there will be an adjustment period. Newlyweds have a lot to learn about becoming a couple. My Edgar and I had a time of it in the beginning. He could be so stubborn, and I was more independent than he expected." She chuckled. "But we found our way."

Emmalin let out a long breath. "I already know Jacob and I don't agree on everything. That became evident when we tried to set out a plan for the house. There was a lot we didn't agree on. But he is such a wonderful man. And I'd be foolish to think we'll be in harmony on everything."

"I don't think I've ever known a couple who were a perfect match."

Emmalin let her hands rest in the bowl in front of her. "I am struggling a bit with the idea of living so far from everyone. I'm afraid of being alone all the way out there."

"When Edgar and I settled here, I felt the same way. Deer Creek was tiny, and it was a bit of a drive into town. But I adjusted, and Deer Creek has grown." She picked up another berry. "And think about all of the challenges you've already overcome. This is just one more and you'll manage well, I'm sure. And Oregon Territory is being discovered. You might well have neighbors out that way before long."

Emmalin offered Margaret a smile. "Thank you. You always know just what to say." When Emmalin finished the last of her berries, she asked, "What do we do now?"

"We set them on the trays and let them dry in the sun." Margaret wiped her hands on her apron and then carried her bowl to the wash table. She put out the trays and placed the berries flesh side up. "Just set them out like this."

Emmalin did just as Margaret had shown her, but gave in to temptation and ate a few. "I think strawberries are the most delicious fruit God created."

Margaret dropped a bite into her mouth. "Quite possibly."

They worked quietly for a few minutes, then Margaret asked, "How are things coming along on the house?"

"Fine, I think. Jacob is working hard." Emmalin pushed some of the berries closer together to make room for more. "I worry about him. He's up there all alone falling trees. I'm afraid he'll get hurt."

"It is dangerous, but Jacob's spent most all of his life in the woods. He knows what he's doing."

"I tell myself that, but I still worry." Emmalin added berries to the cooking sheet. "Even the most experienced man can make a mistake. I tried to convince him to use planed lumber."

"I understand how you feel." Margaret gently shook her pan, spreading out the berries.

"Why do you think Jacob is so against it?"

"It's the only way he knows, and he's confident in his own labor. He wants the best for you two, and he'll do a good job. That house will be strong and secure. You never know what you might get when you trust someone else's work."

"I suppose."

"A man needs to feel like a man, like he's the one taking care of his family. God knew what He was doing when He created men. Though there are some shortcomings that come with that make-up. It's hard for someone like Jacob to accept something like lumber with money from his wife…fiancée."

Emmalin nodded. "Do you think that means I won't ever be able to use my money? What am I supposed to do with it?"

"There will be plenty of need in the days to come. Jacob will get used to the idea of your being able to contribute. But right now, he's adjusting to it all. Plus, you aren't yet his wife. Taking money from you now must make him feel like he's taking advantage."

"I don't want him to feel like that."

"You two will find your way. And I have no doubt that God will show you where your inheritance will best be spent."

"Patience. It's never been one of my strengths."

Margaret added more berries to the sheet. "I thought Charity's brother, John, was going to give Jacob a hand."

"He is, but right now there's so much to be done on the farm that he can only cut out time here and there."

When they finished setting out the berries, Margaret put her hands on her hips and studied their work. "Three full sheets."

"I never imagined we'd have so many and more set aside."

Margaret covered the berries with cheese cloth. "This will keep the bugs out. In a few hours, they'll be ready to put in jars." She dusted off her hands. "I think our men folk would probably like some fresh strawberry pie. Tomorrow we can use the rest for preserves."

"Can I save my berries and make jam the day after? I hoped to take a pie up to Jacob tomorrow."

"Just put them in the root cellar. I'll come by and give you a hand day after tomorrow."

Emmalin tied on an apron. "I can't wait to surprise Jacob."

Chapter Twelve

Jacob woke to the drumming of a woodpecker. He forced his eyes open, slowly awakened, and rolled onto his back. Taking in a deep breath, he listened as the bird routed bugs from a nearby tree.

The bird hadn't made plans for breakfast, he simply knew that with a little bit of effort, it would be there for him. Birds and animals didn't make plans for their lives. They did what was natural and required for each day without worry of what was to come. God provided for them.

What would that be like, to give no thought to what tomorrow might bring? In recent weeks, Jacob had spent too many hours making plans and worrying about all he needed to do to prepare for his and Emmalin's future. Soon their lives would be joined, and he wanted everything to be just right for her. Jacob understood God knew what was best and would make a way and to worry was to lack faith. He needed to be more like the wild birds.

If he listened, God would reveal what He wanted.

Jacob eyed the walls of the tent. In one corner, a spider wove a web. It worked diligently, laying down each strand perfectly. A gust of wind blew in through the door, tossing the web and leaving it imperfect. The spider fell, catching itself on a thin strand. Unintimidated, it returned to work. Jacob understood he needed to be like that, simply doing what came naturally and trusting for the moment.

Still feeling like he could use more sleep, he sat up, scrubbed his face with his hands, and combed back his hair with his fingers. He was tired and his body ached. Working hard was something he was used to but logging was a different kind of beast.

Henry pressed his nose under Jacob's arm. "Hey there, boy. Ready for another day?" Jacob scratched him behind the ears. The dog leaned against him, eyes closed. "Yeah. You like that, don't you." He gave him a pat on the head.

"All right. No time to waste." Jacob pushed to his feet, stepped out of the tent and into the morning air. Sunlight cut through the forest, illuminating nature in a slice of brilliant light.

With the coffeepot in hand, he walked toward the river. Henry darted off into the brush. At the river's edge, Jacob kneeled, scooped water into his hands, and splashed his face. It was icy cold and made him shiver. He dipped the pot into the water and filled it. This would be a good day, he was sure of it.

Back at camp, Jacob set the pot in what remained of hot coals from the previous night's fire. He banked the coals, added firewood, and then scooped coffee into the pot.

He couldn't ignore the blackened trees surrounding the remains of the cabin that had once been his parents'. The fire had burned hot and fast, setting the house and barn ablaze before anything could be saved, except a family photo, which would one day sit on his fireplace mantel. He'd already cut down most of the burned and weakened trees close to the building site. Today he'd bring down the last of them. Many had burned-out roots. Some had been destroyed on the inside and would rot and die. A good number still had healthy interiors and would provide timber for the house, while others would serve well for outbuildings and fencing. He'd put all he could to good use.

With a cast-iron frying pan in hand, he returned to the now crackling fire where he mixed up coals at the edge of the flames, then set the pan in the heat. Tossing a hunk of bacon in, his mouth watered at the sound of sizzling meat. Cutting two biscuits in half, he added them to the pan. Emmalin had baked them. She was determined to keep him well fed. He smiled at the idea of her looking out for him.

Using a spatula, he flipped the sizzling bacon and the biscuits. His stomach ached with hunger. He'd been so exhausted the previous night he'd gone to sleep without eating. The coffee was boiling, so he filled a tin cup with the brew, set the pot back in the coals, then settled on a stump and took a swig. He relished the sharp flavor, though it did taste a bit like the rusted pot.

Jacob gazed into the forest. Already, bees buzzed among the greenery, lighting on wildflowers and newly budding plum trees. Maybe next year Emmalin would make jam from the wild fruit. His mother always had.

A double-edged axe waited for him. It was a reliable tool with a strong blade, but his hands had suffered under hours of swinging it. He opened up his palm. Healing blisters were hardening into calluses. In recent months, he hadn't spent more than a few hours on the end of an axe. Bear grease would help.

The sizzle and aroma of cooking bacon drew his attention back to breakfast. He pulled the skillet out of the coals and cut the bacon slices in half, then he took a biscuit and sandwiched the meat between two halves. He took a bite and chewed. The juicy smoked flavor of the pork along with the buttery taste of biscuit was a perfect blend. He sat back and savored the simple meal, made all the better because of Emmalin's kind attention. She would make a good wife.

He finished off both biscuits and the bacon washing them down with coffee. The brush crackled at the edge of the forest, and he reached for his rifle. Henry appeared, breathing hard, tail wagging. Jacob relaxed and rested the gun against the stump. "Ah, it's you. Looks like you had a good run. You ready for breakfast?" Jacob sliced off a hefty chunk of bacon and offered it to the dog. Henry wasn't one to gobble his food. He carried it to the edge of the clearing where he lay with it between his paws and ate the meat with appreciation.

After a quick wash in the river, Jacob carried the dishes back to camp and put them away in an empty apple box. He sized up the timber waiting for him. There was a blackened tree that needed to come down. It was sizeable, too large for the cabin, but he'd get some good firewood out of it.

Approaching the base of the tree, he gazed up into its limbs. The bark and branches were black at least twenty feet up and the boughs were brown from the flames. It would die and eventually come down. He stepped back a few paces to get a better idea how best to fall it. It was pretty nearly straight and shouldn't be too much trouble. One of the dangers of falling burned trees was weaknesses that couldn't be seen. There might be hollow places or pockets of pitch hidden within.

Taking hold of the double-bitted axe with a strong grip, he clasped it at the belly, then moved his blistered hands down to the throat and gave it a light swing, getting the feel of it. Taking a broad stance, he hefted the axe up and above his right shoulder, then swung it toward the tree. It hit hard, biting into the blackened bark and exposing the lighter meat of the tree's interior. He took another swing and another, feeling the blood begin to work through his muscles, giving him strength. He kept at it, working the angles of each cut, shifting the angle slightly as the blade dug into the wood. Each gash brought him closer to bringing down the big fir.

He pulled the blade free and heard a sharp pop and splintering noise from above. He looked up to see a branch plummeting through the limbs. At the last moment, he leaped away from the tree and the branch dropped and hit him in the shoulder, knocking him to the ground.

Pain seared his arm. He clasped his hand over it and sucked in a breath, sweat breaking out on his face. He bent at the waist, still grasping his shoulder. "Oh Lordy, that hurts." He gritted his teeth and waited for the intensity of the pain to pass.

Gradually it lessened and he straightened, rubbing his shoulder. He should have been more careful. There was a reason loose branches like that were called widow-makers. Many a man had been killed by falling limbs. Best not tell Emmalin. It would only cause her more worry.

After dragging the branch away from the tree, he gazed up into the burned boughs. Were there any others waiting to end his life? He didn't see anything that would cause a problem. And he wasn't about to let fear keep him from doing his job.

Jacob took a swig of water from his canteen, recapped it, and once more studied the fir. It would take only a few more swings of the axe to bring it down.

Once the cabin was completed, Emmalin would realize how much better it was to use the wood growing on the property rather than planed lumber. The very best was right here on the land, and he wasn't about to take any shortcuts, not when it came to their own place. Emmalin was counting on him to provide a sturdy home for them.

He set the canteen aside and moved back to the tree. With sweat running down his back and his arms aching, he made the final cuts. The base of the tree cracked, the fir swayed, tipped, and plunged to the earth with the explosion of its weight slamming against the forest floor. Quickly, using the heel of the bit, he moved along the tree, cutting away its branches, then he continued on to a young healthy tree. It would make a good log for the house. It came down without mishap.

By midday he'd managed to cut and limb a half a dozen trees. He was quickly adding to the timber he'd need for the cabin. One more and he'd take a dinner break. After that, he'd work until sunset. He was driven by the image of Emmalin. She couldn't be his wife until they had a home, and he didn't want to take one day longer than needed. If only there was help available. This time of year, it was hard to find anyone not already overworked. He'd considered asking one of the miners from down south, but without knowing a man, there was no way to judge his character. With any luck, Charity's brother John would find some free time.

Sweeping off his hat, Jacob wiped sweat from his face, then approached a tree he'd avoided all day. It was a good straight tree, and the limbs didn't start until halfway up. The only problem with it was that it grew at an angle. He'd have to plan his cuts with care to make sure it fell true and not come back on him.

He calculated the angle of the cuts he'd need, then stepped up to the hefty cedar and swung the axe, getting a clean first bite. He took another and another. With each swing, he imagined Emmalin greeting him at the door of their cabin. Her thick luxurious hair would fall onto her cheek, and she'd smile seductively as she stepped into his embrace. He'd kiss her, deeply, and she'd kiss him back. He'd lift her into his arms and carry her inside as she hugged his neck.

Henry leaped out of the brush and ran up to Jacob. "Ah, so there you are." Jacob gave him a pat. "Just one more tree, then we'll have dinner. Get back now. Nearly got this one down. Don't need you in the way."

He didn't want to drop the tree into the river, so he'd angle the cut from the inside. Only a few more notches and he'd be done for the day.

Henry settled a few paces away and watched. Jacob took a couple of deep breaths. He was tired and his muscles ached. This was a cedar, and the bark was dense. He chipped away, one swing, then another. It was nearly ready to come down. He pushed against it, but it didn't budge. One more good strike with the axe ought to do it.

He hauled back with the double-bitted blade and swung hard. His bit sank into the interior wood and became stuck as the tree angled back on the blade. He pulled, but it didn't come free. He rubbed the back of his neck. Maybe if he gave it a good shove. It was leaning pretty hard. Might come down.

With determination Jacob approached the tree, pushed against the bark with both hands; it creaked, then cracked as it started to tip. Using his full weight, he leaned in…and finally over it went. All of a sudden, it twisted to his right and fell into another tree where it hung up, momentarily.

Without warning, the cedar bounced off the tree and came back at him. Jacob had only a fraction of a second to decide which way to leap. He dove to the ground and rolled away to his left, but there was no escaping the timber coming at him. Was this the end of his life? All he could think of was Emmalin. He couldn't die. What would happen to her?

The tree crackled as it fell, slamming its weight against his upper back and hitting him in the back of the head. Light and pain exploded in Jacob's skull. And then he plunged into darkness.

Chapter Thirteen

Emmalin pushed her rifle into her saddle holster while she hummed the hymn "Holy, Holy, Holy." It promised to be a grand day. She would see Jacob. Oh, how she'd missed him. She strapped in the rifle. After her encounter with the cougar, she made certain to always have a firearm with her when she traveled. Emmalin had devoted hours into practice and was confident she would be able to defend herself adeptly, if required.

She ran her hand along Sassy's neck and gave her a pat, then took the reins in hand, and pushed up into the saddle. Anticipation hummed through her. She could hardly wait to embrace Jacob. She would hold his handsome face in her hands and kiss him. Today was a special delight because he had no idea she was coming. She'd made a lunch for them, which included slices of strawberry pie. She'd also brought along biscuits, cheese, and dried meat to leave to help sustain him until he returned to town.

Her father stepped onto the porch. "When can I expect you home?"

"I will do my best to get back before dark. If not, Sassy can find the way." She combed the horse's mane with her fingers. "I wish I could come back in the morning. But I'd hate to create a scandal."

"The ladies about town would be wagging their tongues."

"Do you really think so? It would be perfectly proper. Jacob is an honorable man. And we did travel together when I came down from Oregon City last summer."

"I have no worries about Jacob. He's a decent man. But there are always a few people who like to stir up trouble. Do you really want to bring that on yourselves?"

Emmalin leaned back in the saddle. "No. Of course not." She tipped her head to the side. "I'll see you tonight." She turned Sassy toward the road that led to Deer Creek and trotted off, the hymn returning to her. "*Holy, Holy, Holy Lord God almighty, early in the morning our song shall rise to thee.*"

Delicate clouds reached across the sky like a lace coverlet above the hillsides. The air was cool with a hint of the promised warmth that would most certainly come with the day. There was no sign of rain. A perfect day.

As she moved through town, Emmalin kept Sassy at a rapid pace. She didn't want to stop, not even for a chat with Margaret. She turned onto the trail that followed Deer Creek to the northeast. Soon she rode through tall spring grasses that pressed in on the edges of the trail. Their fragrance was heady. Bees hummed as they hovered among the wildflowers, and a doe and two fawns grazed in the midst of an oak grove. Hunting wouldn't begin until fall, so for now deer were only to be admired. Emmalin would never shoot a doe with fawns anyway. One of the youngsters eagerly ate its breakfast of mother's milk, its tail wagging with pleasure. Warmth rose up in Emmalin's heart. God's creation was so delightful.

Sadly, His creation also included predators. She hoped there were none nearby. She rested her hand on the butt of her rifle and scanned the hillsides. There was no need to be afraid.

In the distance she spotted a black bear shuffling up a rocky ridge. It had likely seen her and was doing its best to avoid an encounter. Generally black bears stayed away from humans, something Emmalin was grateful for. Still, she didn't trust any bear and kept her hand on the rifle while she watched it disappear into the shadows of the forest. She tapped Sassy's sides with her heels and moved on.

The trail led up a hill and then down into a forested gorge. She gazed at the mountain foothills, remembering her visit to the native village in the valley the previous Christmas. She knew their summer lodgings were in those hills somewhere. If only she'd had an opportunity to visit before the Indians had been forced to leave.

Jacob said they were gone, every one of them, certainly rounded up by soldiers and forced to live on a reservation. She couldn't imagine being ripped, in such a brutal way, from the only home they'd known. It was a dreadful cruelty. When she left Philadelphia, it had been her choice. Emmalin's heart squeezed at the memory. That had been painful even with the hope of better days ahead.

Did the natives have hope? Would they ever be free again? Jacob would travel north to find his family. But even if he found them, what could be done?

She followed the trail into the darkness of the forest and over a path that wound its way along the North Umpqua River. The summer sun barely penetrated the dense woodland, turning the air chill. The river skipped over shallows, tumbled in a white foam that bounced around boulders, and then washed into quiet deep green pools. A family of ducks skirted along the bank, plucking seeds from overhanging grasses.

Emmalin liked ducks. They were adorable creatures. Normally she would have stopped to enjoy them, but there was no time today. Jacob was all that mattered. She loosened the reins and allowed Sassy to settle into a brisk gait.

An embankment clogged with blackberry vines, ferns, and vine maple rose above her, reaching into heavy forest land. Rocks skittered down from above. What had sent them tumbling? Likely deer or elk. She gazed into the foliage but saw nothing. It could be anything—cougar, bear, or wolf. Rising anxiety kept her moving.

She tried to keep her thoughts on Jacob and their reunion. What was he doing right now, at this moment? Was he downing trees or constructing the cabin? May the Lord keep him safe.

The hillside above rolled down toward the river until it stretched out into a small meadow that hugged the water's edge. It was a good place to stop and get a drink. River water would be more refreshing than what she carried in her flask. She pulled Sassy to a stop and dismounted. She'd been riding for nearly an hour and her muscles were stiff. She stretched from side to side, then moved to the river where a pool washed against the rocks.

She kneeled and scooped water into her hand, then sipped it from her palm. It was cold, clean, and delicious. She dipped out another mouthful and another, then ran a damp palm over her face.

Sassy would be thirsty too. She led the horse to the river and let her drink. The horse moved her ears from side to side, then abruptly lifted her head and blasted air from her nostrils.

"What is it, girl?" Emmalin felt a prickle of fear and searched the forest edge and the trail she'd left behind. For a brief moment she was frightened that it might be Indians, but quickly remembered they were no longer a threat. She reached for the reins, and Sassy backed away with a nervous nicker. Emmalin needed to move on. "Come on, girl." She calmed the horse with a gentle tone. "Everything's fine," she said, even though she feared otherwise. The horse sensed something she didn't.

"There you go." She approached Sassy and got hold of the reins. "Time to be on our way." She kept her tone light and climbed back into the saddle. Sassy had taken only a few steps when a large buck leaped across the trail in front of them. The horse lunged to the side and then reared. Nearly toppling off backward, Emmalin grabbed hold of the saddle horn. "Whoa. Whoa."

Sassy dropped her front feet and pranced, then took a couple of steps forward. Her coat twitched with tension. Finally, she stilled. "Good girl. Just a silly deer." Emmalin tried to catch a glimpse of the woodland creature, but it was gone, swallowed up by the forest.

The incident left Emmalin unsettled. She pushed Sassy into a lope. She needed Jacob. Thankfully it wasn't much farther to his place.

Emmalin saw the charred forest before she spotted Jacob's burned-out cabin and barn. The blackness seemed deeper than it had the last time she'd been here. As she rode through the scorched forest, the image of the trees looked as if they had been screaming when the fire overtook them. The idea of it sickened her.

It was all such a terrible loss. Jacob's history was here where his family had lived and died. She tried to imagine what life with Jacob would be like in this place. Loving him would be easy, but the charred trees and buildings made her heart hurt, reminding her how bleak life could be.

In time it would all be cleared away, and there would be new life.

Today was not a time to think on the sorrows that could befall a person. Today she was here to see Jacob, the man God had given her.

She looked about but didn't see him. Maybe he was down by the river. "Jacob," she called. He didn't call back. There was no sign of him. "Jacob?"

Emmalin climbed off Sassy. She'd check his tent first. Pulling aside the canvas doorway, she peeked inside. No one there. Bedding was in a pile; a shirt and pants had been draped over a wooden box. Provisions were piled inside an apple crate. Where had he gone? Stepping outside, Emmalin scanned the clearing where freshly cut timber for their home had been collected. Clearly, he'd been working hard. She peered into the forest. Smoke stood in the shade, contentedly munching grass. Where was Henry? He should have come running when she rode into camp.

"Henry," she called, then whistled. There was an answering bark, and she headed toward the sound. Henry appeared and trotted toward her. With a whine he pushed his cold nose into her palm. "What is it? Where is Jacob?" Something was wrong. She knew it. "Where is he, Henry?"

As if understanding the question, the dog ran toward a stand of cedars.

Emmalin noticed a newly cut tree. And then she saw Jacob sprawled facedown on the ground beside it, his arms askew. "Jacob!" She ran to him. Was he dead? *Please, no.*

The hair on the back of his head was matted with blood. It dribbled down the side of his head and onto his cheek. She could see there was a wound but didn't dare look at it closely.

"Oh, Jacob." She dropped to her knees beside him. His eyes were closed. "Jacob! Jacob!"

He didn't respond. Blood had pooled on the ground. "Oh, dear Lord! Please don't let him die. Please, God."

She needed to get him on his back. Emmalin grabbed hold of his shoulder and hefted up his chest, pressing her body against him trying to get leverage to haul him over. She cried while she pushed against him. "Please, Jacob." She cried harder, but with strength she didn't know she possessed she rolled him onto his back.

He didn't respond. She laid her hand on his cheek. His skin was warm. His chest rose slightly as he breathed. She pressed her fingers to his neck. There was a pulse.

She gently grabbed hold of his shoulders. "Jacob! Jacob! Wake up!" She patted his cheeks. "Please, Jacob, wake up."

No response. Not even a blink of his eyes. What was she to do?

She stood and ran to the tent. Outside the door, she found a bucket, grabbed it, then ducked inside and snatched up a washcloth before heading to the river. At the water's edge, she fell to her knees and dipped in the bucket, filling it halfway. Scrambling to her feet, she hurried back to Jacob. Water splashed out and soaked the front of her dress. She barely noticed. Kneeling beside him, she wet the cloth and wiped his face. He still didn't respond.

"Oh, Jacob. Please wake up." Tears coursed down Emmalin's cheeks.

He clearly had some sort of injury to his head. She needed to look. Steeling herself for what she would see, she turned his head. He had a deep gash and a large sprawling bump. The back of his neck was black and blue. She cleaned away as much of the blood as possible, then pressed the cloth to the wound. He needed a doctor.

There was no doctor! She scanned the forest as if one might pop out from behind a tree. But of course, that was impossible. There was no one to help.

Emmalin sat on the ground beside Jacob and softly spoke to him, telling him how much she loved him and how he needed to wake up. He showed no sign of awareness. She had to do something. But what?

The truth of what must happen crept around the edges of her mind. How could she do such a thing? But there was no avoiding it. She had to leave him and go for help.

Her heart heavy and quaking with fear, she prepared to go. She went to the tent and grabbed a blanket, then hurried back to Jacob. She draped the blanket over him, tucking it in at his sides. As soon as the sun went down it would be cold.

She set a fresh bucket of water and a cup near Jacob. He might need it if he woke up.

It was time. She had to go. She pressed a kiss to his cheek and stood, then gave the forest a perusal. What if a wolf or a cougar found him?

Henry nudged her. Her heart flooded with gratitude, and she hugged the dog. "You'll stay with him. You'll keep him safe." She got Jacob's rifle and set it beside him, just in case.

"I'll be back soon," she said to Henry, stroking the space between his dark eyes with her thumbs. "I'm counting on you."

She moved once more to Jacob's side, willing him to wake up. He looked as if he were dead. "I'm so sorry, but I have to go. You have to fight to stay alive, Jacob. Fight for me. Fight for us. I love you."

With resolve, Emmalin strode to her horse, climbed into the saddle, and then kicked Sassy in the sides. She dropped down close to the horse's neck and loosened the reins. "Come on, girl."

The horse sensed the urgency and ran full-out down the trail. Emmalin counted on her sure-footedness as they cut across open countryside. It was a faster route than the river trail. "Please, Lord, protect him. I beg you. Please."

Chapter Fourteen

Emmalin continued to push Sassy hard as she rode past the grist mill. She knew the unrelenting pace might be too much for the mare, but she had no choice. Jacob could be dying, or he might already be dead.

When she saw the first house at the edge of town, she let out a quaking breath of relief. Almost there. Her father had to be at the store. He must be. There was no time to ride out to the house or to search for him. She needed help now.

Jacob. Dear Jacob. He'd been so still, so pale. *Lord, please have mercy. Protect him.* She fought against tears. There was no time for them now.

Sassy was lathered up, but she kept running. Poor Sassy.

When Emmalin reached the mercantile, she pulled back on the reins and propelled herself out of the saddle. "Father! Father!" She swung open the door to the mercantile. "Father!"

"Emmalin?" His face lined with worry, he stepped away from a shelf. "What is it?"

"Thank the Lord!" She gulped in air.

"What's happened?" He firmly grabbed her by the upper arms. "Calm down. Catch your breath."

Emmalin choked down a couple of big breaths. "It's…it's Jacob. He's hurt. He's bad." The tears she'd been holding back now spilled down her cheeks. She let out a sob. "I'm not even sure he's still alive."

Her father's brow furrowed into deep creases. "Tell me what happened."

Another sob escaped. "I-I found him on the ground. I thought he was dead. He was so still and pale." She pressed a quaking hand to her chest. "I checked him, and he was still breathing, but I couldn't wake him." Her voice was strident. "I think he was hit by a falling tree. We have to help him."

"Let's go." Samuel kept a hand on Emmalin's shoulder and eased her out the front door, letting it slam behind them. "I'll get a couple of men. You get Margaret."

Emmalin nodded and hurried to the café. She swung open the door. "Margaret," she called and stepped inside. "Margaret?"

Her dear friend hustled out of the kitchen.

"I need your help. Jacob's been injured."

"What can I do?" She gripped a towel. "What's happened?"

"I think he was hit by a falling tree. I found him unconscious at the cabin."

Margaret threw the towel over the back of a chair and untied her apron. "Is he still up there?"

"Yes. We have to get him to town. My father's gone for help."

"I'll get my bag." Margaret ran to the back of the kitchen and reappeared a moment later carrying a carpet bag. She hurried to the door. She flipped the closed sign on the front door and ushered Emmalin out ahead of her just as her father appeared at a full run.

"Pastor Miller's on his way," he hollered as he ran around the side of the mercantile.

Within minutes, a wagon rumbled down the street with Pastor Miller driving. Charity's brother, Chauncey, was with him. Her father arrived, his horse prancing and ready to go.

Emmalin moved to Sassy who was soaked with sweat. "You dear thing." She patted the horse's neck. "You gave everything."

"Thanks for the wagon, Pastor," Samuel said. "We'll need it."

Emmalin's heart sank at the thought. "It will take too long. Can we ride ahead?"

"Of course." Margaret untied her horse from the wooden rail in front of the café. "Your father and I will ride with you." She glanced at Pastor Miller. "Can you find your way?"

"Sure can. I've been to Jacob's more than once." The minister lifted the reins. "This team is sure-footed. We won't be far behind you." Quieting his voice, he said, "He's in the Lord's hands." Without saying more, he slapped the reins, and the team of horses stepped into a brisk walk.

Emmalin looked at her horse, then at her father. "She ran all the way here. She'll never make it back."

"We can get a horse at the livery."

Emmalin took hold of Sassy's reins and led her toward the stables. Her father threw himself onto his horse and ran ahead.

By the time Emmalin reached the stables, her father already had a big piebald stallion saddled and ready to go. "He should do. Not too much for you, I hope."

"I'm sure not." Emmalin moved past him, leading Sassy inside. "Benjamin, can you take care of my horse for me?" She handed the big man the reins.

"No problem. I'll take good care of her. And I'll be praying for Jacob." He gave her a kind smile. "That horse your daddy's got is a good boy. Sturdy and dependable. He'll get you where you need to go." He took Sassy's reins from Emmalin.

"Thank you." Emmalin hurried outside.

"You'll need this." Margaret offered a canteen to Emmalin. "Take a good long drink. I doubt you've had anything since this morning."

"Thank you." Emmalin took a big gulp. She hadn't realized how thirsty she was. She recapped the flask and handed it back to Margaret. With a hand from her father, Emmalin pushed up into the saddle. It felt a bit awkward, being on top of such a large horse, but she didn't have time to ease into the ride. She pulled the reins across his neck and turned onto the road, then gave him a kick. He swiftly stepped into a gallop.

"He's bigger and stronger than Sassy," her father called as he caught up to her.

"Benjamin said he's a good horse. I'm sure he'll be fine. We need to hurry." She leaned forward to encourage the horse to a faster pace. He broke out, as if he was in need of a run.

They quickly overtook the wagon, and Emmalin worried it would take Pastor Miller too long, but there was nothing she could do about any of that. Her thoughts were with Jacob. *Please be alive.* She could see him as he had been when she left him, lying helpless among cedar boughs. *Father, don't let him die. Please don't let him die.*

She pushed forward, tears streaming down her face, fear and sorrow unrestrained.

As they approached Jacob's place, Emmalin's heart pounded hard. They moved past the burned-out cabin and barn as dread reared up like a flame of terror. What would they find?

Her father slowed the pace. "Where is he?"

"Here." Emmalin turned her horse toward the place she'd left Jacob. She couldn't see him. Had an animal taken him? Where was he? Panic shook her. She heard a bark and then spotted Henry. "Oh, Henry!" She almost laughed with relief. Henry hadn't left him.

She reined in the big piebald, and nearly threw herself off his back. She ran toward Henry and then saw Jacob just as she'd left him. She dropped to her knees beside him. "Jacob. Jacob." He didn't respond.

Margaret set her carpet bag on the ground next to him and kneeled beside Emmalin. "Let me have a look." Her voice was somber as she removed the blanket covering him. She rested a hand on Jacob's chest and left it there for several moments, then turned to Emmalin. "He's still breathing, and his heart feels strong."

"Thank the Lord." Tears of relief replaced sorrowful ones.

With a stark expression, Margaret sat back on her heels. She didn't speak. She didn't
move.

"Margaret?" Samuel asked. "Are you all right?"

She turned stricken eyes on Emmalin's father. "Yes. Just remembering Edgar—"

"Oh." Emmalin pressed a hand to her chest. "He died in a logging accident."

"He did." Margaret returned to business. "But that was Edgar. This is Jacob."

Emmalin briefly touched Margaret's shoulder then leaned over Jacob. "I'm here. We're all here—my father and Margaret. Pastor Miller is coming. We'll get you back to town. You're going to be all right."

Margaret ran her hand down Jacob's arms, then stopped and palpated a place just below the elbow. "His arm is broken." She looked at Samuel. "Can you find two pieces of strong straight wood, about this long?" She held up her hands to indicate approximately a foot in length.

"Sure." He set out in search of the needed supports.

Margaret continued her examination. She rested a hand on Jacob's face, lifted his eyelids and looked into his eyes. Gently, she probed the back of his skull and then took a look at the gash. "I'm not surprised he's unconscious. It's amazing he's still alive. That's a bad injury, and he has a terrible knot on his head."

When Samuel returned with the pieces of wood, Margaret asked, "Can you help me get him on his side. I'd like to take a look at his spine."

Samuel kneeled beside Margaret. "Slowly now," Margaret said. The two of them pushed Jacob onto his side while Emmalin kept him from rolling forward onto his stomach. Margaret tugged up his shirt, then probed his back with her fingers. "He's badly bruised and swollen, but I don't feel any irregularities. But that doesn't mean all is well. We need to be very careful when we move him." Her tone was grim.

"Is he going to be all right?" Emmalin asked, afraid to hear the answer.

"There's no way to tell." Margaret changed her stance. "Let's lay him back down." Together, the three of them lowered Jacob onto his back.

Emmalin couldn't tear her eyes away from Jacob. He was so pallid. And though she knew the fear was unfounded, she was afraid if she looked away, he might die.

Margaret rested a hand on Emmalin's arm. "He's still with us and his heart is strong. Just one fracture, as far as I can tell."

Samuel gave the branches he'd found for a splint to Margaret. "I hope these are what you need."

"They're just right." She set them aside. "Let's get him in a more comfortable position."

Emmalin ran to the tent and got a pillow. When she returned with it, she imagined Jacob opening his eyes and smiling at her. If only he would.

"Why don't we wait for that," Margaret said. "Let me get him cleaned up first."

Emmalin held the pillow against her chest. Tears burned her eyes as she fought to hold them back. "Why doesn't he wake up?"

Her father placed an arm around her. "He will. When it's the right time. I've known men to be unconscious for more than a day after an injury like this and then all of a sudden, they come around and are good as new." He gave her a gentle squeeze. "I'm sure he's going to make it back to us. He's a determined man."

Emmalin grasped for the hope offered.

Margaret set Jacob's arm, which should have caused him excruciating pain, but he didn't even flinch. She pulled the blanket up over him, turned his head to the side, and cleaned the wound on the back of his head. "I'll stitch this while we wait for the wagon."

"Is there something I can do?" Emmalin asked. She needed to help.

Margaret looked up at Samuel. "Can you go down to the river and get some clean water?"

"No problem." Samuel set off.

Margaret turned to Emmalin. "I'll need dressings out of my bag."

Emmalin rummaged through the bag and found several sizes of cleaning cloths and bandages. She handed Margaret two and kept others in hand.

When Samuel returned with the water, Margaret dipped a cloth into it and wrung it out, then used it to clean the wound. She worked diligently to remove debris from within the gash.

Emmalin leaned over to get a better look. "How bad?" She sucked in a breath when she saw what looked like white bone deep inside the gash. She fought off wooziness.

"I'll need you to hold this together while I stitch it closed," Margaret said.

Emmalin nodded. But could she actually do it? It was ghastly. She could barely look at it.

"Just so." Margaret showed her how to hold the skin together.

Taking a quieting breath, Emmalin gently pushed the ragged edges of flesh together. "Like this?"

"Yes. Perfect." Using catgut, Margaret deftly sutured the wound closed, pressed a clean dressing over it, and then wrapped a bandage around Jacob's head. "That will take care of it for now."

Margaret glanced up at Samuel.

His expression was one of pride. "You're amazing."

"It's not pretty, but I did my best." She rocked back on her heels. "We'll need a pallet to lift him into the wagon."

"There must be something here we can use." Samuel headed toward Jacob's camp.

By the time the wagon rolled in, a sturdy pallet had been constructed. Samuel placed it beside Jacob who was still unconscious. "Time to get you back into town, my friend." He looked up at Pastor Miller and Chauncey. "I need a hand."

The two immediately leaped out of the wagon. Before they moved Jacob, Pastor Miller closed his eyes and prayed, "Father, we ask You to hold Jacob in Your loving hands and protect his life. We pray for mercy and for healing. Amen."

For a long moment, silence hung over those gathered around Jacob. Emmalin thought her heart might burst with sorrow and fear. Jacob had to be all right.

Chapter Fifteen

Emmalin placed a cool cloth on Jacob's forehead, then ran her finger-tips down his temple. Did he know she was here? It had been nearly twenty-four hours since she'd found him, and he was still unconscious. A dreadful fear burrowed inside of her. What if he never woke up?

The room was hot and stuffy, so she loosened his collar. Her father had surrendered his bed to Jacob and had taken up residence in the barn. He was a kind man. She needed to remember to tell him.

Emmalin moved to the window and opened it. A late morning breeze swept away stale air. She breathed deeply, almost afraid of hanging on to hope and dreading what could be many days of not knowing what would become of Jacob. But God loved him. And Jacob was such a fine person. God would certainly heal him. She just needed to believe.

The door creaked open. It was her father. "Any change?" His tone was hopeful, but his eyes revealed his concern as his gaze went to Jacob.

"No. Nothing yet." Emmalin returned to Jacob's bedside.

"Let me stay with him. You need to rest."

"I can't leave him." Emmalin stared at Jacob, willing him to open his eyes. "What if he wakes up and I'm not here?"

"I'll come and get you." Her father moved closer and placed a comforting hand on her shoulder. "Sitting here and wearing yourself out won't help him."

Emmalin leaned against her father. "I keep praying." She rested her cheek against his shirt. "If only he would wake up."

"Give him time. He'll come around. He's too stubborn not to. He might not look like he's fighting on the outside, but I know he's fighting on the inside."

Margaret stepped into the room and stood at the end of Jacob's bed. "How is he doing?"

"He doesn't move. He's so still." Emmalin tugged out the handkerchief she kept tucked at the cuff of her sleeve and pressed it to her eyes, staunching tears. "I'm so frightened."

"Of course you are." Margaret offered her a kind smile. "But the Lord is with him." She placed a hand on Jacob's forehead. "No fever." She listened to his heart and breathing. "His breaths are shallow, but his heart is strong. He'll come back to us."

"Do you really believe that?"

"I do."

Emmalin dipped the cloth in cool water and returned it to Jacob's forehead. "I've prayed and prayed, but God isn't answering."

"God always answers." Her father rested a hand on her back. "Sometimes not in the way we want. But we can be thankful that Jacob is still alive. And he's strong. God's timing is always perfect. And we can trust Him to do what's best."

Emmalin took in a quaking breath, but it didn't dim the ache she felt inside. She couldn't bear it if Jacob died. Unexpectedly, resentment flared. If he'd done as she suggested and bought planed wood, he wouldn't have been cutting that tree. As quickly as the thought came, Emmalin cast it away. It was shameful to have such feelings.

"All right now, you come with me." Margaret took Emmalin's hands. "I've got some hot soup made. You need to eat and rest. Your father can stay with Jacob."

Emmalin allowed Margaret to guide her out of the room and to the kitchen.

"Now, you sit. Would you like tea?"

"That sounds good. Thank you." She rested her arms on the table. "I hate for you to go to so much trouble when I'm not even certain I can eat."

"It's no trouble. And you must take in some nourishment. How will you be of any help to Jacob if you fall ill?" She dipped out a ladle of soup from a pot heating on the stove and filled a bowl, then put it in front of Emmalin. Cutting into a loaf of bread, she said, "I made this just this morning." She buttered a slice, placed it on a dish, and set it on the table.

Emmalin stared at the soup, but her stomach turned. She hadn't been able to even think of eating since this all began.

"Come on now. That's good soup—I made it with the leftovers from yesterday's roasted chicken."

Emmalin stirred sugar into her tea and took a sip. The warm sweet drink was comforting. She looked up at Margaret. "You're so kind. Thank you."

"It's easy to be kind to the people I love." She smiled.

The tenderness in her voice almost set Emmalin off into a round of fresh tears. She held them inside and took another sip of tea.

"Try some of the soup."

Emmalin set down the cup and dipped out a spoonful of soup. She slurped it quietly, realizing she *was* hungry. "This is delicious. You always know what to do."

"Not always, but I do have a bit of mother hen in me." She sat across from Emmalin. "You know, dear, you feel like the daughter I never had."

Emmalin dabbed at tears that insisted on leaking from her eyes. "I couldn't endure this without you and my father. Even with you both, it's nearly unbearable."

"It is, but I doubt Jacob's even aware of much right now. Sleep is healing and more like a dream than reality. And I'm sure you are in his dreams. And he will be very disappointed when he wakes up if he finds that you've made yourself sick over this."

Margaret was right. Emmalin ate nearly half of her soup and most of the bread. It was fortifying. "How long do you think it will be before he wakes up?"

"One can't know with such things. That was a bad knock on the head."

"And if he doesn't wake up?" The last bite of bread seemed to get stuck mid-swallow.

"We'll just have to cross that bridge when we come to it, if we come to it."

Margaret said the words with confidence, but Emmalin picked up on the concern she failed to conceal.

"Do you think we should go to Eugene City for a doctor?" Emmalin asked.

"I don't know what he would do that we aren't. There's just not a lot to be done. He's not got an infection of any kind, or he would be running a fever. And when I checked his arm this morning it looked fine. I'll freshen his dressings before I leave this evening."

Emmalin took a few more bites of soup.

Margaret refilled her tea. "Drink up and then off to bed with you."

"No. Truly, I couldn't sleep." Emmalin sipped the tea. "I'm afraid to leave him. What if something happens—" She couldn't finish.

"At least lie down for a bit. I'll take care of the dressing on his arm and his head and, if there is any change, I will let you know." She took Emmalin's hand. "Please, you need to take care of yourself."

Emmalin compressed her lips. "All right. I'll try."

Once in her room, she sat on the edge of the bed and slipped off her shoes, then lay down. She didn't close her eyes, but instead stared at the ceiling. Exhaustion and the weight of all that had happened draped itself over her like a heavy quilt. She wasn't with Jacob, but she could still see him. He had been so strong and always seemed invincible. There was nothing he couldn't do.

A tear slipped from the corner of her eye and trailed down her cheek, followed by another. He was the most honorable, kind man she'd ever known. He didn't deserve this. And then, again a voice whispered to her, *In a way, Jacob chose this. He could have used planed lumber. He refused to listen to you.*

Emmalin pushed away the disloyal thoughts. It wasn't right to be angry with Jacob. He couldn't have known.

Another question pressed in. Why would God allow it? *Lord, I don't understand. Please help me, I need Your peace.*

Emmalin closed her eyes, longing for sleep, the only place to escape the pain and fear. Fatigue finally overtook her, and she fell into a troubled slumber. When she awoke, the room was dark, and she was confused. Where was she? Panic swept through her. Then reality. Jacob!

She sat up and pushed out of bed. Dizziness swept over her, and she closed her eyes, pressed a hand against the wall, and waited for the whirling to stop. Had he awakened? She hurried to the door and stepped into the living area. Her father slept in the rocker, his chin resting on his chest. There was no one else present. Emmalin rushed to Jacob's room but stopped at his door and rested her hand against its smooth wood. If only…

She finally dared to push open the door. A single lantern was the only light. Margaret sat in a cane-back chair beside the bed, a Bible in her lap. She was reading out loud, softly. Emmalin listened, recognizing the verses from Jeremiah 29. "For I know the thoughts that I think toward you, saith the Lord, thoughts of peace, and not evil, to give you an unexpected end. Then shall ye call upon me, and ye shall go and pray unto me, and I will hearken unto you. And ye shall seek me, and find me, when ye shall search for me with all your heart."

God's devotion and promises to His people washed over Emmalin in a comforting wave. She covered a sob of gratitude with her hand. She hadn't left Jacob alone. God had been with him every moment. He would not forsake him.

Margaret closed the Bible and looked up. "Emmalin. Were you able to rest?"

She nodded and stepped closer to the bed. "Do you think he hears you?"

"Maybe. God's Word is powerful and a comfort to the soul." Margaret gently patted Jacob's collar flat. "He hasn't left us, not yet. There is always hope with the Lord."

Emmalin needed to believe that. "I can stay with him now."

Margaret set the Bible on the nightstand. "It's past time for me to make something for dinner. I'll get to it. Your father must be hungry and so must you." She pushed out of the chair and walked toward the door.

"My father is not aware of his stomach right now. He's fast asleep."

"Oh. Good. He needs that."

Emmalin sat on the chair and rested a hand on Jacob's arm. "Has he stirred at all?"

"No." Margaret offered an encouraging smile. "I'll get dinner started."

"Thank you." Emmalin picked up the Bible, intending to continue reading to Jacob, but the effort seemed too much. With a sigh, she placed the holy book in her lap and rested her hands on it. For reasons she couldn't fully comprehend, simply holding it gave her strength.

She decided to chat with Jacob. "It was beautiful out today. I wish you could have seen it. The sun was shining and warm, perfect for gardening. And the garden is doing well. Already there are fresh peas and early potatoes. I know Margaret will soon make her marvelous dish of creamed peas and potatoes. And one day, we'll have our own garden. We will. I know it. You just have to wake up."

Her heart squeezed and her voice caught. "Please wake up," she whispered. Weeping threatened to overcome her, but she refused to allow it. That was not what Jacob needed to hear. She took a breath. "The carrots are up, and the corn is looking good."

She gazed out the window into the darkness. "Do you remember how we planned to put our garden in that sunny spot near our cabin? I've been thinking on it and I'm sure there's enough sun there to grow watermelons. What a treat that would be. I hope you like watermelons. I can't imagine that you don't."

She fell silent, remembering the days when she'd gone with Uncle Jonathon to the sprawling garden they had in Philadelphia. They didn't actually work in the garden, they had servants for that, but going together to pick the first ripe watermelon had become a tradition. She and her uncle would walk through the field to search out the best melon. While it was still fresh and warm from the sun, they would slice it into generous portions and sit on the patio together to enjoy its deliciousness.

If only her uncle were here now. He shouldn't have died. Just like Jacob shouldn't die. God could have intervened for her mother and her uncle. Why hadn't He? The ache inside became severe. Emmalin dragged her mind away from wretched thoughts and returned to conversation.

"Yes. We must have watermelons." Melancholy crept back, creating a dark place in her heart. Emmalin picked up the Bible and pressed it against her chest.

A sound came from Jacob. A jolt of surprise shot through Emmalin. Had he said something?

"Jacob?"

He mumbled.

"Oh, Jacob!" Allowing the Bible to slide from her lap to the floor, she leaned over him. "Can you hear me?"

His eyes fluttered, then opened. "Don't…like…watermelon."

Emmalin laughed, pressed her hands to his cheeks, and kissed him on the forehead. "You're awake!"

Jacob gazed at her as if trying to bring her face into focus. He licked dry lips. "How long—" He winced. "How long have I been out?"

"Two days."

He tried to push up on one elbow, but quickly fell back to the mattress.

Emmalin caressed his cheek. "I found you lying in the forest. A tree came down on you." She kissed him again. He closed his eyes and smiled.

She looked over her shoulder. "Father! Margaret! Come quickly!"

"Thirsty," Jacob croaked.

Emmalin picked up the pitcher of water from the nightstand just as the door flew open. Her father stood in the doorway, Margaret behind him. "What is it? Is he all right?"

"Yes! He's awake!" She laughed. "And he's thirsty."

"Oh, my goodness." Margaret shuffled past Samuel to the bed. "My dear boy, how wonderful it is to see you awake." She leaned over him and felt his forehead. "How do you feel?"

He didn't answer right away but pressed his fingers to his temples. "Kind of woozy. My head hurts."

"You took a bad blow." Margaret straightened. "It's not every day a man has a tree come down on him."

"You're lucky to be alive, son." Samuel stood at the foot of the bed.

Jacob pushed up on his arms, then let out a cry and fell back. "My arm!"

"Oh, it's broken. But it will heal," Margaret said.

Using his good arm, he struggled again to sit upright, then he dropped back on the pillows. "My legs. They're heavy. And I don't feel well."

"Of course you don't. You've been unconscious for the last two days."

Margaret sounded cheery, but Emmalin didn't miss the worry in her voice.

"Do you mind if I check your legs?" Margaret asked.

He looked at her as if he were having difficulty seeing. "Go ahead. Figure you seen all of me by now."

Margaret chuckled. "That I have." She pushed back the covers and studied his legs. "They look all right. Straight. No swelling." She ran her hand down his left leg, below the knee. "It feels fine."

"What? What feels fine?"

"Your leg."

Jacob furrowed his brow. "Did you touch it?"

"Yes." She pushed her fingers into his leg.

"Didn't feel anything."

Alarm exploded inside of Emmalin. "You didn't feel that?"

"No."

"How about this." Margaret rubbed his leg harder than before.

"Nothing." There was tension in his voice.

She pinched the skin. "How about that?"

"No."

"Just a moment." Margaret went to her sewing basket that she'd left beside the bedroom chair and took out a needle, then she returned to Jacob's bedside. "All right now. Let me know when you feel this." She gently poked his left calf with the needle. "Just let me know." She poked him again, moving down the leg, then the other leg.

"I don't feel anything."

Emmalin cut off a sob behind a closed fist. Margaret poked the needle into his toes.

Jacob made no reaction.

Margaret sat on the side of the bed. "It appears you've lost the feeling in your legs and feet. I suppose having a tree fall on you could cause all sorts of injuries. My best guess is that you need time to heal." She patted his arm. "It's likely just a matter of time."

As if he hadn't heard the optimism in Margaret's statement, he asked, "You mean I'm paralyzed?"

Emmalin took his hand. "No. Of course not. Your legs just need more time to heal." She squeezed his hand. Was he truly paralyzed? She rested his palm against her cheek. "You're going to be just fine."

Chapter Sixteen

The sun was barely up, but already the unusually warm June temperature heated the air. The house felt stifling. Standing outside Jacob's room, Emmalin patted moisture from her face with a handkerchief and dredged up courage to step inside. If only he were better. And if he wasn't, would he ever be? It had been nearly two weeks since the accident. She dared not even ask herself the question.

She steadied a tray of food, then with a strengthening breath, opened the door and stepped inside. "Good morning." She forced a cheery smile.

Jacob set down a book he'd been reading and awkwardly pushed up on his arms.

"Let me assist you." Emmalin placed the tray on the bureau and hurried to Jacob's bedside. She pulled him forward and plumped his pillows, then helped him sit upright. Anguish swirled through her. "There you go." She picked up the book. "What are you reading?" She looked at the title. *House of Seven Gables*. "Heavy reading."

"Yeah." He said nothing more.

"Are you all right? Do you need anything besides breakfast?"

"I'm fine. And no, I don't need anything." He clipped off his words sharply and glowered at the foot of the bed. He let out a long breath. "I'm not feeling sociable right now."

"Oh. I hoped we might have a visit." Emmalin knew she was being bold, but she so wanted to see improvement.

"I want to be that person you used to know, but all I can think about is my legs. I need to feel them again. I need them to be strong." He stared at his legs as if he willed them to move. "And I need to get out of this bed."

Emmalin set the book on the bureau. "It will happen. But it's going to take time." She tidied the blankets. "You need to restore your strength. A good solid breakfast will help." She placed the tray with bacon, eggs, toast, and two cups of coffee, plus a small bell, on his lap.

He picked up the bell. "I told you I didn't want this."

"That's so you can call for help and not have to holler for someone." She took it from him and jangled it. A soft ring chimed. "So much more pleasant than shouting." She set it on the nightstand, then took a napkin from the platter and started to tuck it into Jacob's neckline.

He swiped it away. "I'm not an infant."

"Of course you're not." Emmalin straightened, her stomach aching. "I just thought you would appreciate something to prevent you from spilling on your shirt."

"I won't spill, but if I do, what does it matter?"

Emmalin knew it needed to matter, but she ignored the harsh question and settled onto the chair beside the bed. "I made us both a cup of coffee." She set one on the nightstand, then took the other and sipped from it.

Jacob forked a bite of egg into his mouth. He said nothing, just chewed, then swallowed and looked at her. "I'm sorry. I didn't mean to snap at you. Just frustrated is all." His face crumpled. "I hate who I've become. I'm not me anymore."

"Of course you aren't the same, at least not right now. I can't imagine how difficult this is for you."

"I never had to depend on anyone else. And now...I can't even do simple things on my own." He gave her a quick glance. "Your father had to help me this morning."

"He's glad to help in any way."

"Sure."

Emmalin put on a smile. "Charity said she would stop by this afternoon with fresh strawberries and a strawberry pie. There's nothing better than strawberry pie." The memory of her trip to the cabin with hopes of surprising Jacob pierced her heart. "That day…I was bringing you straw-berry pie." Tears washed into her eyes, but she blinked them away.

"I wish we'd been able to eat it." He picked up a piece of bacon and tore off a bite, then took a drink of coffee. "This is good. Thank you." His brow furrowed.

"What's on your mind? Perhaps I can help," Emmalin asked, but she had no idea how she could truly help Jacob.

"Just wondering how long it will take. Everything else is healing."

Emmalin set her coffee on the nightstand and leaned over to press a kiss to his forehead. "Not all injuries heal the same. But if the rest of you is recovering, then I think that's a good sign. It shows you're strong and that you will get well."

"What if I don't? What then?" His normally warm hazel eyes were dark. "I'll be nothing but a burden. Useless."

"That's not true." Emmalin was outraged at the notion. "You can't think like that."

"I can't help it. I have a lot I need to do—the cabin, our life… I'm supposed to watch over you, not the other way around. And my native family. I want to help them."

"You shall do all those things." Emmalin sat back. "You have to believe God will bring your legs back. Margaret said it's not unusual for this kind of injury to take a long while to heal."

"And did she also tell you that some people never get better?"

Emmalin pursed her lips. "No. She didn't say that, but of course I know." She took Jacob's hand in hers. "You are strong and determined. You will be one of the people who get well. I know it." She pressed a kiss to the back of his hand, then touched it to her cheek while trying not to cry. "God will not desert you."

"I love you, Emmalin." Jacob's voice was warm with passion, not the kind between lovers, but those who are bound by tragedy.

"I love you too." She tried to look stern. "Now. Eat."

He obeyed, finishing up most of the meal.

"You rest while I wash the dishes and get the house in order."

"All right." He blew out a breath. "I couldn't do this without you."

"It's a good thing you don't have to." She smiled. "We'll fight this together."

He gave her a small nod, then returned to reading.

Emmalin left the room and softly closed the door. She placed the tray and dishes in the kitchen sink then poured hot water from the kettle over them and added water from the hand pump. All the while tumultuous emotions built up inside her. She held back a deluge of weeping.

She'd only begun washing the cups when she heard a wagon out front. Thankful for the distraction, she went to the door. "Charity!" Stepping onto the porch, Emmalin hurried down the steps and threw her arms wide, pulling her friend into a hug. "How good to see you."

"I'm so glad to be here. We've been busy on the farm, and I haven't been able to get away." Charity hugged Emmalin firmly. "Dear friend."

The two stood in an embrace, Charity offering strength and Emmalin soaking it in. Finally, she stepped back. "Until now, I never fully understood how much a hug can mean when it is badly needed."

"Well, I have lots more of them." Charity smiled kindly. "And just as promised, I've brought a pie and some berries."

"You are so thoughtful. Thank you."

"It's my pleasure." She glanced at the house. "How is Jacob? Any better?"

"He's stronger. But he's still unable to feel or move his legs and feet."

"I've been so distressed over this. There must be something that can be done."

"I've been praying. Margaret says we are not to lose hope. His mobility will return in time."

"Yesterday, Arthur and I were talking about Jacob's condition. He thinks we should have the doctor from Eugene City come down and look at him. He said he'd go after him for you. Maybe the doctor knows something that can be done."

"I've considered contacting him."

Charity walked to the back of the wagon and lifted out a bowl of strawberries. Emmalin picked up the pie, and the two friends moved indoors.

Emmalin placed the pie on the counter. "I'll take the berries down to the root cellar." She draped a dish towel over the bowl, then opened the trap door to the storage space beneath the house and carried the berries down the steep stairway. Light from above provided just enough illumination to see. Relishing the coolness of the room, Emmalin set the bowl on a shelf. Reticence accompanied her back up the steps. She put the door in place, then working up a semblance of cheeriness, asked, "Would you like some tea?"

"That sounds good. Thank you." Charity sat at the kitchen table.

Even though Jacob had been reading when Emmalin last saw him, she guessed he wouldn't want company, so she said, "I think Jacob is sleeping. But I know he will enjoy your pie when he wakes up."

She placed delicate teacups on the table and filled them with tea from a kettle. "I'm sorry but I have no milk to offer you. I haven't been into town. But I do have sugar. Would you like some?" She pushed the sugar bowl in Charity's direction.

"I've never been one for milk in my tea anyway." Charity scooped out a spoonful of sugar and sprinkled it into her tea, then stirred. "I've been needing a respite. This is always such a busy season on the farm. The work is never done. And it will stay like this clean through October."

Emmalin dipped out two teaspoons of sugar and and added them to her tea. "Do you truly believe the doctor from Eugene City might help?"

Charity shrugged. "I heard he's quite capable. I had an aunt once who had a terrible experience with apoplexy and he was very helpful. She was nearly fully restored."

Emmalin drank her tea. What could it hurt? "And you said Pastor Miller would be willing to fetch him?"

"Absolutely. He's a kind man and would consider it a privilege. He has great admiration for Jacob."

"I do think it would be wise. Could you ask him?"

"I'll go straight to his place when I leave here." Charity reached across the table and grasped Emmalin's hand. "Don't give up hope."

Jacob woke to find Emmalin asleep on the chair beside the bed. She'd stayed at his side from the very beginning. Love for her welled up, but her devotion would be undeserved if he didn't recover.

A knock sounded at the bedroom door, and Emmalin jolted upright. "Oh dear." She stood, pressing a hand to her back. "I'm so sorry I dozed off."

"Don't apologize. You spend way too much time looking after me. But I have to say, you look very pretty doing it. I enjoyed the view from here." He grinned, then nodded toward the door. "Someone is here."

Tidying her hair, Emmalin hurried to open the bedroom door. "Oh, Reverend Miller, good afternoon." She stepped into the front room.

Jacob heard her father say, "Pastor Miller brought the doctor."

"Oh! Bless you!" Emmalin sounded overly excited.

The pastor said, "This is Dr. Reuben."

"Doctor, what a pleasure." Emmalin opened the door all the way and stepped into the room. "Jacob is in here."

Emmalin returned to Jacob's bedside.

Samuel and Pastor Miller entered the room with a man wearing a tweed cap. "This is Dr. Reuben Bailey from Eugene City," Pastor Miller said.

"Doctor." Jacob gave a nod.

Dr. Bailey removed his cap. "A pleasure. You are the patient, I presume."

He looked to be in his fifties, with a graying beard and kind brown eyes. Jacob liked him right away.

"I understand you have been injured."

"I have." Jacob held his arms out toward his legs. "And these don't work."

"We're so grateful you came," Emmalin interjected.

The doctor never took his eyes off Jacob. "I can't make any promises."

"Of course not." Jacob extended a hand. "Jacob Landon. Thank you for coming." Apprehension welled up and Jacob tried to quiet it. Best not to get his hopes up.

Shaking Jacob's hand soundly, the doctor said, "Well, your young pastor here wasn't about to let me decline." He chuckled. "It's a good thing I don't have an expectant mother just now." He moved to the bedside. "Tell me what happened."

Jacob described what he'd been doing leading up to the accident, then let Emmalin fill in the rest. When she finished, he added, "I haven't been sick, no fever or infection. My broken arm is healing. But I can't feel my legs or my feet. And I can't move them."

"Let's have a look, then."

"We'll leave you to it," Samuel said.

"Can you stay?" the doctor asked him. "I may need your help."

"Of course."

Emmalin and Pastor Miller left the room and closed the door behind them.

The doctor gave Jacob a thorough exam, listening to his heart and lungs, checking his pulse, and carefully examining his spine and limbs. He looked at Jacob's arm and the injury to the back of his head. "Whoever took care of these did a good job."

"That was Margaret. She does a lot of the doctoring around here."

Dr. Bailey took out some peculiar-looking instruments, hooks, and assorted needles, then proceeded to poke and prod while asking Jacob what he could feel or if he could feel.

Jacob's heart raced, and his palms became moist. With each additional display of weakness, anxiety grew. He knew the doctor wasn't going to have good news.

Samuel and the doctor worked together to get Jacob sitting upright on the edge of the bed. Dr. Bailey continued his examination, using a small hammer to tap different places on Jacob's legs, knees, and ankles. Samuel sat alongside Jacob to help hold him steady.

Part of the time, Dr. Bailey ran prickly looking brushes across the bottom of Jacob's feet and across his toes.

Jacob compressed his lips. "I don't feel it. Don't guess that's good."

The doctor stepped back and combed his beard with his fingers. "Your paralysis, while acute for the time being, may become chronic. I can't say it will improve." He placed his hands behind his back and walked to the window and stared out. "Sometimes the condition will resolve on its own." He turned and looked directly at Jacob. "But it's not likely. Bed rest is the only treatment. And I recommend you strengthen your upper body. It will help when you begin to get around on your own."

Jacob felt a heavy weight drop onto his chest. He could barely breathe. He struggled for a moment, then asked, "What is causing this?"

"Damage to your spine. When that tree hit you, it came down on the spinal cord and likely compressed the delicate bone and tissue sheathed inside." The doctor cleared his throat. "You'll almost certainly need a wheelchair."

The room fell away and Jacob thought he might be sick. "No. Never."

Dr. Bailey put a hand on Jacob's shoulder. "The sooner you accept it the better it will be for you."

"There's no hope?"

"I wish I had better news." He glanced at Samuel then back at Jacob. "You're lucky. You still have use of your upper body plus bladder and bowel control. Even so, there is danger of infection and kidney shut down."

"There must be something you can do."

"Make sure you are turned regularly to avoid sores and get into a wheelchair as soon as possible." The doctor closed his bag. "I wish you luck."

A few moments after the doctor left, Emmalin came in. Jacob couldn't look at her.

"Jacob?"

Slowly, he lifted his gaze. The shock and anguish he saw in her eyes matched what he was feeling.

She pressed her hands to her face, tears brimming in her eyes.

"The doctor…he's not hopeful."

Emmalin shook her head in disbelief. "How can he know that? It's only been a few weeks." She turned and ran from the room.

Jacob heard her footfalls cross the front room and move onto the porch, down the steps, and then he envisioned her fleeing from the wreck of the man she'd once hoped to share her life with.

Emmalin flew out the door, across the porch, and into the yard. Her eyes awash with tears, she could barely see where she was going. All she knew was that she must get away.

This couldn't be true. Hadn't God said that "whatever we ask" He would give? No. That wasn't true. It's what Emmalin wanted, but she knew there was more to that verse. He would give what we asked in accordance to His will. Why wouldn't He want to heal Jacob?

She ran into the field. Tall summer grasses caught at her skirt. Her lungs hurt, and she needed more oxygen. When she could no longer run, Emmalin dropped to her knees. Grief swept over her in a huge wave of despair. "Father, why? Why?" She sobbed. "Please. Please don't let this happen."

Spending her tears, she remained there for a long while. Finally emptied, she lay in the grass and rolled onto her back where she gazed at the blue summer sky. She stayed there, exhausted and empty.

She refused to think, concentrating only on things like a drifting cloud, a bird, a roaming wasp. And then she relented. "Lord, I want to hear You. Speak to me."

She closed her eyes and concentrated on the touch of the summer breeze on her cheeks. "Are You saying *no*?"

She waited but didn't feel a response. "Or is Your answer, *not now*?"

Again, she waited. She thought she trusted God, but did she really? Where was her faith?

Lord, if Your answer is no, show me how to help Jacob. Show me how I can be a good wife to him. Sorrow felt like a heavy cape that would smother her. The future seemed so bleak.

She pressed a hand on her abdomen and breathed in deeply, and then let out the breath. She did this several times until she felt the spirit of God and His peace. All right. Whatever God wanted, she could do. She just needed to be patient and wait on Him. God had a plan, and He would reveal it at the proper time.

Chapter Seventeen

Jacob stared at his feet, commanding them to move. Just one toe. "Move!"

It would not obey. He dropped his head back against the headboard. Nothing. He would be like this the rest of his life. He would be a nothing. Why?

He'd done everything he knew to do. Obeyed Margaret and the doctor. Done what Emmalin wanted and had willed himself well. And he'd prayed in earnest.

When Margaret shared about a man she knew who faced the same kind of injury and had recovered when loved ones exercised his legs by moving them for him every day, Jacob swallowed his pride. He allowed Emmalin, Samuel, and Margaret to massage his feet and legs and exercise them by lifting and bending them. They'd helped get him into a chair every day. And he'd relented on the wheelchair. Still, his legs remained heavy and useless.

He'd always seen himself as a man of faith—strong and trusting. Now he felt he had no faith. It was more elusive than he had known.

A soft knock sounded at the door. Jacob forced away his negative thoughts. "Come in."

Emmalin stepped into the room, a tray in hand. "Are you ready for lunch? It's nothing much, just some scrambled eggs and biscuits."

"That sounds good." Jacob tried to keep the darkness at bay, but the sight of Emmalin only reminded him of the life he couldn't give her. He pushed himself more upright in the bed and accepted the tray of food. "Thank you."

"The hens are laying so many eggs, I need to find ways to use them all." She sat on the straight-backed chair beside the bed. "Tomorrow I'll make you something tastier."

"This is fine." Jacob took a bite of the eggs.

"After you finish eating, we can do some exercises if you like. It's a beautiful day. I thought perhaps you'd enjoy getting out of this stuffy room and spend time on the porch."

"Sure." Jacob focused on his food. He didn't want to look at Emmalin. It only made him feel weaker. He was useless to her.

"There are all sorts of wildflowers blooming in the fields. And some of the trees in the orchard have tiny little prunes on them."

Jacob nodded.

Emmalin reached out and brushed a strand of hair off his forehead. "Are you all right?"

A bite of biscuit seemed to swell and stick in Jacob's throat. All right? How could he be all right? He forced down the food and stared at his plate.

"Jacob?"

"No. I'm not all right. And I'm never going to be." He looked at her. "You need to accept that."

Emmalin clutched her hands together.

"You need to find someone else to love. I'm not a whole man any-more." He couldn't stop the words. He knew it was wrong to speak so, but they flew out of his mouth anyway. "I'm nothing. Nothing!" He flung the plate across the room where it slammed against the wall and shattered, spilling food onto the floor.

"Oh!" Emmalin backed up against the wall and hugged herself about the waist. Then as if waking up, she hurried across the room. "I'll clean this up. Don't you worry about it." She kneeled and started picking up pieces of broken glass, her hands trembling.

"Don't do that." Jacob couldn't keep the anger and frustration out of his voice. Emmalin kept on. She didn't look at him. "Stop it!"

Silence, heavy as if a lid had been closed upon a tomb, pressed in around them. Emmalin stood, holding broken pieces of the dish in her hands. She stared at him, eyes awash with tears.

Jacob didn't want to hurt her, but she had to face the truth. They both did.

"I shouldn't have done that. I'm sorry. I'm really sorry." He breathed in deeply, seeking calm. "But Emmalin, I'm no good for you. How can I take care of a wife? I can't even take care of myself."

"We'll find a way." Heavy with sympathy, her voice was barely more than a whisper. "Jacob, is it possible this is why I received the inheritance? God knew we would need that money. I can take care of you."

Jacob felt as if he'd been punched in the gut. Now he knew he couldn't stay with her. He wouldn't have her feeling sorry for him and taking care of him. He could never do that. "No. That's not going to happen."

"It doesn't have to be like that."

"Look at me!" He threw the blanket back and slammed his hands against his legs. "Look! Nothing!"

"I don't care."

"Yes, you do. Maybe you don't know it, but you do." He met Emmalin's eyes and saw the acceptance of reality. "The most I can do is sit in a wheelchair on the porch and admire the scenery." He leaned back against the headboard. "I can't do that to you, to us."

"You're not doing anything to me. I want to be with you. I love you. Nothing will change that. And I'm still praying God will heal you."

"And if He doesn't?"

"We just can't give up. God can do miracles. I've prayed and prayed. He hears me." She pressed a hand to her chest. "I can feel Him here. He's grieving too." Emmalin moved to the bed and sat beside Jacob. She put her hand to his cheek. "Just don't give up, please."

"Emmalin, He isn't going to heal me. I don't know why, but this is what He's chosen for me. It's time to accept that."

"But He loves you."

Jacob made sure to quiet his voice. "Just because He loves me doesn't mean He will heal me. He couldn't have loved anyone more than my mother. She was a saint. And when she got sick, she still died. So did my father and my brother. Sometimes things are just the way they are."

"No. He hasn't told me that. He said that I should wait."

Jacob caught her hands in his. "We aren't going to get a miracle, not this time."

"Even if you are right and I am wrong, it doesn't make a difference. I love you, and whether you can walk or not makes no difference to me. I still love you. I will always love you."

Jacob kissed Emmalin's hand. "I know you do. I love you too. And that's why I'm not going to steal your life from you. You deserve a strong man at your side. And children. I can't let you throw away everything you are so you can take care of me. I won't do it." He clenched his jaw. "I've decided to move to the boarding house."

"You don't have to do that."

"I already had Margaret make inquiries, and they have a room. I'll be moving there tomorrow. Your father said he'll help me."

Emmalin couldn't hold back her tears. "There's nothing I can say to dissuade you?"

"I've made up my mind."

Tears spilled over and trailed down Emmalin's cheeks.

A terrible pain cut into Jacob's heart. "You'll find someone else. There are good men in this territory who would be thankful for a woman like you."

Emmalin lifted her chin. "I love *you*."

The sorrow in her voice was a torment. Jacob wished there were another way, but he knew in the end his weakness would ruin her life. And her kindnesses, her sacrifice, would only make him angry because they would remind him every day of his infirmity.

Emmalin busied herself in the kitchen. This was the day when everything would change. She couldn't look at what was happening. Jacob was preparing to leave. The only man she ever truly loved was moving out of her life.

She set the coffee cups and flatware in the wash bowl, sprinkled washing powder over them, and poured in hot water. Soapy bubbles bounced in the water. She dunked a washcloth and used it to wipe out a cup. She stopped and pressed her hands into the sink. The ache in her chest threatened to steal her breath.

Her father put an arm around her shoulders. "Are you all right?"

"No." She turned and leaned her head against his shoulder. "I'll never be all right again." Fresh tears flowed and she made no attempt to stop them. "How can this be happening?"

He gave her a squeeze. "Give him time. God is in the middle of this. He has a purpose."

"A purpose? What good purpose is there in stealing a man's life? And my life?" She swiped at tears.

Her father pulled her into his arms and held her tightly. "There will always be trouble in life, but the Lord will make a way."

Emmalin pressed her forehead against her father's chest. How would she survive?

Chapter Eighteen

As the boarding house came into view, Emmalin softly pulled back on the reins, and Sassy slowed her pace. Emmalin's stomach tumbled, and her heart beat wildly. She shouldn't have come. Jacob had made it clear—he didn't want her to visit him. Again, he would likely refuse to see her. She pressed her hand against her abdomen and took in a steadying breath. She couldn't give up. Before any of this had happened, they'd talked about how much fun it would be to join the community in the Fourth of July celebrations. In light of what had happened, it seemed rather silly, but perhaps she could convince him to join her.

Emmalin closed her eyes. "Lord, help me. Help us. Remind Jacob how much you love him and that there is hope for our future, even if it isn't what we imagined it would be. Help him to see something new."

She brought Sassy to a stop and dismounted, then secured the mare to a railing near the front entrance. She slipped a pouch filled with oatmeal raisin cookies off the saddle horn where it hung. Jacob's favorite. Taking in a deep breath, she started up the front steps. Her footfalls echoed as she crossed the broad wooden porch. She stopped at the front door and stared at the mahogany wood. She felt as if she were about to enter enemy territory.

Finally, she put her hand on the knob, turned, and then pushed open the door. Stepping inside, Emmalin was enveloped by the silence in the house. No one stood at the front desk, the parlor was empty, no sound came from the kitchen.

"Hello. Hello?"

The rapid tap of footsteps approached from the back of the house. The owner, Grace McDonald, appeared. The round middle-aged woman smiled. "Hello, dear." She tucked dark brown hair into a bun at the nape of her neck. "How nice to see you."

The woman's warmth calmed Emmalin's nerves. "Good morning."

"I suppose you're here to visit Jacob?"

"Yes. How is he today?"

"I really don't know. He keeps to his room most of the time. But Margaret is here. She stops by several times a week."

"Oh. Perhaps I should come back later." Disappointment spread through Emmalin. She so wanted to see him.

"Why don't we let Jacob decide that? It might be good to have you and Margaret here at the same time." She tilted her head. "A force of wills, you might say."

"I hope you're right. I'll go on back."

"That a girl. And while you're there, give him a bit of what for, eh." Grace grinned and walked toward the kitchen.

Wishing she felt the spunk Grace did, Emmalin headed for Jacob's room. As she approached she heard voices. Margaret's was rather forceful. Was she angry? Emmalin strained to hear what was being said. Eavesdropping was impolite, but she couldn't just barge in on a heated conversation.

"That's enough," Margaret said. "It's time you got up and started acting like a man. Stop soaking and souring in that bed. What kind of life is that? Does self-pity make you feel better?" She stopped as if waiting for an answer. When none came, she continued, "It's time to think about someone besides you. Emmalin perhaps?"

Emmalin held her breath and waited for Jacob's response.

"I *am* thinking about Emmalin. I'm protecting her from a miserable life. Let's be honest—what can I offer her? What good am I to her?"

"You're the man she loves. You're the man she wants. You have to fight for a life together. Fight for her. What does it say to Emmalin if you give up and choose to spend your life looking at these four walls? What does it say to God?"

Emmalin's heart ached. If only Jacob would let her take care of him.

Not a word came from Jacob.

"God has something better for you than this room," Margaret said.

The doorknob turned and Emmalin stepped back. She didn't want to get caught eavesdropping.

"I can't make you do anything," Margaret said more softly. "You have to do this. God will give you the strength. But He expects you to make an effort. And if He chooses a wheelchair for you, then you must find a way to trust Him in that too."

Footsteps echoed from the front of the house. It was Charity.

"Oh, Emmalin." Charity hurried toward her, sweeping unruly hair off her face. "I was told Margaret is here. The Sullivans' little girl, Rachel, is sick. They're asking for Margaret's help."

Emmalin moved away from Jacob's door. "I hope it's nothing too serious."

"She's quite ill."

"Margaret is with Jacob."

Charity moved past Emmalin, rapped on the door, then opened it and stepped inside. "Margaret, I hate to disturb you, but the Sullivans are asking for you. Rachel is very sick."

"Of course. I'll come right away." Margaret rushed into the hallway and glanced at Emmalin. "Oh, hello. I didn't know you were here."

"I just arrived."

Margaret looked at Charity. "Did they say what is wrong with Rachel?"

"No. Just that she's very sick and has a high fever."

"All right. I'll see what I can do." Margaret strode toward the front of the house, then stopped and turned back to Emmalin. "I hope you can talk some sense into that man." She hurried on her way with Charity close behind.

Emmalin wasn't optimistic. It didn't sound like Jacob had changed his mind in the least. She considered retreating. Instead, she dredged up courage and entered his room. She had to try at least one more time.

Jacob sat in the wheelchair, staring out the window. He glanced at

Emmalin. "Just in the nick of time. Margaret was giving me a tongue lashing." He returned to gazing out the window. "I suppose you heard."

Emmalin considered lying, then said, "I did." She closed the door. "Did you?"

He didn't reply.

"She's right, you know. You have to fight for a better life, even if you can't fight for me."

He clenched his jaw.

"Jacob, it breaks my heart to see you struggle so. And I understand why you are discouraged. But the man I see in front of me today is not the Jacob I fell in love with."

"I'm not, and I never will be."

Emmalin wanted to allow herself to cry, but she dared not, at least not in front of Jacob. She gathered what tranquility she could muster. "Look at me."

Slowly he turned the chair and met her gaze. What could she say now? Emmalin needed a distraction. She set the cookies on a small table. "Your favorite—oatmeal raisin."

"Thank you."

Jacob's voice was listless. He'd built a wall of protection around himself, and he was the only one who could take it down. He would need God's help.

"I came here hoping to encourage you to try to get well, or if not that, then to find a new way to live. You must realize that the man you are isn't the one on the outside, but rather the person you are on the inside. That's the man I love."

Jacob didn't respond. He didn't even look at her.

"It seems clear there is nothing I can say that will make a difference. I shan't come back again, not until you ask for me." Emmalin's heart felt as if it were being shredded. "I'm not deserting you; I'm simply giving you a chance to do the right thing."

She longed to place a kiss on his cheek and hold him close, to soothe away the sorrow. She didn't dare. Instead, she turned and walked out of the room. Only then allowing tears to flow. She marched rapidly through the house and out the front door, praying God would lift Jacob up out of the pit of despair and set him back on his feet.

The rest of the afternoon, Jacob remained at the window. Margaret's and Emmalin's words sifted through his thoughts. His mind carried him to his childhood—the early days on his parents' homestead where he and his brother used to hunt and fish with their father. He remembered his mother's gentle ways, her faith. He also remembered the dark days when he lost his family and was forced to make a new home with the natives.

He had learned to never give up, to try harder, keep learning, and to believe in a power greater than his own. With God, even on the darkest day, there was light. The Lord had seen him through those terrible days, always at his side. And God was with him now, waiting for Jacob to reach out and take hold of His outstretched hand.

A mix of anguish and hope welled up inside Jacob. "I always believed. I always knew I belonged to You." He dropped his head. "Now I don't know."

God's presence filled the room. And Jacob knew the Lord was with him.

"Forgive me." He broke down, releasing tears of frustration, bitterness, disappointment. "I thought I was a better man. But You haven't given up, even if I did. Help me."

He had to trust more and fight harder. Life hadn't been taken from him. He'd relinquished it. He'd called himself a man of faith, but now that life was hard and demanded more from him, he'd given up.

No. That's not what he was going to do. He would fight.

Renewed, Jacob started working to rebuild strength in his upper body. He would need to be strong if he was going to get around on his own. Every day he spent time trying to move his lower limbs, even though they wouldn't listen to him. Grace came alongside and helped him with his exercises, making sure he had everything he needed.

Jacob worked with weights and learned how to use the wheelchair adeptly so he could spend more time outdoors. Frustration nagged at him, but he held it at bay and pressed on.

An outbreak of fever hit the town, and Margaret was busy caring for the sick, so he saw very little of her, but she encouraged him to continue his fight.

One morning when Grace came into Jacob's room, she was clearly troubled.

"Has something happened?" Jacob asked.

"The little Sullivan girl died last night, and her sister is still very ill. I'm just heartsick. She was such a sweet little thing."

"Does anyone know what it is?"

"Margaret says scarlet fever." She shook her head. "I wish we had a doctor in town. Margaret is doing her best, but she needs help. This is just too much for her."

"The doctor who helped me seemed good. Maybe he'll come down and give Margaret a hand."

"That would be wonderful." Grace sat on the straight-backed chair by Jacob's bed. "We should get to work."

Jacob pushed up on his arms and pulled himself toward the edge of the bed.

Grace gasped. "Jacob!"

"What?"

"You moved your leg!"

Jacob looked at his leg. It didn't feel any different. "No. I was just dragging it. And how could you tell. It's under the blanket."

"I'm sure I saw it! Please try again."

Jacob threw back his blanket and focused on his legs and feet. He willed them to move. Nothing happened. "See, it wasn't anything."

"Please. Give it another try."

Jacob prayed for God's help, then he focused all his energy on moving his leg. The foot twitched. "Oh! Did you see that?" He laughed.

"I did." Grace smiled broadly. "Try again."

Jacob concentrated again, and this time his foot actually moved along with a tremble in his leg. "I did it!" He grinned, then laughed again. "Never thought something like moving my foot a fraction of an inch would be this exciting."

"God be praised! It's a miracle!" Grace hugged him.

"It is a miracle. The doctor said this could happen, but it's been so long, I didn't think it would."

"I can't wait to tell Emmalin!"

"No. Don't say a word. Not yet. I want to surprise her when I can walk across this room." Wearing a smile, he leaned back against his pillows. There was hope that he and Emmalin could have a normal life. He closed his eyes. "Thank you, Lord."

Chapter Nineteen

Emmalin hauled herself up into the wagon, grateful her father had readied it for her. She had learned to harness the team, but this morning she had awakened feeling more tired than usual. When living in Philadelphia, she had languished in bed whenever she desired. She hadn't missed that luxury, but this morning the idea seemed rather delectable.

Once settled on the wooden seat, she lifted the reins, and released the brake. Slapping the leads lightly over the horses' rumps and clicking her tongue, she leaned forward as the team stepped into a brisk gait. Even though it was early yet, the air was hot and the grit rising up around her made it feel oppressive.

It was a struggle to keep an optimistic state of mind. Several families in the county had been sick. Five children had died. And just yesterday, the widow Hanson, who lived on the west side of town, had been found dead. Poor Mrs. Hanson, dying alone. Scarlet fever was a terrible disease.

Emmalin drove past the Pedersons' house. Like many homes in the county, it had a large white X painted on the front door. Their youngest, Eleanor, was sick. Emmalin prayed, then let out a long breath. The weight of the community's struggle only added to her fatigue.

The team of horses knew where they were going and stopped in front of the café. The wagon would be needed to deliver medicines, food, and care to those who had been stricken. Today Emmalin hoped, again, to help Margaret. She pulled back the brake and climbed down. Taking the steps to the café, her legs felt unusually heavy, but she tried to shake off the feeling as she walked indoors. The dining area was empty. Customers had been few since the outbreak of illness. People were cautiously keeping to themselves.

It was a financial hardship for Margaret. Emmalin had been pondering on how she could anonymously donate a financial gift to support the café until better times. With Margaret away from the café so much of the time, slipping money into the cashbox would be easy. Margaret might believe she'd made a bookkeeping error, especially because she was so fatigued these days.

"Oh, good morning, dear," Margaret said, as she stepped out of the kitchen. She looked as weary as Emmalin felt.

"Good morning. I thought you might be in need of help."

"I sure am." Margaret dropped into a chair. She studied Emmalin. "But I worry about you. You've been working so hard. I'd hate to see you get sick."

"I'm in good health. And I have my youth. What about you? No one has worked harder."

Pushing a strand of hair off her face, Margaret smiled. "I have a strong constitution. Always have. I can't recall the last time I took ill."

Emmalin's eyelids felt heavy; she longed to sit but remained standing. "So many have been ill. When I came in this morning, I could have cried when I saw the X painted on the Pederson house. I'd hoped things had improved for them."

"Don't give up hope. Eleanor is holding her own, and no one else in the family is unwell."

"That's good news. I worry about Jacob. What if he were to get sick? In his condition, I can't imagine. Have you seen him recently?"

"I have. And he's quite healthy." A small smile played at the corners of Margaret's mouth.

Did she hold some kind of secret delight? "Is there something you're not telling me?"

"No. Of course not. I'm just pleased that he's remained healthy. But I do hope you two can mend your differences."

"That's up to Jacob." Emmalin felt the sudden sting of tears. "I don't understand him. How can he believe that I am better off without him?"

"It's his pride. I'm afraid he has too much of it. But the Lord loves him, so I'm sure He'll see that Jacob gets his head on straight." Margaret reached out and pressed a hand on Emmalin's arm. "Be patient. God has a way of working things out."

"If only Jacob would pay attention to what He has to say."

"And you?" Margaret lifted a brow.

"Of course." Emmalin folded her arms over her chest. "What are your plans for today?"

"Your father is loading up goods for some of the families who are in quarantine. We can help deliver them, and I'll have to examine those who are sick and make sure they're getting proper care." She untied her apron. "Also, I have some baked goods I want to give away. It might cheer up some of the folks in town."

Emmalin and Margaret packed cookies and cakes into boxes and headed to the mercantile. Just as they reached the door, Emmalin's father opened it. "Come on in. Do you have more?"

"Yes, a few." Margaret moved past him and set a box on the counter. "They're in the kitchen."

"I'll give you a hand."

Margaret gave him a quick hug. "You're a good man, Samuel Morgan."

"I'm glad you think so." Wearing a smile, he followed the ladies. "I'd be more than happy to help with the deliveries. I packed some extra bedding for those who have a need."

"I'd love to have your company, but Emmalin has already volunteered her help."

"Oh." For a moment he looked dismayed, then he turned to Emmalin. "Actually, I was hoping you'd help at the store. Would you mind?"

"No. Of course not. Is that all right with you, Margaret?" She held back a smirk, knowing that both Margaret and her father were happy for any reason to spend time together.

"Either way would be fine with me. I enjoy you both."

"All right then. That's settled." Emmalin's father carried a box of goods to the door. "Might as well load these in the wagon right now. Emmalin, there's stock that needs to be put out and I'm behind on the bookkeeping again. You're much better at that kind of thing than me."

"I'll get right to work." Emmalin didn't mind in the least. Working quietly on her own seemed more manageable. She might even find time for a short nap.

Margaret and Samuel packed the rest of the items into Margaret's wagon. "We should be back before dinner."

"I'll make sure to have something prepared. Margaret, you're welcome to join us."

"I appreciate that. Thank you."

As they headed out the door, Samuel rested his hand on Margaret's back. It warmed Emmalin's heart to see the affection between her father and her closest friend. If only her father would ask Margaret to marry him. She didn't know what was taking him so long.

Emmalin turned her attention to the store. It was quiet and would likely remain so. People came in for absolute necessities only. With the wooden floor creaking beneath her feet, she headed to the storage room. A wooden box of goods had been opened and waited to be unpacked. She dragged it into the store and moved merchandise from it to the shelves. She started with thread goods and enjoyed discovering the new yarns and colorful fabrics. When she came across a pale blue gingham, she held it up to the light. It was bright and cheery. She had the perfect pattern for it, a summer dress with three-quarter length sleeves. It would be much cooler for the hot summer weather. With Margaret's help, she was sure she could make a nice day dress. She set the fabric aside. She would measure off the needed material later.

All of a sudden, she felt flushed and dizzy. Grabbing hold of the shelf, she made her way to a chair and carefully lowered herself to the seat. What was wrong with her? Was she getting ill? The idea frightened her.

She rested a few moments, then went to the back kitchen and filled a glass with water from a hand pump. She drank it down, refilled it, then returned to work, finishing off the fabrics then ribbons, yarns, and threads.

Next, she faced the challenge of shelving canned goods, lining up green beans, waxed beans, corn, and condensed milk. She added cans of fruit—

peaches, pears, and cherries. Winded and weak, she sat to rest. Her head throbbed. She pressed a hand to her cheek. It felt warm.

The bell hanging on the door chimed as someone stepped into the store. Emmalin hurried to the front. "Oh, hello, Charity. How nice to see you."

"I hoped you'd be here today. I thought you might like to share lunch with me. I brought us a small picnic." She held up a basket.

"How kind. Thank you. But I'm not the least bit hungry, although I wouldn't mind taking a rest and having a cup of tea with you."

"Are you all right?"

"I must admit to being a bit under the weather. But I'm sure it's nothing—I've been working too hard lately."

With a furrowed brow, Charity studied Emmalin, then she pressed a hand to her forehead. "You've got a fever." She circled an arm around Emmalin's waist. "Come and sit down. Let me get you something to drink."

"I have a glass of water there on the counter. But the tea kettle is on."

"Tea sounds like just the thing." Charity walked toward the back and disappeared through the door.

Emmalin remained at the table. She really wasn't feeling well.

A few moments later, Charity reappeared with the tea pot and two cups. "I couldn't remember. Do you like sugar?"

"I do."

She set the tea and the cups on the table. "I'll be right back." Taking long strides, she returned to the backroom and returned a few moments later with the sugar. She filled both cups with tea, then spooned a teaspoon of sugar into Emmalin's and stirred. "There you go." She set the basket on the table and opened it. "You're certain you don't want to eat? I have some delicious sandwiches."

Emmalin shook her head. "I fear I may be ill."

"With scarlet fever?" Charity's voice quivered with alarm. "Where's Margaret?"

"She's out with my father helping people in town who are sick."

"Oh dear. Well, we need to get you home and into bed."

"What about the store?"

"We'll just have to close it. People can make do until tomorrow. But first you need to drink your tea." She took a sip of her own.

Emmalin tasted hers. It was good, warm, and sweet.

When they finished their tea, Charity helped Emmalin to her feet. "I'll leave a note for your father."

By the time Charity and Emmalin reached home, Emmalin was alarmed at how ill she felt. She sat on the edge of her bed, and Charity removed her shoes.

"You lie down. Do you have a quilt?"

"In the armoire." Emmalin lay down and closed her eyes. Her throat hurt.

Charity covered her with the quilt. "You sleep. I'll stay until your father gets here."

Emmalin pulled the blanket up under her chin. Despite her aching body, she drifted off to sleep.

When she woke, the room was dark and cool. The door creaked open, and Margaret walked in carrying a lantern. Her father was right behind her.

"Charity told us you are sick," her father said.

Emmalin swallowed past her painful throat. "I am. But it's probably just a little bug."

Margaret sat on the side of the bed and felt Emmalin's face. "You're running a fever." She lifted one of Emmalin's arms and gently pushed up the sleeve. Her expression turned grave.

Emmalin looked at her arm. It was covered with the typical bright red rash of scarlet fever.

Chapter Twenty

There was a light rap on Jacob's door. "Coming." It was late for a visitor. He pushed himself up onto his crutches, moved to the door, and opened it. "Samuel. What brings you here so late?"

Samuel stared at him, shock showing on his face. "You're standing?"

"I am." Jacob smiled broadly. "I've been working hard and getting better. Grace and Margaret are the only ones who know."

"Margaret didn't say a word."

"I made her promise not to. I didn't want anyone to know until I could walk across the room, down the hall, and out the front door on my own. But the game is getting old, so here I am." He lifted his crutches.

"My Lord!" Samuel reached out and grasped his shoulder. "That's fantastic news!" His smile disappeared. "Emmalin would love to hear about this. But she's sick. That's why I'm here."

"Emmalin's sick?"

"Yes—scarlet fever."

"Is she all right, though?"

"We don't really know. She got sick all of a sudden. And she's pretty bad."

"I need to see her."

"I knew you would." Samuel swayed and leaned against the wall.

"You're not looking too good."

Samuel didn't answer, then eyed Jacob. "Can you ride?"

"Maybe. I'll need help getting up into the saddle."

"All right." Samuel let go of the wall. "Let's go." He staggered as he headed for the door.

"You are not well."

Samuel kept moving.

Once Smoke was saddled, Jacob grabbed hold of the saddle horn, lifted his left leg with difficulty, and planted it in the stirrup. He pulled on the saddle horn while Samuel pushed him up, and he managed to get seated. It felt good to be on Smoke again. He leaned forward and gave the horse a pat on the neck.

Samuel mounted and turned toward the road. The men headed for Samuel's place with a full moon lighting the way.

Keeping a hold on the saddle horn and doing his best to keep his feet in the stirrups, Jacob managed to stay mounted. His mind was on Emmalin and his regret at how he had driven her away. How sick was she?

By the time they reached Samuel's place, Jacob was in a full sweat and barely managing to hang on. His legs needed more practice riding. Samuel helped him dismount, and Jacob slung an arm over his shoulder as the two men made their way up the steps to the front porch. "I'm still weak as a newborn colt," Jacob said.

"Maybe so, but a lot better than where you were a few weeks ago." Samuel gave him a pat on the back. "I'm proud of you."

"God brought the healing, but I decided to work hard and live." Jacob stopped at the doorway to catch his breath, then leaning on Samuel, he stumbled into the house.

"Jacob. How good to see you." Margaret eyed him. "And I'm glad you're still improving." She embraced him, holding on for an extra moment as if knowing he needed it.

Jacob's gaze went to Emmalin's bedroom door. "How is she?"

"She got so sick so quickly." Margaret's eyes went to Samuel, who had dropped into a chair. "Samuel, you aren't looking well." She hurried to him and pressed a hand to his forehead. "You're fevered." She checked his arms, exposing the fiery red rash. "You need to get to bed. Right now."

Weak and shaking, Jacob sat at the kitchen table. He wanted to see Emmalin, but not this way. The ride had taken a lot out of him.

Margaret poured a cup of coffee and handed it to him. "Drink this while I get Samuel to bed. Then you can see her." She propped her hands on her hips. "I understand why you're here, but in your condition, I hate to see it. You're likely to come down sick too. And then what am I going to do with all three of you sick?"

"I'll be fine. And there is nothing that would keep me from seeing Emmalin."

Margaret gave him a nod. "I'll be back in two shakes."

By the time she returned, Jacob had recovered most of his strength. Still, he held on to Margaret's arm as he shuffled into Emmalin's room. It was lit by a single lantern, but he could see the flush on her skin and the dampness of fever on her brow.

He lowered himself onto a straight-backed chair beside her bed and took her hand. "I'm here."

Her eyes flickered open and for a moment locked onto his before closing. "Jacob," she whispered and weakly squeezed his hand. She looked at him again, searching his face. "It *is* you. I thought I was dreaming."

"I had to see you." He put her hand to his cheek.

"How did you get here?"

"I rode, just not very well. Smoke was patient with me."

"You rode Smoke?"

"Yes." He chuckled. "I've been keeping a secret from you. I started getting feeling back in my legs a few weeks ago, and I've been working hard to get better, stronger. I wanted to surprise you."

"Oh!" She pressed a hand to her mouth. "Oh, Jacob! Thank the Lord," she whispered.

"We're going to be all right now. You're going to get well, and we'll get married."

"I hope." She stopped and took in a shallow breath. "But—" She stopped and swallowed. "What if...we are not suited to each other? You were..." Another short breath. "So certain it couldn't work."

"I was being foolish and bullheaded. Please forgive me. I never wanted to hurt you."

She studied his face, then gave a slight nod. "All right. We'll try."

Her eyes closed, and she seemed to slip back into sleep. Jacob looked at Margaret. "Is she going to be all right?"

"I think so, as long as she doesn't get rheumatic fever. We can only wait and see."

Jacob spent most of the next few days at Emmalin's bedside, leaving her only for short rests and to practice walking so not to lose his own growing stamina.

Despite his vigil, Emmalin did get worse. Her fever raged, and patches of bruised skin covered her arms and legs. Her joints swelled, and her breathing became shallow and labored.

"Is it rheumatic fever?" Jacob asked Margaret after she finished examining Emmalin.

"I'm afraid so." She moved to the window and gazed outside. "I wish I could stay with her, but there are others who need me."

"I'll take care of her. And Samuel. You do what you have to."

Margaret cast a worried look on Emmalin, then said, "Thank you."

Jacob settled into his task of caring for both Emmalin and Samuel. Samuel wasn't nearly as sick and required less help while Emmalin only seemed to sink deeper into the illness.

Jacob's fear grew and his prayers became more fervent. His thoughts were filled with questions about his own parents. Had his father kept a vigil beside his mother before he was also consumed by the fever? He pushed away the idea of a similar outcome for Emmalin. That couldn't happen to them. Why would God heal his paralysis and then allow such a tragic end?

Early one morning, Margaret returned to the house, clearly exhausted and unable to do more. She sat at the table.

Using one cane, Jacob went to the stove, poured a cup of coffee, and set it on the table in front of her. "You need to get some sleep."

"I do." She eyed Jacob. "You seem to be getting stronger rapidly."

"I think needing to be up more is helping." He scooped stew into a bowl and placed it beside her coffee. "Not the best, but it should bolster you some." He sat down. "You can't keep this up. You need help. And Emmalin needs help. She's not getting any better." He pressed his palms on the table. "I can't lose her."

"What am I to do? So many people are sick. And those who aren't ill are caring for others."

"I'll go to Eugene City. I'll get the doctor."

"You'll never make it. You're not strong enough."

"I can do it." He glanced at the bedroom door. "Emmalin can't die. I won't let her." He pushed to his feet. "I've been thinking on it, and I'm ready to go. Just need to saddle Smoke."

Margaret reached for Jacob's hand. "This is crazy. What if you can't do it and get stuck on the trail somewhere?"

"I'll make it."

She gave his hand a squeeze. "Please be careful."

"I'll be back tomorrow."

Saddling Smoke was nearly more than Jacob could manage, and he began to doubt. Could he do this?

Pink touched the sky as he dragged himself up onto Smoke's back. A wagon would be easier, but it would take too long. And one thing he didn't have was extra time. He kept a tight hold on the saddle horn and urged Smoke into a canter, pressing his heels into the stirrups and his knees against the horse's sides. He must get to Eugene City before dark. And once there, he'd have to convince the doctor to help the people of Deer Creek…and Emmalin.

• → • ┼ • ◆ • ┼ • ← •

Each mile robbed Jacob of strength. Sweat soaked his shirt and more than once, he nearly fell off Smoke's back. The memory of Emmalin fighting to live kept him going.

Nightfall settled over Eugene City when he finally approached. His muscles ached, his feet were numb, his back screamed with pain, and his hands had little grip left in them. Still, he managed to keep moving until he reached the doctor's office. A cooling breeze swept over him as he slid out of the saddle and stood, leaning against Smoke's side and trying not to fall. After a few moments' restoration, he stumbled up the steps to the doctor's office. He opened the door and staggered inside.

Doctor Bailey sat at a desk going over papers.

"I need your help," Jacob gasped. "The folks in Deer Creek need help."

"Calm down." The doctor pushed to his feet and helped Jacob to a chair. "Slow down a minute. Take a breath."

Jacob sat. "It's scarlet fever. A lot of people in Deer Creek are sick. And my fiancée, Emmalin, is really bad. She needs help."

"I'd like to help you, but I can't possibly leave. I have people here who need me."

A young woman entered from the backroom. "I can watch over your patients, Dr. Bailey."

"Are you a doctor?" Jacob asked.

"I am."

"Not yet. She is apprenticing with me."

She lifted her chin. "I was top of my class at Women's Medical College in Pennsylvania. And I'm quite competent. You can leave me in charge and feel at ease."

Dr. Bailey gathered up the papers on his desk and filed them away. He scrutinized her. "All right." He turned to Jacob. "Give me a little time. It's clear you can't make it back tonight. Get something to eat and then sleep. There's a café and hotel a block from here. We'll leave first thing in the morning."

Dr. Bailey studied Jacob. "I don't know how you managed this. I would have bet my life that you would never recover."

"God had other things in mind for me."

"It would appear so." Dr. Bailey chuckled. "But, of course, your fortitude and strength contributed."

"Not mine. Emmalin's strength—her faith. I gave up. She kept praying and believed in me. And now I'm not giving up on her."

Chapter Twenty-One

The door creaked, and Emmalin tried to open her eyes. She was so tired, and her head throbbed.

"Emmalin. It's me."

She felt the bed give and someone took her hand in theirs. It was rough and strong. Jacob. She forced her eyes open.

"How are you?"

"Oh, Jacob," she whispered.

"Here. Drink some water."

Jacob held a glass to her lips, and she sipped. The liquid felt good on her parched lips and aching throat.

"I brought the doctor."

"Hello, Miss Hammond. I'm Dr. Bailey. Do you remember me?"

Emmalin nodded. She didn't have the strength to respond.

"You have a determined young man here."

She looked at Jacob. Oh, how she loved him.

"Well, now let me have a look at you." The doctor pressed his fingers to the inside of her wrist and felt for a pulse, then he placed a thermometer under her tongue.

Emmalin closed her eyes.

The doctor removed the thermometer and read the temperature. "Still rather high."

Margaret stepped around to the other side of the bed. "It has been for many days. We can't get it down, not even with willow tea."

The doctor palpated Emmalin's neck, then examined her bruised arms and legs. "Are you having pain?"

She offered a weak nod.

"Any improvement?"

Emmalin shrugged. She really didn't know.

He held a stethoscope to her chest and listened, his brows furrowing. "Take a deep breath and hold it." She complied. He moved the stethoscope. "Again." She did as he instructed. He straightened and asked. "So, tell me your symptoms."

Emmalin glanced at Margaret. If only she would speak for her.

Margaret stepped in. "Extreme fatigue. She sleeps most of the time. Fever. Very sore throat and headache. General pain."

Emmalin let out a long breath, thankful for Margaret.

The doctor set the stethoscope in his bag. "She's developed rheumatic fever. It's sometimes a complication of scarlet fever."

"Is there anything that can be done to help?" Margaret asked.

"Make sure she is getting enough to drink, keep her warm to help sweat out the fever. And the willow bark tea should be continued." He opened his medical bag. "We've also been having some luck with this." He handed her a bottle of powders. "Belladonna should have her feeling better soon."

Margaret looked at the bottle. "I've never heard of this as a treatment for rheumatic fever."

"It's new."

"We'll begin using it right away."

With round the clock care and intermittent doses of belladonna, Emmalin gradually improved. The doctor graciously remained in town to watch over her and to care for others who were suffering.

The morning Emmalin woke with no fever and decreased pain in her legs, she knew recovery was at hand. Her father had regained his health and he brought in breakfast. Miraculously, she was hungry and completed the entire meal of eggs and toast. She returned the plate to him. "I had forgotten how wonderful it is to feel well."

He gave her a broad smile. "Thank the Lord for His mercy."

Emmalin was grateful for better days, but fatigue and weakness remained. When she asked about it, Dr. Bailey told her it was not unusual after a lengthy illness.

Still, Emmalin was confused by the continuing malaise.

Before returning to Eugene City, Dr. Bailey did a final exam on Emmalin. When completed, he stood at the end of her bed, his expression solemn. "One of the grave dangers of rheumatic fever is the possibility of a weakened heart."

"She's much better, getting stronger every day," Jacob said. "She'll have a normal life, right?"

"She has a good chance of a full recovery. Some people rally faster than others. It's just going to take her some time."

"I will get completely well?"

"I should think so, however, I urge you to be cautious and don't hurry the process too much."

Jacob squeezed her hand. "You're going to be fine."

"Praise be to God," Margaret said.

Jacob held Emmalin's hand against his chest. "You'll be back to your old self before you know it."

"I'll be thankful to be out of this sick bed." Emmalin smiled at Jacob. "Although I have enjoyed your devoted attention."

"It's yours, always."

The doctor rested a hand on Emmalin's shoulder. "I have patients waiting for me in Eugene City. I'm no longer needed here, I'm happy to say." He placed his hat on his head. "I suggest you continue to rest and listen to your body. Do only what it allows you to, don't push too hard."

"I'll see that she doesn't overdo it," Margaret said.

Emmalin scanned the faces in the room. "Why do you all look so serious? This is a good day. The doctor says I'm going to get well." If she'd been able, she would have gotten out of bed and done a pirouette. She turned her attention to the doctor. "Thank you for your skillful care. I'm sure you have much to do with my recovery."

He touched the brim of his hat and left the room.

Jacob sat on the edge of the bed. "I can't wait for us to take a ride up to the house."

"It will be splendid. But right now, all I want to do is sleep." She pressed a kiss to the back of Jacob's hand. "Thank you for all your tender care. And for taking such a risk and going for the doctor."

"I couldn't have done anything less." He hugged her. "I'm so happy you're going to be all right."

Emmalin did improve. It wasn't long before she was able to get up and move about the house, though her activity was limited to mostly just that. One afternoon, her father and Jacob picked green beans from the garden, and Emmalin joined them on the porch to snap them.

"I'm almost feeling like my old self." Emmalin dropped a bean into her bowl.

"The doctor said you would," Jacob said. "I'm about ready to go back to work on the cabin."

"Good idea." Emmalin's father reached for a handful of beans and set them in his lap. "Me and some of the fellas from town are ready to help out."

Jacob rapidly snapped the several beans he had in his hand. "I know you mean well, but I'm able—nearly back to my old self. You all have your own work to do."

Emmalin rested her hands in the bowl on her lap. "You're not fully recovered yet. You can certainly use help."

"Every man in the county could use some help. Our house is my responsibility. And I can do it."

"Jacob, you're being stubborn." Emmalin was unable to keep the frustration out of her voice.

Samuel eyed Jacob. "If getting married soon is important to you I'd reconsider getting help." He stood.

"I'll think about it."

A slight smile lifted the corner of Samuel's mouth. "Well, I'll let you two hash this out. I've got milking to do. Jacob, you do what you have to, but every man in this town has needed help from time to time. That's part of being a community." He said nothing more before walking down the steps and toward the barn.

"All right. I'll see about getting someone to give me a hand."

Emmalin cheered inside.

Jacob and Emmalin worked in silence for several minutes. Emmalin could feel the strength going out of her. She needed rest but hated giving in to it.

She added her father's snapped beans to hers. "These are more than enough for dinner, plus the next couple of days." She pushed to her feet, her legs still feeling dangerously weak. "I'm not up to canning just yet. Soon."

"Margaret said she'd be by to give you a hand later this week."

Emmalin sank back to the chair. "Jacob, we need to talk about something."

He set his bowl of snapped beans on the top of the porch railing. "You sound serious."

"I am. I'm still very weak. I do know something about rheumatic fever. Sometimes people don't get well."

"It hasn't been long."

"I know, but what if I'm one of those people who end up forever weakened?"

"That's not going to happen to you, except when you're a very old woman."

"What if I don't get fully well?"

"You heard the doctor. He said you'll be fine."

"But—"

"Emmalin, I don't want to have this conversation. I think we spent enough time this year thinking the worst was going to happen. I want to believe the best is going to happen. When I couldn't walk, you kept believing I'd get my legs back. Now, believe for yourself."

"And what if I don't get well?"

He leaned on his thighs and met her gaze. "Why all these questions and doubts?"

"Jacob, what about children? I know they are important to you."

"You matter most. And I'm sure you'll be fine. We'll have lots of children."

Emmalin closed her eyes, trying to hold back tears. She nodded. "All right. I believe you."

Jacob moved to Emmalin and gently lifted her out of the chair. "It will be you and me together. I'm here whenever you need help."

Emmalin hugged him around the waist. "I love you. I'll try not to let you down."

He pressed a kiss to the top of her head. "You won't. And it's really not up to you anyway. Either we trust God, or we don't. And whatever He brings our way and leaves with us, He will make a way through."

Emmalin's heart was full. "I love you, Jacob. You make me stronger."

He held her away from him. "Did you hear we're having a Fourth of July celebration in town in two weeks?"

"But the holiday has come and gone."

"True. But so many people were sick, the celebration was postponed and now that most folks are feeling better, the town council decided to go ahead with the plans, fireworks and all. And there will be dancing." He circled his arms around Emmalin. "I can't wait to take my best girl for a spin on the dance floor."

"I love fireworks, but I don't know if I'll be up to dancing."

"I'll carry you if I have to." He lifted her into his arms.

Emmalin squealed, then hugged him around the neck.

By the time Jacob left, Emmalin was ready for a nap, but the idea of dancing played through her mind. She so wanted to dance, but she'd have to increase her strength. Emmalin looked down the steps and decided it was time to begin. Grabbing hold of the railing she moved down one step, then another and another. When she reached the bottom, she took a deep breath. She didn't feel too badly. After waiting a few moments, she started back up. The trip up the steps was more difficult, but she managed. When she walked into the house, she went straight to her room and lay down. Though tired, she was hopeful and imagined what it would be like when she had her strength back.

In the next two weeks, Emmalin took every opportunity to walk the steps. Her vigor increased and so did her hope for a bright future. One afternoon, she decided it was time for a greater challenge. She picked up the egg basket before walking down the steps, and, feeling rather robust, she ambled across the yard to the chicken pen. She glanced back at the cabin. She'd done it!

When she stepped inside the chicken house, the smell of poultry and grain, and the sound of clucking hens, lifted her spirits further. "Hello, ladies. It's a good day. I hope you have a lot of eggs for me."

Her legs quaked, and her heart pounded hard as she made her way from one nest box to another. The favorite two nests had an abundance of eggs with a couple of stragglers in the other boxes. The basket felt heavy. Perhaps she'd asked too much of herself. She stepped out of the shed and studied the ground between her and the cabin. It seemed a long way to walk.

One slow step at a time, she managed to reach the porch. Clinging to the railing, she rested and caught her breath. Feeling defeated, she was nearly ready to give up. She was too weak.

Heavy legs barely carried her up the steps. Tears of disappointment leaked from her eyes as she stumbled into the house. Why was she crying? Fear. It was fear. What if God's will was that she not be fully restored?

She set the basket of eggs on the table, slowly moved to her room, and dropped onto the bed where she lay on her back staring at the ceiling. The celebration was only two days away. How would she ever be strong enough to dance with Jacob?

The morning of the party, Emmalin put in the final stitches on a new gown. It was lovely with a full skirt, nipped waistline, and ruffles on the three-quarter length sleeves. She'd never have managed to create such a beautiful dress without Margaret's help. It was a complicated pattern, but Margaret had been a patient and skillful teacher. Emmalin did most of the work herself but under her dear friend's tutelage. However, even this accomplishment couldn't stir her enthusiasm for the upcoming social.

She was weary and the day had barely begun. Jacob had his heart set on a dance with her, and she didn't want to disappoint him.

She slipped the gown on over her crinoline and did up the buttons, then stood in front of the mirror. She tipped from side to side and the blue gingham gown with its bell-style skirt swayed beautifully. It would be perfect for dancing.

She did up her hair with blue ribbons that matched the dress and then walked into the kitchen.

"So, you managed to bake bread?" her father asked.

"Zucchini. We have so much of it growing, I thought I should do something with it."

"It will be delicious." He held out his hand to her. "You look beautiful."

"Thank you."

"Let's go." He helped keep her steady as they moved down the steps and then he hefted her up into the wagon. "This is going to be a great day," he said as they set off toward town.

Emmalin smiled and kept her uncertainty to herself.

A jumble of wagons and horses crowded the churchyard. Jacob and Margaret spotted Emmalin and her father right off and hurried to greet them.

"Good morning." Margaret cast a smile at Jacob, then said, "Oh, Emmalin, you finished the gown."

"I barely finished. Put in the final stitches just this morning."

Jacob lifted Emmalin down from the wagon. "You look beautiful."

"I agree. That dress is exquisite on you." Margaret gave her a quick hug.

"I only managed because of you." She glanced down at the dress. "But I am kind of proud of it." She took the breadbasket out of the wagon. "I'll set this on the table."

"You made that?"

"I did."

Margaret tucked her arm into Emmalin's. "You are doing so well." The two women walked toward the tables laden with food. There were several sweet breads, and Emmalin proudly added hers to the others.

Charity set a small loaf beside Emmalin's. "I think there is an abundance of zucchini this year." She laughed. Turning to her friend, she said, "It's so good to see you looking more like yourself."

"I'm glad to be out and about again." As she said the words, she realized she was feeling less fearful and was actually looking forward to the afternoon.

Careful not to overdo and save energy for dancing, Emmalin spent much of the day sitting in the shade, visiting with women from the community. When the games started, she had to fend off feelings of discontent, especially when the ladies' three-legged race began. It would have been great fun to run that race with Charity.

After the meal had been announced, people gathered in small groups beneath shade trees to share a picnic. The children couldn't be kept quiet for long and were soon engaged in games of tag and blind man's bluff. With the meal over, the women cleared away the dishes and the musicians set up near the town square.

There were two fiddle players, a man who strummed a guitar, and another who played a cello. The songs were familiar and lighthearted, nothing like the music Emmalin had been accustomed to in Philadelphia. Perhaps one day she'd have a piano and learn to play some of the local songs. She preferred the casual dances enjoyed by Deer Creek residents.

It didn't take long for people to find a partner and dance across the open ground. Jacob walked toward her, and Emmalin inhaled deeply. Was she strong enough?

"We can just watch. That's fine by me."

"No. I'd like to dance."

"You're able?"

She nodded. "Yes. I am."

He took her hand. "I'm still pretty clumsy. My legs don't always work like they should."

"Neither do mine. But I've been doing all I can to get my strength back."

Jacob guided her to the dancing area, and with her in his arms, he cautiously stepped into a waltz. He wasn't a bit clumsy, and Emmalin had no trouble following his lead. She smiled broadly, her hope for the future restored. She had been foolish to allow fear to undermine her faith, which again had proven to be weak. *Lord, increase my faith.*

A gentle voice spoke to her heart, *The faith of a mustard seed is enough.*

Margaret and Samuel danced close by. "My, Emmalin, you're doing wonderfully," said Margaret.

"Thank you."

"Maybe it's time to begin designing your wedding gown."

Emmalin's heart sang. "What do you think? Shall I?"

Jacob scooped her into a hug. "Is a Christmas wedding too soon?"

"Any day will be perfect."

Chapter Twenty-Two

Emmalin made the last notation in the store ledger and closed the book. Business had been off for several weeks during the illness, but trade had picked up. She meandered to the window and looked out at the sleepy town. Ease warmed her. This was home, and she had fallen in love with it. The weeks and months to come were full of promise.

The door opened and her father stepped in. He pulled off his gloves. "I'll be glad when Jacob gets that cabin of yours finished. I could use more of his help around here."

"He feels badly because he knows it makes life more difficult for you. John and Chauncey have been lending him a hand. The work is coming along quite well."

"I'm not angry with him. Just blowing off steam."

"You do realize that even when the house is completed, Jacob won't be taking many trips out of town. I know he won't want to leave for weeks at a time."

"We talked about it. He does want to stay closer to home. And that's as it should be. He agreed to make local deliveries and an occasional trip to Oregon City, but only if it's necessary." He lifted a long-handled ladle off the wall, dipped water out of a barrel, and downed a drink. He finished and wiped his mouth with his shirt sleeve.

"I've got two shipments that need to go out today." Her father returned the ladle to its hook. "One west of town and the other down near Myrtle Creek. I can't take care of both of them."

"Maybe Benjamin Fulsom can take one?"

"I already asked. He has a pile of work at the blacksmith shop. And John and Chauncey are helping Jacob." He shrugged. "I even asked the sheriff, but he's got a prisoner to keep an eye on."

"Can one of the deliveries wait until tomorrow?"

"Tomorrow has work of its own. I can't put Mr. McDonald off another day. He's been waiting on his windows for weeks. He was in again two days ago asking about them." He combed his hair back with his fingers. "He's been doing work for Grace at the boarding house to fill in time while he waits."

"When his brother died, he took on the role of brother-in-law very seriously. He's always watching out for Grace."

"He sure is, which makes me want to get that shipment to him even more."

"Well, then that's what you must do."

"It's not that simple. The other delivery is badly needed dry goods."

An idea flickered in Emmalin's mind. She looked about the store. Things were in order. "I'm not really needed the rest of today. Perhaps I can make one of the deliveries. I'm quite capable of handling a team and wagon. And neither trip is very far."

Her father shook his head. "No. That's not for you to do. Plus, you've barely recovered."

"I won't do the loading. I'm strong enough to drive a team of horses." She planted her hands on her hips.

He hesitated. "Well, windows…those are real touchy. One wrong move and they'll end up broken. That kind of load needs a driver with a lot of experience."

"I understand that. But the dry goods shouldn't be difficult."

"Those go to Myrtle Creek and, as you know, there are some steep grades between here and there."

"Yes, but this time of year the roadway is in good condition." She cocked her head and smiled. "I can take care of it. Is the wagon loaded?"

"It is." He glanced out of the window. "What about customers?"

"I'll leave a sign on the door. If it's urgent they can go next door and get Margaret. She always keeps a key on hand. I'm sure she won't mind."

Her father rubbed a hand over his chin.

"I just completed the books, and if I leave right away, I can be back before nightfall. It will be nice to get out for the day."

"I don't know." He took off his hat and pressed his fist into it. "A woman alone on the road?"

Fear niggled at the edge of Emmalin's mind. Was he right? She pulled together her resolve. "I'll be fine. I'm quite competent. And I'll take my rifle."

"Why don't you ask Charity to join you?"

"That would be fun. But her place is too far out of the way. We'd never make it back before dark."

He studied her. "Are you sure you're strong enough?"

"Oh yes. I've fully recovered. Well, nearly. Well enough to drive a wagon."

"All right. But it's going to get hot today. Make sure to take plenty of water. And don't forget to have some extra bullets on hand. You may feel that you have adjusted, but this is still a wild place, and you never know what you might come across." A deep furrow wrinkled his brow.

Emmalin did know, but she needed to face what might come, whatever it may be. She kissed her father's cheek. "Thank you for trusting me."

He didn't look convinced. Before he could reconsider, she headed to the back of the store where she filled a flask with water. She retrieved her bonnet from where it hung on the wall, placed it on her head, and tied it snugly. This would be one more step toward her independence as an Oregon woman. Traveling from town to town would be required of her.

"I'll see if I can get a sandwich from Margaret to take with me." She dropped another kiss on her father's cheek.

"I'll hang up the sign. You be careful."

"Of course. I'll see you sometime around dinner." She hurried out the door, anxious to be on her way.

———◦•◦•◦•◦———

Margaret had kindly provided Emmalin with a sandwich, an apple, and freshly baked cookies. Emmalin set the lunch beside her on the wagon seat, lifted the reins, and clicked her tongue to get the horses moving. The morning sun was hot, but Emmalin knew she would get some respite from the afternoon heat as much of the roadway between Deer Creek and Myrtle Creek was shaded.

She wasn't far out of town when she spotted vultures circling the skies above an open field. Occasionally one would break away and glide downward until it was just above the tall golden grassland, then it would rise and rejoin others sailing on wind currents. The ugly birds almost looked regal in flight. Most certainly they were in search of some poor animal that had been killed by a predator. A shudder went through her. The idea was hideous.

She scanned the roadside, the idea of predators setting off wariness. There were none to be seen. She slapped the reins, hurrying the team along as they approached an upgrade. It would be a hard pull for them.

Emmalin had believed herself proficient enough to make the trip, but by the time she'd made it to the bottom of the first valley, she was less convinced. Nothing had gone wrong, but the entire descent had filled her with apprehension. She'd kept imagining a failing brake or runaway team. How would she handle such an incident? In frustration Emmalin realized she was, again, worrying needlessly. The horses had managed well, even though she'd held them in a bit tight. She could trust them.

At the bottom of the grade, she pulled to a stop. She needed a few moments to quiet her nerves. *Father, help me to trust You more. Forgive me for my lack of faith.*

Emmalin fanned her face, wishing for a breeze. The road was empty of travelers. She'd seen no one thus far. This was a lonely place. She glanced at the rifle resting against the seat, thankful she'd put time and practice into improving her marksmanship.

A large bull elk emerged from the forest and waded into belly deep grass. He carried an impressive rack, wearing it like a crown. Cropping a mouthful of grass, he chewed, seemingly unafraid. Even wolves would be wise to avoid him. She grabbed her canteen from under the seat and took a drink while continuing to watch him. A herd of cow elk appeared from the forest shadows. Several had calves at their side. Emmalin was mesmerized.

Quietly, so not to scare the herd, she put the lid back on the canteen and set it on the seat, then enjoyed the elk for a few minutes more. She needed to get on. There was no time for dallying if she were to get the supplies to the store, unloaded, and return to Deer Creek before nightfall.

Emmalin focused on the road ahead and, although the horses were moving along steadily, she felt a pull or dragging sensation coming from the back of the wagon. She glanced over her shoulder to see if any of the packages had broken loose. All seemed secure. She kept going, but the sensation got worse until the wagon felt wobbly. Something was wrong.

She pulled to a stop and climbed out, spotting the problem almost immediately. One of the back wheels was sitting at an angle. Was she about to lose it? She walked toward the rear of the wagon to have a better look.

Oh dear. The wheel had nearly worked itself free of the axle. She looked up and down the road. It remained empty.

Emmalin couldn't fix the wheel on her own. And if she kept going, she was almost certain it would break completely. She leaned against the wagon. What should she do? Wait for someone to come along? That could take hours.

It was several miles back and even more going forward. Even so, she would have to walk. If only the team had been trained for riders.

She hated leaving the wagon and dry goods unattended, but what choice did she have? She set the brake and tied back the reins. She gave each of the horses a handful of grain. "I'll be back as soon as I can." With her canteen draped over one shoulder and the rifle over the other she started walking toward Deer Creek.

She'd gone less than a mile when two riders approached from the north. Both were clearly in need of a shower and shave. Likely miners. She hadn't seen either of them in the store or about town. Could she trust them? Her heart rate turned rapid.

They rode up to her and stopped. One had a full beard and shaggy hair. He asked, "What's a pretty thing like you doing wandering around out here all alone?"

Emmalin felt apprehensive, but answered, "I had trouble with the wheel on my wagon."

He removed his rawhide hat. "Name's Ray." He nodded at his partner who was rather swarthy looking with long hair. "That's Charlie."

Charlie gave her a slow nod.

Ray narrowed his eyes and gazed down the roadway. "Figure we came along just in time."

Emmalin's unease increased. She didn't like these men.

"We'll give you a ride back and fix the wagon for you."

She studied them. She didn't want to go anywhere with them, but what choice did she have? She could keep walking, but it would take hours to reach Deer Creek. She had no reason to doubt their intentions. There were many rough-looking men in the Oregon Territory. Accepting help made sense.

"All right."

"Hey, Charlie, you got no manners? Offer the lady your horse." Ray focused on Emmalin. "What did you say your name is?"

"I didn't. But it's Emmalin."

"That's a real pretty name." He looked at Charlie. "Give Emmalin your horse."

Wearing a frown, Charlie climbed off his mount and handed Emmalin the reins. He offered her help up, but not wanting him to touch her, she refused and climbed into the saddle on her own. She draped her canteen over the saddle horn, and kept her rifle on her shoulder, then cantered down the road heading south.

Ray quickly caught up to her.

Charlie hollered, "Hey, wait for me!" He ran after them.

Soon the wagon came into view.

"Yep. Not far. Good thing for Charlie." Ray laughed.

Emmalin didn't find Charlie's situation the least bit funny. She pulled up alongside the wagon and dismounted, then stood back studying the wheel. "Do you think you can fix it?"

Ray and Charlie joined her. Charlie was gasping for breath and looking disgruntled.

Ray kneeled down and took a closer look at the wheel. "I think we can get it up and running." He looked at Charlie. "Give me a hand."

Emmalin watched while the two men removed the wheel and, using a knife to refit it, slid it back into place and tightened the bolts. "That ought to get you home." Ray stepped back. "You headed far?"

"Just to Myrtle Creek." She met his hard gaze and felt sweat bead up on the back of her neck.

"We'll see you get there safely." He tied his horse to the back of the wagon and so did Charlie.

"That's not necessary. I'm quite capable." Emmalin moved her rifle into her hands.

"No need to get touchy. Just trying to be neighborly."

"I appreciate that, but I can get there on my own." She tried to quiet her inner quaking.

"Not likely for a refined lady like yourself. There are all sorts out on these highways." He glanced at Charlie who snickered. "We'll be seeing you make it safely." He stepped toward her.

Emmalin lifted the rifle to her shoulder and sited him in.

He stopped. "What do you think you're gonna do with that? You wouldn't shoot me."

"I'll do what I must, believe me." She met his eyes, hoping she looked fierce. "I'd prefer you not force me to show you." Out of the corner of her eye she noticed Charlie move ever so slightly toward his horse.

"Let's just go," Charlie said. "We don't need nothin' from this highborn floozie."

Emmalin kept her jaw squared and her gaze hard. Inside she quaked.

Ray smiled as if he held some kind of malicious secret. "Fine. We'll go, but you gotta let us get our horses."

"Go ahead." Emmalin stepped away to allow them room to retrieve the horses.

Before she knew what had happened, Ray jumped over the back of the wagon and climbed up front while Charlie threw himself onto his horse. The other remained hitched to the wagon. Ray whipped the reins and hollered, "Hah!"

Emmalin held the rifle to her shoulder and aimed. "Stop! I'll shoot!"

He kept going. Emmalin breathed in resolve and pulled the trigger. Her shot clipped Ray's left arm. He yelled out but kept driving. By the time she got the rifle reloaded and sited in, they were too far away. She lowered the gun and watched the wagon and her father's dry goods disappear into a cloud of dust.

In frustration, she stomped her foot. They had the wagon, the supplies, and the horses. Now what?

She blew out a long breath and tried to quiet her fury and trembling. She wanted to sit down right there in the dirt and cry, but that's what the old Emmalin would have done. She wasn't that person anymore, at least she didn't want to be.

She remained standing. Refusing to allow even a single tear, she turned and walked toward Deer Creek.

Chapter Twenty-Three

When Emmalin had set off that morning, the journey south hadn't seemed that far, but of course she'd been sitting in the wagon and driving a team. Now she had neither.

Just how much farther was it to Deer Creek? She gazed at the deep blue sky. The sun had already passed its peak. Certainly there were not enough hours of daylight left to make it back before dark.

Her feet and legs already ached. Extensive walking was difficult even with well-made boots. She tightened the laces and moved on.

Sweat dripped down her temple and she wiped it away. She was thirsty. If only she had her canteen, but it was still on that demon's horse. She lifted the hem of her skirt out of the dirt for what little good it did. It was already filthy.

"Those men! Those horrible men!"

If not for them she would already have arrived in Myrtle Creek, unloaded the shipment, and been happily on her way home. She'd certainly be weary, but nothing like what she felt now. Perhaps her illness had left her weaker than usual.

Spotting a good-sized log in the shade of an oak tree, Emmalin headed toward it, each step creating insufferable pain in her feet. She was reminded of the long days on the trail when she'd crossed the continent. She'd walked many of those miles, but the wagon had always been available to her when needed.

Before sitting, she checked to make certain there was no poison oak climbing its way over the fallen tree. One entanglement with that noxious plant had been enough for her. She'd barely managed, until Jacob had come to her rescue with the native remedy. Now she kept a jar of it in the root cellar just in case it might be needed.

Seeing no sign of the dreadful vine, she leaned her rifle against the log and sat. Removing a handkerchief from its hiding place at the wrist of her dress, she patted dust and dampness from her face. If only there were a breeze and water. The river shouldn't be far. Part of the time, the road followed the small tributary.

Her stomach grumbled with hunger, again raising her ire. Those men had her lunch.

Emmalin groaned. How had the weakened wheel escaped her father's scrutiny? He must have checked the wagon before loading it. The team, wagon, and goods were a substantial loss. How would they ever recover them?

The caw of a raven cut through the quiet of the forest. If only he were announcing the arrival of a traveler. She glanced up and down the roadway but saw no one. With a sigh, she pushed to her feet and continued on.

Occasionally Emmalin came across a patch of blackberries and stopped to pick some. They held back some of her thirst and hunger. She plodded along, keeping watch for the river and wondering how far it was before she reached an outlying farm.

When she'd nearly given up hope of reprieve, she heard the sound of the river. She spotted it down an embankment, shallow and washing over rocks. Bless the Lord!

She fought the urge to carelessly scramble down the steep bank, and instead searched for a more hospitable trail. It didn't take long before she found what looked like a deer trail. Before starting down, she double-checked for travelers. Still no one.

With a resigned sigh, she gathered up her skirt and made her way along the path, grabbing hold of grass and bushes to keep from falling. The river splashed with white water. The sight and sound made Emmalin thirstier. When she reached the river's edge, she gave no thought to proper etiquette, or the cleanliness of her dress, but dropped to her knees and scooped up handfuls of water to drink. Finally with her thirst satiated, she splashed her face and neck with the cold water. It was pure delight.

She slurped a few more handfuls, then sat in the deep grasses that grew along the river's edge. She lay on her back and gazed at the azure sky. A breeze tousled the limbs of oak and maple that reached out over the river, sending their leaves down as if in a dance to the tripping music of the river. For a moment, she forgot her situation, which was rather dire. She had a long way yet to travel, on foot, without a reliable water source.

She sat up and stared across the river. A heavy bough dropped onto the bank. But it kept moving. It wasn't a bough. It was a bear! And it was walking toward the river's edge.

Slowly and quietly, Emmalin grabbed her rifle and stood.

The animal put his nose in the water to drink, then lifted his head and looked right at her. Emmalin held absolutely still and prayed she blended into the background. The bear made a huffing noise and stepped into the river. He'd seen her. She backed away from the water.

He didn't charge toward her, but he didn't retreat either. He kept moving. Her heart in her throat, her mouth dry as dirt, Emmalin took a few more steps backward until she was up against the bank.

He was still coming.

Emmalin lifted her rifle, braced it against her shoulder and took aim. She slowed her breathing. She needed a steady hand. If she was forced to shoot, there would only be one chance to do it right. If she missed, or wounded him, he'd be on her before she could reload. She took one more step back and up the trail where she braced against a tree.

Eyes fierce and mouth open, the animal revealed terrifying teeth. He came slowly as if stalking her. She wanted to shoot but needed him closer.

The grizzly reached her side of the bank, just north of her, and stopped. He stood on his hind legs, as if to make himself appear larger. Emmalin thought him big enough. He dropped and bounced on his front paws while swinging his huge head back and forth. The brute's eyes glinted with fury. Just a few more steps and she would fire. What if she missed? *Lord, help me.*

The bear continued its threats. In a huff of anger, it charged forward, then stopped. Emmalin had to capture a scream and hold it inside. He stared at her, made a couple more hard bounces on his front legs and, using his huge paws, brushed up dirt from the earth in front of him. And then, as if losing interest, he turned and walked up the river away from her.

Emmalin didn't lower her gun.

He kept moving and crossed the water to the opposite bank. With a glance back, he let out a huff, and then lumbered up the hillside and into the forest. Emmalin remained still, holding the rifle at her shoulder. He might circle back. Several minutes passed. He didn't reappear. Emmalin finally lowered the rifle and took in a quaking breath. She felt like she might vomit. Pressing a hand to her stomach, she took several deep breaths. Home. She needed to get home.

Still trembling, Emmalin scanned the river up and down, then with the gun draped over her left shoulder by a sling she climbed up the bank to the road. The sun had dropped behind the trees and shadows reached across the roadway. She needed to hurry, or she would have to spend the night somewhere along the way.

She closed her eyes. "Lord, I want to be brave, but I'm afraid. Please bring someone to help me."

Emmalin set out, taking quick steps, and keeping watch on the forest. Any number of predators could be lurking there, possibly even the bear she'd encountered. It could be following her. She'd heard of them doing that.

Dusk descended, but Emmalin kept on, ignoring the pain in her feet and legs. She prayed as she went, and soon felt less afraid. She'd lost the wagon but had stood up to those men. She'd even shot one of them. And she'd faced down a grizzly, the most dangerous predator in the territory. God had enabled her. With Him, she done what was needed. If she had to spend the night along this road, then that's what she would do, and in the morning, she would walk the rest of the way to Deer Creek. She only hoped her father and Margaret weren't worrying too much.

She heard a scuffling sound on the road ahead of her and immediately stopped and readied her rifle. She stood waiting for whatever was coming.

All of a sudden, Henry emerged from the near darkness. With a short woof, he ran straight for her. She kneeled and caught him around the neck. "Oh, Henry! How wonderful to see you!"

"Emmalin?"

She saw a rider in the deepening gloom and straightened. "Jacob?"

He galloped toward her. Before he reached Emmalin, he launched himself off Smoke's back. "Thank the Lord!" He pulled her into his arms. "You scared me. I came into town to get supplies, hoping to see you. I was told that you'd gone out to make a delivery and when you didn't come back, I got worried. I couldn't wait. I had to look for you."

"I'm so glad you did." Emmalin held him tightly. "I've never been so happy to see you."

They stood like that in the gathering gloom for several moments and then Jacob held her away from him. "Why are you walking? Where's the wagon?"

"I'll tell you, but can we start back first? I'm so hungry and thirsty."

"Here. I've got water." He handed her his canteen.

She drank from the flask. "I never thought tepid water from a canteen could taste so good."

He helped Emmalin up into the saddle and climbed on behind her.

Emmalin leaned against him. "So, I don't know where the wagon is. I had a broken wheel and had started back on foot when two men came along. They took it."

"Did they hurt you?"

"No. You would have been proud of me. They were true hooligans, but I held them off with my rifle. And I hit one of them. It might just be a graze, but that man has a sore arm."

Jacob tightened his hold on her. "Emmalin." He was silent for a few moments. "I'm proud of you. You're a brave woman."

"I was scared, but mostly angry. How dare they?"

"We'll report this to the sheriff. No doubt we'll find the wagon and horses, and those men will pay."

"Those two villains are only the beginning of today's tale." She told him about her encounter with the bear, then rested against him, feeling her exhaustion. Her eyes were heavy. "It was quite a day."

"You have to be more careful."

She chuckled. "I agree." She felt warm and comfortable in Jacob's arms. "I must admit that when that bear charged at me, I nearly fainted." She smiled up at him. "Perhaps it's a good idea that I not travel alone anymore."

"I won't argue with you."

"Jacob, what am I to do when we're living in the cabin? You can't always be with me."

Jacob didn't answer right away. "I guess there will be times when you'll have to make the trip into town on your own and we'll have to trust God."

"We either trust Him or we don't. I do."

Jacob gave her a light squeeze. "Me too."

Emmalin was overthinking. Life could never be perfectly safe, but God's Word said the Lord was with her always, just as He had been today. But maybe it was all right to rely on others, on Jacob to help her, even rescue her.

She would think on it more, but right now she was just thankful to feel safe.

Chapter Twenty-Four

Emmalin scooped out the last of the grain and let the calf snuffle it out of her hand. "There you go." The sound of a wagon came from outside. Emmalin stepped out of the stall, latched it, and hurried to see who had arrived.

"Margaret! What a nice surprise."

Her friend smiled from beneath a broad-brimmed hat. "Last week when I was fishing, I saw a wonderful patch of blackberries down by the river. I'm headed there now and thought you might like to join me."

"That would be marvelous. Father's in town, and all I planned to do were indoor tasks. Blackberry picking sounds much nicer."

"I saw your father at breakfast. He came in for a pastry."

"He does like his sweets. But I think you're what entices him into the café most days."

Margaret laughed. "Possibly."

Emmalin moved toward the house. "Let me get my bonnet and a pail."

"You'll likely need a couple of buckets. And don't worry about lunch. I already prepared something for us."

Now eager for the day, Emmalin gathered up her skirts and quickly took the porch steps. "I'll be right out, just need to get the buckets from the root cellar."

Emmalin hurried down the steps into the coolness of the cellar, retrieved two buckets off a shelf, and climbed back up the steep stairway.

After grabbing a bonnet, she stepped out of the house and walked to the wagon where she set the buckets in the back. "This should be fun," she said, tying on her bonnet. She climbed up and settled on the seat beside Margaret. "Where is this special berry patch?"

"Not far." Margaret slapped the reins over the backsides of the horses, and they set off down the road. "These will add nicely to what I already have."

In little more than thirty minutes, Margaret pulled the horses to a stop at a wide shady place along the river. "This is one of my favorite fishing spots."

"And you've never shared it with me?" Emmalin asked in a teasing manner.

"I need to keep *some* secrets. But your father fishes here too."

"Hmm. So, this place is just for the two of you?" Emmalin tossed Margaret a playful look. "I've been pretty certain your relationship with my father would bloom. Is something happening between you two?"

"I think so. But your father is taking his own sweet time about it. I'll just have to be patient." Margaret laughed, then climbed out of the wagon. "My golly! There are more berries now than last week." She grabbed two of the buckets and handed one to Emmalin.

"Are these special? There are blackberries all over the county." Emmalin approached the patch.

"Yes, there are, but most are not this plentiful and not this plump." She swung her bucket as she walked. "And I love it here. It's always peaceful with the sound of the river and the profusion of bird song. Sometimes I feel as if I'm being serenaded by nature."

"It is nice. But I have to admit that, no matter where I'm berry picking, I worry about bears. They like berries as much as we do. Perhaps more."

"I don't think about them much. We just need to keep talking and let them know we're here. If they hear us, they'll stay clear."

"You might want to tell that to the one I came across the day those scoundrels stole my father's wagon and horses. He wasn't scared of me one bit. Rather, he was something of a bully."

"That must have been frightening. What an adventure you had."

"I'll be quite satisfied if I never have such an adventure again."

"It truly was an ordeal."

"I did quite well, but only because of God. I could feel His presence."

"Well, I hope He deals with those awful men. Has there been any word on them and the things they took?"

"Not yet. We reported it right away, but it seems the troublemakers and my father's belongings have just disappeared. The sheriff expects the wagon and horses to show up eventually." Emmalin picked a plump berry and, after close inspection to its cleanliness, popped it in her mouth. The combination of sweet and tart exploded on her tongue. "These will be perfect for pies."

"And preserves."

The two women set to work.

"How is Jacob doing?" Margaret asked.

"Wonderfully. He's not fully healed, but nearly so. Just as you said, all he needed was time."

"And God's healing touch." Margaret smiled warmly.

"He's working on the cabin today. I don't worry so much with Charity's brothers helping him. I'm hoping he'll be back this evening." She imagined a quiet evening interlude on the porch, where they could enjoy a cool breeze accompanied by singing crickets.

A bee buzzed close to her head, and she swiped it away, then settled into a rhythm of picking, careful not to catch her sleeves on thorns. Her bucket filled rapidly.

Margaret patted her damp face with a handkerchief, fanned herself with her hat, and then resettled the hat on her head. "My goodness, it's hot."

"It is. But isn't that typical for August? It was very hot last summer as I recall."

"Yes. These are the most difficult days of the season—so much work to be done in the midst of all this heat." She looked at the river. "I believe it's time for a break." She headed toward the wagon.

Emmalin followed, careful not to spill her berries. "My bucket is nearly full."

"Mine too." Margaret exchanged her pail of berries for the basket that contained lunch. "Let's eat down by the river, shall we."

Emmalin grabbed a green checkered tablecloth and joined Margaret. She spread the cloth out on the grass near the bank. "I need to refresh myself." She held up her hands, stained a deep maroon from picking. "Berry juice—it's sticky." Emmalin took a napkin and moved to the water where she kneeled and washed her hands, then dipped the cloth into the river. She wrung the excess water out of it, then used it to pat her face and neck. It was deliciously cold. She closed her eyes and sighed. "Oh, that's wonderful."

Margaret sat on the bank and removed her shoes and stockings. "I dare not do this with anyone else, but it's just the two of us." With a devilish grin, she lifted her skirt and waded into the water. "It's heavenly." She kicked water at Emmalin. "Join me."

With a squeal, Emmalin leaned back.

"I want to immerse myself. If I had one of those new swim dresses I would."

"I don't know how to swim."

"It's easy. I can teach you." Margaret splashed water onto her neckline. "I think it's time for a trip to the coast. It's much cooler there."

"But what about our gardens?"

"We'd be gone only three or four days. We can work extra hard before we go. And when we get back, we'll be refreshed and ready to go back to work." She scooped up a mouthful of water.

"I haven't been since I was a little girl and that was on the Atlantic. I'd love to see the Pacific Ocean."

"It's the loveliest place. We must go." Margaret splashed more water on her face. "I'm thinking your father and Jacob might like the idea too. We could all travel out there together."

"It sounds fabulous, but we might have difficulty dragging them away from work."

Margaret studied her for a moment. "Do you think you're up to it? I know you're feeling so much better, but it's quite a long ride."

"I'm doing well, really. I get tired easier than I did before I got sick, but I have no doubt that I can make the trip."

"All right then. I'll speak to your father. And you convince Jacob." Margaret smiled mischievously.

"I can take care of the costs. Would you mind?"

Margaret smiled. "That is very kind of you. But we'll have to keep it from the men."

"I oversee the books at the store, so that shouldn't be a problem." Emmalin grinned. "But we'll have to find someone to watch over the store and deliveries while we're out of town."

"Maybe Charity's younger brother, Matthew, can help with that. And Charity might keep an eye on the store, if she has the time."

Emmalin pressed her palms together. "Oh, I hope we can go."

All had worked out perfect, and only three days later, early in the morning, Emmalin, Samuel, Margaret, and Jacob set out for the coast on horseback with one pack mule carrying supplies. Henry trotted along beside them. Even at the early morning hour, the air felt hot. The sky was a pale blue and cloudless. Vultures had already sailed into the skies and circled a nearby field.

"How awful. Do you think they've found something?" Emmalin asked.

Jacob eyed them. "Could be, but they spend a lot of time looking before they find."

Emmalin glanced back at the house. "It was kind of Matthew to look after both of our places."

"He's a good fellow," Jacob said, tapping Smoke in the sides with his heels and moving into the lead.

After a time, the roadway narrowed into a trail that followed a tributary west. They moved steadily, until the sun was high in the sky, then stopped to rest the horses and to refresh themselves at the river. Emmalin sat in green grasses that grew in the shade of an oak tree. Jacob dropped down beside her and offered her a drink from his canteen. "Fresh, out of the stream."

She gulped down the cool water. "So good. Thank you." She handed the flask back to him and turned to Margaret. "This trip was a wonderful idea."

"Well, we'll see if you agree by the end of the day. We still have a lot of hours to spend in the saddle." She grinned. "I'm already feeling it."

"It is such a pleasure, though. And I can barely wait to see the ocean. I know it's going to be spectacular." A splash sounded from downriver. "Oh! An otter!"

Henry leaped to his feet and let out a sharp bark. He stared at the animal as it cavorted in the shallows and then dove into deeper water and swam to the opposite bank with a small fish in its mouth. The animal scurried into the brush where he most certainly settled down to devour a midday meal.

"I never tire of the wildlife here. Something like that would not have happened in Philadelphia."

"I've been here a lot of years, and I still enjoy the animal life and the natural beauty." Samuel pushed to his feet and gave Margaret a hand up. "We've got a lot more to see. Time to move on."

Before the day was through, they admired a herd of elk roaming through heavy forest, plus a hungry fox who trotted across a grassy field with a meal in its mouth. They crossed the river, splashing through shallows, took another short break for lunch, and kept moving, stopping only because the setting sun forced them to. At dusk, they set up camp.

Exhausted, Emmalin could easily have collapsed into bed without eating, but she forced herself to help Margaret build a fire and prepare dinner while the men put up tents, gathered firewood, and cared for the horses.

Biscuits baked in a Dutch oven while Margaret stirred up a stew of salted beef and fresh vegetables. Emmalin prepared coffee and set the pot in coals at the edge of the fire. She sat on a log. "I don't think I've ever been more tired or sore."

With a groan, Margaret stood. "It was a long day, and I'm not as young as I once was. Still, it was lovely." She gazed up through the trees as a starling hopped from branch to branch, then her eyes settled on Samuel as he moved toward camp, his arms loaded with firewood. "I wish Samuel and I could spend more time like this."

Emmalin glanced at him, then back at Margaret. "I think he cherishes your time together."

A pained expression flitted across Margaret's face. "I know you're right, but he's been awfully quiet about it."

"You two belong together. I don't know what is taking my father so long to do something about it."

"There has been a lot going on—Jacob's accident, the scarlet fever outbreak, and just keeping up with all that needs to be done. I know he cares for me. I just have to be patient."

With Henry at his side, Jacob appeared from within the shadows, his arms loaded with firewood. "I think we've got enough to see us through the night." He dropped branches on the ground beside the fire, then sat beside Emmalin. "How long until dinner. I'm as hungry as a one-legged coyote."

"Nearly ready," Margaret said, with a glance at Samuel who tended to the horses.

He gave them each a pat and moved into the light of the fire. Hands in his pockets, he stared at the flames. "I'll sleep well tonight."

"We all will," Emmalin said. "Even though the ground makes for a hard mattress."

After a hearty meal, the travelers climbed into their beds. The women shared one tent, the men the other. Henry kept watch near the fire. In spite of the uncomfortable ground, Emmalin quickly dropped into a deep sleep.

⸻

In the morning, Emmalin was the first to awaken. Feeling stiff, she was glad to get up. Light barely touched the sky as she left the tent. The soft twitter of awakening birds welcomed her to a new day. She added wood to the hot coals left from the previous night's fire, then set the pot with leftover coffee from dinner in them to heat.

Her father joined her. "You're up early."

"I don't think I could manage one more minute on the hard ground."

"Me too." He reached his long arms over his head and stretched to the side.

Soon Margaret and Jacob were up, breakfast was eaten, and the gear packed up. The four were back on the trail with the early morning sun. Samuel took the lead. "If we keep a steady pace, we should make it by early afternoon."

"I can hardly wait to stand on the beach and wade into the icy tide." Margaret kicked her horse and moved past him. "And it will be wonderful to watch a glorious ocean sunset tonight."

Emmalin's insides quivered with excitement. She had only a vague memory of standing on a sandy beach as a child. She remembered feeling as if the world was bigger and brighter than usual. Would it feel the same here?

As the Deer Creek travelers approached the coastline, they followed a trail to the southwest that moved alongside a small tributary. Jacob leaned on his saddle horn and gazed into the water. "Last time I was out this way, I did some fishing. Got more fish than I could take home. Course back then, the local natives were happy to take any I didn't need." He smiled, but it quickly melted away as he gazed toward the north as if looking for something.

"I'd like to get a line in the water," Samuel said.

Jacob turned to Emmalin. "We'll give it a try tomorrow."

"That would be nice, but I truly want to spend as much time on the beach as possible. It's not something a person does often."

"We're nearly there," Margaret said. "Coos Bay can't be more than a couple of miles more. Feel that air—cool and damp. And the wind is picking up."

Emmalin had noticed the change in climate. The late August heat had dissipated.

The trail finally broke open along a ridge above the coastline. Emmalin pulled Sassy to a stop alongside Jacob and gazed out over a broad expanse of beach below with a shimmering blue ocean reaching toward the edge of the earth. "How incredibly beautiful." Emmalin couldn't recall ever seeing anything more magnificent. She straightened in the saddle, closed her eyes, and listened to the muffled sound of breaking surf.

"Oh, my goodness. It always takes away my breath," Margaret said.

Practical as always, Emmalin's father turned his horse back onto the trail. "Let's get to the camp site." He headed north, and the others followed.

The air was chilly, the wind brisk, and the sharp smell of brine stung Emmalin's nose. She trusted Sassy to keep her footing and did as much gazing at the sparkling sea as she could. Gradually they moved down a draw and reached the beach where a slough spilled into the ocean.

Samuel dismounted. "This looks like a good spot. We've got a couple of hours before nightfall. Let's make camp and then walk to the beach."

Emmalin withheld a moan. Couldn't camp wait? She itched to stand on the sand.

Just as they had done the night before, two tents were set up, firewood gathered, and the horses cared for. Emmalin worked fast. When she finally inspected the camp, she was grateful to see no further tasks needed to be done.

It was time.

Their hands clasped, Emmalin and Jacob headed toward the beach. Her father and Margaret were close behind.

Tall sharp grasses growing amongst sand dunes were whipped briskly by the wind. Though they could smell the pungent sea and hear the breaking surf, piles of sand blocked any view of the ocean.

Emmalin hurried her steps, but her legs soon felt heavy and weak from the effort. Then she crested a small dune and a strong cold wind caught hold of her hair and her skirts. Her heart thrummed with awe. Pale gray sand darkened as it met waves washing ashore. Emmalin couldn't stop smiling. This was much better than what her memory had revealed. "Oh, Jacob." She squeezed his hand.

"Yeah. I love it here." He circled an arm around Emmalin and pulled her close.

Huge dark waves rolled toward shore, breaking into white boiling surf as they came ashore. The reflection of the sun on the ocean's surface was like a brilliant light shimmering on glass.

"It's spectacular!" Emmalin extracted herself from Jacob's arms and led him toward the water. "I've never seen anything like it!" When she reached the wet sand close to the water's edge. All she wanted to do was run.

Margaret sat and unlaced her shoes, then pulled off her stockings. She laughed at Emmalin's look of shock. "I'm not going to allow convention to steal the moment." She pushed to her feet and raced across the sand.

Her father's eyes shimmered with admiration as he watched Margaret. "Isn't she something?"

"Yes, she is." Emmalin's heart warmed at the love she saw in her father's eyes. "Maybe you should tell her."

"Maybe I should." He hurried after Margaret.

Jacob stopped and stripped off his boots and socks. He glanced at Emmalin. "How about you?"

Did she dare? It took only a moment's thought. Emmalin turned away from Jacob and, as discreetly as possible, removed her shoes and stockings. She left them on the sand, then grabbed hold of Jacob's hand, and the two of them headed to the water's edge.

Bits of shell and rock were embedded in the beach. Emmalin tried to avoid them, but a few pierced the tender skin on the bottom of her feet. She didn't care. All she could think about was wading into the surf. Margaret was already frolicking in the waves.

When Emmalin reached the water, she stopped and watched foam rush toward her. It swept beneath her feet, icy cold and prickly with sharp grains of debris and sand. As it washed back out, it sucked the sand from beneath her feet. "Oh! My goodness!" A sense of dizziness swept over her.

Jacob waded in beside her. "I don't know why it's taken me so long to get back here." He laughed as a wave swept in, soaking the bottom of his trousers.

Emmalin held up her skirt and waded in deeper. A shiver of fear went through her. Could the waves sweep her out into the massive ocean? She reached for Jacob. "I don't know how to swim."

"Yes. I know. And you need to learn. But not here." He laughed. "No one learns to swim in this kind of wild water." He pulled her into his arms. "When we get back to Deer Creek, we'll find a quiet pool at the river, and I'll teach you."

Samuel and Margaret waded out of the water and strolled up the beach, hand in hand. As Emmalin watched them, a wave hit her from the side and nearly swept her off her feet. It felt colder than before. She grasped Jacob more tightly, and they moved into the shallow surf and then walked along the beach in search of treasures offered up from the sea. Emmalin found a flat round shell and picked it up. It was nearly white with what looked like a star, or some type of flower, etched on the back of it. "What is this?"

"People call them sand dollars."

"Oh yes. I can see. It nearly does look like a silver dollar."

"It's a living animal."

"Really?" Emmalin examined the creature more closely then returned it to the sand.

She and Jacob continued on their way. Emmalin noticed Jacob had a slight limp. "Are your legs holding up all right?"

"A little tired, but not bad. I never thought this kind of day would ever happen for me."

Emmalin took both his hands in hers and looked up at him. "God knew." Love and gratitude welled up inside of her.

"I'm grateful. But a lot of people never get a miracle. Why me?"

Emmalin shrugged. "The Bible says God is sovereign. Only He decides such things. I'm not sure we're supposed to know the answers. At least not until heaven. Then we'll understand. Until then, I am simply grateful."

She stopped. Her father and Margaret were embracing. Emmalin didn't want to intrude, so she turned and started back. "I'm cold. And the sun will be down soon."

"Let's get back to camp and start a fire."

"I'll make dinner."

With a fire crackling and dinner cooking, Emmalin huddled within a blanket. She waited for the coffee to boil.

Her father and Margaret stepped into camp.

"Thank goodness. I was preparing to search for you."

"No need." Margaret's face was pink and her hair windblown. Emmalin thought she'd never looked more beautiful. Margaret snuggled into the crook of Samuel's arm.

"We have some news," he said. He and Margaret glanced at one another, then together, they said, "We're getting married. Tomorrow."

Chapter Twenty-Five

Emmalin picked wildflowers as she and Margaret walked toward town. "There's so much to be done. Have you talked to a minister?"

"Your father left early so he could do just that. He has it all arranged." Margaret stopped and pressed her hands to her cheeks. "I can hardly believe this is happening. I've been in love with your father for a long while now, and I'd nearly given up hope of him ever asking me to marry him. I knew he cared for me, but he's been a bachelor for so long."

Emmalin pushed a wild daisy into Margaret's hair. "I knew he loved you. But after what happened with my mother, I wasn't certain he'd dare take the risk." The realization of God's perfect plan being played out filled Emmalin with wonder. "I'm so glad he's chosen you. We'll truly be family."

"And you have no misgivings? I mean, it should have been your mother who shared your father's life."

Emmalin felt a pinch of sadness which left as soon as it came. "I feel badly about what happened to my mother and father. It is something of a tragedy. But that was many years ago, and all I want now is for my father and my dearest friend to find happiness."

"Oh, you are a dear." Margaret embraced her.

Emmalin looped her arm through Margaret's. "I am wondering, though, what about your friends in town? They will all want to attend your wedding. You and Father could wait and get married in Deer Creek."

"I know. We talked about that and decided we don't want to wait. And we both love this place." She hugged Emmalin's arm. "We will have a reason to return every year on our anniversary." She started walking. "We can have a party when we return home. It will be such fun." Margaret stopped and faced Emmalin. "And the two people we love most are here to share this." Her eyes misted.

"I'm so happy for you."

"Me too."

With arms linked, the two friends continued toward town.

"I hope there's a shop with an appropriate gown." Margaret looked down at her traveling dress. "I never thought I'd have reason to bring anything special. I know it shouldn't matter, but it does. I want to look my best. After all, it's my wedding."

"No need to fear. We'll find something."

Coos Bay sat along a small inland quay. It was a friendly little hamlet, and Emmalin soon spotted what looked like a dress shop. "Here we are," she said, hurrying her steps. A window display showed off a lovely yellow gown with a full skirt. "What about this?"

"It's pretty, and no bustle. Thank goodness. It's getting more and more difficult to buy a dress without one these days. All the more reason to make my own dresses." Margaret the frock. "I wonder if it's my size. Let's go in."

A young woman with golden hair arranged in a fashionable coiffure approached them. "May I help you?"

"Yes, thank you." Emmalin walked toward the display. "My friend, Margaret"—she nodded at Margaret—"is getting married, and she's looking for a suitable gown."

"I do have a few in stock, but I'm a good seamstress and can make one that would be fitted especially for the bride." She smiled at Margaret. "When is the wedding?"

"Today." Margaret blushed. "I know it's very short notice, but I had no idea…and we'll be traveling back to Deer Creek tomorrow morning."

"Oh, my goodness. I guess readymade will have to do." The woman took stock of Margaret, then smiled. "I believe I have something that will be just right." Taking short quick steps, she moved toward the back of the store where several gowns hung inside an open closet. She thumbed through them, then pulled out a soft green dress with a bell skirt and lace bodice.

"That's lovely," Margaret said.

The clerk held the dress up to Margaret. "I think the color is perfect for your complexion."

"It looks expensive. And I'll need a crinoline as well."

Emmalin was not going to allow Margaret to deprive herself. "I'd like to make your wedding ensemble a gift. And there's no need to concern yourself with cost."

"Oh dear, that's so generous of you, but I couldn't."

"Of course, you can." Emmalin flashed a smile and leaned close enough to whisper. "I love to help my friends, and what better way to spend my money. Jacob won't allow me to use a dime on our home, at least not yet." Again, she held the gown up against Margaret. "I think it's perfect, and the color is especially nice with your hair."

Margaret smiled brightly and took the dress. "All right. I'll try it."

"The dressing room is just there," the saleswoman said, pointing toward a room with a heavy brocade drapery across the doorway.

Margaret disappeared inside while the salesclerk went to a display of shoes, returning with delicate mint green slippers. "These should match perfectly. I hope they fit." She reached a hand through the drapery and set them on the floor.

"I'm going to need help with these buttons." Margaret poked her head out of the curtain. "Would you mind?"

"Of course not." Emmalin stepped into the tiny room, and Margaret turned her back to her. "My goodness. There are so many buttons I can't even count." She proceeded to loop each small eyelet. "Can you breathe in a little. It's a bit snug here at the waist."

Margaret sucked in her breath.

When Emmalin finished, she turned Margaret around to face a large mirror. The two gazed at the image in the glass.

"It's beautiful." Margaret pressed a hand against her abdomen. "It is snug. I can barely breathe."

"I don't think I've ever seen you look prettier. My father will be swept away."

Margaret continued to gaze at her reflection, turning from side to side. "I suppose I can keep my breathing to a minimum during the wedding." She laughed softly.

Emmalin picked up the shoes. "Try these on."

Margaret slipped her feet into the dressy shoes. "Perfect." She did a little twirl. "I think this will do nicely." She hugged Emmalin. "Thank you."

Emmalin's heart swelled. "It's a pleasure. I'm so happy for you."

"I can barely believe I'm to be blessed with a wonderful man like your father." Margaret's eyes filled with tears, and she turned her back to Emmalin. "Now you need to unbutton this dress. And then we'd better be on our way. We still have much to do."

The men met with the minister while Emmalin and Margaret made dinner arrangements with a local café, then hurried back to camp, picking more wildflowers as they walked. When Emmalin had a decent bunch, she held them up. "These should do nicely. And we can use extras for your hair."

"They're very pretty."

After a refreshing dip in the river, Margaret prepared for the wedding. "Your father said we're to meet them at the little church on the edge of town, the one that sits along the quay."

Emmalin felt prickles of excitement. "All this makes me think about Jacob and me. I wish I was preparing for our wedding."

"It will happen. The day will be here before you know it."

"It seems so far away. I'd be happy to move onto the property and live in a tent if it meant we could marry right away."

"You say that but spending months in a tent is no picnic."

Emmalin compressed her lips, then said, "I know. I remember how difficult it was to live in a wagon all those months on the Oregon Trail." She shimmied a cotton dress over her head and buttoned up the bodice. "I wish I'd brought one of my nicer gowns."

"You look very pretty." Margaret brushed her hair up onto her head and twisted it into a sophisticated bun. She pinched her cheeks and wet her lips, then turned to face Emmalin. "How do I look?"

"Stunning. But one last thing." Emmalin deftly arranged delicate wildflowers into Margaret's coiffure. "Now you look perfect. My father will wonder why it took him so long to ask you."

"Even if I bathed in a river and dressed in a tent?" Margaret giggled.

"I think he would consider that a plus."

"I'm feeling giddy. Am I too old for such feelings?"

"You're never too old. Love *should* always make a woman giddy." Emmalin reached out a hand. "Are you ready?"

"I am."

The two friends walked into town, hands clasped.

Jacob stood on the church steps with Henry at his side. He removed his hat when he saw the ladies. "You are a beautiful sight," he told Margaret.

"Thank you, Jacob." She gave a little dip, her cheeks dimpling. "Where is Samuel?"

"Inside. Waiting for you." He walked up to the church entrance. "The preacher found a woman to play the piano."

"Wonderful."

The door opened, and a nice-looking middle-aged man stepped out. Wearing a warm smile, he moved toward Margaret. "I'm Reverend Greenwald. And my guess is you are Margaret."

"Yes. Margaret Clark." She shook his hand. "It is a pleasure to meet you."

"The pleasure is mine. Weddings are one of my favorite events."

He turned his eyes on Emmalin. "And this is?"

"I'm Emmalin. Samuel is my father."

"Ah, yes." He nodded, then turned to Jacob. "You can go on in and stand with Samuel. Do you have the ring?"

Jacob patted his breast pocket. "Yes, I do."

"A ring?" Margaret asked.

Jacob smiled. "He was determined to find one, and he did."

Margaret's face flushed, and she put her hands to her cheeks while tears filled her eyes.

Jacob turned to Henry. "You stay." The dog sat, his tail wagging. Jacob gave Emmalin a wink and disappeared inside the church.

The minister faced Margaret. "Do you have any questions?"

"No. I don't believe so."

"Are you ready to pledge your life to Samuel Morgan?"

"I am."

"All right, then. Though this is a spontaneous decision, I've been told you've given it adequate thought."

"Yes. I have."

"Fine then. I'll wait at the front of the church, and when the music begins, Emmalin, you walk up the aisle to the front and stand to my right, opposite the groom and his best man."

Emmalin nodded agreement, goose bumps skittering up her arms.

"Margaret, it will then be your turn. You and Samuel will stand in front of me when you take your vows."

The reverend stepped inside and closed the door. Emmalin and Margaret waited, standing side-by-side.

Margaret whispered, "I'm so nervous."

"Of course you are, even if you're the one who is never shaken."

"I try always to remain calm, but this is not just any average event. My life is about to change forever." She pressed a hand to the base of her neck. "My heart is racing."

Piano music came from inside. Margaret handed Emmalin a small batch of her flowers. "You should have a bouquet too."

"Thank you." Emmalin stepped inside. The church was small, with only six rows of pews and an aisle running down the middle. At the front was a small rise with a wooden lectern. A cross had been burned into the wood. Candles flickered on two small tables placed on either side of the podium. She started down the aisle, keeping her eyes straight in front of her, taking only a glance at her father and then Jacob. She felt heat rise in her cheeks. Soon she would be the bride and Jacob would be her groom.

She took her place in front and watched the door, waiting for Margaret. When the door opened and Margaret stepped in, a light from a side window caught her face. She looked radiant. Emmalin never recalled a time when she'd seen her friend happier. This priceless moment would always remain etched in her heart.

Margaret moved toward the front, her eyes on the man waiting at the altar for her. Her expression was one of devotion.

Emmalin's heart swelled with joy for these two people whom she loved.

Her father took Margaret's hand, and the two turned to face the minister. Emmalin and Jacob's eyes met. A charming half-smile rested on Jacob's lips. He sent Emmalin's heart racing. Soon it would be their turn. Soon they would promise themselves to one another. Soon they would begin their lives together. Soon.

Chapter Twenty-Six

Emmalin rolled onto her side and was immediately aware of a rock burrowing into her shoulder. She forced open her eyes, then pushed up on one elbow. The time here had been divine, but she had to admit to missing her bed at home. The smell of coffee brought her more awake.

Was Margaret already up? Memories of the wedding swept over her. It had been delightful. And now she and Margaret were family, which pleased her a great deal.

Emmalin sat up and, using her fingers, combed her long hair away from her face. She grabbed a brush out of her pack and ran it through her hair, then caught it up in back with a ribbon. Pushing to her feet, she smoothed creases out of her dress, though some stubbornly remained. She hated the idea of facing the day looking disheveled, but there was no way around it.

She poked her head out of the tent door. No sign of Margaret or her father. The previous evening, they had moved their tent to a discreet distance. She'd slept in the remaining tent, and Jacob had stretched out by the fire. Now, in the morning mist, he sat on a log, gazing at a small fire. His jaw was set, and his brow furrowed. Was he upset?

Emmalin stepped out into the fresh air. "Good morning."

He looked up with a smile. "Good morning. I was beginning to think you would sleep until noon."

Henry lifted his big head and groaned a greeting, then rested his head back on his front paws.

Emmalin warmed herself at the fire. "Are Margaret and my father up?"

"They left for the beach about an hour ago. Margaret said they wanted one last look at the ocean before heading back."

Emmalin sat on a stump. "I'd love to take a walk on the beach. Will we have time?"

"I don't see why not." He poured a cup of coffee and handed it to Emmalin. "Drink this and then we can go down."

She sipped the bitter drink. It could do with a little sugar. "I hope we can come back here soon."

"I was thinking maybe early October when most of the harvesting is done."

"Won't it be awfully cold by then?"

"Maybe. But there are usually a lot of sunny days and little rain. We just need good warm clothes and bedding."

"Will our house be done by then?"

"Probably not."

"How long do you think it will be before it is completed? We talked about a wedding around Christmas. It would be amazing if we could spend Christmas together in our new home." Emmalin knew she sounded whiny and hated that.

He offered a patient smile. "I want that too, and I know we talked about it, but with working for your father when I can and not being back to my full strength, I don't think that's going to happen after all. The fellas can't work all the time. Their family depends on them." He picked up a stick and poked the coals. Sparks flew into the air.

Disappointment soaked into Emmalin, but she tried not to reveal it. She'd been considering a proposal, but hesitated to ask, knowing how Jacob felt about her money. She took a drink of the dark coffee. "Would it be possible to hire a few more men?"

Jacob didn't look up but stared at the fire. "I'm already digging deep to pay John and Chauncey." He looked at her.

Emmalin knew not to press. "I suppose everything will fall into place as God wills."

He nodded.

She studied him. He seemed troubled. "Is something worrying you?"

Jacob took a drink of his coffee, then holding the cup in both hands, he rested his forearms on his thighs. "I've been thinking about my native family. There's been word that the natives are being treated harshly. I need to know what's happening and see if I can find my family."

"Of course."

"I want to travel to Grand Ronde, to the reservation there, to see if that's where they are. And find out if they're all right."

"I understand." Emmalin took another sip of coffee, unsettled over whether it was a good idea. "Will it actually be of help? I've heard that conditions at some reservations are deplorable. If that is the case, wouldn't their circumstances only haunt you?"

"Maybe. But I have to know. Maybe I can do something to help."

Emmalin's heart squeezed. "Of course. When will you go?"

"Today. That is if you don't mind traveling back to Deer Creek without me."

Emmalin was immediately disappointed but tried not to let on. "No. I don't mind. But why leave from here?"

"Grand Ronde is close to the northern coast. It will take less time if I head there from here."

"That makes sense." Emmalin rested her cup in one hand. "I can't pretend I wasn't looking forward to our journey back to Deer Creek."

"I was too, but if I leave from here, the trip will go faster. John and Chauncey know what needs to be done. But I want to get back to work with them on the house as soon as possible." He grinned. "We both want that."

"I most certainly do. How long will you be gone?"

"Two or three weeks, I figure."

"I'm going to miss you." She reached across the space that separated them and took his hand.

❖ ❖ ❖ ❖

Jacob and Emmalin shared a lingering kiss. She wrapped her arms around him and held on tight. Jacob felt a pinch of doubt and guilt. It didn't feel right to leave her even if she was with her father.

"Please be careful. I need you to come home."

"Don't worry. I'll be back soon." He helped Emmalin onto Sassy's back, then mounted Smoke. He turned to Samuel. "Take care of her."

"We'll be fine."

"I'll see you all in Deer Creek in a few weeks. Come on, Henry." The dog pranced around the horse's legs. Jacob lifted the reins and lay them over the side of Smoke's neck, turning the horse northward. They moved along the trail leading up the coast. Jacob took a glance back and waved, then tapped Smoke's sides with his heels, and the horse stepped into a trot.

About midday, Jacob turned onto a trail that cut toward the northeast and away from the coastline. It was less traveled, but well-marked. Jacob remembered taking this route only once before, but he was certain it would lead him to Grand Ronde.

He'd heard the army had used this track to move Indians from the south coast to the reservation at Fort Yamhill. Many died along the way. His ire rose at the thought of people being taken from their homes and herded like animals to federal lands where they had no roots, no homes. Throughout the Indian wars, wrongs had been committed on both sides, but the brutality of the U.S. Army sickened him.

Knowing that negative thinking served no good purpose, he pushed aside such thoughts. Instead, he turned his attention to the beauty of the heavy timbered forest of cedar, pine, and fir. The woodlands were alive with birds and buzzing insects. The sun had risen into the sky and now heated the earth. Sweat traced a line down the back of his neck, attesting to the rising temperature.

When the trail dipped down to a small stream, he pulled Smoke to a stop and dismounted. Henry waded into the water, lapping it up as he went. Smoke stepped into the shallow tributary and buried his nose in the stream. Moving up the creek away from muddied water, Jacob squatted along the bank and scooped up handfuls of water. He drank until satisfied, then splashed his face. He looked up through the trees at patches of blue sky and lifted a prayer to God for the health and welfare of his family. His muscles tightened with anxiety. What would he find? Were they all right?

Jacob led Smoke out of the stream and tied him to a birch tree. He removed a knapsack from the saddle and walked to a cedar where he sat and rested his back against its heavy trunk. Henry dropped into deep grass alongside him. "You hungry, boy?" Jacob stroked the dog's head and scratched him behind the ears, then opened the satchel and took out a piece of deer jerky. He gave it to Henry, who captured it between his paws and tore into it. Jacob fished out another piece, took a bite and leaned back, chewing leisurely. The smoky flavor came alive in his mouth. It had been a good batch. He finished off the jerky, then took out hardtack, giving one to Henry and keeping one for himself.

With the melody of birds echoing about him, Jacob closed his eyes, relishing the breeze that cooled his hot skin. Taking a deep breath, he allowed peace to seep into him.

Through the many months since his family's disappearance, he'd tried not to think about them, but here in the quiet, Mother Blossom's, friendly face filled his mind. He missed her. She'd been kind to him always. His father, Makya, and brother, Songa, had been true to their names. Songa had been strong and taught him how to build the strength of his body and his mind. Makya helped him when he hunted his first eagle. He'd kept three tail feathers from that first hunt, but they had been lost in the fire. An ache tightened in his chest. Jacob had nothing left from that part of his life.

He ate another biscuit, thinking he'd prefer meat. Maybe he'd come across a deer. Even rabbit would be good. He finished eating, then packed up and set out once more.

He met no one on the trail that day or the next. His only companions were the forest wildlife. He'd spotted a cunning bobcat as it leaped into a covey of quail. They flew in all directions, but he came up with one in his mouth and disappeared into the shadows. Jacob didn't bother shooting one. They'd only offer a couple bites of meat—a waste of a bullet.

Heavy mist greeted him on the morning of the fourth day. He set out, hunkered low in the saddle, and huddled deep inside his coat. Careful to keep his hat tipped slightly to one side to keep water from pooling on the brim, he felt optimistic. He was getting close. Henry trotted a few steps ahead of him. All of a sudden, the dog stopped and barked. A man with two boys approached from the opposite direction.

The stranger eyed him suspiciously. Jacob put on what he hoped was a friendly face. "Hello. I'm no threat. Just traveling to Fort Yamhill."

The man relaxed the set of his shoulders. "Morning. It's a wet one, ain't it? Thought I was glad to be done with the heat, but right about now I'd welcome it." He settled back in his saddle. "You have business at the fort? You a soldier?"

"No. Just hoping to see friends of mine."

The man studied him with a question in his eyes. "You've got about a day's travel left. A lot going on there these days."

"Oh?"

"They've been bringing Indians from up north down. And they're building more quarters for soldiers. Some of them are still camped out. But there's plenty of them, so no need to worry about renegades."

"Good to know." Jacob decided it was wiser to play along with what most people feared. No reason to start an unwinnable argument.

"I wish you well." The man gave his horse a light kick and moved past Jacob. The boys followed, barely giving Jacob a glance.

The reality of what waited for him weighed on Jacob. Should he have come at all? The question was answered even before he was done asking. Yes. He had to know.

At dusk the next day, Fort Yamhill came into view. Walls of cut timber stood tall, like soldiers standing shoulder to shoulder. Garret towers sat at each end of the front wall, and a large double gate stood in the center. Were the Indians shut behind those walls?

He approached the gate. A guard stood. "You have business here?"

Jacob wasn't sure what he ought to say. "I have family to see."

The man visibly relaxed his stance. "You'll have to wait till tomorrow. You gotta get permission from the commander, and he won't be available till then."

"I'll just take a few minutes."

"Sorry. No exceptions."

Clearly, he'd get no answers tonight, so he swallowed his disappointment. "Can you suggest a place to stay for the night?"

"Nothing much around here. Might want to set up camp by the river. Just stay to the west of the fort."

Jacob turned Smoke back the way he'd come. Maybe he would find his family tomorrow.

Disturbed in his spirit, Jacob settled down for the night along the riverside. The rain had stopped, and hot muggy air hugged the earth. Biting flies and mosquitoes tormented him while he started a fire. He walked to the river's edge and dipped a coffeepot into the water, then set it in the coals at the edge of the fire. After scooping coffee into the pot, he took out a piece of hardtack with disappointment. He'd not come across any game. Maybe tomorrow.

Henry settled just out of the firelight. He watched Jacob. "Ah, you thought I forgot you." Jacob grinned and took out a piece of jerky, tossing it to the dog. Henry hunkered down and ate it. "Maybe I'll have something better tomorrow."

Jacob put out his bedroll and lay down.

Birds perched within the trees, quietly trilling to one another as the night settled over them. The hoot of an owl was answered by another. Coyotes sang. Weary to the bone, Jacob closed his eyes, thoughts on his family. Was *reservation* just another word for prison?

Chapter Twenty-Seven

An overly ambitious rooster crowed in the early morning darkness. Jacob pulled his blanket up over his shoulder, hoping for more sleep. But it was too late—his mind was awake. He rolled onto his back and looked up into the pre-dawn sky. Stars were few and faint. Birds rustled in the trees and occasionally twittered to one another as they came awake.

He sat up and rested his arms on bent knees. Heaviness sat on his chest. What would he discover today? A dark and menacing presence lurked in the hidden places. Would he learn anything about his family? Would the news be grave?

Henry laid his head on Jacob's thigh. "How you doing, boy?" Jacob scratched the dog behind the ears, thankful for his company. With a heavy sigh, he pushed to his feet. "God be with me," he spoke into the darkness.

After a breakfast of coffee and hardtack, it was time to go. Soft light touched the sky and illuminated puffs of clouds. He scanned the hillside where the post stood. Were Indians locked behind its walls? Jacob set off for the fort on foot. He approached what looked like the main gate where two soldiers stood guard.

One stepped forward. "State your purpose."

Jacob responded boldly, "I have family here."

The soldier raised a questioning eyebrow. "You'll need to speak to the base commander. His accommodation is marked. It'll be to your left." He eyed Henry. "The dog will have to stay out."

Jacob fought to dampen down his frustration and turned to Henry. "You stay. I'll be back soon."

Henry sat and stared at Jacob.

"Stay."

The soldier opened the gate.

Jacob gave him a nod and walked through into the interior. His nerves hummed. Keeping his spine straight, he took long strides as he walked toward the commander's office. He spotted a building with a cross at its peak and assumed it was the fort's church. What influence did the chaplain have over the men who lived and worked here? More importantly, what influence did God have on them?

The quarters were two long structures standing side-by-side. The base was mostly quiet. A few men wandered about, most headed into what he imagined was the dining hall. He turned to the commander's office and stopped in front of a wooden door and knocked.

"Come in," a gravelly voice responded from inside.

Uncertain what to expect, Jacob opened the door. He stepped into a sparsely furnished room where only a single small window allowed in light. A man who looked to be in his forties sat behind a well-worn desk. He was dressed in traditional army blues. His hat hung from a post on the wall beside the door. "I'm Captain Levenger."

"Jacob."

"What can I do for you?"

Jacob hadn't been sure what he would say. Most people didn't understand the idea of a white man and Indians being family. "I want to check to see if my native...family is living here on the reservation."

The captain stared at him, suspicion in his eyes. "You Indian?"

"No." Jacob didn't trust the man and said simply, "I used to live with a band, and I think they might be here."

"We have a lot of Indians here from all over the territory. Have a seat." He motioned toward the only chair in the room, then leaned back and rested the heels of his boots on the desk. "Don't know why you'd come looking for them." He studied Jacob, a question on his face.

Jacob lowered himself into the chair. "As I said, I used to live with them. Years ago, my parents were missionaries, and after they died, the local tribe took me in."

"Highly unusual."

"Yes, sir." If Jacob was going to get any help from this man, he needed to be respectful, but he couldn't refrain from adding, "I owe them my life."

"In the beginning, we tried to keep them in their tribal groups, but they had a mind of their own. It'll be tough to point out your...family." He took a pipe off a shelf, packed in some tobacco, and struck a match to light it. Holding the tiny flame to the pipe, he drew on it, then let out a puff of smoke. He took another draft. "Might want to check down by the river, east of here. And there are a lot of them living up on the tree line. I'll have one of my men go with you. He might know who is living where."

Jacob didn't like the idea of having a soldier with him. It would only make this place feel more like a prison. "I'm sure I can find them, if they're here."

"How can I know to trust you?"

Jacob met the captain's gaze. "I'm just a simple man. Not looking for any trouble."

Measuring Jacob, the captain took another puff off his pipe. "Go ahead and have a look."

Jacob pushed out of the chair and started toward the door, then stopped and faced Captain Levenger. "If they live on their own here, why couldn't they remain on their own lands?"

The commander smirked. "They need us to watch out for them, to keep them from stirring up trouble. And they're not on their own. The government takes care of them—food, clothing, medical care, schooling. We're teaching them how to be decent Americans."

Immediately anger rose up within Jacob. Decent Americans? He wanted to punch the smug look off Levenger. "They don't need anyone to teach them that." Before he gave in to the baser part of himself, he turned and walked out.

His stomach churned. The government had stripped away the native's honor. They were dependent, and in another generation, they would forget who they were.

The reservation was large. Jacob returned to camp, saddled Smoke, and, with Henry padding along beside him, he followed the river. Groups of natives eyed him warily. Most lived in lodges made of animal hides. It wasn't what his people had used before, but the shelters seemed adequate. But what did they do against animal attacks? They had no weapons to defend themselves. He felt ill as his mind mulled over the disheartening circumstances.

Jacob searched both sides of the river but found no sign of his mother or father. With the sun rising higher into the sky and the air heating up, he moved past the walls of the fort and spotted several wickiups along the tree line. Many were grouped together, but some stood on their own. It didn't look like the village life his people had once known.

He spotted a group of children who were taking turns throwing a stick, as one would a spear. After each toss, they measured to see who had thrown the farthest. It was an age-old test that helped prepare them to become hunters. Now that seemed highly unlikely, and the wretchedness of their circumstances grew heavier on his heart.

When he rode past, the children stopped the game and stared at him. He smiled, but none smiled back or waved. He didn't recognize any from the Umpqua. He couldn't help but notice that they all looked thin, too thin.

He headed toward a small group of wikiups partially hidden within the trees. As he got closer, he recognized two of the children. He tipped his hat to them, then using their native tongue, he said, "Hello. It is me, Adahy. Remember, the one who Lives in the Woods."

One of the girls smiled. "Adahy! Adahy!"

The other said, "You have come!"

"Do you know where my mother is?"

The little girl turned and pointed toward one of the wikiups. "There."

"Thank you." Exhilarated, he nudged Smoke forward. His family was here.

When he approached, he recognized several of the natives and greeted each warmly, but there were no smiles from them. It was as if all joy had been stripped away.

At the last lodge, he saw Mother Blossom. He stopped and dismounted. She was mixing what looked like cornmeal in a wooden bowl. "Mother."

She glanced up, but the sun was at his back, and there was no recognition in her eyes. She squinted and shaded her brow with her hands. "Who is it?"

"Me. Jacob…Adahy." The name seemed to stick in his throat.

She smiled and her eyes came alive, then she leaped to her feet. "Adahy!" She hurried to Jacob and pulled him into her arms, holding him tightly. "My son."

A wave of joy swept through him, and he held her tightly. She was no longer plump; he could feel protruding bones. "I have missed you." Jacob hadn't spoken the native tongue in months. Now, wrapped in Mother Blossom's embrace, the Umpqua language came to him as easily as breathing. "When I went to your camp in the forest and discovered you were gone, I didn't know where you were or what had become of you. But it is as I feared."

She stepped back and looked up into his face. Her eyes looked shadowed and weary. "There was no way to tell you. We had no time. Now we are here. It is not our home. It will never be our home." She could not disguise the bitterness that mingled with her sorrow.

"Someday you will return to the Umpqua."

"We pray to the Great Father for such a thing." She moved back toward her house. "Are you hungry?"

"Yes. I am."

"Let us eat and we will talk."

Jacob sat. Others greeted him. Many of the group he'd known on the North Umpqua were not here. His mother gave him something similar to corn bread. He took a bite and chewed, afraid to ask the question foremost on his mind. Finally, he found the courage. "Where is my father and my brother?"

His mother glanced at a group of children sitting in the shade of a tree, then looked straight at him. "Your father is gone. He died from a disease of the lungs. This place is good at taking lives."

Jacob felt as if someone had hit him in the chest. Dead?

"And your brother refused to let them take him. He escaped into the mountains. If you go there, you might find him. But I do not think he will let himself be found."

She looked about. "Many have died. And more will follow."

The doorway flap rustled, and Wild Dove stepped inside. "Adahy." She smiled shyly. "It is good to see you."

Her appearance had changed greatly. Jacob struggled to disguise his shock. She looked wan, tired, and painfully thin. The fire that once danced in her eyes had been extinguished. "I am glad to see you," Jacob said. "Please come and eat with us."

"No. I must go to the fort. I have work there."

"All right. I'll see you again?"

"Maybe. Only God knows such things." She gave a slight bow and moved off.

Jacob leaned toward his mother. "What's wrong? What's happened to her? To everyone?"

His mother closed her eyes for a moment. "They have taken everything from us. Our ways are no more. We are not even allowed to speak our language."

Fury ignited inside Jacob.

They took their land! Their freedom! And their culture too? Hatred grew. The white man had done this. And then he remembered...he was white. The woman he loved was white. And his closest friends were white. Were they the enemy? Was he?

He scooted closer to his mother and draped an arm over her shoulders. "I'm sorry. I am one of them."

"You are not." She pressed her hand against his chest. "In here, you are one of us."

"It was the army. The United States government who did this."

"Jacob." His mother's voice was gentle. "I see the anger inside of you. You must release it, or it will grow, and you will learn to hate. Hatred destroys people."

He was so consumed by rage, Jacob barely heard her.

She released a heavy sigh and clasped her hands in front of her. "The children don't know what they have lost. They are hungry and go to the white man's school, but they play and think they have a future." She glanced around. "There is no future for them. And Wild Dove...I fear for her. She is beautiful. The soldiers like her. But not in the right way."

Jacob gritted his teeth. "No one can touch her." Even as he said the words, he knew they were preposterous. He had no power here.

Blossom pressed her hand on his arm. "For now, there is one soldier who protects her, but if he leaves..."

"I won't allow this. You and Wild Dove will come with me. Come to my home."

Blossom shook her head. "The soldiers watch us all the time. And those who try to leave are dragged back."

Her eyes were haunted with images Jacob could only imagine.

"I think about your brother, and it is sad that I hope I will never see him again." She turned an anguished look on Jacob. "You go. You live your life. Remember what you shared with us. You are free as you should be. I will think of you and my heart will be glad as I remember the happy days."

"I can't walk away. I won't."

"You think there is a choice?" She squeezed his arm. "You have no choice, Jacob."

He met her eyes. Was she right? There must be something he could do.

"I'll return to Deer Creek, but I will be back. I won't leave you here like this."

Chapter Twenty-Eight

Emmalin glanced out the window, hoping to see Jacob on the street. He should be back by now, but there had been no sign of him. Had he found his family? May the Lord protect them all.

She turned her attention back to the mail order catalog and thumbed through the pages. It wasn't the same as strolling the streets of Philadelphia and visiting shops in search of gifts, but it was still fun. Since receiving her inheritance, she'd managed her funds conservatively, but she'd decided to splurge on Christmas gifts. The holiday was still months away, but it was time to begin shopping. Placing and receiving orders was a slow process.

She spotted a nice-looking cast-iron cookstove. It was big with four burners and a warming plate, large wood box, and a full-sized oven with two warming shelves. Margaret needed a new stove. The one at the house was far too small and well worn. This one would be perfect.

Emmalin wrote down all the information, including the cost, and moved on. Her father desperately needed a more modern harvester, especially now that he'd decided to add an additional field plus the prune orchard. She tapped her finger on the counter as she studied the options.

The door opened and Emmalin looked up. Jacob! She could hardly believe it. He looked weary, but when he saw her his eyes brightened and he smiled.

"Jacob!" She hurried to him and threw her arms about him. "Thank the Lord! You're home! You've been gone so long I was beginning to worry."

"No need." Jacob held her close and rested his cheek on the top of her head. "It feels good to hold you."

"I missed you so." Emmalin forced herself to release him and stepped back so she could look into his face. She rose onto her tiptoes and kissed him. "I love you."

Jacob kissed her back. "I love you too."

They embraced again, then Emmalin asked, "Can I get you something to eat or drink?"

Jacob removed his hat, placing it on the table as he sat.

"Maybe a glass of water and a cup of coffee?"

Emmalin moved to the back of the store. "Was it a difficult journey?" She filled a glass of water from the hand pump at the sink.

"Just long."

She returned to him with the water. "You look so tired."

"I am."

"I have a few doughnuts from the café."

"Sounds good."

"I'll get them with your coffee." Emmalin fetched his refreshments and hurried back, eager to hear what he'd learned.

She settled in a chair across from Jacob. After adding sugar to her coffee and serving them each a sweet, she sat back and admired him. Even in his present exhausted state, he was a handsome man with his deep brown hair, hazel eyes, and lips that looked like they might smile at any moment. She was certain she'd never tire of looking at him.

He spooned out sugar and stirred it into his cup, then glanced at her. "You're looking playful. What is it?"

"What, I can't admire you?"

His face flushed pink. "I can't be much to look at right now, covered in days of trail dust."

"Dirt or not, there is much to regard," Emmalin teased.

He leaned on his forearms and gazed at her. "You bring out the best in me. And being here sitting across from you is just what I've been needing."

Emmalin lay a hand over his. "Without you, the days seemed interminably long."

"Well, I'm back now."

Emmalin took a drink of coffee. "Tell me what happened at Grand Ronde."

His expression darkened. "It wasn't what I expected. I'm not even sure what I did expect. But I found my mother. Blossom."

"That's wonderful news!"

"It was good to see her." He stared down into his cup, anguish showing on his face. "But my father is dead, and my brother ran off into the mountains."

Emmalin covered her mouth. "Oh, Jacob, I'm so sorry."

"Conditions there are bad. The government has stolen the heart of the people. They have no breadth of life. They are just existing."

Emmalin's heart hurt for Jacob and his family. If only there were something she could do to ease the suffering.

"There are a lot of different native groups from all over the territory living at the fort. Every one of them has had their lives stolen. They live off the government. They don't hunt and can't pass on the old ways. They're not even allowed to speak their own languages."

Emmalin reached for his hand and squeezed it gently. "That's awful. Will they be able to leave soon?"

He looked at her, his eyes bleak. "They won't be leaving. It's prison. Anyone who escapes gets hunted down and forced back."

"Is there nothing to be done?"

"I'm told not, but I can't leave them there. I have to get them out somehow."

Alarm shook within Emmalin. "But how? The army would only re-arrest them. And you'll be in trouble."

"I need time to think, to figure it out. I'll come up with something. And I don't want you worrying about it." He took a sip of coffee then a bite of the doughnut. "What have you been doing while I was gone?"

Emmalin was glad to move on to another topic. She hoped Jacob could release this sorrow and go on with his life. "Actually, I've been Christmas shopping."

"Already?"

"It can take months to get some items. And this year I want to do something special for the people I love."

"Oh, you do? Please don't spend a lot on me."

"I have more money than I can spend, so please give me this pleasure."

His lips twitched. "Us living in our own place by Christmas is all I need."

"Do you think it's possible?"

"Maybe." He leaned back in his chair. "There's still a lot of work to do. And I need to work for wages as well."

"I can't wait to order items for the house. But whether it's completed or not, just knowing it is going to happen is enough for me."

"How are Samuel and Margaret getting on?"

"They're happy. Very happy. I never knew my father could be so romantic. It's almost embarrassing to be around them. I imagine they would prefer that I not be sharing the house right now."

He chuckled.

Emmalin cut off a bite of her doughnut and poked it with a fork. "Margaret is selling her home."

"That makes sense."

"It's a fine house with good land for gardening and for livestock."

"With all the settlers moving into the territory, she shouldn't have any trouble finding a buyer."

"That's what I was thinking." Emmalin knew better than to speak her next thought but ignored the caution. "Perhaps we should consider purchasing it. After all, it is completed, which means we could get married right away. And it's a good solid home—and with your injury, I know the work is difficult for you."

Jacob looked into his cup, then at Emmalin. "I know building the cabin is more work, but I've learned that just because something's difficult isn't reason to quit. Where would I be if I'd done that?"

"Of course, but I thought that maybe just for a while."

"A temporary place? Do you really think that is best?"

"Maybe not, but it would allow us to begin our life together sooner."

"I like that idea." He took both her hands in his. "But it really isn't sensible to spend all that money."

The money, of course. Her money wasn't his, and he needed to be the one who provided for them. All of her life, money had been available to

Emmalin. There had never been a need to be careful with it, except after her uncle died, and she didn't yet know of her inheritance.

She kissed the back of his hand. "Of course. You're right. I'm simply being impatient." She'd known his agreeing to such an idea was a remote possibility, but she had to try. Even though his was the wiser choice, it created worry about whether he would ever accept her wealth.

"Jacob, do you think there is something we can do for the natives? I have so much, and they have so little."

He turned pensive. "They need just about everything, and with winter coming on, blankets and warm clothing will be really important."

"Wonderful! I'll put a list together and begin ordering items. Then we'll make a trip up."

"All right." Jacob nodded, but his tone sounded tentative. "You know that will keep me away from work on the house. It will mean another delay for our wedding."

Emmalin hadn't thought of that, but how could she be so small-minded as to put her wedding date ahead of the welfare of the natives? "They are more important. I can wait a bit longer."

"With that and everything else that's happened, it will be spring before the house is ready."

Emmalin nodded.

"But early spring." He lifted a strand of hair off her face. "I figured I'd stay in town tonight and get a good sleep, then head out to the cabin tomorrow."

"Margaret and I are going to start designing my wedding gown tomorrow." She smiled. "And make plans for the wedding."

"You'll be a beautiful bride. I can't wait for that day." He leaned across the table and kissed her gently. "Having you as my wife sooner could almost convince me to buy Margaret's house." He lifted his brows. "Almost."

Trying to maintain a good humor, Emmalin gave him a soft slap across his nose with her napkin. "Oh, you."

❖◦❖◦❖◦❖◦❖◦❖◦❖

The following day, Emmalin would have liked joining Jacob, but she was excited about wedding plans. And she'd decided to create her gown, with Margaret's help of course. The song, "Praise Him, Praise Him" had been dancing through her mind all morning. She'd been waiting for Margaret, but she still hadn't shown up, and Emmalin didn't want to wait so she hurried to the café, singing the tune, which accompanied her as she stepped inside the establishment. She didn't see Margaret. "Hello. Are you ready?"

Margaret stepped out of the kitchen. "Just finished up the breakfast dishes. And I'm closed the rest of the morning." She removed her apron and hung it on a hook on the wall. "I can't wait to see the fabric."

"It arrived just two days ago. I've been dying to show you." Emmalin gave Margaret a quick hug. "You were gone before I got up this morning."

"If I wanted to take time off today, I had to do my baking early. And your father came in to make a delivery, so I rode along with him." She smiled blissfully. "I love traveling into town together when the day is just beginning." She clasped her hands in front of her. "I never thought I'd feel this way about a man again. I love him so."

Emmalin laughed. "I'm happy for you both."

"Now it's time to focus on you and Jacob." Margaret hooked her arm through Emmalin's. "We have a lot to do in the weeks to come. I guess we'd best get to it."

When they stepped into the mercantile, Emmalin could barely quiet her excitement. She'd looked at the fabric when it first arrived but had forced herself to save another viewing until Margaret could join her.

She'd kept the trunk in the back of the store. "I do hope you like it."

"I have no doubt. You have impeccable taste."

Emmalin lifted the lid of the trunk. White satin fabric nearly shimmered. She held it up.

"Oh my, that is exquisite." Margaret touched the material, then gently grasped it, and held it out in the light.

"I was thinking this would be perfect for the body of the gown."

"Oh yes."

"And then…" Emmalin handed the satin to Margaret and retrieved a piece of lace. "Do you think this would work well for an overlay and for the sleeves?"

"Absolutely. It is so delicate. We could also use this for your veil. If there's enough fabric."

"That's exactly what I was thinking. I ordered extra."

Emmalin held the fabric against her body. It was beginning to feel real. She and Jacob were truly going to be married. "You know I don't have the skills and will have to rely on you a great deal."

"I am pleased to do it." Margaret felt the lace. "Did this come from back east? I don't believe I've ever seen this fine a quality of fabric."

"Yes. I sent for this months ago, before Jacob was injured." She pressed the lace against her chest, feeling emotion well up. "I was so afraid I'd never have use of a gown."

"It all turned out just as it should." Margaret refolded the lace and returned it to the trunk. "Do you have a pattern?"

"I do. It arrived a few weeks ago. I want to make changes, but I'm sure you know how to do that." She moved to a cabinet, opened a drawer, and lifted out a packet and handed it to Margaret.

She studied the picture on the front of the envelope. "This is lovely. And perfect for your figure." She turned the package over and read the information. "We'll need to measure you and then lay this out on your fabric. Then we can pin it on you to make sure it fits exactly right." She looked about. "Hmm. Where should we do this? I'm not sure this is the place. It would be a disaster if Jacob were to come in and see. And there is always some sort of shipment coming and going."

"We don't need to worry about Jacob today. He's out at the property. But I do agree, we need to find a place to do the sewing and fittings."

"I don't see why we can't use my house. It's empty and no one goes out there. I don't need to put it up for sale right away. I haven't even moved most of my things over yet."

"It would be perfect." Emmalin folded the satin fabric and returned it to the trunk. A smidge of disappointment settled over her. "I was thinking that perhaps Jacob and I could buy your home."

Margaret covered a laugh with her hand. "Jacob? In my house?"

"I knew it wasn't the perfect solution, but that way we wouldn't have to wait so long to get married. He thinks we should wait."

"I would love to have you two so close by." She pressed a hand over Emmalin's. "But Jacob wouldn't be happy there."

"Of course I know that, but I told myself, nothing ventured nothing gained." Emmalin found straight pins in the cabinet drawer.

"How did his trip to Grand Ronde go?"

"He found his mother and some of the group from upriver, but his father died, and his brother escaped."

"What terrible news for Jacob."

"Jacob said conditions are deplorable. We've decided to get some needed items up to them and the poor souls who are living there."

"That sounds like a fine idea."

"Yes. But it means delaying the wedding again."

"The day will come."

"Jacob is determined to rescue his mother from the reservation."

The words felt like a bomb going off in the room.

"Isn't that dangerous? I mean, couldn't he get into trouble with the law, maybe even go to prison?"

"I don't know. I hope not. He is highly disturbed about what he saw, and he's determined to do something about Blossom's situation. He's planning to bring her here." She closed the lid of the trunk. "I'm afraid something terrible might happen."

"I'm sure Jacob will use caution. He's not a foolish man."

"I know, but ever since he told me, I've been feeling anxious. Fear is like a nemesis to me. I struggle with it all the time."

"We all do, dear. Just don't let it control you." She offered an encouraging smile. "We can trust the Lord with all our worries."

Emmalin knew in her head that she could trust God, but it was the heart she struggled with. And there was something more than Jacob's safety that was concerning her. Jacob planned to build a cabin for Blossom on their property. What would that be like, having her so close by?

Blossom didn't approve of her. She'd made it clear she wanted Jacob to marry Wild Dove. The idea of having her as part of their life felt threatening.

And where was Wild Dove? Was she with Blossom? Jacob hadn't mentioned her, and Emmalin was afraid to ask.

Chapter Twenty-Nine

The summer season had stretched into October. The good weather turned out to be a blessing as Jacob had decided he must get supplies to the reservation before winter set in. With a bit of coaxing, Emmalin convinced him to allow her to join him. Margaret went along to help and as a chaperone to keep any gossip under control. Though nervous about what she would find at Grand Ronde, Emmalin needed to be of help.

What she'd discovered, hunger and distress, assured her she'd made the right decision. The natives were in great need. Plus, the time spent with Blossom and Wild Dove, though a bit awkward, was a first step in building a friendship between Emmalin and the two women.

With winter weather, it was too distant to make a Christmas trip with gifts for the children, like she had the previous year, but spring might work out well. Perhaps she and Jacob could do that following their wedding and then go on to Oregon City for a honeymoon stay.

They celebrated Emmalin's twenty-fourth birthday on the trip back to Deer Creek. She enjoyed the simple celebration more than she'd expected, feeling less like a spinster with her marriage approaching.

They reached home in plenty of time for the holidays. When family and friends had gathered for Thanksgiving, they'd hoped they might be surprised by an early snowfall, but the holiday had been unusually warm. The weather, however, did not place a damper on the festivities. It had been a grand day with good food, good conversation, and even a game of chess, which Emmalin was rather inept at, but now felt she'd gained some proficiency.

Emmalin awakened to the sound of wind whistling beneath the eaves. She pushed up on one elbow and gazed at the window. The light seemed muted. She climbed out of bed and, with cold spiking into her feet, she padded to the window. Low hanging clouds scuttled across a gray sky. She shivered. Winter had finally rolled into the valley.

Emmalin moved away from the window. There was much to do. She dressed hurriedly and went to the kitchen. The smell of brewing coffee perked up her appetite.

Margaret gave her a cheery smile. "Good morning."

"Good morning." Emmalin covered a yawn. "I had a terrible time waking up. The weather has changed dramatically."

"It's about time. I was a bit disappointed with our Thanksgiving weather—no frost, no snow. But I think that's about to change." Margaret glanced out the window. "I'm beginning to feel the excitement of the season."

Emmalin poured a cup of coffee. "Do you think we'll get snow today?"

"Almost certain of it. But hopefully not this morning. I was counting on doing another fitting for your gown."

A bubble of happiness welled up inside Emmalin. "That would be lovely." She took another look at the clouds. "If it doesn't snow, we might get caught in the rain."

"It wouldn't be the first time." Margaret chuckled. "If we waited for clear weather to do what needed doing, we'd never get anything done."

"That's true. When would you like to leave?"

"Right after breakfast."

"That sounds perfect." Emmalin loved their time together, and with each fitting, the wedding felt closer. She would soon be Mrs. Landon. The thrill of it rolled through her, and she caught a momentary glimpse of herself in the role of wife.

The women shared a simple breakfast of hot oatmeal then cleaned up the kitchen in something of a hurry. As they set off in the wagon, Emmalin bundled deeper into her wrap, scanning the clouds as they drove. "They do have the look of snow in them."

"December weather."

"It's time to get a Christmas tree put up at the store. Customers have been asking about it. I saved the decorations donated by everyone last year, so I can't wait to get started."

"You had such a beautiful tree. And the project for the native children was so popular people are remembering. It made the holiday more cheerful."

"I loved it all. It's hard to believe there are no longer local natives. It doesn't seem right."

"It's not."

"I wish we could make another trip to the reservation with gifts for the children, but it would be foolish with the unpredictable weather."

Margaret clicked her tongue and slapped the reins. The horses picked up their pace. "Has Jacob said any more about rescuing his mother?"

"No. And I'm ashamed to say I'm thanking the Lord for that." Emmalin watched a rain shower move toward them. "They are living in wretched conditions, but I don't want Jacob to put himself in danger. He could get into terrible trouble." Emmalin opened her umbrella and held it so it would protect her and Margaret. "Do you think there is any chance the government will allow natives to return home?"

"I doubt it. After all, there are treaties, and the reservation lands have been given to the Indians. I heard they intend to keep them on the reservations indefinitely."

"Oh dear." Emmalin felt an aching weight in her middle. "I wish none of it would have happened—not the attacks on the Indians or their retribution toward the whites. It's all so horrible."

Margaret patted Emmalin's thigh. "It is. But there's nothing we can do about it. It's in the Lord's hands."

"I know you're right, but it's all so wrong. I pray God will bring justice."

"He will, one day. I'm sure of it. But for now, it's out of our hands. All we can do is pray and trust God."

Emmalin didn't quite disagree with Margaret, but somehow her answer seemed rather trite. While trusting God was always wise, sometimes circumstances required action.

By the time they reached Margaret's house, Emmalin was chilled to the bone, and there was no warm fire to greet them. The two went to work immediately building a fire to ward off the frigid cold. Soon wood in the hearth popped and crackled, and coffee was brewing. Gradually the house warmed up.

Margaret helped Emmalin into the gown. "This is going to be beautiful."

"Can I look in the mirror?"

"Not yet."

"When?"

"After this fitting, I'll complete the modifications and then you can see. You will be able to request any changes you like."

"I'm sure it will be perfect." Emmalin looked down at the white satin and pressed it with her hand. "I can't wait to wear this and walk down the aisle in the church."

"It's going to be wonderful." Margaret chuckled and stepped back to study the fit. "It's truly going to be the loveliest gown I've ever seen. And it will be worn by the prettiest stepdaughter I've ever had." Margaret winked at Emmalin.

Emmalin hugged herself. "If only Jacob and I were getting married sooner. There have been so many delays. Spring seems far away."

"It does, but you and Jacob have done your best and the time away was important." She offered a compassionate smile. "The weeks will pass quickly. And your special day will be here before you know it."

By the time they set out for home, Emmalin's heart was full, and waiting to become Jacob's wife felt even more difficult. They'd no sooner left Margaret's house when snow started coming down. "I'm glad we're not far from home."

Emmalin tried to stay warm, but her cloak wasn't enough protection and she shivered. Margaret studied her. "Are you all right, dear?"

"Yes. Fine. Just cold."

"It hasn't been all that long since your illness. And I worry some about your robustness."

"Truly, I'm fine." Emmalin smiled. "There's no need to worry."

With a nod, Margaret turned her attention back to the horses.

When the house came into sight, Emmalin breathed a sigh of relief. Yet, her thoughts were with Jacob. "I hate to think of Jacob being out in this weather with only a tent to protect him. The house isn't complete enough to be a proper shelter."

"How much longer do you think before it's completed?"

"He says we won't likely be able to move in until March."

"A spring wedding will be perfect."

"I think so too." Emmalin hugged Margaret's arm. "And thank you so much for my dress."

"I didn't do it alone."

"You've done most of it."

Margaret smiled. "You chose the fabric, which is sublime, and made design decisions that make your dress extra special. And you've done a fair share of sewing." She leaned against Emmalin. "You're going to be a beautiful bride."

Emmalin closed her eyes, imagining the scene at the church—Jacob standing at the front of the sanctuary...waiting for her as she walked down the aisle. "It will be wonderful."

By the time they reached the house, the winds had picked up, snow swirled and had started piling up against the house. Would Jacob remain at the cabin? As much as Emmalin hated the idea of him riding out the storm in a tent, she was more concerned about him traveling in this terrible weather.

She stood at the window and watched the snow fall and deepen, transforming the outdoor world into a white dreamland. She warmed inside, thinking about how special Christmas would be this year. She was glad she'd ordered the gifts months early because they had all arrived. It would be such fun to watch the people she loved discover their presents on Christmas morning.

A figure emerged out of the swirling white. Jacob! Emmalin clapped her hands together and rushed to the door.

She threw it open and stepped onto the covered porch. "Jacob!"

He peered at her from beneath the brim of his hat. "Looks like winter finally got here." He dismounted.

Emmalin hurried down the steps, and, in spite of the icy snow blanketing his coat, she captured him in a hug. "I'm so happy to see you."

Henry tromped up the steps and onto the porch where he immediately shook the wetness off his coat.

Jacob dropped a kiss on Emmalin's forehead. "When the weather started to change, I thought it better to be here, than being stuck up there in that tent."

"How wonderful it will be when the cabin is finished, and we can enjoy a winter storm there together."

"On my way back, I saw a couple of nice trees that should do well for Christmas. We could put one of them in the store like you did last year. And the other one would look nice here."

"I can't wait to see them."

"Maybe, if the weather clears, we can go out tomorrow and cut them?"

"I'd love that." Emmalin circled her arm into his. "You must be hungry. Dinner is nearly ready."

"Sounds good. Let me put Smoke away and then I'll be in."

⁕⁕⁕

That evening, Emmalin felt content and convinced all in life was just as it should be. She was tucked safely inside her father's home, protected from the bitter cold of winter. A fire burned warm and bright indoors. And she was surrounded by those she loved most. The days to come could be nothing less than delightful. And the wedding was getting closer; she didn't have long to wait.

Jacob stayed over, sleeping on the floor of the cabin. He assured Emmalin he didn't mind. She did her best to make the floor more comfortable by creating a bed of quilts.

They lingered in front of the fire for as long as was proper, then Emmalin reluctantly went to her room. She stood at the door for a moment. "Good night."

"Good night, Emmalin." His tone was warm with devotion.

"I love you."

"I'll hang on to that tonight. It will help me sleep." He smiled at her. "I love you too."

She closed the door softly and changed into her nightgown. She blew out the candle and burrowed beneath her blankets. It was cold with the door closed. But she didn't mind. Her thoughts were with Jacob. He was so close. Soon he would be her husband. Snuggling deeper into her bedding, thankfulness filled her. She couldn't imagine a better man for her and marveled at how God had brought them together. The love she felt for him was so powerful, it felt like it would consume her. She rolled onto her back, tucked the blanket up under her chin and gazed at the ceiling and wondered if he was awake too, thinking of her.

Anxiety intruded on her thoughts. Life could be marvelous, or it could be terrifying. There was much that couldn't be counted on. The wilderness outside of town was vast enough to swallow a person up like the sea. And hidden there were all kinds of dangers, and many unknowns she and Jacob would face. She bunched more of the quilt up around her neck. *Father, help us navigate this new life. Protect us.*

In spite of the dark thoughts that had washed over Emmalin before sleep, she woke with a sense of well-being. It was lovely to waken in the morning and know that Jacob was there.

When she emerged from her room, he sat at the table with her father and greeted her with a smile. "It's a perfect day to cut a tree. The sun is bright, and the world is white."

"Wonderful." She looked at her father and Margaret. "Would you two care to join us?"

"I wish I could," Margaret said. "But I've got a terrible amount of baking to do today."

"And I have to stock shelves." Her father set down his cup. "I'd better get to it. The trip into town is going to be more of a challenge today."

"I'll ride in with you." Margaret set her dishes in the sink.

"Don't worry about those," Emmalin said. "I'll take care of them."

"You're such a dear. Thank you."

While Emmalin washed and dried the dishes, Jacob had gone out to ready the horses. When she saw him approaching the house, horses following, she hurried to finish. After kicking his boots free of snow, Jacob hurried up the steps and opened the door, a burst of cold air sweeping inside. "All set," he announced.

"Nearly done." Emmalin set a cup in the cupboard, wiped her hands dry on a dish towel, and then laid it on the counter. She pulled on her coat, put on a hat, and snugged on a pair of gloves. "Is it very cold?"

"Freezing."

The frigid air didn't bother Emmalin. She was dressed for it, and the day was gloriously beautiful.

When they set out, Emmalin was impressed by the overnight transformation. Pillows of snow glistened in the sunlight, while evergreens dressed in white stood like watchmen of the wilderness. "I've never done anything like this. When I lived in Philadelphia, my uncle always went out and purchased a tree."

Jacob laughed. "I can't imagine that."

"This is much more fun, but through the years, we did have many lovely trees. Of course, I missed out on something as exhilarating as this." Sassy tossed her head and chewed on the bit. "Thank you for including me." Emmalin couldn't remember ever feeling happier. "I never knew life could be so exhilarating."

"And it's going to get better." Jacob grinned.

Emmalin cast him a smile. "I believe you're right."

Jacob tapped Smoke with his heels. He headed off the trail, Smoke plunging into deep snow and Henry following in the horse's tracks.

Slightly unnerved, Emmalin kept going. She hadn't ridden in these kinds of conditions before. Was she in any danger? She couldn't imagine Jacob putting her at risk, and Sassy wasn't struggling.

"There they are."

Emmalin spotted the trees. "They're perfect."

Jacob leaned forward, and Smoke charged toward one of the trees. Emmalin tried to keep up.

He beat her there and jumped off Smoke, then helped her dismount. Jacob held her as she slid from the saddle, and, when Emmalin's feet touched the ground, he kept his arms around her and gazed down at her. "The cold makes you look even more beautiful." He kissed her tenderly.

Emmalin quivered inside. "It's happiness you see. I am absolutely bliss-ful."

"I'm not sure if men are blissful, but if they are then that's what I am." He kissed her again, then lifted her just slightly and set her down away from her horse. "Now then, would you like to learn how to cut a tree?"

"Yes. I would."

Jacob pulled a small axe out of the saddle pack and tromped toward one of the trees. After shaking the snow from its limbs, he went to work and had it down in a matter of minutes. "See, not hard at all." He handed the hatchet to her. "Your turn."

They moved to the other tree, and Jacob shook the snow out of it.

Emmalin had never used an axe for anything except to cut firewood on occasion.

"I'll hold it while you chop."

Using both hands, Emmalin tried to swing the axe.

"No. That won't work." Jacob showed her how to hold it with one hand.

She tried again. Her first swing was weak, and she barely nicked the tree.

"Try again with a little more force."

She took another swing and this time managed to cut out a good bite. It was thrilling. Such a small thing, and yet it mattered. Again and again, she chopped, and finally the tree came down. "I did it!" she cheered.

Jacob laughed. "And now we have a perfect tree for the house and one for the store. I think your father and Margaret will like these."

"Oh yes. At least Margaret. I don't know that my father cares all that much."

Emmalin was suddenly struck by the importance of the moment. She spoke in a tone of wonderment. "Jacob, it's our first Christmas tree that we've obtained together." She imagined all the Christmases yet to come and her eyes teared. She swiped away the moisture. "It must seem silly to you, but—"

"No. It's not silly. It's the beginning of our future. How could that be silly?"

Chapter Thirty

Emmalin held a hand-blown glass ball up to the light. It glistened. It was one her mother had brought home from an overseas trip. Emmalin hung it on the tree in the store window display. It was the last of the ornaments. She'd always loved decorating the tree with her mother. Sometimes Uncle Jonathon had joined them, though he usually watched from his leather chair. Heaviness of spirit pressed down on Emmalin. She missed her mother and her uncle. If only they could share the holidays with her. Emmalin was pretty sure they would enjoy an Oregon Christmas. And they would be so pleased to see how marvelous life had turned out for her.

She stepped back and admired the tree. All it needed now was a topper. She had a lovely Bethlehem star that Charity had donated, but she'd have to wait for her father to return from a delivery to help her with it. With Christmas only a few days away, he'd been busy transporting merchandise and food.

Her insides quivered with excitement. This year would be extra special, what with Margaret officially part of the family and Jacob soon to become her husband. She had splurged on gifts and wasn't about to feel guilty about any of them.

Keeping them a secret had been a challenge. Her father's harvester and Margaret's new stove were both hidden at Charity's house. Her brothers had offered to help deliver them the day before Christmas. After that,

Emmalin would have to keep everyone out of the barn until Christmas morning. Jacob's new rifle and clothing were already wrapped and ready to put under the tree. Tomorrow she planned to take Charity's gift out to her. She'd found an exquisite day dress. It was a deep blue with a moire skirt and jacket and a white silk blouse. It would be suitable for a day reception or even a special evening event. Emmalin could barely wait to see her in it. She was sure Charity would be surprised and pleased. And with any luck, Pastor Miller would see her in a new light when she wore it.

The door opened along with a gust of cold winter air and pulled Emmalin out of her reverie. Jacob stepped into the store.

"What a wonderful surprise!" She hugged him. "I didn't expect to see you today."

"I needed a few things, more nails and some bracing for the windows." He continued to hold her. "I was hoping we could have lunch together before I head back."

"I'd love that. Shall we go to the café? I believe Margaret has chicken pot pie today, and I saw a chocolate cake when I was there earlier this morning."

"Sounds good."

Emmalin and Jacob were soon sitting across from each other at one of the small café tables. "So, you are working on windows for the cabin? That sounds like excellent progress."

"Not too bad." Jacob spooned out a big bite of chicken pie.

"Are you staying warm enough? It's been dreadfully cold."

"I'm managing, but I must admit that a tent is not the most obliging winter home. I'll be glad to get the cabin sealed up. As soon as that's finished, I can stay indoors. But there's still work to be done on the fireplace."

"I'd love to help with that." Emmalin took a drink of tea.

"The sooner you can come, the better."

"Are you missing me?" Emmalin asked coquettishly as she gently set the cup back on its saucer.

"I've had company."

"Oh, really? I thought John and Chauncey were helping their father put up a new barn."

"They are, but that doesn't mean I'm alone." Jacob grinned.

"Oh, well Henry of course."

He propped his elbows on the table. "A fox comes into camp every morning. I share breakfast with him."

"Oh, my goodness. But what about Henry?"

Jacob shrugged. "He tolerates him."

"I'd love to see that."

"Maybe you can come out for a day after Christmas. I'll plan to work on the fireplace that day. You can choose from the stones I've hauled up from the river. I've got a big pile of them."

"I'd love that, if the weather permits."

"We can ride out together." Jacob finished his meal. "Well, I better get moving if I want to get back before dark." He leaned across the table and gave Emmalin an affectionate kiss. "I'll return Christmas Eve."

"I wish you didn't have to go." She pouted. "I hate having to spend so much time apart."

"Not much longer." He briefly rested his hand on her cheek, then stood and left the café.

Christmas Eve couldn't have arrived soon enough. Emmalin didn't remember a time when she was more excited. The past year, her faith had been sorely tested, but her life had also been richly blessed. She had much to be thankful for—good health, family, friends, Jacob and his miraculous recovery, and this place that was more home to her than Philadelphia had ever been.

There was to be a Christmas Eve service, so at dusk Emmalin walked into the church sanctuary with her father and Margaret. Candles flickered in the window alcoves and the candelabras were ablaze. There was a reverent hush among the parishioners. Had Jacob arrived? She searched but didn't see him.

She caught Charity's eye and gave her a wave. Charity wore the new gown and looked stunning in it.

Charity approached, her eyes alight and her cheeks flushed. "I can hardly believe I own such an exquisite dress. Thank you so much! I've never possessed anything so fine." She hugged Emmalin.

"I'm so glad you like it. I knew it would look lovely on you."

Charity held the skirt out from her legs, then let it fall. She looked as if she might cry. "I never imagined."

"It's long past time you had something elegant."

Charity smiled and lifted her brows as she glanced at the front of the church where the minister reviewed his notes. "Pastor Miller couldn't conceal his pleasure when he saw me."

"I wouldn't be surprised if you have a proposal soon."

"Oh, I do hope so."

Someone rested their hands on Emmalin's shoulders. She turned to find Jacob smiling down at her. "You made it."

He took her hands and stepped back to admire her. "You look beautiful."

"Thank you. I think it appropriate to wear something special on Christmas Eve." Emmalin teetered back on her heels slightly and glanced down at her velvet maroon dress. "And I do like this gown." She looked back at Jacob. "Margaret is making a special meal for after the service. Would you like to join us?"

"I wouldn't miss it."

The service began with one of Emmalin's favorite hymns, "O Come, All Ye Faithful." What a perfect beginning to the evening. Next the congregation sang "Hark! The Herald Angels Sing" then "Joy to the World" and "O Little Town of Bethlehem." Emmalin's happiness increased with each additional hymn. The music carried her back to the joy she'd once had while sitting at her piano in the music room of her uncle's home. Oh, how she'd loved to play.

The church reverberated with the voices of the faithful, and Emmalin's longing for the spring and summer melodies of the valley was satisfied.

Pastor Miller then stepped up to the podium and delivered a stirring message about the humanity of Christ. It was just what Emmalin needed to hear—Jesus fully man and fully God. He chose to come to earth, to lower Himself to a mere human who lived a life of humility and sacrifice. The incredible gift of God's love cut into her heart and brought tears of gratitude. He had given so much. All she needed to do was embrace Him and accept His mercy and protection.

As the reverend finished, he led the people in a final hymn—"O Holy Night." As Emmalin sang, tears spilled onto her cheeks. Jacob grasped her hand and gave it a gentle squeeze, which only created more tears. She dabbed at her cheeks, thanking God for loving her just as she was.

After the service, jubilant emotions accompanied Emmalin and her family home. The sky was cloudless with stars winking down from the black canopy. Cold penetrated the land, turning patches of snow into glistening white islets. The only sound was the creaking of the wagon, crunching steps of the team, and Smoke as Jacob rode alongside the family. In the distance, a wolf called out to its pack.

"I've been a believer all of my life," Margaret said. "And no matter how much I mull over the truth of God's Son coming to earth as a baby to live His life as a human and then give it up again, I can't fathom it."

"It's love," Samuel said. "He's all about love."

Emmalin pressed her heels together. "I'm not certain it's possible to fully comprehend."

A reverent silence settled over the group as they continued on through the night.

Jacob broke the silence. "I appreciate God's creation, but it sure is cold."

Everyone broke out in laughter.

"I'm looking forward to the warmth of your fire." He pulled his coat closed.

"I stoked it up before we left." Samuel clicked his tongue to hurry the horses. "Maybe new snow for Christmas, eh?"

"We'll need clouds." Emmalin looked up at the night stars.

"They're coming," her father said. "You'll see, we'll be building a snowman tomorrow."

"Oh, I do hope so." Emmalin breathed in the cold, which made her chest hurt just a bit.

As they pulled up at the cabin, it looked warm and cozy, lantern light glowing in the windows and the smoke of the fireplace drifting in the air.

"Oh my. We left the lanterns burning." Margaret climbed down from the wagon. "Such a waste of oil."

"I'll put the wagon away later." Samuel climbed down and escorted

Margaret up the steps. When he reached the front door, instead of going inside, he and Margaret waited for Emmalin and Jacob. Mischief stirred. He winked at Emmalin, then turned to Jacob.

She couldn't imagine what was going on.

Jacob stepped up to the door. Wearing a crooked smile, he said, "Some gifts can't wait until Christmas morning." He opened the door and motioned for Emmalin to step inside.

"What?" Emmalin walked into the house. Her eyes immediately went to an upright piano that stood in the center of the room. "Oh my!" She put her hands to her mouth. "What is this?"

"I figured you deserved one since I ruined the other one you had."

Without thought, Emmalin crossed the room. She ran her hand over the rich dark mahogany wood of the piano, then allowed her fingertips to trip over a floral engraving that meandered across the front panel. She moved her hand down to the keys and across the ivories. "It's beautiful. I can't believe it." Her eyes filled with tears. "It's mine?"

"Well, it's looking for someone who plays well." Jacob grinned. "And that wouldn't be me."

"Oh, Jacob! Thank you." Emmalin hugged him around the neck. "Thank you."

"It will look perfect in our new home, don't you think?" he asked with a smile.

"Oh yes! Yes, it will." Emmalin couldn't imagine where he got the money for such an extravagance but didn't dare ask.

"Try it out," Margaret said.

Emmalin released Jacob, and he pulled out the bench for her. Joy bubbling up from deep inside, she sat and placed her hands on the keys, and then the music spilled out of her—"Ode to Joy." She played to the end, her own joy blended with the music, filling the room. When the song came to an end, she broke down and cried. "I've never received such a beautiful gift."

"We are the ones who have received a gift," said Jacob. "And it will bless us through the years."

"You are so wonderful." She looked at her father and Margaret. "And you two kept it from me."

Her father leaned his tall frame against the piano. "You would expect something different?"

Emmalin turned back to the piano. "Would you like me to play some Christmas hymns?"

"That would be perfect," Margaret said, tucking herself in beside Samuel. She and everyone in the room lifted their voices, filling the house with the holiness of Christmas through their worship.

It was nearly ten o'clock when Margaret and Samuel went off to bed.

Emmalin poured two mugs of hot chocolate and joined Jacob by the fire. She gave him one of the mugs, then sat across from him and gazed into the flames. "This is the best Christmas I've ever had."

"It's not actually Christmas yet."

"Perhaps not, but it's still the best. I never imagined I'd have a piano again so soon."

"I was envisioning you sitting in our home and playing. Me working around the place and music coming from inside. You teaching our children how to play."

"It all sounds so lovely." Emmalin felt as if her heart would melt with happiness. "Life feels nearly perfect."

"It does."

"Earlier I thought I couldn't be happier, but now I am."

Jacob's expression turned serious.

"What is it? Something's troubling you."

"I am thankful for you, for my life…but it would be better if Mother Blossom could share our happiness. It's not right for her to be locked up at that reservation."

"You are still thinking about rescuing her? Even if it means you could go to prison?"

He nodded. "I have to. It's a tragedy what's happened to her and the rest of them is evil. We can't ignore evil. Sometimes we have to do what's right. No matter what the consequence. I have to go after her. And Wild Dove."

Emmalin's stomach clenched. Her eyes met Jacob's. She'd known it would come to this. "I can't leave them there, as if they don't exist."

Emmalin knew he was right. "When will you go?" Emmalin tried to quiet rising anxiety.

"Probably not before February. Hopefully the weather will be better by then."

What of Wild Dove? Emmalin didn't want less for her, but she was afraid of what could happen with the native woman being a part of their lives. There was nothing she could do about that, except to trust it to God. She reached across the distance between them and took Jacob'd hand. "I know you must go."

Chapter Thirty-One

Clouds parted and sunshine pushed away the rain. They'd had downpours throughout the day.

Emmalin faced the January sun and closed her eyes, soaking in what little warmth it had to offer. The air was cold. Still, it had been a good day. She had worked on the house all day, at Jacob's side. Now it was time to head home where a warm fire and a hot meal waited.

"Are we ready?" she asked.

"Just about." Jacob picked up some loose nails, set them in a can, and placed them inside the cabin. He looked at the work in progress. "We're making headway."

"We are." Her voice carried the wonderment she felt. "I can hardly wait. Tomorrow I'll order some of the items we'll need to make it a real home." She planted her hands on her hips and studied the nearly completed fireplace. "The hearth will be so nice, but there's nothing quite as efficient as a good cooking stove."

Jacob nodded. He walked to the place where the kitchen window would soon be installed and gazed out. "Nice view from here."

"I might even enjoy washing dishes." Emmalin circled an arm around his waist. He'd been somewhat glum during the day. She turned and looked at him. "Jacob, is something troubling you?"

He let out a huff of air. "I guess you could say that." He glanced toward the north. "I was going to wait another month, hopefully finish the house, before leaving for the reservation. But I feel this nagging urge to go, almost as if something bad will happen if I wait. It's time to get my mother."

"Oh." A surge of panic coursed through Emmalin. She calmed herself. "Do you think it wise while we're still in the middle of winter?"

"The temperatures have been mild, no snow."

Emmalin hugged him. "You do what you must."

"When I get back, I'll work extra hard."

"I know you will. Don't worry about that, just do what you must and come back safely."

He put his arm around her. "I love you."

"Everything will be fine. The house will get done and we will share our lives together." In spite of her brave words, Emmalin was scared, and tried to focus on their future rather than the dangerous journey Jacob was about to make. "How soon will you be leaving?"

"In the morning."

Alarm went off inside Emmalin, but she said nothing about her fear as they walked outside and saddled their horses.

Jacob finished before Emmalin and stepped up to tighten the belly strap for her. He helped her into the saddle and draped a wool blanket over her skirt. "It's going to be a cold ride home."

Jacob climbed onto Smoke, settled in the saddle, and then headed down the trail. Emmalin followed. Once the track widened, they rode side-by-side.

Emmalin did her best to avoid muddy ruts. The meadow grasses had been flattened from the heavy rains. She missed the summer fields that swayed in warm breezes and closed her eyes, imagining how it would be in a few months. There were good days coming.

"Perhaps you should wait for the weather to improve before going to Grand Ronde. It's bound to warm up."

"It's not so bad, just wet. And I don't want to wait. Every day is a hardship for her—not enough food and poor housing. I'm afraid she won't make it to spring."

Emmalin didn't argue. He had to make this decision for himself, and she had to trust him and God.

"I hope Margaret has something ready for dinner when we get home."

"She will." Jacob pulled his coat collar up.

"You'll stay and eat, won't you?"

"I'd be a fool not to." He smiled at her.

Emmalin watched as a martin darted into hiding at the base of an oak. "Will you be doing any trapping this winter?"

"No time. I have a house to finish. I'll do the trapping next year."

"I don't mind actually. I hate to see the animals killed."

"Never liked it much, but it's a way to make money. Even out here in the Oregon Territory, I need that."

He didn't actually have to make money. Emmalin had plenty. But she said nothing. He needed to make his own way, for the both of them. Clearly, it would be a struggle to fully grasp the reality that what was his was hers and what was hers was his. Jacob would eventually adjust, but she had no idea how long it would take. She hoped soon. His determination to ignore her assets felt awkward and almost like a rebuff.

They moved on, both mulling over their own thoughts. When they approached Deer Creek, a sharp wind kicked up and the icy cold cut through Emmalin. Was there another storm blowing in?

As they rode into town, someone on horseback tore down the street toward the store.

"I wonder what that's about?" Jacob gave Smoke a tap with his heels and picked up his pace.

Emmalin hurried Sassy. Had something happened? Anxiety prickled through her.

When they reached the store, the rider they'd seen earlier ran out and propelled himself back onto his horse. Emmalin's father followed him out and hollered after him. "I'll get a wagon and some men. We'll be there as quick as we can."

The rider glanced back but didn't slow down.

"What's happened?" Jacob asked.

"Mud slide. South of town," Samuel said. "Several injured. At least one dead."

"Oh no!" Emmalin pressed a hand to her stomach. "What can I do?"

"Get Margaret and set up a medical post at the church. We'll bring the injured there."

Jacob galloped off with Samuel while Emmalin ran to the café. "Margaret!"

Margaret was washing down tables. "What is it?"

"There's been an accident!"

Margaret straightened. "What's happened? Not Jacob."

"No. A mud slide. Father said we should set up a place in the church to care for the injured."

"We'll need towels, washcloths, and washing bowls. Do you have bandages and gauze at the store?"

"We do."

The two packed a bag with items from the café, then hurried next door to the store. Margaret grabbed gauze and bandages and plucked a bottle of carbolic acid off the shelf. "We'll need this. Nothing filthier than a mud slide."

Emmalin hurried to the back of the store where a wheelbarrow had been stored. She pushed it into the storefront. "This should help."

"Perfect. Do you have blankets?"

"Some." Emmalin grabbed three quilts and several wool blankets off a shelf and placed them in the wheelbarrow.

Margaret added the other items. "I think that's all we need for now. There may be additional blankets at the church."

With Emmalin pushing the wheelbarrow, they hurried out of the store and down the street. Emmalin nearly tipped the wheelbarrow. "I wonder how many are injured."

"I pray not many." When they reached the church, Margaret moved to the front of the wheelbarrow and pulled while Emmalin pushed it up the steps. Margaret opened the door and stepped inside.

Emmalin parked the wheelbarrow in the foyer. Hopefully there would be enough room for all the injured.

"We can lay the quilts and blankets out here for people to lay on." Margaret handed some to Emmalin, then sorted through the other items, setting them out on a table. "Can you see if there are more blankets?"

Emmalin entered a room off the foyer and searched through cupboards until she found several. She hauled them out, setting them on the table.

"Oh good. That should be more than enough."

With everything set out and ready, Emmalin and Margaret waited as darkness settled over the town.

Emmalin's empty stomach gnawed at her. "I'm hungry. Are you?"

"I am. There's a beef roast at the café. I cooked it up for tomorrow's lunches. And there's fresh baked bread."

"I'll go and get it."

"I expect some of the people we're taking care of tonight might be hungry so bring all the meat and some extra bread."

When Emmalin returned with the food, she and Margaret sliced off meat and bread to make sandwiches, then sat down to eat. The meat was still warm.

Emmalin's hunger overrode apprehension, and she was able to eat. "This is good."

"I'm glad you can eat. You'll need all the energy you can get."

"Another crisis. It seems there is always something awful happening. And I don't feel adequate to cope."

"You've been through a lot since you arrived here in Deer Creek, but you're doing wonderfully."

"Not really. I'm always scared."

"We all are, some of the time." Margaret reached out and took Emmalin's hand. "But we don't give up. We do what we must. You're one of us, an overcomer."

"I don't feel like that but thank you."

Charity strode into the church. "I heard about what happened. Can I help?"

"Of course," Margaret said. "But right now, we're waiting."

Sounds of riders and a wagon came from outside.

"It seems, you were just in time." Margaret set aside her sandwich and went to the door. "They're lifting someone out of the wagon."

Emmalin crowded up behind Margaret. "Who is it? Do you recognize him?"

"I can't see from here." She stepped out on the porch. "Bring the victims in here. This way." She motioned for the men to come inside.

Pastor Miller and Jacob carried one man. "I think this is one of the miners camped on the river between here and Myrtle Creek. Evidently there was a group of them on their way to Myrtle Creek for a night of merry making."

Jacob carried the man under the arms. "They're not very merry now." He set him on one of the blankets.

The miner was unconscious and covered with dried mud from head to foot. Even his eyes had mud in them. Emmalin had never seen such a thing and for a moment thought she might get sick.

Margaret kneeled beside him. She quickly examined the man, clearing mud from his mouth and his eyes. She checked for breathing and a pulse. She sat back on her haunches. "I can't imagine being engulfed in mud." She glanced at Emmalin. "Can you get me some water and a washcloth?"

Thankful for something to do, Emmalin retrieved the items. "Is he going to be all right?"

"Only time will tell." She dipped the washcloth in the water and wiped mud from the man's face.

Shock swept through Emmalin. "Oh, my Lord!"

Margaret looked up at her. "What is it?"

"That's one of the scoundrels who accosted me and stole the wagon. His hair is shorter, but I'd recognize him regardless. His name is Charlie."

"Oh dear." Margaret turned back to the man.

Emmalin stared at him, fury welling up inside. The scene of what happened charged through her mind. "I wonder if his sidekick is here too?" She glanced at the door.

"This fellow isn't going anywhere." Margaret stood. "You can check out the rest of the injured as they come in."

More men were carried inside. Watching for the other man who had stolen the wagon, Emmalin cleaned them up so Margaret could examine them. She didn't recognize any. Most were not seriously injured, but there were contusions, broken bones, and head injuries. As Margaret worked on them, there was a fair amount of moaning and groaning and a few outcries.

Samuel stood in the doorway. "There's one left. He was alive when we loaded him, but I think he died." He removed his hat. "And there were two others we'll have to go back for. They didn't make it."

"Emmalin, maybe you should check out the man who's still in the wagon," Margaret said. "Make sure he's actually gone. I can't leave this man right now."

"Of course." Grabbing hold of her courage, Emmalin carried a lantern and hurried out to the wagon parked in front. "Is he in here?"

"Yeah," Jacob said. "You sure you want to do that?"

"I'm fine." Emmalin climbed into the back and kneeled beside a man. What if he was the other one? He was in terrible shape, caked with mud from head to foot. The slide must have swallowed him as it tumbled down the hillside. Emmalin's stomach roiled at the sight. She could barely make out that he was human. She couldn't imagine a worse way to die.

She placed her hand on his chest. It did not rise. There was no heartbeat. She scraped away mud and pressed her fingers to his neck. No pulse. She cleared away more mud, trying to get a better look at him. She held a lantern up close and then nearly swooned. It was him—Ray. He'd shaved his beard, probably to avoid recognition after she'd given a description to the authorities. His skin had a pale blue tinge to it, and his lips were nearly purple, but even so she would never forget that face.

Samuel stood alongside the wagon.

"He's gone. Someone needs to take him to the funeral parlor." She grabbed her father's hand. "He's one of the men who stole your wagon and the goods. The other one is inside."

Shock showed in her father's eyes. "I'll be darned. Never thought we'd find them this way."

She nodded.

"And the fella inside?"

"He's alive, but unconscious. You need to contact the sheriff."

"I'll do that. He's out at the site of the slide right now." Samuel turned and headed inside the church. "I'll check on him. I'm not about to let him get away."

"His name is Charlie. Margaret can show you."

Emmalin pushed to her feet and moved toward the back of the wagon. Out of the corner of her eye, she caught sight of something. A child? A little girl huddled in the corner of the wagon. Frightened brown eyes looked out at her. She was native. How had she escaped being rounded up by the soldiers?

"Oh dear. You startled me." She reached out to her. "Let me help you."

The girl drew back, staring at Emmalin's outstretched hand as if it were a snake ready to strike. She didn't make a sound.

"I won't hurt you. I promise." Emmalin made her voice as kind and gentle as possible.

The girl kept staring.

"Are you hungry? I have some fresh bread and beef inside."

Slowly the child's expression softened, and she reached out and grasped Emmalin's hand.

Emmalin pulled gently toward her and helped the child to her feet. "Come on." She circled an arm around bony shoulders. "We'll get you something to eat."

Emmalin led her to the back of the wagon, climbed out and then lifted the little girl to the ground. She held her close for just a moment, unable to imagine the trauma she had experienced.

Was the child related to one of these men? *Please not one of the ones who had died.*

Keeping ahold of her hand, Emmalin said, "Come with me. Everything will be all right."

Chapter Thirty-Two

Emmalin's father and Jacob returned to the slide to help with the clean up, while the ladies nursed the injured. With all the victims cleaned and bandaged, Emmalin turned her attention back to the little girl. She had eaten the bread and milk Emmalin had given her. "Would you like something more to eat?"

She nodded.

Emmalin made up a plate with meat and another piece of bread and handed it to the mite. "It's good."

She picked up the bread and took a bite, then another. As if suddenly awakening, the child ate ravenously until the meat and bread were gone.

Oh dear. Poor thing must have been so hungry. Emmalin offered her more milk, and she drank most of it. She'd stayed close to the little one, hoping she would say something, but she didn't.

Margaret approached. "Would you like some dessert? I have cookies at the café."

Charity pulled a blanket up under the chin of one of the injured miners. "I can get them."

"Thank you, Charity. You've been such a help."

"It's a good thing I was in town." She headed for the door. "I'll be back shortly."

Margaret moved among the injured, checking one and then another.

"It could have been so much worse. All these people will recover." She returned to the little girl. "Are one of these folks your family?"

Her eyes widened momentarily, then narrowed beneath her furrowed brow. She shook her head.

Knowing came to life. Emmalin knew. "Was the man in the wagon your father? The man who died?"

Tears brimmed. "No. Daddy drove."

Emmalin took hold of her hands and kneeled in front of her. "Is your father one of the men they left at the slide?"

The child pressed a closed fist to her mouth and nodded.

"I'm so sorry."

Tears spilled over.

"Aww, sweet darling." Emmalin pulled the child into her arms and caressed her hair. The child held her body stiff. Emmalin eased away slightly and swept a strand of hair off the child's face. "We want to help you. Can you tell us your name?"

The little girl pressed her lips together, but finally mumbled, "Annie."

"And do you have a last name, Annie?"

"Last name?" She frowned. "My daddy is dead?"

Emmalin didn't want to lie. Besides, the child had seen what happened to her father. "Yes. I'm sorry, sweetheart." She rested a hand on Annie's head. "Do you have a mother?"

"She flew to heaven."

Margaret sat beside her. "Was your mother an Indian?"

Annie raised her shoulders in a slight shrug.

"Do you know how old you are?"

She held up three fingers.

"You're very grown up for three years old." Margaret smiled. "Would you mind coming to my house just for tonight?"

Looking to Emmalin, Annie asked, "Will you be there?"

"Yes. I live there too."

Puzzlement touched the child's face. After a few moments, she said, "I will go."

The church doors opened and cold air swept in. Charity appeared with a plate of cookies. "Look what I found." She smiled brightly and held out the plate to Annie. "Applesauce cookies."

Plucking a cookie from the plate she examined it, then tasted it.

Margaret stood and faced Charity. "I need to get this little one home. Do you think you and your mother can stay with the men tonight? Everyone should be fine, just need to stay warm and sleep. Most of them should be fit enough in the morning to set out for their camps. I hope the roadway will be cleared by then."

"I'm more than happy to stay. And I'm sure my mother won't mind." Charity glanced at her mother who kneeled beside a man, helping him with a drink of water.

"All right, then." Margaret looked down at Annie. "I think we all need some sleep." She turned to Emmalin. "Time to head home."

"I'd like to wait for Jacob. Do you think they'll be much longer?"

"I'd be surprised if we see them before daylight. There's certainly a lot of cleanup to be done. And then the other two men." She glanced at Annie.

"Is Charlie awake?"

"He is."

"I don't want to leave him until the sheriff comes back."

"He's not going anywhere. One leg is broken and the ankle on his other leg is badly sprained."

"I'll keep an eye on him," Charity said. "Don't worry about him."

"Oh, thank you, Charity." Emmalin took Annie's hand. "Come on, sweetie. You can stay with me tonight."

"My daddy?"

"He is being taken care of."

"Is he in heaven?"

Emmalin's heart broke, and she barely managed to say, "Yes. He is."

"With Mommy?"

"Yes."

Annie's big brown eyes were awash with tears. But instead of releasing them, she set her mouth and refused to cry. She took hold of Emmalin's hand and allowed herself to be led to the wagon.

Emmalin made a stop at the mercantile, and then they headed home.

No one spoke. They were all weary and had seen and heard too much suffering.

When they arrived at the house, Margaret fed the fire while Emmalin dragged in the bathing tub and filled it with warm water. She removed Annie's muddy clothing and lifted her into the bath. "We'll get you all clean and warm. And I have a lovely nightgown that should fit you perfectly."

"Where did you get a child's nightdress?" Margaret asked.

"The store."

"Oh, of course."

"I grabbed a couple of them since we don't know how long she'll be here. Maybe tomorrow she and I can pick out a couple of play dresses."

"That's a good idea." Margaret headed for Emmalin's room. "I'll make up the bed."

Emmalin smiled at Annie. "I hope you don't mind sharing a bed with me."

"I don't mind."

Emmalin bathed her with soap and a washcloth, then removed her braids and washed her hair. It clearly hadn't been cleaned in a while. She retrieved a towel and held it up for her. "All done."

Annie stood, water dripping from her. "I'm clean now."

"Yes, you are." Emmalin lifted her out of the tub, wrapped the towel around her, then gently dried her off. "I suppose you are very tired."

"No." She blinked extra hard.

Emmalin chuckled, then held up a little girl's nightdress. "I think this should fit you just right."

Annie touched the cotton fabric. "It's soft and pretty."

"Arms up," Emmalin said. Annie stuck her arms in the air and allowed Emmalin to slip the nightgown over her head and button it up. "All ready." Emmalin carried her into the bedroom. She sat at the dressing table and stood Annie in front of her. Gently she combed out her wet hair and braided it into a single plait.

Margaret had put clean bedding on and draped two colorful quilts over the bed. "All right, then." Emmalin lay her on the bed and pulled up the covers. "Do you say prayers?"

She shook her head.

"Would you like to?"

Annie shrugged. "I guess."

"All right. Just fold your hands like this and close your eyes. I'll pray."

Annie pressed her palms together and shut her eyes. Emmalin's heart warmed at the child's innocence. "Our dear heavenly Father," she prayed. "We thank you so much for keeping Annie safe. Please give her Your peace and help her to sleep well. Help her to know that she is safe here. Thank You for all that You do and will do. In the Lord's name, Amen."

"Amen," Annie whispered.

Emmalin pressed a kiss to her cheek. "I'll be right out there." Emmalin nodded toward the front room.

"Can you stay?" Annie's voice was quiet but pleading.

"Of course." Emmalin lay down beside the little girl and rolled onto her side so she was facing her. She was so tiny. What kind of terrible things had she known in her young life? At the very least the loss of both parents. It didn't seem right. Now, what would happen to her? An Indian girl on her own had a bleak future.

"Thank you for helping me," Annie said in a tiny voice. She snuggled close to Emmalin and was soon fast asleep.

Rain returned and pounded on the rooftop. When Emmalin lay down, she hadn't climbed beneath the covers, and now she shivered from the chill in the room. She lifted her arm from around Annie and edged away from the little girl, careful not to wake her. She quietly slipped out of the room. Margaret was just finishing the cleanup from the bath. "I'm so sorry. I didn't mean to leave that for you."

"It's no trouble. I'm just thankful we were able to help the poor little dear."

Emmalin sat at the table. "What will become of her?"

"Maybe there is family nearby." Margaret moved to the stove. "I'm still cold from the ride home and was thinking about having another cup of coffee. Would you like some?"

"Yes. Thank you."

Margaret poured them each a cup, then joined Emmalin at the table. "Are you hungry?"

"No. I couldn't eat." She glanced at the bedroom door. "I'm worried about Annie. She said her mother died and now her father."

"Poor thing. We need to see if we can get her last name from one of the injured miners. The men who do the placer mining down south rarely have much in the way of family."

"Most likely, her mother was Indian. There is no home for her with the Indians. She said her father was driving the wagon. Maybe he wasn't a miner and lives in the area."

"I pray so."

It was late when Emmalin climbed into bed beside Annie. She'd waited up, hoping Jacob would return, but he was still gone, and she was too weary to wait longer. She prayed for God's protection for him and all those who were helping with the slide. In spite of her concerns, she quickly fell asleep. The next thing she knew was the sound of her father's voice.

Emmalin climbed out of bed, pulled on a dressing gown, and hurried into the living room. "Thank goodness, you're home. Where is Jacob?"

"He's putting away the horses."

Margaret was already preparing a cup of coffee along with a hearty breakfast of eggs and bacon. "I prayed for you. Were there more injured miners?" She handed him the coffee.

"Yes." He ran a hand over his face, lined with fatigue. "Two, but they were dead. It was a pretty bad slide and took a lot of work to open the road. We are lucky there weren't more injuries or deaths."

He slurped down the coffee. "I found out a little more about the two who died at the slide. The little girl's father is James Thompson. He was a miner and had been raising her on his own since his wife died two years ago."

"Oh dear."

"There's no family. No friends, except other miners."

Jacob stepped into the house. "When I lost my parents there was no one but mountain men to look out for me. That's how I ended up with the Indians."

Emmalin moved to Jacob. "Thank the Lord you're home and safe."

"I'd give you a hug, but don't think you'd like that much." He looked down at himself. He was a muddy mess.

Emmalin leaned toward him and dropped a kiss on his cheek, while making sure to keep distance between them. "Even with the mud, you're still quite handsome."

Margaret got him a cup of coffee. "Have a seat. You've had a long night."

"Shouldn't I clean up first?"

"You got your hands washed?"

He held out clean hands.

"Well, then sit. You can worry about the rest later."

He obeyed. "Thought you might want to know. The man, Charlie, he's awake and he's being moved to the jail house. He swears he has no idea about our wagon or the horses."

"That's outrageous," Margaret said.

"He'll be held to account. He can't get away with lying. Emmalin can identify him. There'll be a trial when a judge comes to town."

"Well good." Margaret returned to the stove. "We have other things to sort out right now. What are we going to do with that little sweetheart?"

"We can't let her end up at the reservation," Emmalin said.

"I agree, but what can we do?" her father asked. "There are no orphanages around here."

"I don't know. But not a reservation." Jacob's expression was set and determined.

Margaret moved to Samuel and rested a hand on his shoulder. "Maybe we could keep her, at least for now. She needs someone. Why not us?"

"Us? We're not exactly young."

"Young enough. She just needs a place for now."

"You've never had a child and neither have I, at least not one I raised." He glanced at Emmalin apologetically.

"I don't have to have had a child to know how to love one. We're decent people with a lot of love to give. Why shouldn't we help her?"

The room went silent. Emmalin was trying to imagine her father as a parent to this little girl. "You both would make good parents." She looked at her father. "And even if you didn't meet me until I was grown up, you've been a fine father to me."

"Thank you, Emmalin."

"I think she's right." Margaret draped her arms around Samuel's neck and shoulders. "Annie has no one. Why not us?"

"Maybe. We need to give it a little time, more thought."

Margaret kissed his cheek. "Of course. But she is such a dear little thing."

Emmalin looked at Jacob. What about them? Her heart warmed at the idea of being a mother to Annie. Maybe they could take her in after she and Jacob were married. "Jacob, perhaps you should wait a bit before heading north? At least a week or so while Annie gets used to this new situation."

"I hate to wait…" His eyes warmed. "Whatever's best for Annie."

Chapter Thirty-Three

Jacob and Samuel sat on the porch as the sun slipped toward the horizon, sending splintered colors of pink and orange across the sky. Jacob watched Emmalin and Annie walk toward the chicken yard. Annie's tiny hand was securely clasped inside Emmalin's. The little girl swung the egg basket back and forth as she walked, and she looked up often and smiled at Emmalin. He felt something akin to cherishing the child, though he'd only known her for a couple weeks.

"I think those two are a pair," Samuel said.

"I agree. They're smitten with one another." He leaned forward on his thighs. "I'm wondering if we ought to take her in. After Emmalin and I are married of course."

"Actually, Margaret was saying just that. She loves Annie but sees the wisdom of a young couple adopting her. And, of course, it's clear those two have connected."

The chicken house door creaked as Emmalin opened it. Annie slipped inside ahead of her, excitedly talking about how many eggs she thought might be in the nest boxes.

Jacob's mind went to his mother, Blossom. She was still locked up at the fort, and she and Wild Dove needed to be set free. He couldn't wait any longer, February was already here and soon it would be spring. He'd already been delayed too long.

When Emmalin and Annie returned to the house, Annie proudly

showed off several eggs nestled inside the basket. "I didn't break any. The chickens were nice to me."

"She did a wonderful job." Emmalin placed a hand on Annie's back. "But it's time to get ready for bed."

"Read a story?"

"Of course. Which one would you like?"

"The mermaid?"

"I love that one."

Jacob took hold of Emmalin's hand as she passed. "Can we talk later?"

"Of course. Just as soon as I've got Annie safely into bed." The tone in her voice held a question. She reluctantly released his hand before walking inside.

Jacob leaned back in the chair. "Warm for February."

"Yep. Something I like about this place. The weather's changeable. And sometimes it gives us a break from winter."

"I'm grateful for it."

Samuel pushed out of his chair. "I better go in. I need to check my spreading rifle. Make sure it's in good shape so I can count on it when I need it. Won't be long before the geese start flying through, especially if the weather stays nice." He opened the door. "Good night."

"Good night."

The door closed softly, leaving Jacob alone to listen to the croaking frogs as darkness took hold. He'd stay in the barn tonight and leave early in the morning. He had a plan on how to free his mother, but he'd need help. God would have to provide.

He was still thinking on it when Emmalin stepped out of the house and onto the porch. "Nice evening," he said.

She sat in the chair beside him and pulled her shawl closed around her shoulders. "Wouldn't it be nice if spring has actually arrived early? It seems the frogs think so. Here every season has a different song to share throughout the valley." She leaned forward on her thighs. "And now I am privileged to add some of my favorite piano tunes to the valley melodies." She smiled at him.

"When we are married, I will have you play for me every night."

"I fear you will tire of my music."

"Never." He gazed at the darkness. "And I'm sorry to say this, but don't let this lull in winter fool you. It will be back. We get some bad storms in February. Nothing like December and January, but we could still have more snow."

"I'm ready for winter to be over."

"Soon." He reached for her hand. "The cabin is nearly finished, and spring will be here in a month or so, and that means so will our wedding."

Emmalin gave his hand a squeeze. "Is that what you wanted to talk about?"

He cleared his throat. "No. Actually it's time I head to Grand Ronde."

Emmalin released his hand and sat back in her chair, pulling her shawl closer. She stared out into the darkness. "Of course. If not for the mud slide, you would already be gone."

Her voice sounded strained. Jacob hated to cause her more worry, but he had no choice.

"Everything's quieted down. And I've already waited too long. The cabin is nearly done, enough for Blossom and Wild Dove to stay there while I build something else for them."

Emmalin let out a breath. "We are so close to finishing. And they are going to live in our house while you build something for them?"

"I'm sorry, Emmalin. But I can't leave them there any longer. I can't explain it, but I know in my gut that I can't wait any more."

Emmalin sucked in a breath, then drew in another. Her body tight and her lips pursed, she looked at him. "What if you're caught?"

"I won't be."

"You can't know that, not for certain."

"I've got a plan. And once I get them out, no one there will know they're here."

"What about when we took them food and blankets? Doesn't the fort commander know who we are?"

A sly smile settled on Jacob's lips. "I didn't let him know anything. Actually, I misled him, made him think we were from up north."

Emmalin compressed her lips. "I can't bear the idea of something happening to you, or of you spending years in prison."

"Nothing's going to happen. I promise." He pushed out of his chair. "I'll be gone before daylight."

Emmalin stood and stepped into his arms. She rested her cheek against his chest. "You're a good man, but I'm afraid for you."

"God will be with me." Jacob tightened his hold, wishing he didn't have to leave her, but he couldn't imagine, even for a moment, not helping Blossom and Wild Dove. Such a choice would be unforgiveable.

"I love you, Emmalin."

The sky was still dark when Jacob saddled Smoke. He was also taking Margaret's bay gelding for Blossom and Wild Dove. Margaret had assured him she wouldn't need the horse while he was gone. He'd considered taking a wagon but quickly rejected the idea. It would be too conspicuous and too slow. If soldiers came after them, they wouldn't be able to avoid capture.

There had been no rain the previous night and the temperature was warm. Maybe the good weather would hold. He draped his supplies over the back of the gelding and, finally ready, pushed up into the saddle and headed for the road. He heard a soft woof from inside the house. He hated to do it, but this trip he'd be leaving Henry behind. He couldn't risk the dog giving them away if soldiers came after them.

For two days the good weather held, but on the third a storm with strong winds and rain blew in from the west. For nearly a day, Jacob took refuge in a hollowed-out trunk of an old cottonwood tree.

The poor weather continued, though to a lesser degree, and Jacob resumed his trek. He was cold and miserable, and there would be no fire to warm him when he stopped at the end of each day. Huddling inside his coat with his hat down low to protect him from the wet, he tried to focus on his destination. Several days into the journey, just before dark, he stopped at a large oak with broad spreading limbs that created a natural shelter. There he hobbled the horses so they could graze.

Shivering with cold, he huddled beneath two blankets and bundled deep inside his coat. With his back pressed against the trunk of the tree, he managed to sleep until he awakened early in the morning to a moonless sky. The clouds had moved on and daybreak was just close enough to illuminate the way.

That week Jacob encountered rain, snow, and sun and was grateful when on the seventh day he saw the walls of the fort. He reached the fort as the sun went down. He didn't check in at the gate, not wanting anyone to know he was there. Praying he wouldn't be spotted by watchful soldiers, he ruminated on an explanation for his presence if anyone stopped him. He went to his mother's wikiup. She and Wild Dove were inside the pelt walls, huddled close to a small fire.

When Blossom first saw Jacob, her face lit up, and she welcomed him. But quickly a frown replaced her smile. "Why are you here? You said you would stay away."

"No. That's what you told me to do." Jacob grinned. "I'm here to rescue you."

Blossom stared at him, her aging eyes flooding with sorrow. "You may want that, but it cannot be. If we are caught, you will be harshly punished. I will not risk that."

"If I have to, I'll hog tie you and drag you to safety."

She folded her arms over her chest. "Oh, you will?"

"Yes."

"Blossom, you must go," Wild Dove said. "You can have a good life with your son."

Blossom let out a rushed breath and turned to Jacob. "Do you have a plan?"

"Yes. And I have a horse for you. We'll go at night and stay off the roads. I will build a house for you at my place. It's far from town, so you'll be safe there."

"Am I to hide forever?"

"Things will get better. Soon no one will care where you live."

"I hope you are right." Blossom looked at Wild Dove. "She will come too."

"Of course."

Wild Dove stood. "I would be grateful."

"What about the soldier, the one who helps you? Do you care for him?"

"I do. But one day he will return to his home. And I will remain here."

Jacob nodded. "But it can only be you two." Sorrow welled up in him over what it meant to leave others behind.

Blossom didn't speak, but her eyes revealed her sorrow.

"We cannot succeed if we take anyone else."

"So, we will go," Blossom stated. "But how do we get past the soldiers?"

"I've been thinking on that. Wild Dove, do you think your soldier friend will help us?"

"Maybe. We can talk to him."

"All right. Let's do that. When?"

"Now? Maybe."

Wild Dove led the way to the soldier's post. Before they got there, Jacob stopped and asked, "Are you sure he'll want to help?"

She shrugged. "I know nothing for certain. But if anyone will, it is him."

As Jacob walked, he worked through what he should say to the man and how he could convince him without creating more danger for his mother or Wild Dove.

He stopped again. "Are you sure you want to take the risk?"

"To stay means we will die." She said nothing more but continued on.

They didn't have to go far before Wild Dove spotted him. "You wait." Silently, she walked ahead, like a ghost in the night. Jacob could see them talking in the faint light of the moon. And then she motioned for him to join them.

As he approached, Jacob kept his hand on his pistol, just in case. The soldier was tall and thin, and he eyed Jacob warily. Jacob worked at keeping his demeanor cordial. He extended a hand. "I'm Jacob," he said politely, careful not to give his last name.

The soldier tentatively grasped his hand. "George Lee." He stood straight, shoulders back, and met Jacob's gaze. "You want something from me?"

"For Wild Dove. And for my mother, Blossom."

His eyes narrowed. "You don't look like no Indian."

"I'm not, but they are my family. And they do not belong here. I think you know that."

"I do."

"I want to take them home, but we need help. Am I right in believing you are an honorable man? And that you might be the one to help us?"

George stared at Jacob for a long moment before asking, "What can I do?"

"Is there a way to distract the other soldiers? Just long enough so we can get away?"

"Maybe. They're always glad for a game of cards, and we just had our payday. When do you want to go?"

"Tomorrow night."

He thought a moment. "I'll get a game together before the moon rises. You should leave then."

"Good."

"You won't have much time. The soldiers will not leave their posts for long."

"I understand. How will we know it's clear to go?"

"I'll send a runner."

"All right. Thank you."

"I'm not doing this for you." He turned to Wild Dove. "I wanted to take you with me when I leave." He searched her face. "But I know that won't work. This world doesn't look kindly on marriages between Indians and whites."

Wild Dove didn't reply, but Jacob thought he saw something akin to love in her eyes. Was she in love with this man?

"Tomorrow night," George said.

Wild Dove quickly grasped his hand. "Thank you, George. And in case, I will be living in a place close to Deer Creek."

Jacob could have clapped a hand over her mouth. No one was to know where they were going.

She hurried toward the wikiup.

Jacob tipped his hat to George, then followed her while worrying about the disclosure of their destination. George seemed loyal to her, but what if he could be convinced sometime in the future to give away the information?

He caught up to Wild Dove and stopped her. "You can't tell anyone where we are going."

"Of course, I just thought that maybe one day he might come looking for me." She squared her jaw. "I will tell no one else."

⁕⁕⁕

The next day, Jacob took the horses deep into the forest and tied Margaret's horse there while he explored possible escape routes. When he'd found a trail he thought would work, he rested in the shadows of the forest and waited for nightfall.

The women gathered their belongings together and just as the sun set, Jacob returned. Quickly, he packed the horses, including baked corn muffins and tins of meat distributed by the army. Blossom added blankets. After that, they settled down to wait and each ate a corn muffin in readiness for the long night ahead.

A night hawk screeched. An owl hooted and another one answered. A coyote howled. The runner did not come. Soon the glow of moonlight touched the treetops. Had something gone wrong? Had George changed his mind or turned them in?

"We better go," Wild Dove said. "We can't wait longer."

"We'll wait."

"No. We have to go." Her voice sounded frantic.

Blossom set a hand on Wild Dove's shoulder, stopping her from saying anything more.

They sat in silence for what seemed hours. And then Jacob heard something rustling in the meadow grass. Was someone coming?

A small brown body emerged from the tall grass. The young boy bent over, fighting to catch his breath. "I was told that the game has started." He didn't seem to know what any of that meant but had done what was asked.

"Good," Jacob said. "Thank you."

The boy trotted off the way he had come.

"Time to go. No talking, ride low, and follow me." Jacob helped the women onto the bay, then threw himself up onto Smoke's back. His heart pounded ferociously, but he forced himself to take slow breaths. This was their chance. He had to make it work. He glanced over his shoulder to make sure no one had seen them, then kicked Smoke in the sides and moved toward the trail that would lead them to freedom. Moonlight was already touching the sky. They would have to hurry.

Chapter Thirty-Four

Jacob kept moving through the night, staying off the main roads. Blossom and Wild Dove followed without complaint. They made it known that they were thankful for a chance at freedom but were well aware that at any moment a stranger could put an end to their flight.

A cloudless night provided moonlight but drove down the temperatures. There was no way to stay warm, and, as dawn arrived, Jacob looked forward to the little warmth the sun would bring.

"We need to get off the trail." He dismounted and took hold of Smoke's bridle.

Wild Dove easily dismounted, but Blossom was so fatigued she didn't move. Jacob approached her. "Are you all right?"

"Yes. Tired."

He reached up a hand to her. She grasped it and slid from the horse, leaning against the gelding for a few moments before straightening.

"We'll rest." Jacob led the way into the forest until they were far enough off the trail to be hidden from passersby. "This will do." He tied off Smoke and the women's horse. "I'm sorry, but we can't have a fire. It could attract attention. Try to get some sleep."

Jacob sat and rested his back against a cedar tree. "I'll keep watch."

Wild Dove spread out a blanket. "You need sleep too."

"I'll sleep after you." He offered what he hoped was an encouraging smile. "Don't worry about me."

Blossom spread out her quilt and lay down, pulling a wool blanket over her. She studied Jacob, her dark brown eyes warm with gratitude.

"Now, sleep," he said.

Wearing a soft smile, she closed her eyes.

Wild Dove stretched out on her quilt and pulled a blanket up under her chin. She shivered. Resting her cheek on her hands, she closed her eyes. Even with the cold and untamed conditions, she slept.

Jacob's apprehension remained high. Soldiers would soon know of the women's disappearance, and they could come for them at any time. Even if the soldiers didn't pursue them, they were still in danger. If a stranger came along, it would be difficult to explain a white man and two Indians traveling together.

Had he left any clues as to his whereabouts? When he had introduced himself to the fort commander, he'd given only his first name. Did the captain remember? On the second trip, he'd managed to avoid the man. Would he be able to track them to Deer Creek?

Lord, protect us.

Jacob remained awake, listening for any sound that might be out of the ordinary. During the winter months, the forest was quiet with an occasional call of a bird or the drumming of a woodpecker. He longed for the relief that waited at his own place. But even there they would have to be cautious—Deer Creek also had a few who hated Indians and might strike out if given an opportunity, but most of those were people just passing through. And most who were placer mining down south didn't set down roots. He hoped that in time, the tensions between the government and the natives would die down. If they did, was it possible the Indians would be able to return to their normal lives? More likely it was lost to them forever.

Wild Dove lifted up her blanket. She'd slept only a couple of hours. She pushed to her feet, crossed to Jacob, and sat beside him. Keeping her voice quiet, she said, "I have not thanked you. What you did was very brave. But now what will we do? The soldiers will come for us."

"They don't know where we are. And my place is a long way from Grand Ronde. We'll keep you out of sight, and soon they will forget about you. You and Blossom can stay there as long as you want."

She plucked a blade of grass and ran it between her fingers. "Are you still going to marry the woman, Emmalin?"

"Yes. Nothing's changed since we were here."

"What does she think about me and Blossom living with you?"

"She wants to help."

"Even me?"

"She's a very kind person and feels badly about what has happened to you."

Wild Dove looked as if she might disagree. "I have not forgotten our many years together. Have you? We were good friends, and then we understood we were meant for each other."

"That was a different time. We were different. And as much as I care for you, I never felt like more than a friend."

"Is that so?"

Jacob ignored her implication. "What about George?"

Her expression turned to one of resolve. "He is at the fort, and I am here. It cannot work for us." She retrieved one of her blankets and draped it over her shoulders. "You should sleep now. I will watch."

Jacob didn't want to leave the subject as is. He thought Wild Dove had abandoned her feelings for him long ago. He had to make her understand that there was no place for her in his future if she insisted on more than friendship. He closed his eyes. Now was not the time. But she would soon come to understand.

Jacob woke to Wild Dove shaking his shoulder. She placed a finger to her lips to keep him silent. Alarm shot through him, and he sat up. She pointed toward the trail. Jacob heard the plodding of horse's hooves and the quiet whistling of a traveler.

Blossom pushed up on her elbow. She made no sound, but her eyes were wide.

Jacob barely breathed. Their horses grazed quietly. Were they visible from the trail? He should have moved them farther off.

Silently they waited for the person to move by. He continued whistling and seemed to be in no hurry, and clearly unaware of the group hiding in the woodland. When he was gone, Jacob released a relieved breath. "We have to stay farther off the trail. That was too close."

<hr />

The days that followed left Jacob tense and weary, and longing for an end to their journey. They encountered only one other traveler, but he didn't seem the least interested in why Jacob would be traveling with two Indian women. Even with the miles between him and the fort mounting, Jacob found himself checking over his shoulder from time to time, fearing he'd see a group of soldiers tracking them down. Finally, the day came when they approached the nearly completed cabin, and relief rolled through Jacob.

They moved past the burned-out home of his youth. "This is the place I lost in the fire. I'll clean it all out after I finish the new house." He'd wanted to tear it down and clear away the rubble, but just hadn't had the heart to do it.

"It is a great loss," Blossom said. "I am sorry."

"I have good memories here."

They plodded past the rubble, and the new house appeared in a clearing in the midst of tall healthy trees. "This is the cabin I told you about. Not done yet, but nearly. It's meant for me and Emmalin after we get married, but for now you can stay in it while I build a temporary shelter for you."

Blossom dismounted. She stood with her arms folded over her chest and studied the cabin. "It is so big." She walked inside and moved through the structure. "There are many rooms." Wearing a look of satisfaction, she moved to the kitchen window and stared out at the view. "This is a good house." She turned and smiled at Jacob. "Emmalin will like it."

"She and I planned it together. And she's helped me with some of the building. She's worked hard."

Wearing a frown, Wild Dove walked through the cabin. She didn't speak.

Jacob moved to the nearly completed fireplace. "We don't have a stove yet, but you can use this for cooking and heat. I don't have the floor in yet, and I don't have any hides, but this should still work well."

"A fire will be good. I am worn out by the cold," Blossom said.

"I'll get you set up here, and then I'll go into town for supplies."

"And you will see Emmalin?" Wild Dove asked.

"Of course. She's waiting for my return." He gave Wild Dove a reproving look.

Even Blossom spoke up. "Emmalin is promised to him."

Wild Dove shot her a wounded look. Blossom had always supported the idea of her and Jacob being a couple. "He is not married yet."

Blossom pursed her lips but said no more.

Wild Dove was not unreasonable. Given time, she would see the truth and accept it.

He created a temporary roof and moved the meager goods and rudimentary furniture he'd been using into the house. "This should see to your needs for now. And you might catch a fish for your dinner. There's a good spot just down the river." He climbed onto Smoke's back. "I'll return tomorrow. You can build a fire, but if anyone comes by, hide yourselves. No one can know you are here."

Anxious to see Emmalin, he turned Smoke toward the trail that led to Deer Creek. The life they had imagined together had changed, but he was certain the new one would still be blessed by God.

With a glance at the two women, the reality of what he'd done plowed over him. The responsibility he had taken on was a weighty one. Blossom and Wild Dove would depend on him for all their needs, including keeping them safe. How long would it be before he was free of the obligation? Immediately he reprimanded himself for allowing such a thought. They were his family and not a burden.

For the moment, Jacob put his worries aside and focused on Emmalin. He needed her, to feel her arms about him, and to be reminded of the love between them. Smoke seemed to sense his urgency and kept a brisk pace. Margaret's gelding also pranced, as if knowing he was nearly home. When Jacob rode past the grist mill, delight began to build. He was nearly there.

Smoke settled into a relaxed gallop. Emmalin was probably at the store. Wanting to run, Smoke snorted and tossed his head. Though tempted to let him have his way, Jacob held him back. No reason to put himself or the horses at risk. He would see Emmalin soon enough.

When Jacob reached the mercantile, there was no sign of Samuel's wagon, but Emmalin might have ridden Sassy and left her at the livery. He stopped and tied the two horses to the hitching post, then in three strides, he reached the door of the store and stepped inside. "Emmalin?" His eyes went to the front counter. She wasn't there.

"Jacob?" Her voice came from the back. "Jacob?"

She emerged from an aisle, and he rushed to her, scooping her into his arms. He buried his face in her hair. "Emmalin."

She squeezed him so tight, he thought his lungs might deflate. "I'm so happy to see you." She kissed him.

Holding her against him, all thoughts of Blossom and Wild Dove evaporated. The stress of the past days slipped away. Reluctantly he held her from him so he could see her clearly. "You are a sight for sore eyes." Her ivory complexion, and the soft flush in her cheeks. Her auburn hair was caught up in a ribbon while some was left to cascade onto her shoulders. Adoration lit the sky blue in her eyes.

"I don't ever want you to go away again. I don't know that I can bear it."

"I'm home, for a long while now."

"And your mother? Wild Dove? How are they?"

"Good. They're at the cabin."

He moved to the window and looked out on the street. "I'll have to build a shelter for them, before I can finish our house."

"That's what you said before you left." Disappointment showed in Emmalin's eyes.

"I'll work fast. And I'll get some more help." His lips lifted into a crooked smile. "We could all share the house, but I don't want to begin our lives living with them. I want it to just be us."

"I understand. And I can't wait until it's just us."

He hugged her again. "Do you think you can come out with me tomorrow? I have to get supplies and start work on their place."

"Yes. I'd like that. Can Annie come also? I'm sure she'll want to meet people of her own kind."

"Sure. We'll make a picnic of it. A winter picnic. We can take the wagon, and then you can drive it back to town at the end of the day. The road isn't very muddy. I'll have to stay. I don't want to leave Blossom and Wild Dove there alone. They're not used to living on their own. They've always had a village to depend on." He saw uncertainty flash in Emmalin's eyes. Was she unhappy about what he'd done? "Is that all right with you?"

"Of course." She took in a deep breath. "I was just hoping you and I would have a little time together, alone."

"We'll have that. As soon as I get their cabin up. I'll see if John and Chauncey can come back up and maybe a couple of other fellas. You'll see, we'll get it done fast."

"Of course you will," she said.

Her voice wasn't convincing. Did she really understand?

Chapter Thirty-Five

Emmalin had nearly decided not to drive out to the cabin with Jacob. She wasn't sure what to expect from Blossom and Wild Dove. Even though they had been cordial when she'd gone to the reservation with Jacob, this was different. Now they were part of Jacob's life. Emmalin was certain that both women still believed Jacob should marry Wild Dove.

As she climbed up into the wagon, she felt trembly inside. What would Blossom have to say now?

Jacob handed up an apple cake. "Can't wait to taste this."

"It's all I had as a welcoming gift."

Jacob lifted Annie into the back. "Time to go, Henry," Jacob said, and the dog leaped into the wagon. Annie hugged him about the neck, and the two of them stood together expectantly.

Jacob climbed into the wagon. "You'll have to make another cake for your father."

"Margaret already said she'd bake one today. He was complaining, though as politely as he could." She tipped her mouth up into a half-smile.

Releasing a long breath, Emmalin looked toward the road. It would be a rough ride out to the property. She glanced into the back. Annie was sitting on a box. "Are you ready?"

"Yes." She smiled brightly.

Emmalin turned to Jacob. "You've packed enough supplies to last quite some time."

"I plan to work steady, so the fewer trips into town the better."

"I hope you'll come to visit me once in a while," she said, trying to ignore a twinge of disappointment.

"I won't be able to stay away." He put his arm around her. "I hate being separated as much as you do, but there just isn't another choice." He gave her a little squeeze. "You'll see, it won't be that long."

He picked up the reins, clicked his tongue, and the horses moved forward. Secured by a lead, Smoke trotted along behind.

Her stomach in knots over the upcoming meeting, Emmalin focused on the weather. At least it wasn't raining, though clouds threatened. Wind whipped up the edge of her collar, and she smoothed it down. "I hope it doesn't decide to rain."

Jacob studied the sky. "Well, you never know."

Though not as bad as it might be, the road was muddy, which could hardly be avoided in February. As they made their way, more than once, it seemed they would be mired down, but Jacob knew how to navigate winter roadways and kept the horses moving.

"So, your father said that man, Charlie, confessed to taking the horses and wagon."

"Yes. He did. I suspect he knew there was no other choice." She snugged her gloves up a bit. "But he sold off everything, including the horses. And he has no idea what has become of them."

"Too bad."

"At least he'll be going to jail."

"Both paid a price." Jacob slapped the reins, and the horses picked up their pace.

Emmalin wasn't sure if she wanted the trip to be over quickly or to never end. She couldn't quite account for her nervousness. There was nothing to be afraid of. Blossom would accept her as Jacob's choice. And Wild Dove would certainly understand that the friendship she'd had with Jacob would continue, though without a future marriage.

Annie stood behind the seat and stared ahead between Jacob and Emmalin. "Are we there?"

"Yes. We're here." They approached the cabin, and Emmalin's stomach tightened.

Seeming to comprehend her apprehension, Jacob took her hand. "It's all going to be fine."

Jacob pulled the wagon to a stop, and Henry leaped out of the back. When Blossom appeared from inside the partially built cabin, Henry let out a short bark and approached her with his tail wagging. She gave him a pat and walked toward the wagon. "Hello." She offered a friendly smile.

After climbing out, Jacob gave Emmalin a hand down, while juggling the apple cake in his free hand. When Emmalin found her feet, she took the cake and approached Blossom. "Welcome," she said.

"I am glad to be here." Blossom smiled in a motherly way.

Emmalin's tension eased. "I brought you something. It's just an apple cake, but I thought you might enjoy it."

"It looks good." Blossom took the cake and sniffed it. "And smells good. We can eat some today."

An excited Annie nearly leaped into Jacob's arms. "This is Annie. She's living with Emmalin right now."

Annie stepped alongside Emmalin and took her hand.

"Hello, Annie," Blossom said.

"Hello."

Wild Dove appeared from around the side of the house. She offered a slight smile.

"Hello," Emmalin said. "I am glad you both made it here safely."

"It is because of Jacob."

An uncomfortable silence wedged itself between the two young women.

"I brought supplies," Jacob said.

"I will put this inside." Blossom walked into the cabin, then returned a few moments later and joined the others in unloading the goods.

Emmalin helped to get the supplies put away, then worked with Blossom and Wild Dove to prepare a midday meal. Over lunch, the conversation started off a bit stilted, but the five of them soon settled into an amiable discussion about the simple design of the small cabin and where Jacob had decided to build it. There was real excitement about the garden and what they hoped to grow that summer.

Before she realized it, the time had passed, and Emmalin needed to head for home. She was feeling much better, now convinced that having the two native women living close by would work out well. Her main worry was if the women would be safe, and if they were found out, would Jacob be punished for bringing them to Deer Creek.

⸺•⸺◆⸺•⸺ ⸺•⸺◆⸺•⸺ ⸺•⸺◆⸺•⸺

Emmalin set a bowl of porridge on the table in front of Annie. "There you go. It's a bit hot so be careful."

Wearing a frown, Annie picked up her spoon and took a tiny bite. She chewed slowly and swallowed while making a face of disgust. She scowled at the hot cereal in her bowl, then looked at Emmalin. "Bacon. I want bacon."

"I know, but you had bacon yesterday. This is good for you. You can't eat bacon every day."

"Why not?" She pouted.

"Your body needs all different kinds of food. And porridge is one of those."

Annie glowered at the meal, then reluctantly took another bite.

"I'm going out to the cabin today. Do you want to come?"

"With Wild Dove? And Blossom?"

"Yes. They will be there."

The little girl brightened.

Emmalin felt a tug of hurt in her heart. Annie had strongly bonded with the two Indian women, especially Wild Dove. Emmalin understood. They shared a native ancestry. She and Jacob had decided to adopt Annie, and Emmalin hoped the little girl would have people from her own culture in her life, but she hadn't been prepared to be the less preferred family member. She knew not to take it too much to heart, but it still hurt. She wanted Annie to love her and Jacob the way she would her own parents.

"After you finish eating, we'll go." Annie ate another bite. "I set out your clothes on the bed. Do you need help dressing?"

"I can do it." She shoveled in the porridge, then scooted off the chair and ran into the bedroom.

Emmalin made a lunch, including apples and oatmeal cookies. Just as she finished, Annie bounced out of the bedroom. She'd done a good job of dressing, leaving only one button undone. Emmalin did up the button. "Let me help you with your hair."

Squirming, Annie sat in front of Emmalin and allowed her to braid her hair into two plaits. Emmalin added blue ribbons to match the fabric of her dress. "Soon we will live at the cabin. Will you like that?"

"Wild Dove will be there too, right?"

"She will be living there, but in a different cabin. You will live in the big house with me and Jacob. We'll be a family."

Annie's expression turned pensive. She didn't respond.

Emmalin picked up the picnic basket. "All ready. Get your coat."

Scrambling up onto the bench, below the coat rack, Annie grabbed her cloak. Emmalin gave her a hand with it, then pulled on her own. Annie ran ahead and jumped down the steps with her feet together. "The wagon is ready."

"My father did that for us."

"He's nice." Her eyes turned shimmery. "My daddy used to do that. He liked to drive a wagon."

"That's the kind of thing that fathers do." Emmalin circled an arm around Annie, steering her toward the wagon. Losing her father was a huge loss to the little girl. Emmalin hadn't known him, but he must have been a good father to have raised such a charming, well-mannered child.

"I wish my daddy was here." Tears spilled onto her cheeks. "I miss him."

"I know you do. I wish he was here too." Emmalin hugged her. "One day you will see him again in heaven."

"Will I? For sure?"

Of course, Emmalin couldn't know Annie's father's spiritual beliefs, but he had stuck by his child so maybe he was a godly man. "Yes. I'm sure." She helped Annie up into the wagon.

Emmalin walked around to the back and checked to make sure the lumber was secure. She had decided to buy planed wood for Blossom's house. Jacob had agreed to using it instead of falling trees himself but hadn't had time to pick it up. She hoped he didn't mind her taking charge and acquiring it for him.

She climbed into the wagon and set the basket on the seat. "It is a beautiful morning. Sun with just a little bit of clouds is perfect for a drive and a picnic."

"I think so too." Annie leaned against Emmalin.

Emmalin lifted the reins, and the horses immediately set off trotting through the midst of a spring display. The fields were alive with color from early spring flowers, and the grasses were already deep.

The trip to Jacob's place seemed longer than usual. Jacob had been working hard and Emmalin hadn't seen him in several days. She could barely wait. Would this excitement ever fade? She hoped not.

"Oh look!" Annie pointed at a great heron rising up out of a pond, its long legs dragging behind. Emmalin stopped the horses so she could watch. "He's beautiful."

The heron's flight had startled a herd of deer who sprinted across the meadow.

Annie clapped her hands together. "I love deer!"

"Me too. I never tire of watching them." A memory of Emmalin's early days in the Oregon Territory flashed through her mind. It had all seemed so big and frightening. Now, it was a place she loved and felt a part of.

By the time they reached Jacob's camp, Annie had fallen asleep. Emmalin pulled up the team and set the brake carefully so not to wake the little girl. She gently lowered her to the seat and left her sleeping there, then climbed down from the wagon.

Jacob strode toward her. "I was hoping to see you today." He caught her in a hug and held her tight.

"I wish I could be here all the time."

Jacob eyed the wagon. "What do we have here?"

Emmalin's stomach did a nervous flip. "I thought it might be wise to get the lumber our here for Blossom's cabin."

"I was rethinking that some and started cutting timber."

"Oh. I thought we decided."

He set his jaw.

A flutter of fear stirred inside. It almost felt like he was choosing Blossom and Wild Dove over her. "If you do that it will take much longer and we'll have to put off the wedding. Is that what you want?"

Blossom approached and placed a hand on the wood. "It looks like fine lumber and should make a good, strong cabin." She gave Jacob a knowing smile. "Emmalin is wise. And it will be nice to have a house."

Emmalin could have hugged her but refrained.

Jacob rubbed his chin. "Well, I could use the timber I've cut for a barn. And I want to get married soon. Don't ever think otherwise." He gave her a smile, then moved to the back of the wagon and lifted a piece of the lumber. "It's enough to get started."

"Wonderful!" Relief filled Emmalin.

Wild Dove climbed onto the wagon seat and lifted Annie.

"Oh. No. She was sleeping," Emmalin said as Wild Dove pulled the little girl into her arms.

"She will sleep better with me." She held her close.

Feeling rebuffed in some way, Emmalin said nothing as Wild Dove held Annie against her shoulder and carried her down from the wagon. She'd wanted the little girl to nap.

Annie woke up and smiled at her friend. "Hello, Wild Dove." She hugged her around the neck.

Emmalin swallowed her hurt and walked to the wagon to retrieve the picnic basket. "I brought lunch."

"Thank you," Blossom said. "I will get water." She carried a kettle to the river.

After setting the basket on a makeshift table Jacob had built from a slab of wood, Emmalin sat on a stump that was being used as a chair. "So, now you'll be able to start construction on the new cabin?"

"I've already set logs in place as a foundation. I wasn't expecting the lumber but thank you. We can get to work on it right away."

"Can I help?"

"Of course."

Feeling lighthearted, she removed sandwiches from the basket and set them on the table, while watching Wild Dove and Annie. They were huddled over a batch of early spring flowers. Annie picked one and handed it to Wild Dove. Emmalin's heart constricted. The friendship between them had developed so easily. And obviously the little girl had great affection for Wild Dove. Emmalin sighed, frustrated with herself for being jealous.

"Are you all right?" Jacob asked.

"Me? Yes. Of course."

"You sure? You looked distressed."

"Oh no." She tidied her hair. "I'm fine."

"Here's some fresh clean water," Blossom said, placing the kettle on the table. "Such a fine place here for a home." She looked about. "How kind of my son to share this with me. I like how it is hidden by the trees. Makes me feel secure. And we can be close without seeing each other."

Wild Dove stepped up on the other side of Jacob and circled an arm around him. "I am very grateful."

"He's a good man." Emmalin felt a sense of separation between her and Jacob. He might not share their blood, but he did share their heart. Emmalin felt as if she were fighting for the man she loved while he was being drawn into a relationship with his past.

Everyone sat down. Annie insisted on sitting between Blossom and Wild Dove. Emmalin served the meal.

"Thank you," said Wild Dove. "This is very good."

"It's my pleasure. I'm so glad you are here with us." As she said the words, she was surprised to realize that she actually meant them, at least where Blossom was concerned. She was still uncertain about Wild Dove.

Talk about the table was animated and pleasant. Emmalin soon found herself feeling more content and happier. There was no reason for her to fret. She pushed down the hurt and decided to enjoy the day.

Working alongside Jacob was fun. Emmalin ended up feeling silly over her earlier emotional battle. Annie helped both her and Jacob and seemed to enjoy everyone's company equally. Soon she and Jacob would be married, and Annie would be part of their family. Emmalin needed to accept that Jacob would always be tied to his roots, and that was as it should be.

With many hands, the work went relatively fast. By the end of the day, one side had been framed in. Blossom was excited about the idea of a home close to her son and the hope of a future here in the place so close to the land where she had grown up. Occasionally Blossom would look into the forest, searching as if fearing intruders would spoil the dream, but then she would turn back to her work with a smile and strength.

As the afternoon wore on, the wind increased, and the air turned chill.

"It feels like a storm is moving in." Emmalin studied the clouds. "Annie and I should set out for home."

"Good idea. I'll be in town in a few days; I'll need more lumber."

"We'll have to make time to be together." She gave him a squeeze. "I better find Annie. She's gone off somewhere with Wild Dove."

Emmalin had seen them head toward the trail, likely in search of wildflowers and perhaps skunk cabbage, which Emmalin found distasteful. The natives used the plant to treat a variety of maladies.

She didn't see them right away and then she heard Annie's voice. She was about to call out when she heard her name mentioned, so instead she stayed out of sight and listened. She knew better but gave in to the temptation to eavesdrop.

"I want to stay here. With you," Annie said.

"No. You must go with Emmalin. At least for now. One day you will live right here, and we will see each other every day."

Emmalin's stomach dropped. What was Wild Dove referring to? Was she planning to steal Jacob from her and then take Annie too?

Annie shook her head. "I want you."

Emmalin sucked in a breath, feeling the wound of rejection.

Wild Dove pulled the child into a hug. "I want you too."

"Please, ask Emmalin."

Wild Dove stroked Annie's hair. "All right. I will ask."

Chapter Thirty-Six

On the trip back to Deer Creek, Emmalin didn't let on that she'd overheard the conversation between Annie and Wild Dove. What could she say? Annie was just a child, and all she'd done was speak her heart to someone she trusted. Emmalin had to consider what would be best for Annie. Could it possibly be Wild Dove?

Her mind wouldn't release the questions and the hurt she felt. What if she had to let Annie go? She hadn't known her long, but already she felt like a mother to the little girl.

Annie leaned against her, and Emmalin put her arm around the child. It didn't take long before the rocking of the wagon put the young one to sleep. Emmalin pulled the horses to a stop and moved Annie so she was lying flat on the wooden seat. Emmalin needed both hands if she were going to safely control the team.

She looked down at the little girl. Her long lashes rested on pudgy brown cheeks. Wisps of black hair framed her round face. She was a beautiful child.

Emmalin was glad Annie slept and wasn't peppering her with questions and comments. She needed time to reflect on what she'd seen and heard and to consider what would truly be best for the child. Did she belong with her people? If only Jacob was with her. He'd spent so much of his life with people of a different culture and could offer insights she had no understanding of.

Despite overhearing the conversation between Annie and Wild Dove, it had been a good day. Yes, her spirits had been knocked down when she learned how close the relationship was between them. She wanted to be the most important person in Annie's life. But recognizing that she felt that way made those needs seem petty. What mattered most was Annie's happiness and well-being.

And what about Jacob? He and Wild Dove had been close friends since childhood. Though he had reassured Emmalin that he loved her and not Wild Dove, the tie between them could not be ignored. How could she compete with it? Was it possible that Jacob, Wild Dove, and Annie belonged together? The idea cut her to the quick.

Emmalin felt the rise of tears but held them in check. How many times had Jacob reassured her of his love? He would never deceive her. He was a good and honorable man.

It was dusk when Emmalin pulled up to the house. As much thinking as she'd done on her trip home, she hadn't managed to sort out her questions and doubts.

Annie let out a small moan and pressed balled fists to her eyes. She sat up. "We are home? Already?"

Emmalin chuckled. "You slept most of the way."

Annie smiled at Emmalin, then hugged her. "It was a good day. Thank you."

"I'm glad you enjoyed it. I did too."

Annie scrambled off the seat. "I'm hungry." Emmalin helped her out of the wagon, and the little girl ran to the porch just as Margaret appeared at the door.

"I was beginning to wonder if you were going to make it back tonight." She bent and held out her arms for Annie. "How good to see you." She lifted the little girl and held her in a bear hug, then propped her on her hip. "So, you're hungry?" Annie nodded. "Well, dinner is ready. Go in and wash up."

She set Annie on her feet and watched as she ran indoors, then turned to face Emmalin. "I've got a chicken ready along with mashed potatoes and gravy and some green beans. They're one of my last jars. We'll have to get the new beans planted soon."

"I'll put the wagon and horses away and be right in." Emmalin was worn out but tried not to let it show.

"Do you need help?" Margaret walked down the steps and stood at the back of the wagon. "Ah, I see the wood was unloaded."

"We actually got a lot done on the small cabin today."

"I know that John and Chauncey have been helping some, but maybe we can get a team of men together to help finish your place so you and Jacob can get married."

"That would be wonderful," Emmalin said, but on the inside, she wasn't sure she should be celebrating. What if she and Jacob weren't meant to get married? She could barely even consider the possibility. Too many times she'd been in this place, feeling uncertain and afraid. *Speak to my heart, Father.*

"I'll be in as soon as I get the team put away." She lifted the reins and clicked her tongue, driving toward the barn.

❖❖❖

Over the next several days, there was no evidence that Annie had any doubts about living with Emmalin and Jacob. Emmalin began to wonder if she'd misunderstood the conversation. She desperately needed to speak to Jacob and waited anxiously for his return. He had said he'd be back to visit in a few days, and it had already been nearly a week.

On the sixth day, she was ready to close up the store when Jacob stepped in. "Oh, my goodness! I'm so glad to see you. I've been missing you so." She nearly leaped into his arms.

"You're a sight for sore eyes." He pulled her close and kissed her. "I can't wait until I can do this every day." He straightened and smiled. "And it won't be long. The little cabin is done."

"Already? But you never came back for more lumber."

"John showed up and he came in for the rest of the lumber. With his help, and Mother and Wild Dove doing all they could, we finished, at least enough to live in. We can spruce it up more later. And I need to buy a couple of windows and a cookstove, but Blossom moved the makeshift table in and made up some mats for sleeping. They plan to sleep in their cabin tonight."

"That's wonderful news!" Maybe her imagination had been playing tricks on her. "Margaret suggested we get a team of men together to work on the house." She looked into his eyes, hoping he would see how much it meant to her. "I know you don't want to pull men away from their own families but—"

"It's not what I wanted."

Disappointment rolled through Emmalin.

"But I think you're right. What harm can it do to ask? And I've just about had my fill of building." His hazel eyes filled with mischief.

"Oh, Jacob. Really?"

He gave a firm nod. "I'd rather be your husband than an overworked carpenter."

She hugged him close. "I'm so happy."

"It's time for us to settle down."

Emmalin hated to break the joyful interlude, but there was a conversation they needed to have. "Can we ride down to the river before we go out to my father's place?"

"I like the sound of that."

After closing the shop and retrieving her horse, she and Jacob were on their way. The air was chilly, but the last of the day's sun warmed them. The river was flowing heavy with spring runoff, churning muddy water and carrying logs downriver.

Emmalin dismounted and tied Sassy to a vine maple. Jacob did the same. Together they walked to a log that overlooked the water. There they stood side-by-side, hands clasped, neither speaking.

"This is nice," Jacob said, breaking the silence. "I've been needing time alone with you. It's all I could think about. I'm surprised I got any work done."

"You don't know how good it is to hear that." Emmalin looked into his eyes and knew she needed to be honest with him.

"I have been worried. I couldn't help it. Clearly Wild Dove is still in love with you. And the history you two share and the life you knew as children is a powerful bond. I—"

Jacob pressed a finger to her lips. "Stop. I know what you're going to say, and you're wrong. Wild Dove and I have a past, not a present, not a future. I've told you that before."

"I know that in my head. But when I see you together I feel afraid. Here." She moved her hand to her heart. "You seem to be so right for each other, and I feel as if I'm a barrier between you."

"The enemy is lying to you. I don't love her, except as a sister. I love you, only you." He took her hands in his. "I don't know what I can say to convince you."

"I don't know what's wrong with me—why I have these doubts?" Emmalin leaned against him. "When I'm with you, I believe." She gazed at the turbulent river.

"Do you think it's about faith? Do you have faith in me?"

"I do."

"Then believe me." Jacob pulled her into his arms. "I don't want anyone else."

"And I don't want anyone but you." Emmalin straightened. "There is something else. I overheard Annie talking to Wild Dove when I was there last week. Annie wants to live with her, not with us."

"Are you sure?"

"Yes. And Wild Dove told her she would speak to us about it. Did she say anything to you?"

"No."

"I have to admit, it crossed my mind that the three of you and Blossom seem like a good fit. You and Wild Dove would be good parents for Annie. You would all be happy together."

He set her away from him. "Emmalin. Stop it." He studied the river for a moment, looking as if he was reining in his emotions. "There's only one thing wrong with that picture. I wouldn't be happy. You and I belong together. And Annie will be happy with us. We just have to give her time."

Emmalin stepped into his arms. "I am so thankful for you."

"I will love you for the rest of my life. There will never be anyone else for me."

He kissed her gently, then more deeply. His passion left Emmalin breathless. She'd been so foolish. But what to do about Wild Dove? She would be living close by, and the idea of her vying for Jacob's affections was unthinkable. She couldn't live with that.

Jacob released her. "It's time for you to take care of the plans for our wedding. I'm going to find a team of men and we'll finish the house. I ran into Mr. Henderson when I was in town last, and he asked me if we'd gotten married yet. When I explained about the house, he offered to help. I'll contact him. And there are a few others I know I can count on. We should have the cabin done in no time." He smiled broadly. "It's about time you became Mrs. Landon."

On the ride home, Emmalin felt giddy. Mrs. Landon. She loved the sound of it. "What day should we get married? I have to set a date so I can invite our guests."

Jacob thought a moment. "How about the first Saturday in April."

"That will be perfect, only weeks away."

Jacob left her at the house with plans to head back to the cabin the next day after making arrangements for help. He also had to order some items for the small cabin and the main house to complete the interior. Emmalin was already waiting on an order she'd placed weeks before.

The following morning, Emmalin walked out to the garden, her spirits still high. Margaret had taken Annie into the café with her, and her father was on a delivery, so she was on her own.

The garden had been prepared for planting, and today she planned to put peas in the ground. They were always one of the first vegetables to ripen. She could almost taste the sweet delicate flavor.

She rolled the small, shriveled orbs around in her apron pocket. When she reached the patch of ground that had been designated for peas, she walked the line between posts and tied a string from one to the other, then hoed a furrow for planting. Once the green shoots were up, she would string the rows to encourage the plants to climb, which made picking easier.

She noticed someone walking along the roadway. Emmalin squinted, trying to make out who it could be. Wild Dove? Her heart rate picked up. Was she here for Annie?

Wild Dove didn't wave, and as she approached, her expression was serious. When she reached the garden, she stood and studied the tilled ground. "What are you planting?"

"Peas. Have you grown them?"

"No. But I would like to."

"I'll be happy to teach you, but I'm only just learning. Jacob knows so much more."

Wild Dove nodded, focusing on Emmalin. "I must speak to you—that is why I am here."

"Did you walk all the way?"

"Yes." She looked at the house. "Is Annie here?"

"No. She went into town with Margaret."

"Good."

"Would you like something to drink? Some water or tea?"

"No." She clasped her hands in front of her. "When you were at the property, Annie talked to me about something important."

Emmalin tried to prepare for what was to come.

"She asked if she could live with me."

"I know. I didn't mean to eavesdrop, but I overheard her ask you."

"I love Annie and want her to stay with me, but I cannot do that. She needs a home with a mother and a father. And I am not safe. The soldiers could come for me. What would happen to her then? She might be forced to live on the reservation. I would never want that for her."

Emmalin's heart felt as if it were cracking open. She'd been so unfair and unkind in her assumptions. Wild Dove was the one who lived with daily sorrow. "Thank you for thinking first of Annie. She loves you and Blossom." Emmalin leaned on the hoe. "It would be a tragedy if she were to be forced onto a reservation."

"It cannot happen. We can't let it."

"But Wild Dove, you are good for Annie."

She nodded ever so slightly. "And she is good for me."

"You do not have to give up your friendship with her. She can have all of us in her life. She will be able to see you and Blossom every day, if she likes. We can all be her family."

Wild Dove smiled. "Yes. That's what I want."

Emmalin scraped up a small bit of dirt with the hoe, then looked at Wild Dove. "Now." She took a breath for courage. She had been praying for wisdom and for a merciful heart. "We must speak of something else. Jacob. He is going to be my husband, and I will not share him." She met Wild Dove's gaze. "Your flirtations with him must cease. At once. Otherwise, we cannot share the land."

Wild Dove's expression was receptive. "I know. I didn't want to understand, but I do. Jacob belongs to you. I surrender any claim I thought I had. He does not want me. I am his sister only."

Relief flooded Emmalin. She was surprised at how easily Wild Dove had yielded. "I know we come from very different backgrounds, but I would like us to be friends."

"That would be good." Wild Dove smiled. "We are like a family."

Emmalin felt the thrill of being part of God's intentional plan. How much simpler life would be if she would surrender to God more easily. "Yes. Family."

Chapter Thirty-Seven

Emmalin cast her line into the river and watched the current carry it downstream. This was one of her favorite spots on the Umpqua. Soon she would be fishing far from here and close to her new home with Jacob. She would have a new favorite fishing hole. The idea was exciting and a little frightening, a new direction on her journey. She'd experienced many over the last year and a half. So much had changed.

When she'd first gone fishing with Jacob, she had known nothing about how to fish the river, but with his help, she'd landed her first salmon. A dreadful storm had blown up, and they'd been forced to take shelter in Jacob's cabin. She'd been frightened and injured, but even in the midst of the melee, Jacob had made her feel safe. He still did, but she knew Jacob couldn't always be there for her. God was the only one who would always be present, especially in times of need.

Emmalin reeled in some of the line and set the pole on the ground. She was thirsty. She walked to Sassy and took her flask off the saddle where she'd hung it and took a long drink, then studied the tumbling river. Fear had become her adversary, always teasing her, waiting to tear her down. If she were going to find happiness, she needed to find a way to overcome that enemy.

Her Bible was in the saddlebag. It held the answers to all of life. She cast up a prayer to God. *Show me.*

Holding the Bible close, she sat in a grassy spot in the sunshine. Expectantly, she opened the Book and turned to Ephesians. Her eyes went to chapter six where she read, *"My brethren, be strong in the Lord, and in the power of his might. Put on the whole armour of God that ye may be able to stand against the wiles of the devil."*

As she read, the Holy Spirit spoke to her. *Her adversary was the devil. He was the one who raised up the fear inside of her. But she could win the battle because she possessed the armor of God.*

She knew the truth. She would never fight alone, for the Lord loved her just as she was. The faith she needed was given by God, a gift, not something she must invoke. Her salvation was trustworthy, obtained only through the death and resurrection of Jesus Christ. And each day, she could grasp the sword of the spirit more firmly, for the Word of God was alive and it was active. It would bring down the enemy.

These words were not new to her, but until now she had never truly comprehended them and the power they possessed. She pressed the open pages of the Bible against her chest. Tears washed into her eyes as the joy and certainty of God's provision swept through her. Life would bring challenges, but she was prepared to face them for the battle would be won in the heavenlies not on her own strength.

She gazed across the river to the trees on the far bank. They tossed gently in the breeze. There was no threat, only the chirp of frogs singing a familiar melody. "Lord, make me worthy," she whispered.

One more day and she would be Jacob's wife. The idea was almost too wonderful to comprehend.

The journey to this place had been unexpected. She'd been lost, confused, and afraid when she arrived in Oregon and had no notion that the rough and frightening place would become home. It would be a place where love grew.

Closing her eyes, she breathed in the fragrance of spring grasses and wildflowers, and she thanked God for all He had given her. She would truly be an Oregon pioneer and the wife of a mountain man, a good and godly man. Jacob. She took in a deep breath and slowly released it. *Lord, thank You for all You have given me. With You I know I can be a good wife.*

Marriage wouldn't be easy, and no couple was completely happy all of the time, but she and Jacob belonged together. And they would begin their life as a family because of Annie. She was the dearest child, a gift from God. Life was richer because of her. *Thank you, Father.*

All of a sudden, she realized her pole was being dragged toward the water. Emmalin jumped up and grabbed it. She yanked on the line, stretching it taut and reeling hard, pulling the fish into the shallows. There was a flash of silver in the water, then it broke through the surface and danced on the end of the line. She reeled and fought back, pulling it close to shore, then tossed it onto the bank, where it flopped on the rocks. She picked it up and removed the hook from its mouth. It would make a grand meal, but it didn't feel right to end its life just as she was about to begin a new one. She set the fish back in the river and released it, watching as it flipped its tail and swam away.

Oh, how she loved this life.

She gazed at the azure sky. It was getting on to afternoon. She'd best be on her way if she was going to help set up at the church.

———— ✦•✦•✦ ————

Emmalin and Jacob had volunteered to help Charity set up tables and other preparations at the church the night before the wedding. In the morning, Charity would decorate.

Margaret also took a few minutes to show Annie what she would do as the flower girl and gave instructions to Emmalin and Charity. "Alice Sullivan will play the piano. I wish you could, Emmalin, but you'll be a bit busy." She chuckled, and the three friends fell into giggles.

Jacob and Emmalin lingered on the church steps, gazing into the quiet evening. Emmalin never wanted to part from him, and she remained in his arms. Their kisses were passionate and full of promise.

"I can't wait until tomorrow." Jacob tightened his embrace.

Emmalin leaned against him, the slight fragrance of sweat and soap alluring. She studied his hand. It was callused and strong. She kissed his palm and snuggled closer. "I don't want to go home."

"I don't want you to go."

She smiled up at him. "It will only be a few hours until we return here." She glanced at her father who sat obligingly in the wagon. "My father is being very patient with us. I must go." She gave him one last kiss. "Tomorrow."

The trip home seemed extra sweet. No one spoke, understanding that everything was about to change. There was a sense of wonderment, and the silence was companionable. Annie slept in the back on Margaret's lap. Margaret stroked her hair. "Little mite is all worn out."

"She's excited for tomorrow."

"Aren't we all. It seems like such a long time coming."

"It seems so. Now I just want to sleep so tomorrow can arrive."

"You think you'll be sleeping?" Margaret chuckled.

"I can hope."

Finally with the house silent, Emmalin settled into bed beside Annie. Her mind whirled with all the possibilities of her future. Sleep was illusive, but somehow in the wee hours of the morning, Emmalin drifted off into beautiful dreams and remained there until the crowing of the rooster.

She allowed herself the luxury of waking slowly, then sat up and looked at Annie, who still slept, her hands tucked under her cheek and a soft smile on her lips. Emmalin moved gently, careful not to awaken the little girl. She climbed out of bed, pulled on a dressing gown, and met Margaret in the kitchen. "You're up early."

"And so are you." Margaret winked at her.

"I barely slept."

"Me either. I'm so giddy, you'd think this was my wedding." Margaret laughed. "You sit, and I'll get us some coffee and make breakfast."

"I don't know if I can eat."

"You must. This will be a day of excitement and stress. We don't need you getting weak and woozy in the middle of the ceremony."

"Oh, that would be horrible."

Margaret set a cup of coffee in front of her, then poured one for herself and sat across from Emmalin. She looked a bit sad.

"Is something wrong?"

"No. I was just thinking this will be our last breakfast together like this." She reached across and pressed her hand over Emmalin's. "I'm going to miss you."

"Oh, me too. You have been the dearest friend, and, in many ways, you are like a mother to me."

Margaret smiled. "I remember the first time I saw you, the day you rode into town with Jacob. I knew right away that I was going to like you. But I had no idea how much that young city gal would change all of our lives." She took another sip of coffee and stood up. "I'd better get busy. We have a wedding to get to."

Nearly an hour later, Annie wandered out of the bedroom, and at the same time, Blossom and Wild Dove arrived. They had agreed to watch over the little girl while Margaret and Emmalin went to the church to make final preparations.

"Good morning," Blossom said. "I am wondering if we should go to the church. There will be people there."

"There will be, but we've only invited our friends. None of them will say a word about you and Wild Dove." She rested a hand on Blossom's arm. "Jacob is your son. You should be there."

Blossom smiled tremulously and nodded.

Margaret stepped out of the bedroom, carrying a traveling bag with Emmalin's dress. "Oh, how wonderful. You're here."

"Margaret, you look stunning."

"Well, you're the one who picked out my dress. You have wonderful taste." Her eyes went soft. "Thank you for asking me to be your matron of honor."

"Who else would I ask?" She hugged Margaret. "I love you."

Annie caught Emmalin around the legs. "I want to go with you."

"You still have to get dressed. Wild Dove said she'll help you. And Blossom is going to put some pretty ribbons in your hair." She bent and pressed a kiss to her forehead. "When you're all done, then you can come to the church."

"All right. Today is your wedding." Annie smiled broadly.

"Yes, it is. And we have to get moving." Margaret opened the door. "No dawdling. Come on."

When Emmalin and Margaret arrived at the church, Charity was already there. She hurried down the steps. "Good morning. I'm so excited!"

Emmalin hugged her. "Me too." They smiled at each other.

"We have everything prepared. The church looks so pretty. Several ladies brought flowers from their gardens. And the tables are already set for the lunch reception."

"My goodness. What time did you get here?"

"A while ago. But I couldn't wait to start."

"You are such a good friend. Thank you." Emmalin could barely contain her joy. It was really happening. She was actually going to become Mrs. Jacob Landon. She studied Charity. "You look fabulous."

"It's this dress. It's the prettiest one I've ever worn." She grasped Emmalin's hands. "Thank you so much for asking me to be your bridesmaid."

"Of course. You are such a dear, dear friend. And a bridesmaid needs a special dress."

"You two need to stop gabbing," Margaret said. "It's time to get ready. We only have two hours."

Emmalin sat at the dressing table that had been brought over for the wedding. "Have you seen Jacob?"

"He and your father just arrived. He looks so handsome."

"He always looks handsome." Emmalin gave her a sideways smile and lifted her brows.

"You two are going to have the most beautiful children," Charity said.

"Charity! Oh my. We're not even married yet."

"I'm only stating the obvious." Charity did a little twirl and grinned.

"Be still. I'll never get this right." Margaret braided Emmalin's hair into three plaits, then tucked them each into a classic coiffure, pinning it in place with a gold tone filigree and mother of pearl hair clip. "This is a stunning barrette."

"It was my mother's. She always wore it for special occasions."

"I can see where you got your exquisite taste."

"I wish she was here." Emmalin felt the sting of tears. "She would have loved Jacob, and I think she would be proud of my father. He made a good life for himself." She glanced up at Margaret. "And he found a good woman to share it with."

Margaret placed a hand on Emmalin's shoulder. "And she would be very proud of you and the woman you've become."

"I hope so. I know she would be surprised. This is not the life we had imagined for me."

Using the tips of her fingers, Emmalin rubbed in just a touch of rouge, then added a hint of lipstick.

"All right now." Margaret gave Emmalin a hand mirror. "What do you think of it?"

Holding up the mirror so she could see the coiffure from every direction, Emmalin turned this way and that. "It's lovely."

"I agree. And so are you. Now, let's get your dress on. It's almost time for the ceremony."

Emmalin's stomach flipped, barely able to grasp that the day she had dreamed of—prayed for and about, and thought she'd lost—was actually upon her. Charity and Margaret presented her gown. It was spectacular and possibly more beautiful than she had imagined it would be. They held it while she lifted her arms over her head and allowed them to drop it over her head, careful not to muss-up her hair. They adjusted it on her shoulders. Margaret did up the pearl buttons in the back, then fluffed out the gown and arranged it so it flowed away from her in back. Emmalin looked into the dressing mirror. "It's absolutely stunning, Margaret. You are a wonder of a seamstress."

"And you're a beautiful woman who is able to make any dress look fabulous." Margaret studied Emmalin's reflection. "Although I must say I am proud of my work." Her smile held a bit of mischief.

Resting her hands on her abdomen where the gown caught her snugly at the waist, Emmalin studied her image. The satin had been the perfect choice and the lace overlay gave it a most delicate beauty.

"I don't think I've ever seen a prettier bride," Charity said. She kissed Emmalin's cheek. "I'd better get out there and make sure everything is going smoothly." She quickly slipped out of the room.

"Now, let me see," said Margaret. "You have something new, the dress. And something old, your mother's pin. And here is something borrowed."

She held out a delicate gold cross necklace. "This is mine. I wore it when my first husband and I were married."

"It's lovely. Thank you." Emmalin turned so Margaret could set the clasp in back.

"And here's a blue satin handkerchief. All you need is the veil." She retrieved the veil from a hanger. "This is the most delicate lace." She placed the veil over Emmalin's perfectly coiffed hair and pinned it in place. She draped one side over her shoulder and turned Emmalin to face the mirror.

Emmalin stared at herself. She had been transformed. "I look like a princess."

"Jacob won't be able to take his eyes off of you."

"Oh, I hope so." She giggled.

The door opened and Annie flew in. She stopped and gazed at Emmalin. "You are beautiful!"

"Thank you. And you look very pretty." She retrieved the basket of flower petals that had been prepared for the ceremony. "Here are your flowers." She smiled at Wild Dove and Blossom who waited at the door. "She knows what to do, but you might need to make sure she doesn't get distracted."

"I will do that." Wild Dove took the little girl's hand. "You look very beautiful, Emmalin."

"Thank you." Emmalin offered her a kind smile.

Wild Dove led Annie out of the room.

Charity poked her head in. "Are you ready?"

"I believe so." Emmalin took a deep breath. Everything was happening so fast. She'd waited and waited, and now she wished she could slow it down. She looked about the room. "My bouquet."

"Here it is." Margaret took the bouquet of wildflowers and handed them to Emmalin. "I guess it's time for me to take my place." She smiled warmly and dropped a kiss on Emmalin's cheek. "I love answered prayers. And you are an answer to prayer."

"I love them too."

Margaret hugged Emmalin and held her for a few moments before moving toward the door.

Emmalin watched her leave the room.

Charity smiled at her. "I'll go out and wait my turn. I can hear the music."

It was time. Emmalin's skin tingled.

She waited until Annie started down the aisle followed by Charity and then Margaret. The wedding march began. Emmalin stepped into the vestibule where her father waited.

His eyes lit up when he saw her. "You take my breath away." He shook his head. "I wanted to take a few minutes with you, but it seems we've run out of time." He gazed at her. "I'm proud of you. And so thankful you found me and then allowed me to be part of your life. This moment wouldn't have happened for me if not for your courage and your heart of forgiveness."

Emmalin laid her hand on his arm. "I am deeply grateful for you, and for God's mercy and love. He's the one who led me to you."

He escorted her to the sanctuary doors.

"We missed a lot of years, Father, but we have so many more left to share."

He nodded, his eyes wet with unshed tears. "You ready?"

"Yes."

The doors opened and Emmalin searched for the man who had changed her life—the man she knew God brought to her. Jacob stood to the minister's left, at the front of the church, his dark suit setting off the deep tan of his skin and the hazel fire in his eyes. He stood straight and tall. Her eyes locked with his, igniting a flame she knew would burn through eternity. They belonged to one another for all time.

Her father moved forward, and she matched his steps. Her eyes remained on Jacob. She was scarcely aware of friends and family who had gathered as witnesses. The music seemed to flow through her and carried her to the front of the church. She could barely breathe as she gazed upon the man who loved her more than any other. She belonged to him and him only.

Joy and thankfulness filled her. How did such a beautiful gift come to her? An ache of gratitude swelled at the base of her throat, and her eyes filled with unshed tears. She never knew there could be such a powerful love as what she carried within her for Jacob.

They stopped at the front of the church, suspended in a moment of time. Pastor Miller looked at her and smiled, then turned to her father. "Who gives this woman to be married?"

"Margaret and I do."

Jacob took a step toward Emmalin. Her father placed her hand in Jacob's. His grip was sure and strong as he drew her toward him.

The presence of God was all around them and the songs of the valley rose in her spirit, reminding her that love was all that mattered in beginnings and endings.

Acknowledgments

A book is not created by one person. It takes a team. I am grateful for all the warriors who have been part of my team. I especially owe gratitude to my Heavenly Father who walked with me through this process, lifting me up when I fell, and kept me moving forward when I felt less than empowered.

This story was born in the midst of a grueling time: the Archie Creek Fire that devastated my community and the world of COVID that devastated the planet. The writing was difficult, and my mind was preoccupied by what was going on around me. In the end, the story came together because of those who came alongside to help.

There are a few I must mention. My many friends who knew the battle and lifted me in prayer. It was your faithfulness and love that made the writing possible. Thank you, dear friends. You know who you are. And there are some that I don't even know, faithful servants of God who give so much for the Lord. May He bless you.

And thanks to Sarah Sundin who was the first to see my efforts. You read this story and returned the pages to me with personal remarks and suggestions. I am grateful for your input, Sarah, my fellow writer.

I must also mention my daughter, Kristina, who is a fine writer. She read each chapter, some more than once, and her sharp eye and innate comprehension of good storytelling caught many blunders and aided in the refining process.

I also owe much to the many authors who diligently recorded Oregon's history, compiling the account of its early beginnings as a territory of the United States. This project would have been impossible without their work. The recorded history is intriguing, surprising, and inspiring.

And I can't forget those at WhiteFire Publishing who took my work and made it better. Thank you, David and Roseanna White. And to my editor Janelle Leonard, I appreciate your gentle touch. You could see what needed polishing, but allowed the work to remain my own, which is precious to this author.

There is also a team of editors who work for WhiteFire Publishing who contributed to this project. I do not know your names, but I appreciate your hard work and dedication.

Thank you all.

ALSO BY
Bonnie Leon

THE NORTHERN LIGHTS SERIES
The Journey of Eleven Moons
In the Land of White Nights
Return to the Misty Shore

To Dance with Dolphins

One Hundred Valleys

CPSIA information can be obtained
at www.ICGtesting.com
Printed in the USA
LVHW091155290822
727088LV00006B/284